D0784929

Mills & Boon Romance brings you

CHRISTMAS TREATS

For an extra-special treat this Christmas
don't look under the Christmas tree or in
your stocking—pick up one of your favourite
Mills & Boon® Romances, curl up and relax!

Experience the warmth, wonder and the
true spirit of Christmas with Liz Fielding
and Jessica Hart in these two festive tales.

Enjoy our new 2-in-1 editions of stories
by your favourite authors—

for double the romance!

CHRISTMAS ANGEL
FOR THE BILLIONAIRE
by Liz Fielding

UNDER THE BOSS'S MISTLETOE
by Jessica Hart

*And look out for Christmas extras this month
in Mills & Boon® Romance!*

Annie wants anonymity…

TRADING PLACES

…Lydia wants the spotlight.

Can they both find love…?

This month:
CHRISTMAS ANGEL FOR THE BILLIONAIRE
Lady Roseanne Napier has been in the media spotlight
most of her life and wants a break from being the
'nation's angel', so she goes undercover—
and meets breathtakingly handsome George Saxon…

Next month:
HER DESERT DREAM
Her lookalike, girl-next-door Lydia Young,
takes Annie's place for the week! Lydia thinks that a
holiday in the desert kingdom of Ramal Hamrah with
an irresistible sheikh doesn't sound like much of a
chore…but she's in for a surprise!

CHRISTMAS ANGEL FOR THE BILLIONAIRE

BY
LIZ FIELDING

First published in Great Britain 2009
Harlequin Mills & Boon Limited,
Eton House, 18-24 Paradise Road, Richmond, Surrey TW9 1SR

© Liz Fielding 2009

ISBN: 978 0 263 86977 4

Set in Times Roman 12½ on 14 pt
02-1109-53143

Harlequin Mills & Boon policy is to use papers that are natural, renewable and recyclable products and made from wood grown in sustainable forests. The logging and manufacturing process conform to the legal environmental regulations of the country of origin.

Printed and bound in Spain
by Litografia Rosés, S.A., Barcelona

Liz Fielding was born with itchy feet. She made it to Zambia before her twenty-first birthday and, gathering her own special hero and a couple of children on the way, lived in Botswana, Kenya and Bahrain—with pauses for sightseeing pretty much everywhere in between. She finally came to a full stop in a tiny Welsh village cradled by misty hills, and these days mostly leaves her pen to do the travelling. When she's not sorting out the lives and loves of her characters she potters in the garden, reads her favourite authors, and spends a lot of time wondering 'What if…?' For news of upcoming books— and to sign up for her occasional newsletter—visit Liz's website at www.lizfielding.com

PROLOGUE

Daily Chronicle, 19th December, 1988

MARQUESS AND WIFE SLAIN ON CHARITY MISSION

The Marquess and Marchioness of St Ives, whose fairy-tale romance captured the hearts of the nation, were slain yesterday by rebels who opened fire on their vehicle as they approached a refugee camp in the war-torn region of Mishona. Their driver and a local woman who worked for the medical charity Susie's Friends *also died in the attack.*

HM the Queen sent a message of sympathy to the Duke of Oldfield, the widowed father of the Marquess, and to the slaughtered couple's six-year-old daughter, Lady Roseanne Napier.

The Marchioness of St Ives, Lady Susanne Napier, who overcame early hardships to train as a doctor, founded the international emergency charity with her husband shortly after their marriage.

Daily Chronicle, 24th December, 1988

WE MUST ALL BE HER FAMILY NOW...
Six-year-old Lady Roseanne Napier held her grandfather's hand as the remains of her slain mother and father were laid to rest in the family vault yesterday afternoon. In his oration, praising their high ideals, the grieving Duke said, 'We must all be her family now...'

Daily Chronicle, 18th December, 1998

A PERFECT ANGEL...
Today, on the tenth anniversary of the slaying of her parents while helping to co-ordinate relief in war-ravished Mishona, Lady Rose Napier opened Susanne House, a children's hospice named to honour her mother. After unveiling a plaque, Lady Rose met the brave children who are being cared for at Susanne House and talked to their parents. 'She was so caring, so thoughtful for someone so young,' one of the nurses said. 'A perfect angel. Her mother would have been so proud of her.'

Her mother isn't here to tell her that, so we are saying it for her.

We are all proud of you, Lady Rose.

CHAPTER ONE

ANNIE smothered a yawn. The room was hot, the lingering scent of food nauseating and all she wanted to do was lay her head on the table in front of her, close her eyes and switch off.

If only.

There was a visit to a hospital, then three hours of Wagner at a charity gala to endure before she could even think about sleep. And even then, no matter how tired she was, thinking about it was as close as she would get.

She'd tried it all. Soothing baths, a lavender pillow, every kind of relaxation technique without success. But calming her mind wasn't the problem.

It wasn't the fact that it was swirling with all the things she needed to remember that was keeping her awake. She had an efficient personal assistant to take care of every single detail of her life and ensure that she was in the right place at the right time. A speech writer to put carefully chosen words into her mouth when she got there. A style consultant whose job it was to ensure that whenever she appeared in public she made the front page.

That *was* the problem.

There was absolutely nothing in her mind to swirl around. It was empty. Like her life.

In just under a minute she was going to have to stand up and talk to these amazing people who had put themselves on the line to alleviate suffering in the world.

They had come to see her, listen to her inspire them to even greater efforts. And her presence ensured that the press was here too, which meant that the work they did would be noticed, reported.

Maybe.

Her hat, a rich green velvet and feather folly perched at a saucy angle over her right eye would probably garner more column inches than the charity she was here to support.

She was doing more for magazine and newspaper circulation than she was for the medical teams, the search units, pilots, drivers, communications people who dropped everything at a moment's notice, risking their lives to help victims of war, famine, disaster—a point she'd made to her grandfather more than once.

A pragmatist, he had dismissed her concerns, reminding her that it was a symbiotic relationship and everyone would benefit from her appearance, including the British fashion industry.

It didn't help that he was right.

She wanted to do more, *be* more than a cover girl, a fashion icon. Her parents had been out there, on the front line, picking up the pieces of ruined lives and she had planned to follow in their footsteps.

She stopped the thought. Publicity was the only gift she had and she had better do it right but, as she took her place at the lectern and a wave of applause hit her, a long silent scream invaded the emptiness inside her head.

Noooooo…

'Friends…' she began when the noise subsided. She paused, looked around her, found faces in the audience she recognised, people her parents had known. Took a breath, dug deep, smiled. 'I hope I've earned the right to call you that…'

She had been just eighteen years old when, at her grandfather's urging, she'd accepted an invitation to become patron of Susie's Friends. A small consolation for the loss of her dream of following her mother into medicine.

All that had ended when, at the age of sixteen, a photograph of her holding the hand of a dying child had turned her, overnight, from a sheltered, protected teen into an iconic image and her grandfather had laid out the bald facts for her.

How impossible it was. How her fellow students, patients even, would be harassed, bribed by the press for gossip about her because she was now public property. Then he'd consoled her with the fact that this way she could do so much more for the causes her mother had espoused.

Ten years on, more than fifty charities had claimed her as a patron. How many smiles, handshakes? Charity galas, first nights?

How many children's hands had she held, how many babies had she cradled?

None of them her own.

She had seen herself described as the 'most loved woman in Britain', but living in an isolation bubble, sheltered, protected from suffering the same fate as her parents, it was a love that never came close enough to touch.

But the media was a hungry beast that had to be fed and it was, apparently, time to move the story on. Time for a husband and children to round out the image. And, being her grandfather, he wasn't prepared to leave anything that important to chance.

Or to her.

Heaven forbid there should be anything as messy as her own father's passionate romance with a totally unsuitable woman, one whose ideals had ended up getting them both killed.

Instead, he'd found the perfect candidate in Rupert Devenish, Viscount Earley, easing him into her life so subtly that she'd barely noticed. Titled, rich and almost too good-looking to be true, he was so eligible that if she'd gone to the 'ideal husband' store and picked him off the shelf he couldn't be more perfect.

So perfect, in fact, that unless she was extremely careful, six months from now she'd find herself with a ring on her finger and in a year she'd be on every front page, every magazine cover, wearing the 'fairy-tale' dress. The very thought of it weighed like a lump of lead somewhere in the region of her heart. Trapped, with nowhere to turn, she felt as if the glittering chandeliers were slowly descending to crush her.

She dug her nails into her palm to concentrate her mind, took a sip of water, looked around at all the familiar faces and, ignoring the carefully worded speech that had been written for her, she talked to them about her parents, about ideals, about sacrifice, her words coming straight from the heart.

An hour later it was over and she turned to the hotel manager as he escorted her to the door. 'Another wonderful lunch, Mr Gordon. How is your little girl?'

'Much improved, thank you, Lady Rose. She was so thrilled with the books you sent her.'

'She wrote me the sweetest note.' She glanced at the single blush-pink rose she was holding.

She yearned to be offered, just once, something outrageous in purple or orange, but this variety of rose had been named for her and part of the proceeds of every sale went to Susanne House. To have

offered her anything else would have been unthinkable.

'Will you give her this from me?' she said,
offering him the rose.

'Madam,' he said, pink with pleasure as he took
it and Annie felt a sudden urge to hug the man.
Instead, she let her hand rest briefly on his arm
before she turned to join Rupert, who was already
at the door, impatient to be away.

Turned and came face to face with herself.

Or at least a very close facsimile.

A look in one of the mirrors that lined the walls
would have shown two tall, slender young women,
each with pale gold hair worn up in the same elegant
twist, each with harebell-blue eyes.

Annie had been aware of her double's existence
for years. Had seen photographs in magazines and
newspapers, courtesy of the cuttings agency that
supplied clippings of any print article that contained
her name. She'd assumed that the amazing likeness
had been aided by photographic manipulation but
it wasn't so. It was almost like looking in the mirror.

For a moment they both froze. Annie, more ex-
perienced in dealing with the awkward moment,
putting people at their ease, was the first to move.

'I know the face,' she said, feeling for the
woman—it wasn't often a professional 'lookalike'
came face to face with the real thing. With a smile,
she added, 'But I'm afraid the name escapes me.'

Her double, doing a remarkable job of holding her poise under the circumstances, said, 'Lydia, madam. Lydia Young.' But, as she took her hand, Annie felt it shaking. 'I'm s-so sorry. I promise this wasn't planned. I had no idea you'd be here.'

'Please, it's not a problem.' Then, intrigued, 'Do you—or do I mean I?—have an engagement here?'

'Had. A product launch.' Lydia gave an awkward little shrug as she coloured up. 'A new variety of tea.'

'I do hope it's good,' Annie replied, 'if I'm endorsing it.'

'Well, it's expensive,' Lydia said, relaxing sufficiently to smile back. Then, 'I'll just go and sit down behind that pillar for ten minutes, shall I? While I'm sure the photographers out there would enjoy it if we left together, my clients didn't pay me anywhere near enough to give them that kind of publicity.'

'It would rather spoil the illusion if we were seen together,' Annie agreed. About to walk on, something stopped her. 'As a matter of interest, Lydia, how much do you charge for being me?' she asked. 'Just in case I ever decide to take a day off.'

'No charge for you, Lady Rose,' she replied, handing her the rose that she was, inevitably, carrying as she sank into a very brief curtsey. 'Just give me a call. Any time.'

For a moment they looked at one another, then Annie sniffed the rose and said, 'They don't have much character, do they? No scent, no thorns…'

'Well, it's November. I imagine they've been forced under glass.'

Something they had in common, Annie thought.

She didn't have much character either, just a carefully manufactured image as the nation's 'angel', 'sweetheart'.

Rupert, already through the door, looked back to see what was keeping her and, apparently confident enough to display a little impatience, said, 'Rose, we're running late…'

They both glanced in his direction, then Lydia looked at her and lifted a brow in a 'dump the jerk' look that exactly mirrored her own thoughts.

'I don't suppose you fancy three hours of Wagner this evening?' she asked but, even before Lydia could reply, she shook her head. 'Just kidding. I wouldn't wish that on you.'

'I meant what I said.' And Lydia, taking a card from the small clutch bag she was carrying, offered it to her. 'Call me. Any time.'

Three weeks later, as speculation in the press that she was about to announce her engagement reached fever-pitch, Annie took out Lydia's card and dialled the number.

'Lydia Young…'

'Did you mean it?' she asked.

George Saxon, bare feet propped on the deck rail of his California beach house, laptop on his knees, gave up on the problem that had been eluding him for weeks and surfed idly through the headlines of the London newspapers.

His eye was caught by the picture of a couple leaving some gala. She was one of those tall patrician women, pale blonde hair swept up off her neck, her fabulously expensive gown cut low to reveal hollows in her shoulders even deeper than those in her cheeks.

But it wasn't her dress or the fact that she'd so obviously starved herself to get into it that had caught and held his attention. It was her eyes.

Her mouth was smiling for the camera, but her eyes, large, blue, seemed to be looking straight at him, sending him a silent appeal for help.

He clicked swiftly back to the program he'd been working on. Sometimes switching in and out of a problem cleared the blockage but this one was stubborn, which was why he'd left his Chicago office, lakeside apartment. Escaping the frantic pre-Christmas party atmosphere for the peace—and warmth—of the beach.

Behind him, inside the house, the phone began to ring. It would be his accountant, or his lawyer, or his office but success had insulated him from the need to jump when the phone rang and he left it for the machine to pick up. There was nothing, no one—

'George? It's your dad…'

But, then again, there were exceptions to every rule.

* * *

Tossing a holdall onto the back seat of the little red car that was Lydia's proudest possession, Annie settled herself behind the wheel and ran her hands over the steering wheel as if to reassure herself that it was real.

That she'd escaped…

Three hours ago, Lady Rose Napier had walked into a London hotel without her unshakeable escort—the annual Pink Ribbon Lunch was a ladies-only occasion. Two hours later, Lydia had walked out in her place. And ten minutes ago she'd left the same hotel completely unnoticed.

By now Lydia would be on board a private jet, heading for a week of total luxury at Bab el Sama, the holiday home of her friend Lucy al-Khatib.

Once there, all she had to do was put in an occasional appearance on the terrace or the beach for the paparazzi who, after the sudden rash of 'Wedding Bells?' headlines, would no doubt be sitting offshore in small boats, long-range cameras at the ready, hoping to catch her in flagrante in this private 'love-nest' with Rupert.

She hoped they'd packed seasick pills along with their sunscreen since they were going to have a very long wait.

And she grinned. She'd told her grandfather that she needed time on her own to consider her future. Not true. She wasn't going to waste one precious second of the time that Lydia—bless her heart—had given her thinking about Rupert Devenish.

She had just a week in which to be anonymous, to step outside the hothouse environment in which she'd lived since her parents had been killed. To touch reality as they had done. Be herself. Nothing planned, nothing organised. Just take life as it came.

She adjusted the rear-view mirror to check her appearance. She'd debated whether to go with a wig or colour her hair but, having tried a wig—it was amazing what you could buy on the Internet—and realising that living in it 24/7 was not for her, she'd decided to go for a temporary change of hair colour, darkening it a little with the temporary rinse Lydia had provided.

But that would have taken time and, instead, in an act of pure rebellion, of liberation, she'd hacked it short with a pair of nail scissors. When she'd stopped, the short, spiky result was so shocking that she'd been grateful for the woolly hat Lydia had provided to cover it.

She pulled it down over her ears, hoping that Lydia, forced to follow her style, would forgive her. Pushed the heavy-framed 'prop' spectacles up her nose. And grinned. The sense of freedom was giddying and, if she was honest, a little frightening. She'd never been completely on her own before and, shivering a little, she turned on the heater.

'Not frightening,' she said out loud as she eased out of the parking bay and headed for the exit. 'Challenging.' And, reaching the barrier, she encountered her first challenge.

Lydia had left the ticket on the dashboard for her and she stuck it in the machine, expecting the barrier to lift. The machine spat it back out.

As she tried it the other way, with the same result, there was a series of impatient toots from the tailback building up behind her.

So much for invisibility.

She'd been on her own for not much more than an hour and already she was the centre of attention…

'What's your problem, lady?'

Annie froze but the 'Rose' never came and she finally looked up to find a car park attendant, a Santa Claus hat tugged down to his ears against the cold, glaring at her.

Apparently he'd used the word 'lady' not as a title, but as something barely short of an insult and, like his sour expression, it didn't quite match the 'ho, ho, ho' of the hat.

'Well?' he demanded.

'Oh. Um…' *Concentrate!* 'I put the ticket in, but nothing happened.'

'Have you paid?'

'Paid?' she asked. 'Where?'

He sighed. 'Can't you read? There's a notice ten feet high at the entrance.' Then, since she was still frowning, he said, very slowly, 'You have to pay before you leave. Over there.' She looked around, saw a machine, then, as the hooting became more insistent, 'In your own time,' he added sarcastically.

And *Bah! Humbug...* to you, she thought as she grabbed her bag from the car and sprinted to the nearest machine, read the instructions, fed in the ticket and then the amount indicated with shaking fingers.

She returned to the car, calling, 'Sorry, sorry...' to the people she'd held up before flinging herself back into the car and finally escaping.

Moments later, she was just one of thousands of drivers battling through traffic swollen by Christmas shoppers and visitors who'd come up to town to see the lights.

Anonymous, invisible, she removed the unnecessary spectacles, dropping them on the passenger seat, then headed west out of London.

She made good time but the pale blue winter sky was tinged with pink, the trees black against the horizon as she reached the junction for Maybridge. A pretty town with excellent shops, a popular riverside area, it was not too big, not too small. As good a place as any to begin her adventure and she headed for the ring road and the anonymous motel she'd found on the Internet.

Somewhere to spend the night and decide what she was going to do with her brief moment of freedom.

* * *

George Saxon's jaw was rigid as he kept his silence.

'No one else can do it,' his father insisted.

A nurse appeared, checked the drip. 'I need to make Mr Saxon comfortable,' she said. Then, with a pointed look at him, 'Why don't you take your mother home? She's been here all day.'

'No, I'll stay.' She took his father's hand, squeezed it. 'I'll be back in a little while.'

His father ignored her, instead grabbing his wrist as he made a move.

'Tell me you'll do it!'

'Don't fret,' his mother said soothingly. 'You can leave George to sort things out at the garage. He won't let you down.'

She looked pleadingly across the bed at him, silently imploring him to back her up.

'Of course he'll let me down,' his father said before he could speak. 'He never could stand getting his hands dirty.'

'Enough!' the nurse said and, not waiting for his mother, George walked from the room.

She caught up with him in the family room. 'I'm sorry—'

'Don't! Don't apologise for him.' Then, pouring her a cup of tea from one of the flasks on the trolley, 'You do realise that he's not going to be able to carry on like this?'

'Please, George…' she said.

Please, George…

Those two words had been the soundtrack to his childhood, his adolescence.

'I'll sort out what needs to be done,' he said. 'But maybe it's time for that little place by the sea?' he suggested, hoping to get her to see that there was an upside to this.

She shook her head. 'He'd be dead within a year.'

'He'll be dead anyway if he carries on.' Then, because he knew he was only distressing his mother, he said, 'Will you be okay here on your own? Have you had anything to eat?'

'I'll get myself something if I'm hungry,' she said, refusing to be fussed over. Then, her hand on his arm, 'I'm so grateful to you for coming home. Your dad won't tell you himself…' She gave an awkward little shrug. 'I don't have to tell you how stubborn he can be. But he's glad to see you.'

The traffic was building up to rush-hour level by the time Annie reached the far side of Maybridge. Unused to driving in heavy traffic, confused by the signs, she missed the exit for the motel, a fact she only realised when she passed it, seeing its lights blazing.

Letting slip a word she'd never used before, she took the next exit and then, rather than retracing her route using the ring road, she turned left, certain that it would lead her back to the motel. Fifteen minutes later, in an unlit country lane that had meandered off in totally the wrong direction, she admitted defeat and, as her headlights picked up the gateway to a field, she pulled over.

She found Reverse, swung the wheel and backed in. There was an unexpectedly sharp dip and the rear wheels left the tarmac with a hard bump, jolting the underside of the car.

Annie took a deep breath, told herself that it was nothing, then, having gathered herself, she turned the steering wheel in the right direction and applied a little pressure to the accelerator.

The only response was a horrible noise.

George sat for a moment looking up at the sign, George Saxon and Son, above the garage workshop. It was only when he climbed from the car that he noticed the light still burning, no doubt forgotten in the panic when his father had collapsed.

Using the keys his mother had given him, he unlocked the side door. Only two of the bays were occupied.

The nearest held the vintage Bentley that his father was in such a state about. Beautiful, arcane, it was in constant use as a wedding car and the brake linings needed replacing.

As he reached for the light switch he heard the familiar clang of a spanner hitting concrete, a muffled curse.

'Hello?'

There was no response and, walking around the Bentley, he discovered a pair of feet encased in expensive sports shoes, jiggling as if in time to music, sticking out from beneath the bonnet.

He didn't waste his breath trying to compete with whatever the owner of the feet was listening to, but instead he tapped one of them lightly with the toe of his shoe.

The movement stopped.

Then a pair of apparently endless, overall-clad legs slid from beneath the car, followed by a slender body. Finally a girl's face appeared.

'*Alexandra?*'

'*George?*' she replied, mocking his disbelief with pure sarcasm. 'Gran told me you were coming but I didn't actually believe her.'

He was tempted to ask her why not, but instead went for the big one.

'What are you doing here?' And, more to the point, why hadn't his mother warned him that his daughter was there when she'd given him her keys?

'Mum's away on honeymoon with husband number three,' she replied, as if that explained everything. 'Where else would I go?' Then, apparently realising that lying on her back she was at something of a disadvantage, she put her feet flat on the concrete and rose in one fluid, effortless movement that made him feel old.

'And these days everyone calls me Xandra.'

'Xandra,' he repeated without comment. She'd been named, without reference to him, after her maternal grandmother, a woman who'd wanted him put up against a wall and shot for despoiling her little princess. It was probably just as well that at the time he'd been too numb with shock to laugh.

Indicating his approval, however, would almost certainly cause her to change back. Nothing he did was ever right. He'd tried so hard, loved her so much, but it had always been a battle between them. And, much as he'd have liked to blame her mother for that, he knew it wasn't her fault. He simply had no idea how to be a dad. The kind that a little girl would smile at, run to.

'I have no interest in your mother's whereabouts,' he said. 'I want to know why you're here instead of at school?'

She lifted her shoulders in an insolent shrug. 'I've been suspended.'

'Suspended?'

'Indefinitely.' Then with a second, epic, I-really-couldn't-care-less shrug, 'Until after Christmas, anyway. Not that it matters. I wouldn't go back if they paid me.'

'Unlikely, I'd have said.'

'If you offered to build them a new science lab I bet they'd be keen enough.'

'In that case *I'd* be the one paying them to take

you back,' he pointed out. 'What has your mother done about it?'

'Nothing. I told you. She's lying on a beach somewhere. With her phone switched off.'

'You could have called me.'

'And what? You'd have dropped everything and rushed across the Atlantic to play daddy? Who knew you cared?'

He clenched his teeth. He was his father all over again. Incapable of forming a bond, making contact with this child who'd nearly destroyed his life. Who, from the moment she'd been grudgingly placed in his arms, had claimed his heart.

He would have done anything for her, died for her if need be. Anything but give up the dream he'd fought tooth and nail to achieve.

All the money in the world, the house his ex-wife had chosen, the expensive education—nothing he'd done had countered that perceived desertion.

'Let's pretend for a moment that I do,' he said, matter-of-factly. 'What did you do?'

'Nothing.' She coloured slightly. 'Nothing much.' He waited. 'I hot-wired the head's car and took it for a spin, that's all.'

Hot-wired...

Apparently taking his shocked silence as encouragement to continue, she said, 'Honestly. Who'd have thought the Warthog would have made such a fuss?'

'You're not old enough to drive!' Then, because she'd grown so fast, was almost a woman, 'Are you?'

She just raised her eyebrows, leaving him to work it out for himself. He was right. He'd been nineteen when she was born, which meant that his daughter wouldn't be seventeen until next May. It would be six months before she could even apply for a licence.

'You stole a car, drove it without a licence, without insurance?' He somehow managed to keep his voice neutral. 'That's your idea of "nothing much"?'

He didn't bother asking who'd taught her to drive. That would be the same person who'd given him an old banger and let him loose in the field out back as soon as his feet touched the pedals. Driving was in the Saxon blood, according to his father, and engine oil ran through their veins.

But, since she'd hot-wired Mrs Warburton's car, clearly driving wasn't all her grandfather had taught her.

'What were you doing under the Bentley?' he demanded as a chill that had nothing to do with the temperature ran through him.

'Just checking it out. It needs new brake linings…' The phone began to ring. With the slightest of shrugs, she leaned around him, unhooked it from the wall and said, 'George Saxon and Granddaughter…'

What?

'Where are you?' she asked, reaching for a pen. 'Are you on your own…? Okay, stay with the car—'

George Saxon and Granddaughter…

Shock slowed him down and as he moved to wrest the phone from her she leaned back out of his reach.

'—we'll be with you in ten minutes.' She replaced the receiver. 'A lone woman broken down on the Longbourne Road,' she said. 'I told her we'll pick her up.'

'I heard what you said. Just how do you propose to do that?' he demanded furiously.

'Get in the tow-truck,' she suggested, 'drive down the road…'

'There's no one here to deal with a breakdown.'

'You're here. *I'm* here. Granddad says I'm as good as you were with an engine.'

If she thought that would make him feel better, she would have to think again.

'Call her back,' he said, pulling down the local directory. 'Tell her we'll find someone else to help her.'

'I didn't take her number.'

'It doesn't matter. She won't care who turns up so long as someone does,' he said, punching in the number of another garage. It had rung just twice when he heard the clunk as a truck door was slammed shut. On the third ring he heard it start.

He turned around as a voice in his ear said, 'Longbourne Motors. How can I…'

The personnel door was wide open and, as he watched, the headlights of the pick-up truck pierced the dark.

'Sorry,' he said, dropping the phone and racing after his daughter, wrenching open the cab door as it began to move. 'Turn it off!'

She began to move as he reached for the keys.

'Alexandra! Don't you dare!' He hung onto the door, walking quickly alongside the truck as she moved across the forecourt.

'It's Granddad's business,' she said, speeding up a little, forcing him to run or let go. He ran. 'I'm not going to let you shut it down.' Then, having made her point, she eased off the accelerator until the truck rolled to a halt before turning to challenge him. 'I love cars, engines. I'm going to run this place, be a rally driver—'

'What?'

'Granddad's going to sponsor me.'

'You're sixteen,' he said, not sure whether he was more horrified that she wanted to race cars or fix them. 'You don't know what you want.'

Even as he said the words, he heard his father's voice. *'You're thirteen, boy. Your head is full of nonsense. You don't know what you want…'*

He'd gone on saying it to him even when he was filling in forms, applying for university places, knowing that he'd get no financial backing, that he'd have to support himself every step of the way.

Even when his 'nonsense' was being installed in every new engine manufactured throughout the world, his father had still been telling him he was wrong...

'Move over,' he said.

Xandra clung stubbornly to the steering wheel. 'What are you going to do?'

'Since you've already kept a lone woman waiting in a dark country lane for five minutes longer than necessary, I haven't got much choice. I'm going to let you pick her up.'

'Me?'

'You. But you've already committed enough motoring offences for one week, so I'll drive the truck.'

CHAPTER TWO

ANNIE saw the tow-truck, yellow light flashing on the roof of the cab, looming out of the dark, and sighed with relief as it pulled up just ahead of her broken-down car.

After a lorry, driving much too fast along the narrow country lane, had missed the front of the car by inches, she'd scrambled out and was standing with her back pressed against the gate, shivering with the cold.

The driver jumped down and swung a powerful torch over and around the car, and she threw up an arm to shield her eyes from the light as he found her.

'George Saxon,' her knight errant said, lowering the torch a little. 'Are you okay?' he asked.

'Y-y-yes,' she managed through chattering teeth. She couldn't see his face behind the light but his voice had a touch of impatience that wasn't exactly what she'd hoped for. 'No thanks to a lorry driver who nearly took the front off the car.'

'You should have switched on the hazard warning lights,' he said unsympathetically. 'Those sidelights are useless.'

'If he'd been driving within the speed limit, he'd have seen me,' she replied, less than pleased at the suggestion that it was her own fault that she'd nearly been killed.

'There is no speed limit on this road other than the national limit. That's seventy miles an hour,' he added, in case she didn't know.

'I saw the signs. Foolishly, perhaps, I assumed that it was the upper limit, not an instruction,' she snapped right back.

'True,' he agreed, 'but just because other people behave stupidly it doesn't mean you have to join in.'

First the car park attendant and now the garage mechanic. Irritable men talking to her as if she had dimwit tattooed across her forehead was getting tiresome.

Although, considering she could be relaxing in the warmth and comfort of Bab el Sama instead of freezing her socks off in an English country lane in December, they might just have a point.

'So,' he asked, gesturing at the car with the torch, 'what's the problem?'

'I thought it was your job to tell me that,' she replied, deciding she'd taken enough male insolence for one day.

'Okaaay…'

Back-lit by the bright yellow hazard light swinging around on top of the tow-truck, she couldn't make out more than the bulk of him but she had a strong sense of a man hanging onto his temper by a thread.

'Let's start with the basics,' he said, making an effort. 'Have you run out of petrol?'

'What kind of fool do you take me for?'

'That's what I'm trying to establish,' he replied with all the long-suffering patience of a man faced with every conceivable kind of a fool. Then, with a touch more grace, 'Maybe you should just tell me what happened and we'll take it from there.'

That was close enough to a truce to bring her from the safety of the gate and through teeth that were chattering with the cold—or maybe delayed shock, that lorry had been very close—she said, 'I t-took the wrong road and t-tried to—'

'To' turned into a yelp as she caught her foot in a rut and was flung forward, hands outstretched, as she grabbed for anything to save herself. What she got was soft brushed leather and George Saxon, who didn't budge as she cannoned into him but, steady as a rock, caught her, then held her as she struggled to catch her breath.

'Are you okay?' he asked after a moment.

With her cheek, her nose and her hands pressed against his chest, she was in no position to answer.

But with his breath warm against her skin, his

hands holding her safe, there wasn't a great deal wrong that she could think of.

Except, of course, all of the above.

She couldn't remember ever being quite this close to a man she didn't know, so what she was feeling—and whether 'okay' covered it—she couldn't begin to say. She was still trying to formulate some kind of response when he moved back slightly, presumably so that he could check for himself.

'I think so,' she said quickly, getting a grip on her wits. She even managed to ease back a little herself, although she didn't actually let go until she'd put a little weight on her ankle to test it.

There didn't appear to be any damage but she decided not to rush it.

'I'm in better shape than the car, anyway.'

He continued to look at her, not with the deferential respect she was used to, but in a way that made her feel exposed, vulnerable and, belatedly, she let go of his jacket, straightened the spectacles that had slipped sideways.

'It was d-dark,' she stuttered—*stuttered?* 'And when I backed into the gate there was a bit more of a d-drop than I expected.' Then, realising how feeble that sounded, 'Quite a lot more of a drop, actually. This field entrance is very badly maintained,' she added, doing her best to distance herself from the scent of leather warmed by a man's body.

From the feel of his chest beneath it, his solid shoulders. The touch of strong hands.

And in the process managed to sound like a rather pompous and disapproving dowager duchess.

'Good enough for a tractor,' he replied, dropping those capable hands and taking a step back. Leaving a cold space between them. 'The farmer isn't in the business of providing turning places for women who can't read a map.'

'I…' On the point of saying that she hadn't looked at a map, she thought better of it. He already thought she was a fool and there was nothing to be gained from confirming his first impression. 'No. Well…' She'd have taken a step back herself if she hadn't been afraid her foot would find another rut and this time do some real damage. 'I banged the underside of the car on something as I went down. When I tried to drive away it made a terrible noise and…' She shrugged.

'And what?' he persisted.

'And nothing,' she snapped. Good grief, did he want it spelling out in words of one syllable? 'It wasn't going anywhere.' Then, rubbing her hands over her sleeves, 'Can you fix it?'

'Not here.'

'Oh.'

'Come on,' he said and, apparently taking heed of her comments about the state of the ground, he took her arm and supported her back onto the safety of the tarmac before opening the rear door of the truck's cab. 'You'd better get out of harm's way while we load her up.'

As the courtesy light came on, bathing them both in light, Annie saw more of him. The brushed leather bomber jacket topping long legs clad not, as she'd expected, in overalls, but a pair of well-cut light-coloured trousers. And, instead of work boots, he was wearing expensive-looking loafers. Clearly, George Saxon hadn't had the slightest intention of doing anything at the side of the road.

Her face must have betrayed exactly what she was thinking because he waved his torch over a tall but slight figure in dark overalls who was already attaching a line to her car.

'She's the mechanic,' he said with a sardonic edge to his voice. His face, all dark shadows as the powerful overhead light swung in the darkness, matched his tone perfectly. 'I'm just along for the ride.'

She? Annie thought as, looking behind her, he called out, 'How are you doing back there?'

'Two minutes…'

The voice was indeed that of a girl. Young and more than a little breathless and Annie, glancing back as she reached for the grab rail to haul herself up into the cab, could see that she was struggling.

'I think she could do with some help,' she said.

George regarded this tiresome female who'd been wished on him by his daughter with irritation.

'I'm just the driver,' he said. Then, offering her the torch, 'But don't let me stop you from pitching in and giving her a hand.'

'It's okay,' Xandra called before she could take it from him. 'I've got it.'

He shrugged. 'It seems you were worrying about nothing.'

'Are you sure?' she asked, calling back to Xandra while never taking her eyes off him. It was a look that reminded him of Miss Henderson, a teacher who had been able to quell a class of unruly kids with a glance. Maybe it was the woolly hat and horn-rimmed glasses.

Although he had to admit that Miss Henderson had lacked the fine bone structure and, all chalk and old books, had never smelt anywhere near as good.

'I'm done,' Xandra called.

'Happy?' he enquired.

The woman held the look for one long moment before she gave him a cool nod and climbed up into the cab, leaving him to close the door behind her as if she were royalty.

'Your servant, ma'am,' he muttered as he went back to see how Xandra was doing.

'Why on earth did you say that to her?' she hissed as he checked the coupling.

He wasn't entirely sure. Other than the fact that

Miss Henderson was the only woman he'd ever known who could cut his cocky ten-year-old self down to size with a glance.

'Let's go,' he said, pretending he hadn't heard.

Back in the cab, he started the engine and began to winch the car up onto the trailer but, when he glanced up to check the road, his passenger's eyes, huge behind the lenses, seemed to fill the rear-view mirror.

'Can we drop you somewhere?' he asked as Xandra climbed in beside him. Eager to be rid of her so that he could drop the car off at Longbourne Motors.

That took the starch right out of her look.

'What? No… I can't go on without my car…'

'It's not going anywhere tonight. You don't live locally?' he asked.

'No. I'm… I'm on holiday. Touring.'

'On your own? In December?'

'Is there something wrong with that?'

A whole lot, in his opinion, but it was none of his business. 'Whatever turns you on,' he said, 'although Maybridge in winter wouldn't be my idea of a good time.'

'Lots of people come for the Christmas market,' Xandra said. 'It's this weekend. I'm going.'

All this and Christmas too. How much worse could it get? he thought before turning to Xandra and saying, 'You aren't going anywhere. You're grounded.' Then, without looking in the mirror, he said, 'Where are you staying tonight?'

'I'm not booked in anywhere. I was heading for the motel on the ring road.'

'We'd have to go all the way to the motorway roundabout to get there from here,' Xandra said before he could say a word, no doubt guessing his intention of dropping the car off at Longbourne Motors. 'Much easier to run the lady back to the motel through the village once we have a better idea of how long it will take to fix her car.'

She didn't wait for an answer, instead turning to introduce herself to their passenger. 'I'm sorry, I'm Xandra Saxon,' she said, but she was safe enough. This wasn't an argument he planned on having in front of a stranger.

Annie relaxed a little as George Saxon took his eyes off her and smiled at the girl beside him, who was turning into something of an ally.

'Hello, Xandra. I'm R-Ro...'

The word began to roll off her tongue before she remembered that she wasn't Rose Napier.

'Ro-o-owland,' she stuttered out, grabbing for the first name that came into her head. Nanny Rowland... 'Annie Rowland,' she said, more confidently.

Lydia had suggested she borrow her name but she'd decided that it would be safer to stick with something familiar. Annie had been her mother's pet name for her but, since her grandfather disapproved of it, no one other than members of the household staff who'd known her since her mother was alive had ever used it. In the stress of the moment, though, the practised response had gone clean out of her head and she'd slipped into her standard introduction.

'Ro-o-owland?' George Saxon, repeating the name with every nuance of hesitation, looked up at the rear-view mirror and held her gaze.

'Annie will do just fine,' she said, then, realising that man and girl had the same name, she turned to Xandra. 'You're related?'

'Not so's you'd notice,' she replied in that throwaway, couldn't-care-less manner that the young used when something was truly, desperately important. 'My mother has made a career of getting married. George was the first in line, with a shotgun to his back if the date on my birth certificate is anything—'

'Buckle up, Xandra,' he said, cutting her off.

He was her father? But she wasn't, it would appear, daddy's little girl if the tension between them was anything to judge by.

But what did she know about the relationship between father and daughter? All she remembered was the joy of her father's presence, feeling safe in his arms. If he'd lived would she have been a difficult teen?

The one thing she wouldn't have been was isolated, wrapped in cotton wool by a grandfather afraid for her safety. She'd have gone to school, mixed with girls—and boys—her own age. Would have fallen in and out of love without the eyes of the entire country on her. Would never have stepped into the spotlight only to discover, too late, that she was unable to escape its glare.

'Are you warm enough back there?' George Saxon asked.

'Yes. Thank you.'

The heater was efficient and despite his lack of charm, he hadn't fumbled when she'd fallen into his arms. On the contrary. He'd been a rock and she felt safe enough in the back of his truck. A lot safer than she'd felt in his arms. But of course this was her natural place in the world. Sitting in the back with some man up front in the driving seat. In control.

Everything she'd hoped to escape from, she reminded herself, her gaze fixed on the man who was in control at the moment. Or at least the back of his head.

Over the years she had become something of a connoisseur of the back of the male head. The masculine neck. All those chauffeurs, bodyguards…

George Saxon's neck would stand comparison with the best, she decided. Strong, straight with thick dark hair expertly cut to exactly the right length. His shoulders, encased in the soft tan leather of his jacket, would take some beating too. It was a pity his manners didn't match them.

Or was she missing the point?

Rupert's perfect manners made her teeth ache to say or do something utterly outrageous just to get a reaction, but George Saxon's hands, like his eyes, had been anything but polite.

They'd been assured, confident, brazen even. She could still feel the imprint of his thumbs against her breasts where his hands had gripped her as she'd fallen; none of that Dresden shepherdess nonsense for him. And his insolence as he'd offered her the torch had sent an elemental shiver of awareness running up her spine that had precious little to do with the cold that had seeped deep into her bones.

He might not be a gentleman, but he was real—dangerously so—and, whatever else he made her feel, it certainly wasn't desperation.

Annie didn't have time to dwell on what exactly he did make her feel before he swung the truck off the road and turned onto the forecourt of a large garage with a sign across the workshop that read, George Saxon and Son.

Faded and peeling, neglected, it didn't match the man, she thought as he backed up to one of the bays. He might be a little short on charm but he had an animal vitality that sent a charge of awareness running through her.

Xandra jumped down and opened the doors and then, once he'd backed her car in, she uncoupled it, he said, 'There's a customer waiting room at the far end. You'll find a machine for drinks.' Dismissed, she climbed down from the truck and walked away. 'Annie!'

She stopped. It was, she discovered, easy to be charming when everyone treated you with respect but she had to take a deep breath before she turned, very carefully, to face him.

'Mr Saxon?' she responded politely.

'Shut the damn door!'

She blinked.

No one had ever raised their voice to her. Spoken to her in that way.

'In your own time,' he said when she didn't move.

Used to having doors opened for her, stepping out of a car without so much as a backward glance, she hadn't even thought about it.

She wanted to be ordinary, she reminded herself. To be treated like an ordinary woman. Clearly, it was going to be an education.

She walked back, closed the door, but if she'd expected the courtesy of a thank you she would have been disappointed.

Always a fast learner, she hadn't held her breath.

'Take no notice of George,' Xandra said as he drove away to park the truck. 'He doesn't want to be here so he's taking it out on you.'

'Doesn't…? Why not? Isn't he the "and Son"?'

She laughed, but not with any real mirth. 'Wrong generation. The "and Son" above the garage is my granddad but he's in hospital. A heart attack.'

'I'm sorry to hear that. How is he?'

'Not well enough to run the garage until I can take over,' she said. Then, blinking back something that looked very much like a tear, she shrugged, lifted her head. 'Sorry. Family business.' She flicked a switch that activated the hoist. 'I'll take a look at your car.'

Annie, confused by the tensions, wishing she could do something too, but realising that she'd been dismissed—and that was new, as well—said, 'Your father mentioned a waiting room?'

'Oh, for goodness' sake. It'll be freezing in there and the drinks machine hasn't worked in ages.' Xandra fished a key out of her pocket. 'Go inside where it's warm,' she said, handing it to her. 'Make yourself at home. There's tea and coffee by the kettle, milk in the fridge.' Xandra watched the car as it rose slowly above them, then, realising that she hadn't moved, said, 'Don't worry. It won't take long to find the problem.'

'Are you quite sure?' she asked.

'I may be young but I know what I'm doing.'

'Yes…' Well, maybe. 'I meant about letting myself in.'

'Gran would invite you in herself if she were here,' she said as her father rejoined them.

In the bright strip light his face had lost the dangerous shadows, but it still had a raw quality. There was no softness to mitigate hard bone other than a full lower lip that oozed sensuality and only served to increase her sense of danger.

'You shouldn't be in here,' he said.

'I'm going…' She cleared her throat. 'Can I make something for either of you?' she offered.

He frowned.

She lifted her hand and dangled the door key. 'Tea? Coffee?'

For a moment she thought he was going to tell her to stay on her own side of the counter—maybe she was giving him the opportunity—but after a moment he shrugged and said, 'Coffee. If there is any.'

'Xandra?'

'Whatever,' she said, as she ducked beneath the hoist, clearly more interested in the car than in anything she had to say and Annie walked quickly across the yard, through a gate and up a well-lit path to the rear of a long, low stone-built house and let herself in through the back door.

The mud room was little more than a repository for boots and working clothes, a place to wash off the workplace dirt, but as she walked into the kitchen she was wrapped in the heat being belted out by an ancient solid fuel stove.

Now this was familiar, she thought, relaxing as

she crossed to the sink, filled the kettle and set it on the hob to boil.

This room, so much more than a kitchen, was typical of the farmhouses at King's Lacey, her grandfather's Warwickshire estate.

Her last memory of her father was being taken to visit the tenants before he'd gone away for the last time. She'd been given brightly coloured fizzy pop and mince pies while he'd talked to people he'd known since his boyhood, asking about their children and grandchildren, discussing the price of feedstuff, grain. She'd played with kittens, fed the chickens, been given fresh eggs to take home for her tea. Been a child.

She ran her hand over the large, scrubbed-top table, looked at the wide dresser, laden with crockery and piled up with paperwork. Blinked back the tear that caught her by surprise before turning to a couple of Morris armchairs, the leather seats scuffed and worn, the wooden arms rubbed with wear, one of them occupied by a large ginger cat.

A rack filled with copies of motoring magazines stood beside one, a bag stuffed with knitting beside the other. There was a dog basket by the Aga, but no sign of its owner.

She let the cat sniff her fingers before rubbing it behind the ear, starting up a deep purr. Comfortable, it was the complete opposite of the state-of-the-art kitchen in her London home. Caught in a nineteen-fifties time warp, the only concession to modernity here was a large refrigerator, its cream enamel surface chipped with age, and a small television set tucked away on a shelf unit built beside the chimney breast.

The old butler's sink, filled with dishes that were no doubt waiting for Xandra's attention—George Saxon didn't look the kind of man who was familiar with a dish mop—suggested that the age of the dishwasher had not yet reached the Saxon household.

She didn't have a lot of time to spare for basic household chores these days, but there had been a time, long ago, when she had been allowed to stand on a chair and wash dishes, help cook when she was making cakes and, even now, once in a while, when they were in the country, she escaped to the comfort of her childhood kitchen, although only at night, when the staff were gone.

She wasn't a child any more and her presence was an intrusion on their space.

Here, though, she was no one and she peeled off the woolly hat and fluffed up her short hair, enjoying the lightness of it. Then she hung her padded jacket on one of the pegs in the mud room before hunting out a pair of rubber gloves and pitching in.

Washing up was as ordinary as it got and she was

grinning by the time she'd cleared the decks. It wasn't what she'd imagined she'd be doing this evening, but it certainly fulfilled the parameters of the adventure.

By the time she heard the back door open, the dishes were draining on the rack above the sink and she'd made a large pot of tea for herself and Xandra, and a cup of instant coffee for George.

'Oh…' Xandra came to an abrupt halt at the kitchen door as she saw the table on which she was laying out cups and saucers. 'I usually just bung a teabag in a mug,' she said. Then, glancing guiltily at the sink, her eyes widened further. 'You've done the washing-up…'

'Well, you did tell me to make myself at home,' Annie said, deadpan.

It took Xandra a moment but then she grinned. 'You're a brick. I *was* going to do it before Gran got home.'

A brick? No one had ever called her that before.

'Don't worry about it,' she replied, pouring tea while Xandra washed her hands at the sink. 'Your gran is at the hospital with your grandfather, I imagine?'

Before Xandra could answer, George Saxon followed her into the kitchen, bringing with him a metallic blast of cold air.

He came to an abrupt halt, staring at her for a moment. Or, rather, she thought, her hair, and she belatedly wished she'd kept her hat on, but it was too late for that.

'Has she told you?' he demanded, finally tearing his gaze away from what she knew must look an absolute fright.

'Told me what?' she asked him.

'That you've broken your crankshaft.'

'No,' she said, swiftly tiring of the novelty of his rudeness. A gentleman would have ignored the fact that she was having a seriously bad hair day rather than staring at the disaster in undisguised horror. 'I gave my ankle a bit of a jolt in that pothole but, unless things have changed since I studied anatomy, I don't believe that I have a crankshaft.'

Xandra snorted tea down her nose as she laughed, earning herself a quelling look from her father.

'You've broken the crankshaft that drives the wheels of your car,' he said heavily, quashing any thought she might have of joining in. 'It'll have to be replaced.'

'If I knew what a crankshaft was,' she replied, 'I suspect that I'd be worried. How long will it take?'

He shrugged. 'I'll have to ring around in the morning and see if there's anyone who can deal with it as an emergency.'

Annie heard what he said but even when she ran through it again it still made no sense.

'Why?' she asked finally.

He had the nerve to turn a pair of slate-grey eyes on her and regard her as if her wits had gone begging.

'I assume you want it repaired?'

'Of course I want it repaired. That's why I called you. You're a garage. You fix cars. So fix it.'

'I'm sorry but that's impossible.'

'You don't sound sorry.'

'He isn't. While Granddad's lying helpless in hospital he's going to shut down a garage that's been in the family for nearly a hundred years.'

'Are you?' she asked, keeping her gaze fixed firmly on him. 'That doesn't sound very sporting.'

He looked right back and she could see a pale fan of lines around his eyes that in anyone else she'd have thought were laughter lines.

'He flew all the way from California for that very purpose,' his daughter said when he didn't bother to answer.

'California?' Well, that certainly explained the lines around his eyes. Screwing them up against the sun rather than an excess of good humour. 'How interesting. What do you do in California, Mr Saxon?'

Her life consisted of asking polite questions, drawing people out of their shell, showing an interest. She had responded with her 'Lady Rose' voice and she'd have liked to pretend that this was merely habit rather than genuine interest, but that would be a big fat fib. There was something about George Saxon that aroused a lot more than polite interest in her maidenly breast.

His raised eyebrow suggested that what he did in the US was none of her business and he was undoubtedly right, but his daughter was happy to fill the gap.

'According to my mother,' she said, 'George is a beach bum.'

At this point 'Lady Rose' would have smiled politely and moved on. Annie didn't have to do that.

'Is your mother right?' she asked.

'He doesn't go to work unless he feels like it. Lives on the beach. If it looks like a duck and walks like a duck…'

She was looking at George, talking to him, but the replies kept coming from his daughter, stage left, and Annie shook her head just once, lifted a hand to silence the girl, waiting for him to answer her question.

CHAPTER THREE

'I'M AFRAID it's your bad luck that my daughter answered your call,' George replied, not bothering to either confirm or deny it. 'If I'd got to the phone first I'd have told you to ring someone else.'

'I see. So why didn't you simply call another garage and arrange for them to pick me up?' Annie asked, genuinely puzzled.

'It would have taken too long and, since you were on your own…' He let it go.

She didn't.

'Oh, I *see*. You're a gentleman beach bum?'

'Don't count on it,' he replied.

No. She wouldn't do that, but he appeared to have a conscience and she could work with that.

She'd had years of experience in parting millionaires from their money in a good cause and this seemed like a very good moment to put what she'd learned to use on her own behalf.

'It's a pity your concern doesn't stretch as far as

fixing my car.' Since his only response was to remove his jacket and hang it over the back of a chair, the clearest statement that he was going nowhere, she continued. 'So, George...' use his name, imply that they were friends '...having brought me here under false pretences, what do you suggest I do now?'

'I suggest you finish your tea, Annie...' and the way he emphasized her name suggested he knew exactly what game she was playing '...then I suggest you call a taxi.'

Well, that didn't go as well as she'd hoped.

'I thought the deal was that you were going to run me there,' she reminded him.

'It's been a long day. You'll find a directory by the phone. It's through there. In the hall,' he added, just in case she was labouring under the misapprehension that he would do it for her. Then, having glanced at the cup of instant coffee and the delicate china cups she'd laid out, he took a large mug—one that *she'd* just washed—from the rack over the sink and filled it with tea.

Annie had been raised to be a lady and her first reaction, even under these trying circumstances, was to apologise for being a nuisance.

There had been a moment, right after that lorry had borne down on her out of the dark and she'd thought her last moment had come, when the temptation to accept defeat had very nearly got the better of her.

Shivering with shock at her close brush with eternity as much as the cold, it would have been so easy to put in the call that would bring a chauffeur-driven limousine to pick her up, return her home with nothing but a very bad haircut and a lecture on irresponsibility from her grandfather to show for her adventure.

But she'd wanted reality and that meant dealing with the rough as well as the smooth. Breaking down on a dark country road was no fun, but Lydia wouldn't have been able to walk away, leave someone else to pick up the pieces. She'd have to deal with the mechanic who'd responded to her call, no matter how unwillingly. How lacking in the ethos of customer service.

Lydia, she was absolutely certain, wouldn't apologise to him for expecting him to do his job, but demand he got on with it.

She could do no less.

'I'm sorry,' she began, but she wasn't apologising for being a nuisance. Far from it. Instead, she picked up her tea and polite as you please, went on. 'I'm afraid that is quite unacceptable. When you responded to my call you entered into a contract and I insist that you honour it.'

George Saxon paused in the act of spooning sugar into his tea and glanced up at her from beneath a lick of dark hair that had slid across his forehead.

'Is that right?' he asked.

He didn't sound particularly impressed.

'Under the terms of the Goods and Services Act,' she added, with the poise of a woman for whom addressing a room full of strangers was an everyday occurrence, 'nineteen eighty-three.' The Act was real enough, even if she'd made up the date. The trick was to look as if you knew what you were talking about and a date—even if it was the first one that came into her head—added veracity to even the most outrageous statement.

This time he did smile and deep creases bracketed his face, his mouth, fanned out around those slate eyes. Maybe not just the sun, then…

'You just made that up, Annie Rowland,' he said, calling her bluff.

She pushed up the spectacles that kept sliding down her nose and smiled right back.

'I'll just wait here while you go to the local library and check,' she said, lowering herself into the unoccupied Morris chair. 'Unless you have a copy?' Balancing the saucer in one hand, she used the other to pick up her tea and sip it. 'Although, since you're clearly unfamiliar with the legislation, I'm assuming that you don't.'

'The library is closed until tomorrow morning,' he pointed out.

'They don't have late-night opening? How inconvenient for you. Never mind, I can wait.' Then added, 'Or you could just save time and fix my car.'

George had known the minute Annie Ro-o-owland had blundered into him, falling into his arms as if she was made to fit, that he was in trouble. Then she'd looked at him through the rear-view mirror of the truck with those big blue eyes and he'd been certain of it. And here, in the light of his mother's kitchen, they had double the impact.

They were not just large, but were the mesmerizing colour of a bluebell wood in April, framed by long dark lashes and perfectly groomed brows that were totally at odds with that appalling haircut. At odds with those horrible spectacles which continually slipped down her nose as if they were too big for her face…

As he stared at her, the certainty that he'd seen her somewhere before tugging at his memory, she used one finger to push them back up and he knew without doubt that they were nothing more than a screen for her to hide behind.

Everything about her was wrong.

Her car, bottom of range even when new, was well past its best, her hair was a nightmare and her clothes were chain-store basics but her scent, so faint that he knew she'd sprayed it on warm skin hours ago, probably after her morning shower, was the real one-thousand-dollar-an-ounce deal.

And then there was her voice.

No one spoke like that unless they were born to it. Not even twenty-five thousand pounds a year at Dower House could buy that true-blue aristocratic accent, a fact he knew to his cost.

He stirred his tea, took a sip, making her wait while he thought about his next move.

'I'll organise a rental for you while it's being fixed,' he offered finally. Experience had taught him that, where women were concerned, money was the easiest way to make a problem go away. But first he'd see how far being helpful would get him. 'If that would make things easier for you?'

She carefully replaced the delicate bone china cup on its saucer. 'I'm sorry, George. I'm afraid that's out of the question.'

It was like a chess game, he thought. Move and countermove. And everything about her—the voice, the poise—suggested that she was used to playing the Queen.

Tough. He wasn't about to be her pawn. He might be lumbered with Mike Jackson's Bentley—he couldn't offload a specialist job like that at short notice as his father well knew—but he wasn't about to take on something that any reasonably competent mechanic could handle.

Maybe if she took off her glasses…

'As a gesture of goodwill, recognising that you have been put to unnecessary inconvenience,' he said, catching himself—this was not the moment to allow himself to be distracted by a pair of blue eyes, pale flawless skin, scent that aroused an instant go-to-hell response. He didn't do 'instant'. It would have to be money. 'I would be prepared to pay any reasonable out-of-pocket expenses.'

Check.

He didn't care how much it cost to get her and her eyes out of the garage, out of his mother's kitchen, out of his hair. Just as long as she went.

'That's a most generous offer,' she replied. 'Unfortunately, I can't accept. The problem isn't money, you see, but my driving licence.'

'Oh?' Then, 'You do *have* a valid licence?'

If she was driving without one all bets were off. He could ground his daughter for her reckless behaviour—maybe—but Annie Rowland would be out of here faster than he could call the police.

But she wasn't in the least bit put out by his suggestion that she was breaking the law.

'I do have a driving licence,' she replied, cool as you like. 'And, in case you're wondering, it's as clean as the day it was issued. But I'm afraid I left it at home. In my other bag.' She shrugged. 'You know how it is.' Then, looking at him as if she'd only just noticed that he was a man, she smiled and said, 'Oh, no. I don't suppose you do. All a man has to do is pick up his wallet and he has everything he needs right there in his jacket pocket.'

He refused to indulge the little niggle that wanted to know whose wallet, what man…

'And where, exactly, is home?' he asked, trying not to look at her hand and failing. She wasn't wearing a ring but that meant nothing.

'London.'

'London is a big place.'

'Yes,' she agreed. 'It is.' Then, without indulging his curiosity about which part of London, 'You must know that no one will rent me a car without it. My licence.'

Unfortunately, he did.

Checkmate.

'Oh, for goodness' sake!' Xandra, who'd been watching this exchange with growing impatience, said, 'If you won't fix Annie's car, I'll do it myself.' She put down her cup and headed for the door. 'I'll make a start right now.'

'Shouldn't you be thinking about your grandmother?' he snapped before she reached it. 'I'm sure she'd appreciate a hot meal when she gets back from the hospital. Or are you so lost to selfishness that you expect her to cook for you?'

'She doesn't…' Then, unexpectedly curbing her tongue, she said, 'I'm not the selfish one around here.'

Annie, aware that in this battle of wits Xandra was her ally, cleared her throat. 'Why don't I get supper?' she offered.

They both turned to stare at her.

'Why would you do that?' George Saxon demanded.

'Because I want my car fixed?'

'You won't get a better offer,' Xandra declared, leaping in before her father could turn down her somewhat rash offer. 'My limit is baked beans on toast. I'm sure Annie can do better than that,' she said, throwing a pleading glance in her direction.

'Can you?' he demanded.

'Do better than baked beans on toast?' she repeated. 'Actually, that won't be…' She broke off, distracted by the wild signals Xandra was making behind her father's back. As he turned to see what had caught her attention she went on. 'Difficult. Not at all.'

He gave her a long look through narrowed eyes, clearly aware that he'd missed something. Then continued to look at her as if there was something about her that bothered him.

She knew just how he felt.

The way he looked at her bothered her to bits, she thought, using her forefinger to push the 'prop' spectacles up her nose. They would keep sliding down, making it easier to look over them than through them, which made wearing them utterly pointless.

'How long do you think it'll take?' she asked, not sure who she was attempting to distract. George or herself.

He continued to stare for perhaps another ten seconds—clearly not a man to be easily distracted—before he shrugged and said, 'It depends what else we find. Your car is not exactly in the first flush. Once something major happens it tends to have a knock-on effect. You're touring, you say?'

She nodded. 'That was the plan. Shropshire, Cheshire, maybe. A little sightseeing. A little shopping.'

'There aren't enough sights, enough shops in London?' he enquired, an edge to his voice that suggested he wasn't entirely convinced.

'Oh, well…' She matched his shrug and raised him a smile. 'You know what they say about a change.'

'Being as good as a rest?' He sounded doubtful. 'This isn't a great time of year to break down, especially if you're stranded miles from anywhere,' he pointed out.

He didn't bother to match her smile.

'It's never a good time for that, George.'

'It's a lot less dangerous when the days are long and the nights warm,' he said, leaving her to imagine what it would be like if she broke down way out in the country, in the dark, with the temperature below freezing. Then, having got that off his chest, 'Are you in a hurry to be anywhere in particular?'

He sounded hopeful.

'Well, no. That's the joy of touring, isn't it? There's no fixed agenda. And now Xandra has told me about the Christmas market in Maybridge this weekend…' she gave another little shrug, mainly because she was certain it would annoy him '…well, I wouldn't want to miss that.' It was a new experience. Annoying a man. One she could grow to enjoy and, taking full advantage of this opportunity, she mentally crossed her fingers and added, 'Ho, ho, ho…'

That earned her another snort—muffled this time—from Xandra, who got a look to singe her ears from her father before he turned back to her and, ignoring her attempt at levity, asked, 'Have you spoken to your insurance company?'

'Why would I do that?'

'Because you've had an accident?'

'Oh. Yes.' The prospect of contacting her insurance company and what that would mean took all the fun out of winding up George Saxon. 'I suppose I have. It never occurred to me…'

'No?' He gave her another of those thoughtful looks. 'Maybe you should do it now although, bearing in mind the age of the car and the likely cost of repairs, their loss adjuster will probably decide to simply write it off.'

'What? They can't do that!'

'I think you'll find they can.'

'Only if I make a claim.'

He didn't answer. And this time Xandra didn't leap in to defend her.

'I *am* insured,' she said hurriedly, before George asked the question that was clearly foremost in his mind.

She didn't blame him. First she wasn't able to produce her licence and now she didn't want her insurance company involved. Anyone with two brain cells to rub together would believe she had something to hide.

Obviously not whatever scenario was going through his mind right now, but something. And they'd be right to be suspicious.

But she was insured.

She'd checked that Lydia's car was covered by her own insurance policy but now, faced with the reality of accidental damage, she realised that it wasn't that simple. If, on the day she made a claim for an accident in Maybridge, the entire world knew she was flying to Bab el Sama—and they would, because she'd made absolutely sure that the press knew where she was going; she wanted them there, establishing her alibi by snatching shots of 'her' walking on the beach—well, that really would put the cat among the pigeons.

She couldn't tell him that, of course, but she was going to have to tell him something and the longer she delayed, the less likely it was that he would believe her. From being in a position of power,

Annie now felt at a distinct disadvantage in the low chair and, putting down her cup, she stood up so that she could look him in the eye.

'You needn't worry that I won't pay you. I have money.' And, determined to establish her financial probity at least, she tugged at the neck of the V-neck sweater she was wearing, reached down inside her shirt and fished a wad of fifty-pound notes from one cup of her bra and placed it on the table.

'Whoa!' Xandra said.

'Will a thousand pounds cover it?' she asked, repeating the performance on the other side before looking up to discover that George was staring at her.

'Go and check the stores to see what spares we have in stock, Xandra,' he said, not taking his eyes off her.

His daughter opened her mouth to protest, then, clearly thinking better of it, stomped out, banging the back door as she went.

For a moment the silence rang in her ears. Then, with a gesture at the pile of banknotes, George said, 'Where did that come from?'

Realising she'd just made things ten times worse, that she was going to have to tell him at least some version of the truth, Annie said, 'It's mine.' He didn't move a muscle. 'Truly. I don't want to use credit cards for the same reason I can't call my insurance company.'

'And why is that?' he asked, stony-faced as a statue.

'It's difficult…'

'No licence, no insurance and a pile of hard cash? I'll say it's difficult. What exactly is your problem, Annie?' he asked. 'Who are you running away from? The police?'

'No! It's nothing like that. It's…' Oh, help… 'It's personal.'

He frowned. 'Are you telling me that it's a domestic?'

Was he asking her if she was running from an abusive husband?

'You're not wearing a ring,' he pointed out, forestalling the temptation to grab such a perfect cover story.

'No. I'm not married.'

'A partner, then. So why all the subterfuge?' he said, picking up one of the wads of banknotes, flicking the edge with his thumb. 'And where did this come from?'

'My parents left me some money. I daren't use credit cards—'

'Or claim on your motor insurance.'

She nodded.

'Is he violent?'

'No!'

'But unwilling to let you go.'

She swallowed and he accepted that as an affirmative. This was going better than she'd hoped.

'How will he trace you? You understand that I have to think about Xandra. And my mother.'

'There's a security firm he uses, but they think I've left the country. As long as I don't do anything to attract attention, they won't find me.'

'I hope you didn't leave your passport behind.'

'No. The clothes I'm wearing, the car, belong to the friend who helped me get away,' she said before he asked her why her 'partner' was in the habit of hiring a security firm to keep tabs on her. 'You can understand why I feel so bad about what's happened to the car. Will you be able to fix it?'

He looked at her for a long time before shaking his head. 'I knew you were trouble from the first moment I set eyes on you,' he said, 'and I know I'm going to regret this, but I'll see if your car is salvageable so I can get you on your way. I just hope I don't live to see the name Annie Rowland linked with mine in the headlines.'

'That won't happen,' she promised.

'Of course it won't. The only thing I am sure of where you're concerned is that your name isn't Rowland.'

'It *is* Annie,' she said, glad for some reason that she couldn't begin to fathom that she had chosen to use her own best name.

'Then let's leave it at that,' he said, putting down the mug as he pushed himself away from the table. 'But whatever you plan on cooking for dinner,

Annie, had better be worth all the trouble you're causing.'

'I can guarantee that it'll be better than beans on toast,' she promised. 'Thank you for trusting me, George.'

'Who said I trusted you?' He looked at her as if he was going to say more, but let it go. 'Save your thanks and put that out of sight,' he said, pointing at the pile of notes lying on the kitchen table. Then, as she made a move to stuff it back in her bra, 'No! I didn't mean…' He took a deep breath. 'Just wait until I've gone.'

She blushed furiously. 'Sorry.'

'So am I,' he muttered as he left the kitchen. 'So am I.'

CHAPTER FOUR

ANNIE hadn't been aware of holding her breath, but the minute the back door closed she covered her hot cheeks with her hands and let out something very close to a, 'Whew.'

That had been intense.

She appeared to have got away with it, though. For now, at any rate. And she hadn't told any outright lies, just left George to answer his own questions. A bit of a grey area, no doubt, but she was sure he'd rather not know the truth and twenty-four hours from now she'd be miles away from Maybridge with no harm done.

The cat leapt from the chair as she crossed to the fridge, chirruping hopefully as it nuzzled its head against her ankle.

'Hello, puss. Are you hungry too?'

She poured a little milk into a bowl, then sat back on her heels, watching the cat lap it up.

'Trouble,' she said, grinning in spite of everything that had happened. 'He said I was trouble. Do you know, puss, that's the very first time anyone has ever looked at me and thought "trouble".' The cat looked up, milk clinging to its muzzle, and responded with a purr. 'I know,' Annie said. 'It is immensely cheering. Almost worth wrecking Lydia's car for.' Then, since the cat made a very good listener, 'Tell me, would you describe George Saxon as a likely beach bum?'

The cat, stretching out its tongue to lick the last drop from its whiskers, appeared to shake its head.

'No, I didn't think so, either.'

Surely 'laid-back' was the very definition of beach-bum-hood, while George Saxon was, without doubt, the most intense man she'd ever met.

With Xandra on his case, she suspected, he had quite a lot to be intense about, although if he really was an absentee father he undoubtedly deserved it. And what was all that about closing down the garage? How could he do that while his own father was in hospital? It was utterly appalling—and a private family matter that was absolutely none of her business, she reminded herself.

She just wanted to get the car fixed and get back on the road. Take in the sights, go shopping unrecognised. But, despite Xandra's build-up and her assurance that she wouldn't miss it, she'd be giving the Maybridge Christmas market a wide berth.

Less ho, ho, ho… More no, no, no…

The thought made her feel oddly guilty. As if she'd somehow let the girl down. Which was stupid. If it hadn't been for Xandra, she would have been picked up by some other mechanic who wouldn't have given her nearly as much grief.

A man without the careless arrogance that was guaranteed to rouse any woman with an ounce of spirit to a reckless response. One who wouldn't have held her in a way that made her feel like a woman instead of a piece of porcelain.

Someone polite, who would not have made uncomplimentary comments about her driving, but would have promised to deliver her car in full working order the next day because that was on the customer relations script he'd learned on his first day on the job.

In other words, all the things that she wanted to get away from.

Whatever else George was, he certainly didn't follow a script. And locking horns with a man who didn't know he was supposed to show due deference to the nation's sweetheart was a lot more interesting than being holed up in a budget hotel room with only the television remote for company.

For all his faults, George Saxon did have one thing in his favour—he was the complete opposite of Rupert Devenish, a man who had never rated a single 'whew'. Not from her, anyway.

There was nothing textbook about George.

Okay, so he was tall, with shoulders wide enough to fill a doorway—no doubt like the lines carved into his cheeks, around those penetrating grey eyes, they came from hard use.

And he was dark.

But he wasn't, by any stretch of the imagination, classically handsome. On the contrary, his face had a lived-in quality and there was enough stubble on his chin to suggest a certain laissez-faire attitude to his appearance. He certainly wasn't a man to wait for some woman to pluck him off the 'ideal husband' shelf, she thought. More the kind who, when he saw what he wanted, would act like a caveman.

The thought, which was supposed to make her smile, instead prompted the proverbial ripple down her spine. Something which, until today, she'd foolishly imagined to be no more than a figure of speech.

He was, by any standard, anything but ideal and she had the strongest feeling that her wisest course of action would be to make his day and get out of there, fast.

But, then again, why would she when, for the purposes of this adventure, he could almost have been made to order.

Exciting, annoying, disturbing.

She'd wanted to be disturbed, jolted out of her

rut. Wanted to be excited and, maybe, just a little bit reckless.

She swallowed as she considered what being reckless with George Saxon would entail.

He was right. She should definitely leave. As soon as possible. Not because the idea appalled her. On the contrary, it was much too excitingly disturbing, recklessly appealing and she'd call a taxi to take her to the motel.

Just as soon as she'd cooked the hot meal she'd promised them.

Her stomach rumbled at the thought. Lunch had been a very long time ago and she'd been too nervous to eat more than a mouthful of that. Not that she'd eaten much of anything lately, a fact that had been picked up by one of the gossip magazines looking for a new angle. An eating disorder was always good copy.

Now, for the first time in months, she felt genuinely hungry and, leaving the cat to its ablutions, she stood up and returned her attention to the fridge.

It was well stocked with the basics, but it wasn't just the bacon, eggs, cheese and vegetables that were making her hungry. She'd already seen the large homemade meat pie sitting on the middle shelf, gravy oozing gently from the slit in the centre, just waiting to be slipped into the oven.

Presumably it had been made by George's

mother before she'd left to visit her husband in the hospital. That Xandra knew it was there was obvious from her earlier performance but, anxious to keep her grandfather's garage functioning, desperate, maybe, to prove herself to her father, she was prepared to take any chance that came her way and she'd grabbed her offer to make dinner for them all with both hands.

Good for her, she thought. If you had a dream you shouldn't let anyone talk you out of it, or stand in your way. You should go for it with all your heart.

Annie put the pie in the oven, then set about the task of peeling potatoes and carrots. It took her a minute or two to get the hang of the peeler, then, as she bent to her task, the annoying glasses slid down her nose and fell into the sink.

She picked them out of the peelings and left them on the draining board while she finished.

Her only problem then was the vexed question of how long it took potatoes to boil. She'd left her handbag in the car, but she'd put her cellphone in her coat pocket after calling for help. She wiped her hands and dug it out to see what she could find on the Web.

The minute she switched it on she got the 'message waiting' icon.

There was a text from Lydia with just a single code word to reassure her that everything had gone exactly according to plan, that she'd reached the airport without problem—or, as she'd put it, being twigged as a 'ringer'.

Even if they hadn't agreed that contact between them should be on an emergency-only basis— you never knew who was tuned into a cellphone frequency—she'd still be in the air so she couldn't call her and tell her everything that had happened, confess to having cut her hair, wrecking her car. Instead, she keyed in the agreed response, confirmation that she, too, was okay, and hit 'send'.

There was, inevitably, a voicemail from her grandfather asking her to call and let him know when she'd touched down safely. Using any excuse to override her insistence that she wanted to be left completely alone while she was away.

'You'll have to call me at King's Lacey,' he said. 'I'm going there tomorrow to start preparations for Christmas.' Piling on yet more guilt. 'And the Boxing Day shoot.'

As if he didn't have a housekeeper, a game-keeper, a houseful of staff who were perfectly capable of doing all that without him.

'And of course there's the Memorial Service. It will be twenty years this year and I want it to be special. You will be home for that?'

It was the unexpected touch of uncertainty in his voice that finally got to her.

'I'll be there,' she murmured to herself, holding the

phone to her chest long after the voicemail had ended.

It was twenty years since her parents had died in a hail of gunfire in the week before Christmas and every year she'd relived that terrible intermingling of grief and celebration that made the season an annual misery.

And worse, much worse, the centuries-old Boxing Day shoot that nothing was allowed to interfere with. Not even that first year. Cancelling it would have been letting her parents' killers win, her grandfather had said when he'd found her hiding beneath the stairs, hands over her ears in terror as the guns had blasted away.

'God help me,' she said again, 'I'll be there.'

Then she straightened, refusing to waste another minute dwelling on it. Having come so close to losing this little bit of freedom, she was absolutely determined to make the most of every moment. Even something as simple, as unusual for her, as cooking dinner. But as she clicked to the Net to surf for cooking times, the sound of something hitting the floor made her jump practically out of her skin.

She spun round and saw George Saxon in the doorway, her bag at his feet.

How long had he been there? How much had he heard?

* * *

George hadn't intended to eavesdrop, but when he'd opened the door Annie had been half turned from him, so tense, the cellphone so tight to her ear that she hadn't noticed him and he'd frozen, unable to advance or retreat.

He'd heard her promise to 'be there', but the 'God help me…' that had followed as she'd clutched the phone to her chest had been so deeply felt that any doubts about the kind of trouble she was in vanished as, for a moment, all control had slipped away and she'd looked simply desolate.

At that moment he'd wanted only to reach out to her, hold her. Which was when he'd dropped her bag at his feet.

And she'd visibly jumped.

'I'm sorry,' he said. 'I didn't mean to startle you.' Just shatter the spell that she seemed to be weaving around him.

'You didn't,' she said, a little too fiercely. Then blushed at the lie. 'Well, maybe just a bit.'

She looked down at the cellphone, then crammed it quickly into the back pocket of her jeans. Unlike her clothes or the holdall he'd just brought in from the car, which was definitely from the cheap-and-cheerful, market-stall end of the spectrum, it was the latest in expensive, top-end technology. He had one exactly like it himself and knew how much it had cost. And he wondered what kind of wardrobe she'd left behind in

London, along with her driving licence, when she'd made her bid for freedom.

A woman whose partner could afford to employ a security company to keep an eye on her would be dressed from her skin up in designer labels. Silk, linen, cashmere. Would wear fine jewels.

What had he done to her to make her run? If not physical, then mental cruelty because she was running away from him, not to someone. His hands bunched into fists at the thought.

'I was just catching up on my messages,' she said.

'Nothing you wanted to hear, by the look of you.' For a moment she stared at him as if she wanted to say something, then shook her head. 'You do know that you can be tracked by your phone signal?' he asked.

Not that it was any of his business, he reminded himself, forcing his hands to relax.

'It was only for a minute. I need to know what's happening.'

Long enough. Who was important enough to her that she'd take the risk? Make that kind of promise?

A child?

No. She'd never have left a child behind.

'Use some of that money you've got stashed away to buy the anonymity of a pay-as-you-go,' he advised abruptly.

'I will,' she said, clearly as anxious as he was to

change the subject. Then, lifting her chin, managing a smile, 'I found a pie in the fridge so I've put that in the oven. I hope that's all right?'

'A pie?'

'A meat pie.'

'Ah…'

A tiny crease puckered the space between her beautifully arched brows.

'Is that a good "ah" or a bad "ah"?' she asked. Then, raising her hand to her mouth to display a set of perfectly manicured nails, she said, 'Please don't tell me you're a vegetarian.'

'Why?' he demanded. 'Have you got something against vegetarians?'

'No, but…'

'Relax. You're safe. What you've found is the equivalent of the fatted calf…'

'I'm sorry?'

'For the prodigal son.'

'I'm familiar with the metaphor.' She regarded him intently. 'Just how long is it since you've been home?' she asked.

'A while,' he said.

Which was why his mother, even with his father in hospital, had taken the time to make him one of her special steak-and-mushroom pies, just as she'd been doing ever since he'd gone away on his first school trip. More to avoid his own sense of guilt than tease her, he said, 'Judging by your reaction, I suspect we've both had something of a narrow escape.'

'Escape?' Annie, swiftly recovering from whatever had upset her, placed a hand against her breast in a gesture perfectly calculated to mime shocked surprise and said, 'Are you suggesting that I can't cook, Mr Saxon?'

Despite everything, he found himself grinning at her performance. 'I sensed a lack of conviction in your assurance that you could do better than Xandra.'

'That was no more than simple modesty,' she declared.

'You'll forgive me if I reserve judgement until I've tasted your mashed potatoes.'

'Mashed?' The insouciant air vanished as quickly as it had come. 'Is that another favourite?'

'Food for the gods,' he assured her. 'At least it is the way my mother makes it.'

'Well, I'm not your mother, for which I'm deeply grateful since you appear to be as casual a son as you are a father, but I'll do my best not to disappoint.' Then, as he scowled at her, 'I don't suppose you've any idea how long it takes to boil potatoes?'

Which suggested he'd been right about the narrow escape.

'Sorry. That's not my area of expertise.'

'No?' She lifted those expressive brows, inviting him to tell her what he was an expert in, then, when he didn't oblige, she gave a little shrug and said, 'I don't suppose there's a lot of call for potato mashing on the beach.'

'You know how it is with sand,' he replied, wondering what kind of woman didn't know how to cook something as basic as potatoes.

The kind who'd never had to cook, obviously. Or close car doors behind her.

Who the devil *was* she?

'It gets in everything?' she offered. Then, because there really wasn't anything else to say about potatoes, 'Thanks for bringing in my bag.'

'I didn't make a special journey,' he said and, irritated with himself for getting drawn into conversation, he took a glass from the dresser and crossed to the sink to fill it.

'Thirsty work?' she asked, watching him as he drained it.

'No matter how much water I drink on long-haul flights, I still seem to get dehydrated.'

'Excuse me?'

He glanced back at her as he refilled the glass.

'Are you telling me that you flew from California *today*?' she demanded, clearly horrified.

'Overnight. I slept most of the way,' he assured her. The first-class sky-bed he could afford these days was a very different experience from his early cattle-class flights.

'Even so, you shouldn't be working with machinery. What about Health and Safety?'

'Goods and Services, Health and Safety? What are you, Annie? A lawyer?'

'Just a concerned citizen.'

'Is that so? Well, if you don't tell, I won't,' he replied flippantly, refusing to think about how long it had been since anyone, apart from his mother, had been concerned about him. It was his choice, he reminded himself.

'I'm serious,' she said, not in the least bit amused. 'I wouldn't forgive myself if you were hurt fixing my car. It can wait until tomorrow.'

'You're *that* concerned?' Then, because the thought disturbed him more than he liked, 'Don't worry, I'm only there in a supervisory capacity. Xandra's doing all the hard work.'

'Is that supposed to make me feel better?'

'It's supposed to make you feel grateful,' he said, determined to put an end to the conversation and get out of there. 'Since you're so eager to be on your way.' Then, as he noticed her glasses lying on the draining board, he frowned. 'And actually,' he said thoughtfully as he picked them up and, realising that they were wet and muddy, rinsed them under the tap, 'I'm hoping a taste of the real thing will encourage her to reconsider a career as a motor mechanic and finish school.'

'Always a good plan,' Annie agreed. 'How old is she?'

'Sixteen.'

He picked up a dish cloth and, having dried the frames, began to polish the lenses.

'In that case, she doesn't have much choice in the matter. She can't leave school until she's seventeen.'

'I know that. You know that. Which may go some way to explain why she went to so much trouble to get herself suspended from her boarding school.'

Annie frowned. 'She's at boarding school?'

'Dower House.'

'I see.'

She could sympathise with her father's lack of enthusiasm at her career choice after he'd sent her to one of the most expensive boarding schools in the country. The kind that turned out female captains of industry, politicians, women who changed the world. The school where, two years ago, she'd given the end-of-year address to the girls, had presented the prizes.

She clearly hadn't made that much of an impression on young Xandra Saxon. Or maybe the haircut was worse than she thought.

'Obviously she's not happy there.'

'I wanted the best for her. I live in the States and, as you may have gathered, her mother is easily distracted. It seems that she's on honeymoon at the moment.'

'Her third,' Annie said, remembering what Xandra had said.

'Second. We didn't have one. I was a first-year student with a baby on the way when we got married.'

'That must have been tough,' she said.

'It wasn't much fun for either of us,' he admitted. 'Penny went home to her mother before Xandra was due and she never came back. I don't blame her. When I wasn't studying, I was working every hour just to keep us fed and housed. It wasn't what she'd expected from the son of George Saxon.'

'I'm sorry.'

'So am I.'

Then, because he clearly didn't want to talk about it and she didn't much want to hear about a youthful marriage that appeared never to have had a chance, she said, 'So, what did she do? Xandra. To get herself suspended.'

'She borrowed the head's car and took it for a joyride.'

'Ouch.' Sixteen years old, so she wouldn't have a licence or insurance. That explained a lot. 'Attention-seeking?'

'Without much success. Presumably anticipating something of the sort, Penny had the foresight to switch off her cellphone.'

'Then it's just as well Xandra has you.'

His smile was of the wry, self-deprecating kind. 'I'm the last person she'd have called, Annie. Much as I would have wished it otherwise, I'm little more to my daughter than a signature on a cheque.'

'You think so?'

George held the spectacles up to the light to check, amongst other things, that they were smear-free before looking at Annie.

'I know so. I'm only here because my father had a heart attack,' he said, taking a step towards her and, as she looked up, he slipped her spectacles back on her nose, holding them in place for a moment, his thumbs against the cool skin stretched taut over fine cheekbones.

Her lips parted on a tiny gasp but she didn't protest or pull away from him and for what seemed like an eternity he simply cradled her face.

There was no sound. Nothing moved.

Only the dark centre at the heart of eyes that a man might drown in widened to swallow the dazzling blue. He'd have had to be made of ice to resist such a blatant invitation, but then, according to any number of women he'd known, he was ice to the bone...

'The first rule of wearing a disguise, Annie...' he began, touching his lips briefly to hers to prove, if only to himself, that he was immune.

Discovering, too late, that he was not.

CHAPTER FIVE

ANNIE'S lips were soft, yielding, as they parted on a little gasp of surprise. Not the response of a seductress bent on luring a man to his doom, he thought, more the reaction of a girl being kissed for the first time.

Arousing in a way that no practised kiss could ever be.

And when, slightly breathless, he drew back to look at her, her eyes were closed and the mouth that had tempted him to take such outrageous liberties was smiling as if it had discovered something brand-new.

'The first rule of wearing a disguise,' he tried again, his voice barely audible as he struggled not to kiss her again, 'is never to let it slip, even for a moment.'

It took a moment for his words to get past the haze of desire but then her eyes flew open and he felt the heat beneath his fingertips as colour seared her cheekbones. Whether at the way she'd responded to his touch or at being found out in her deception, he'd have been hard put to say.

'H-how did you know?' she asked, making no effort to put distance between them, which appeared to answer that question. The innocent blushes had to be as fake as her glasses.

'Since you weren't wearing them when you checked your messages, it seemed likely that they were purely for decoration,' he said.

'Decoration?' The beginnings of a smile tugged once more at the corners of her mouth. 'Hardly that.'

'I've seen prettier,' he admitted, struggling not to smile back.

'The wretched things fell into the potato peelings. I put them on the draining board and then forgot all about them.'

As clear an admission of guilt as he'd ever heard.

'You should have tossed them into the bin with the peelings.'

'I doubt they'd have added much to the compost heap.'

'Maybe not, but if you're afraid of being recognised, I'd advise getting yourself a pair that fits properly instead of sliding down your nose.' He waited, hoping that she might tell him the truth this time. 'Maybe go for tinted lenses.'

Something to tone down the distracting blue.

'I bought them on the Internet. I had no idea they

came in different sizes.' She gave a little shrug. 'Maybe I should get some little sexy ones with lenses that react to the light.'

'Maybe. I have to tell you, though, that if anyone has put together a photofit of you, you can forget the glasses. It's the hairdo that's the dead giveaway.'

'Oh…' she lifted a hand to her hair in a self-conscious gesture '…no. No danger there.' She pulled a face. 'I cut it myself this morning with a pair of nail scissors.'

Well, yes. Obviously. No woman would walk around with hair like that for a minute longer than she had to.

'I'd have bet on the garden shears,' he said, accepting that she wasn't going to trust him with her secret. Or was, perhaps, protecting him from something he was almost certainly better off not knowing?

Just as he'd be wiser not to imagine how her hair might have looked before she'd hacked it off.

Adding long, creamy-coloured silky hair to the image that was building up inside his head was not helping him drop his hands, take the necessary step back.

'I'd better get back,' he said, forcing himself to do just that. 'Before Xandra, in her enthusiasm, strips your car down to the frame.'

He picked up the glass of water he'd abandoned but at the door he stopped, looked back. Despite a natural poise, a look-him-in-the-eye assurance that was so at odds with her innocent blushes, there was a lack of knowingness in the way she'd responded to his kiss that didn't quite fit with the jealous-partner scenario.

But then, presumably, if she was any kind of con woman, she'd have that down pat.

When the silence, the look, had gone on for too long, he said, 'You might find the answer to the vexed question of how to boil a potato in one of my mother's cook books. They're over there, behind the television.' He didn't bother to check that they were still there. Nothing had been changed in this room in his lifetime. 'And, in case you're interested, I'm partial to a touch of garlic in my mash.'

'Garlic?' She pushed the glasses, already sliding down her nose again, back into place. 'Good choice,' she said. 'Very good for the heart, garlic.'

'Are you suggesting that mine needs help?'

'Actually, I was thinking about your father. Isn't heart disease supposed to be hereditary? Although, now you come to mention it, maybe yours could do with some work in other departments.'

'What makes you think that?' He wasn't arguing with her conclusion, merely interested in her reasoning.

'Well, let me see. Could it be because you're the one with your daughter up to her elbows in axle-grease while you stand back telling her what to do?'

The smile that went with this, reassurance that she was teasing, was no mere token but shone out of her, lighting up her face in a way that could make a man forget that she was too thin. Forget the hair. Forget anything…

'I'm not telling her anything. She wasn't exaggerating when she said she knew what she was doing.'

Her smile became a look of sympathy. 'That must be a worry.'

'My father never forgave me for not wanting to follow him into the business. Given a second chance with Xandra, it's clear that he hasn't made the same mistakes with her that he did with me.'

Or maybe, being a girl, she'd had to beg to be allowed to 'play' cars with her granddad.

He wondered if his old man had seen the irony in that. Probably not. He'd doted on Xandra since the moment she'd been born. Indulged her, as he'd never been indulged. Maybe that was the difference between being a father and a grandfather. There was not the same responsibility to be perfect, do everything right. And getting it wrong.

'She might just love it,' Annie pointed out.

'I'm sure she does, but there's a world of difference between doing something for fun in the school holidays and it being your only option.'

'So if she stayed at school, took her exams, went to university and at the end of it all she still wanted to be a garage mechanic?' she asked.

'If only. She wants to drive rally cars too.' He took a deep breath. 'I don't suppose you have a handy Health and Safety regulation you're prepared to quote on the subject of sixteen-year-olds doing dangerous jobs?'

'I don't have one on the tip of my tongue,' she said, 'but, even if I did, I don't think I'd use it.'

'Not even if I promised to fix your car myself?'

'Not even then. This is something she wants, George. Something she can do. That she believed no one would take away from her.'

'That sounded heartfelt.'

'Yes, well, at her age I had a dream of my own, but I allowed myself to be persuaded against it for what at the time seemed sound reasons. Not that I believe Xandra is going to be the walkover I was. She's nowhere near as eager to please.'

'A daddy's girl, were you?'

She paled, shook her head, but before he could take a step back towards her, say sorry even though he didn't know why, she said, 'You do realise that if you close the garage it will make her all the more determined?'

'It's not an option. No matter how much he fights it, the truth is that my father won't be able to carry on.'

'What about you? This is your chance to prove to your daughter that you're more than just a signature on a cheque. That you really care about what she wants. Or is there a Californian beach with a

Californian beach girl stretched out in the sun who you can't wait to get back to?' She didn't wait for an answer but, having planted that little bombshell, said, 'I'll give you a call when dinner's ready, shall I?'

'Do that,' he snapped, turning abruptly and leaving her to it.

Annie didn't move until she heard the outside door close. Only then did she raise her hands to her face, run her fingertips over the warm spots where George Saxon had touched her.

He'd been so close as he'd slipped the glasses on her nose, held them in place, his thumbs against her cheek, fingertips supporting her head. There had been an intimacy about the way he'd looked at her that had warmed her, made her pulse leap, stirred something deep inside her so that when his lips had touched hers it had felt like two pieces of a puzzle finding the perfect fit.

And if he could do that with a look, a touch, a tender kiss, what could he do if…?

She whirled around, refusing to go there.

Instead, she crossed to the corner to root through the small collection of old cookery books before pulling out a heavy black bound book that was re-assuringly familiar.

She'd kept all her mother's books—medical text-books, mostly—and a copy of this basic cookery book had been among them, the inscription on the flyleaf from the foster mother who'd taught her to cook and passed on her own cookery book when she'd left for university.

How much strength of will must it have taken her mother to get to medical school? More than she'd had, she thought, swallowing hard as she opened the book to check the index.

Potatoes…

Potatoes, it seemed, took around twenty minutes to boil, depending on whether they were old or new and, once cooked, should be creamed with a little pepper and margarine. Clearly post-war austerity had still been part of life when this book had been published. And a sprinkle of parsley was as exotic as it got back in the days when garlic was considered dangerously foreign.

But, despite the fact that Mrs Saxon's cookery book and fridge appeared to be from the same generation, the large bulb of garlic tucked away in the salad crisper suggested that she, at least, had moved with the times. Or had that been bought specially for the prodigal's homecoming too?

She laid the table, put plates to warm and was energetically mashing butter, milk and finely chopped garlic into the potatoes when she heard the kitchen door open.

'Perfect timing,' she said, concentrating on the job in hand. 'Just enough time to scrub up.' Then, when there was no answer, she turned round. 'Oh!'

Not George or Xandra, but a slender middle-aged woman who bore a clear resemblance to both of them. 'Mrs Saxon,' she said, wiping her hands on the apron she'd found hanging behind the door and offering her hand. 'I'm Annie Rowland. I hope you don't mind me making free with your kitchen, but George thought you'd be tired when you got back from the hospital. How is your husband?'

'As bad-tempered as any man who's being told to change the habits of a lifetime and give up everything he loves…'

Before she could say any more, Xandra burst through the door and flung her arms around her grandmother.

'Gran! How's Granddad?'

'He'll be fine. He just needs to take more care of himself. But what about you, young lady? What are you doing here? Why aren't you at school?' Then, clearly knowing her granddaughter better than most, 'I suppose it's got something to do with your mother?'

'I don't care about my mother. I just wanted to be here so that I can help Granddad with the garage.'

'Oh, Xandra!' Then, with a sigh, 'What have you done?'

'You didn't know she was here?' George asked, following his daughter into the kitchen and this time he'd been getting his hands dirty—presumably in an effort to get the job done as quickly as possible so that he could get rid of her and close down the garage.

'I would have mentioned it.'

'You've a lot on your plate.' He crossed to the sink and, squishing soap on his hands, began to wash them thoroughly. 'How are things at the hospital?'

'It would help if he wasn't fretting so much. The garage is his life.'

'He's going to have to widen his horizons.' He picked up a towel. 'If it's any help, tell him I'll take care of the Bentley myself,' he said, drying his hands. 'But I'll have to get in touch with the owner of the restoration job in the end bay. The baby Austin. He'll need to start looking for another garage—'

'It's mine,' Xandra cut in with a touch of defiance as she anticipated disapproval.

George frowned. 'Yours?'

'Granddad bought it for my birthday,' she said, swiftly bending to make a fuss of the cat, as if she knew she'd just thrown a hand grenade into the room. 'It's a restoration project. We've been doing it together.'

No one else was looking at George and only she saw the effect that had on him. As if he'd been hit, winded, all the air driven from his body. A big man destroyed by a few words from a slip of a girl.

Love, she thought. Only love could hurt you like that and she ached to go to him, hold him.

'I'll go and give Mike Jackson a call about the Bentley,' his mother said, oblivious to the tension— or perhaps choosing to ignore it. 'He's got a wedding next week and I know how worried he's been.'

'I'll do it,' George said, clearly needing to get out of the room for a moment. 'I need to talk to him.' Then his eyes met hers and in an instant the barriers were back up. Nothing showing on the surface. 'Sorry, Mum, I should have introduced Annie.'

'We've met.' Mrs Saxon turned to her with a smile. 'I'm so sorry, my dear. I didn't thank you for getting on with dinner.' She patted her arm distractedly. 'We'll talk later but right now I really must go and call my sister-in-law, let her know how her brother is. Xandra, come and say hello to Great-Aunt Sarah.'

Annie wanted to say something, talk about Xandra, ask him what had gone wrong, but this didn't come under polite conversation and she had no idea where to begin.

As if sensing the danger, George crossed to the stove, hooked his finger through the mash and tasted it.

'Not bad for a first effort,' he said.

'Not bad? I'll have you know I've eaten in some of the finest restaurants in London and that stands comparison with the best.'

'Which restaurants?'

Annie had reeled off the names of half a dozen of the most expensive restaurants in the capital in her absolute determination to impress him before she realised that she was giving away rather more than she'd ever intended.

He lifted a quizzical brow. 'What was that you were saying about modesty?'

She pulled a face. 'No point in being coy. Of course you'd only get a tiny spoonful.'

'The more you pay, the less you get,' he agreed, taking a second dip in the potato. 'Maybe that's why you're so thin. You'd have been better occupied doing a little home cooking and saving your money for a more roadworthy car for your getaway.'

She rapped his knuckles sharply with a spoon and having scooped the potato into a serving bowl, bent to put it in the warming oven.

George regarded her thoughtfully for a moment before he shrugged and said, 'How long has your friend had that sorry heap?' he asked.

'Are you referring to Lydia's pride and joy? Only a week or two,' she said, concentrating on straining the carrots and peas. Then, realising that it wasn't an idle question, 'You've found something else?'

'I don't suppose there's the faintest chance that she bought it from a garage that offered her some kind of warranty?' he asked.

'No. She bought it from a woman who was going

to use the money to take her grandchildren on holiday for Christmas.'

Lydia had been eager to tell her all about the one careful lady owner when she'd offered to lend it to her. Pride of ownership coming through loud and clear as she'd explained that, although her car wasn't new, it had been well cared for.

'She didn't happen to be a vicar's wife too, by any chance?'

'Excuse me?'

He sighed. 'Did she see any documents? Service record, receipt? Did this kindly grandmother invite her into her house for tea and biscuits while they did the deal or did your friend buy it off the side of the road?'

'I don't know about the documents, but I do know that the woman lived on the other side of London so she offered to bring the car to Lydia to save her the journey.'

'How kind of her.' His intonation suggested she had been anything but kind and he underlined it by saying, 'She must have thought it was her birthday and Christmas all rolled into one.'

'I don't understand.'

'Your friend was sold a cut'n'shut, Annie. A car welded together out of two wrecks. The front half of one car and the back half of another.'

She shook her head. 'That can't be right. She'd bought it new—'

'The classic "one careful lady owner".' He shook his head. 'Your sweet little old lady sold your friend a deathtrap, Annie. If that abomination had come apart while you were driving at any speed…'

He left the outcome to her imagination.

Her imagination, in full working order, duly obliged with a rerun of the carefree way she'd driven down the motorway, relishing her freedom as she'd buzzed along in the fast lane, overtaking slower moving traffic.

All it would have taken at that speed would have been a small piece of debris, a bit of a bump and she could have ended up in the path of one of the lorries thundering west…

And if it hadn't been her, it would, sooner or later, have been Lydia.

'Xandra hadn't seen one before but, when she spotted the welding, she asked me to take a look.'

So that was how he'd got his hands dirty.

'You do understand what this means? It'll have to be crushed. I can't be responsible for letting it back on the road.'

'Crushed?' Right now, she would be glad never to see it again but—

'And any documentation that came with it will be fake,' he added pointedly. 'This would be a good time to come clean if you've been economical with the truth about the car's provenance, since I will have to inform the Driver and Vehicle Licensing Agency.' His look was long and intense, demanding an answer.

'I've got the picture, George.'

'I can leave it a day or two if it's going to be a problem?' he pressed.

It wasn't necessary, but her heart did a little loop the loop that he was prepared to cover for her. Give her getaway time.

'Thanks, but I won't strain your probity, George. The car is properly registered in the name of Lydia Young. She's the only victim here.' Then she groaned. 'Lydia! She's spent all that money on something that's absolutely worthless.' She looked up at him. 'I imagine the question of insurance no longer arises?'

He shook his head and she let slip that new word she was finding all kinds of uses for, but it didn't help. This went far beyond a slightly shocking expletive.

'How could anyone do such a wicked thing?' she asked.

'For money, Annie.' He made a move as if to put his hand on her arm in a gesture of comfort, but instead lifted it to push his fingers through his thick, dark hair. 'This is going to totally screw up your plans, isn't it?'

'I didn't actually have anything as organised as a plan,' she admitted. 'Just a general direction.'

'Running blind is never a good idea.' Then, almost, it seemed, against his will, 'What will you do now?'

She lifted her shoulders in a resigned shrug. 'Call a cab and go to the motel.' She managed a wry smile. 'Spend the evening working on a plan.'

'Have something to eat first,' he said.

'Thank you. Both of you,' she added. 'I mean that. I'm really grateful that you were so thorough.'

'George Saxon and Son might not look much at the moment, but it was the finest garage in the area for nearly a century.'

'Until it ran out of sons.'

'Until it ran out of sons who wanted to be a replica of their father.'

'It's an equal-opportunities world, George.'

'Actually, when I asked what you're going to do, I meant without a car.'

Then, as Xandra returned, he leaned back against the table and folded his arms, rather like a shield, she thought.

'You'll be stranded on the wrong side of the ring road at the motel,' he said, 'and taxis aren't cheap.'

'Isn't there a bus service?'

'One or two a day, maybe, but it's a motel,' he pointed out. 'A motor hotel. There isn't a lot of demand for public transport.'

'Annie could stay here tonight,' Xandra intervened, in just the same casual manner as she'd handed her the door key and invited her to make herself a cup of tea.

George looked at the girl with something close to exasperation.

'What?' she demanded. 'There's plenty of room and Gran won't mind.'

That he did couldn't have been more obvious.

'I think your grandmother has quite enough to cope with at the moment without taking in a total stranger,' Annie said, rescuing him. 'But thank you for the offer.'

She took her cellphone from her back pocket but, before she could switch it on, he took it from her with a warning look.

'Actually,' he said, 'it would be easier if you stayed here. I'll need you to deal with the paperwork in the morning.' Then, 'I'll have more than enough to do without driving over to the motel.'

She doubted that, but she knew better than to take advantage of a man who'd been put in an impossible position. Even if he had taken advantage of her and kissed her.

'No, really. You've done enough.'

'True,' he said distantly, returning her phone, 'but I've no doubt you'll be the perfect guest and help with the washing-up.'

That really was too much.

'Maybe you should be the perfect son and buy

your mother a dishwasher,' she replied, responding in kind.

'Sorry. I flunked that one years ago.' Then, as the door opened behind him, 'You've no objection to Annie staying, have you, Mum?'

'Where else would she go?' Then, as Annie placed the pie and vegetables on the table and she sank wearily into a chair, the phone began to ring.

'I'll go, Gran,' Xandra said, leaping up.

'No… It might be the hospital.'

George followed her from the room but was back in seconds. 'It's one of my mother's friends. She said to start without her.'

'We can wait.'

'The way she's settled herself in the armchair, I suspect it's going to be a long one. No point in letting good food spoil.'

She ducked her head in an attempt to hide the blush that coloured her cheekbones at the simple compliment and, despite everything, he felt an answering warmth as he watched her cut into the pie. She was such a mixture of contradictions.

Assertive, poised, innocent…

She handed him a plate, then, as he helped himself to vegetables, she served Xandra and herself before putting the dishes back in the warming oven for his mother.

Xandra made a deeply appreciative moaning noise. 'Real food. This is worth getting grounded for.'

'It is good,' Annie said swiftly, presumably to stop him from saying something inflammatory. Then spoiled it all by adding, 'For pastry like this I'd come home every week.'

'Once a year would be nearer the mark,' Xandra said.

'Are you suggesting it's up to the standard of all those smart London restaurants you're used to?' he enquired, pretending he hadn't heard. 'Always assuming they served anything as basic as meat pie and mashed potato.'

'It's absolutely delicious,' she said quickly, in an attempt to rescue the blunder. 'But then I can't actually remember the last time I was this hungry.'

From the way she was tucking in, it was clear that her thinness wasn't the result of a desire to be size zero and he wondered what, exactly, she'd been going through that had driven her to fly from home. And, more to the point, who she'd made that *'I'll be there'* promise to.

The one with the desperate *'God help me'* tag.

He pushed away the thought, not wanting to go there.

For the moment there was colour in her cheeks and, as she laughed out loud at something Xandra had said, her face was animated, alive. Then, as if she could sense his eyes on her, she turned, looked at him over those ridiculous frames.

The impact was almost physical.

Forget the fact that she was too thin, that dark smudges marred the porcelain-fine skin beneath her eyes.

It wasn't that instant belt-in-the-gut sexual attraction that normally grabbed his attention and he was honest enough to admit that if he'd passed her in the street, head down, he probably wouldn't have given her a second glance.

But he didn't believe for a minute that she'd ever walk along a street with her head down.

Despite that oddly disturbing vulnerability, she possessed a rare presence, an ability to look him straight in the eye, hold her own in a confrontation.

Not the kind of woman, he'd have said, to run away from anything.

He pushed back his chair the minute he'd finished eating. 'I'd better go and put Mike Jackson out of his misery,' he said, desperate to get away from Annie's unsettling presence. He made a general gesture that took in the table. 'Thanks for doing this…'

'I was glad to help.' She continued to hold him captive with nothing more than a look for what felt like endless seconds. 'Can I get you anything else?' she asked as he lingered.

What on earth was the matter with him?

Annie was the kind of woman that no man with an atom of sense would get entangled with, especially not one who, having learned his lesson the hard way, could spot trouble a mile off.

'Coffee?' she prompted.

'If I need anything I'll get it myself,' he said, forcing himself to move.

CHAPTER SIX

ANNIE felt the tension evaporate as George left the room, but it felt surprisingly empty too. He was very contained, with a rare stillness. He made no unnecessary movements, had been terse to the point of rudeness throughout supper. And yet his presence still filled the room.

What could have happened to cause such a rift between him and his family? Was it just the garage, or had a teenage wedding that had evidently fallen apart faster than the ink had dried on the marriage certificate been the real cause of family friction?

And what about his daughter who, now that her father had left the room, had slumped down in her chair, all that chippy bravado gone.

It was obvious that she craved his attention. She might take every chance to wound her father, but when he wasn't looking her eyes followed him with a kind of desperation.

'Can I suggest something?'

The only response was a shrug of those narrow shoulders, making her look more like a sulky six-year-old than sixteen.

'Write a note to Mrs Warburton.'

She was instantly back on the defensive. 'I'm not sorry for taking the car.'

'Maybe not, but you're old enough to know that you must have given her a very nasty fright.' She waited a moment but, getting no response, said, 'Why did you do it?'

'Because I could?' she offered, giving her the same barbed I-don't-care-what-you-think-of-me stare that she used to hurt her father and she felt a pang of tenderness for the girl.

'If you wanted to come home to see your father I'm sure she would have understood.'

'I didn't! It's got nothing to do with him!' She glared at her. 'I'll write when I'm ready, okay? If I'd known you were going to nag I wouldn't have asked you to stay.'

'You're right,' she said, standing up, gathering the dishes. 'I've abused your hospitality.' Then, 'Time to wash up, I think.'

'Oh, right. Wash the dishes? Write a letter?' Xandra held out her hands as if balancing the choice. 'Very subtle.'

'The two have a lot in common. They both need doing and neither gets easier for leaving. And I'll bet I'm an amateur in the nagging stakes compared with your gran. As for your father…'

'If he cared what I did he'd be here instead of sending me off to school so that he could live on a beach,' she declared sullenly. 'He might be able to fix it so that they'll take me back, but I won't stay so he might as well save his money.'

'Where do you want to go?'

'Maybridge High School. It was good enough for him. I'll stay here with Gran. She'll need help,' she said. Then, leaping from her chair, she grabbed the bag that George had dropped. 'I'll take this upstairs.'

'Where are you rushing off to?' her grandmother asked as she rushed past her.

'I'm taking Annie's bag up to her room.'

'I've made up the front right bedroom,' she said. 'You'll have to make your own bed.' Then, giving her a quick hug, 'Your granddad will be all right.'

'Of course he will,' she said tightly. 'I'm going to bed.'

'Sleep tight.'

She turned to Annie with a shake of her head. 'I suppose this is about her mother getting married again. The woman doesn't have a thought in her head for anyone but herself.'

'I'd have said it was more to do with her father. She did know he was coming home?'

'I told her when I rang to let her know that her

granddad was in hospital. George has always tried to do his best for Xandra, a fact that her mother has used to her own advantage, but it's never been easy and, since she hit her teens…'

'It's a difficult time.'

'And they are so alike. George has probably told you that he and his father had a difficult relationship. It's like watching history repeat itself.'

'I'm sorry to put you to so much trouble when you've already got so much on your plate,' she said, taking the food from the warming oven and placing it on the table.

'What trouble?' she said with a smile. Then, looking at the food, 'Actually, I think I'll pass on that, if you don't mind. I had a sandwich earlier and there's something about a hospital that seems to take away the appetite.'

'How is your husband?'

'Like most men, he's his own worst enemy, but he got treatment very fast. The doctor said he's been lucky and if he behaves himself he'll be home in a day or two.'

'And then your problems will really begin.' They exchanged a knowing look. Her grandfather had never been seriously ill but he could make a simple cold seem like double pneumonia. 'Could I make you a cup of tea, Mrs Saxon?'

'Hetty, please.' Then, 'Actually, what I really need is a bath and my bed. You must be tired too.'

She patted her arm. 'Your room is on the right at the top of the stairs. It's not fancy, but it's comfortable and it has its own bathroom. There's plenty of hot water. Just make yourself at home, dear.'

People kept saying that to her, Annie thought, as Hetty, clearly exhausted by long hours at the hospital, took herself off to bed.

She smiled to herself as she got stuck into the dishes. This wasn't anything like being at home, but that was good. Just what she wanted, in fact. And she was happy to help, to be able to repay in some small way this unlooked for, unexpected kindness, hospitality.

And she could think while she was working.

The loss of Lydia's car had thrown her simple non-plan off the rails and now she needed a new one.

A new plan, a replacement car and a haircut, she decided, pushing her hair back from her face.

She should make a list, she thought, twitching her nose to keep the glasses in place.

Or maybe not.

Her life had been run by her diary secretary for years. A list of monthly, weekly, daily engagements had appeared on her desk, each month, week, morning without fail.

Everything organised down to the last minute. Even her escape had been meticulously planned. The how. The where. The when.

She'd still been doing things by the book until the wheels had come off. Literally.

At the time it had seemed like a disaster. Now it seemed like anything but. Hadn't kicking back, taking whatever life threw at her, been the whole point of this break from reality? Cooking and washing up hadn't figured on any list of things to do, but it certainly came under the heading of 'different'.

George hadn't reappeared by the time she'd finished, put the dishes away, wiped everything down, so, remembering his aversion to instant coffee, she made a pot of tea and then ventured into the main part of the house to find him.

The front hall had that shabby, comfortable look that old houses, occupied by the same family over generations, seemed to acquire. It was large, square, the polished floor covered by an old Turkish rug. There was a scarred oak table along one wall, piled with mail that had been picked up from the mat and left in a heap. Above it hung a painting of an open-topped vintage car, bonnet strapped down, numbered for a race, a leather-helmeted driver at the wheel.

A small brass plate on the frame read: 'George Saxon, 1928'. It was full of life, energy, glamour and she could see how it might have caught the imagination of a teenage girl in much the same way as photographs of her mother working at a clinic in an African village had inspired her to follow in her footsteps.

Despite George's misgivings, she hoped Xandra was more successful in achieving her dreams.

The living room door stood ajar but George wasn't there. The next door opened to reveal the dining room and, after tapping lightly on the remaining door, she opened it.

The study was a man's room. Dark colours, leather furniture.

There was an open Partner's desk against one wall, but George was sitting in a large leather wing chair pulled up to the fireplace, head resting against one of the wings, long legs propped on a highly polished brass fender, cellphone held loosely in his hand, eyes closed.

Fast asleep.

'George?' she murmured.

He didn't stir but the soft cashmere of his sweater was warm to the touch and she left her hand on his broad shoulder long after it became obvious that he wasn't going to wake without more vigorous intervention.

Eventually, though, she took it away, eased the phone from his long fingers and put it, carefully, on the table, then stood watching him for a moment, wondering whether to try harder to rouse him.

He looked exhausted and, instead, she reached out as if to smooth the strain lines from his face. But the intimacy of such a gesture made it unthinkable and she curled her fingers into her palms before they quite touched his skin.

She wouldn't have done that to a man she'd known for years and George Saxon was practically a stranger.

But then that was the difference.

He didn't know who she was. Didn't feel the need to treat her with kid gloves. He'd kissed her because something in her face had told him that was what she wanted, and he'd been right. For the first time in her adult life she didn't have to be guarded, careful about how everything she said, did, would be interpreted. Didn't have to worry about reading 'all about it' in the morning paper.

The sheer dizzying freedom of that hit her in a rush and she knelt at his feet, uncurled her fingers and let them rest lightly against his face.

Fingertips against the smooth skin at his temple, palm against the exciting roughness of a day-old beard. And then she leaned forward and touched her lips to his.

Not a wake-up-and-kiss-me-back kiss, but a promise to herself to be brave enough to embrace life, embrace every new experience that offered itself.

To be wholly and completely herself.

He didn't stir and after a moment she leaned back on her heels, then, leaving him to sleep, stood up and let herself quietly out of the room before taking the stairs that rose through the centre of the house.

She followed Hetty's directions and opened the first door on the right. Her bag was at the foot of an ornate wrought iron bed and, reassured that she was in the right room, she switched on the light and closed the door.

The house was old and the room was large, with high ceilings. The en suite bathroom, a more recent addition, had taken a bite out of the room and the bed was tucked into the larger section of the remaining L.

The walls were decorated with old-fashioned flower-strewn wallpaper that went perfectly with the bed, the patchwork comforter, the dark oak antique furniture. The velvet button-back nursing chair, oval cheval mirror.

A moss-green rug that matched the velvet curtains lay in front of a dresser on the wide oak boards and she drew them to shut out the winter dark before taking a look at the bathroom.

The huge roll-top claw-footed bath with its brass fittings was, like everything else in the house, gleaming with care.

She turned on the taps and then, leaving the water to run, returned to the bedroom to open her bag, see what Lydia had packed for her.

She'd sent her a cheque to cover the basics. Underwear, a nightdress, toiletries. Just enough to see her through until she could buy what she needed. There was a pink T-shirt nightie, plain white underwear, a couple of brushed cotton shirts, socks.

Basic as you like, she thought with a smile. Perfect.

But, when it came to toiletries, the clean, simple lines of the packaging disguised a world of luxury and she clutched the bag to her, hoping that her lookalike would get as much pleasure from the special treats she'd packed for her.

Smiling, she picked up a towel from a pile on the chair and then returned to the bathroom.

She uncapped a bottle and poured a little oil into the bath and the scent of lime blossom rose with the steam, enveloping her as she stripped off, piling up the cash she'd stowed about her body.

Not just the thousand pounds in her bra, but the rest of her running-away money that, on Lydia's insistence—who seemed to believe she'd be mugged the minute she stepped outside the hotel—she'd tucked around her waist inside her tights. Fortunately, Lydia hadn't felt the need to lose weight to keep the likeness true, so there had been ample room in the baggy jeans she'd been wearing.

Bearing in mind George's reaction to the thousand pounds she'd produced, it was probably a good thing that it had been safely out of reach, she thought as she sank beneath the water and closed her eyes, letting the warmth seep into her bones.

He'd been suspicious enough as it was. If she'd let him see just how much she was carrying on her, he would have called the police on the spot. Unless she'd owned up to her real identity, she'd be languishing in a police cell right now, up to her neck in hot water, instead of lying back in this deliciously scented bath.

Her mind drifted to the image of how she'd left him, dark head resting against the leather wing of his chair. The unfamiliar feel of the day-old beard shadowing his chin.

Her smile faded into a sigh of longing as she wondered how it would feel against her cheek, her neck, the delicate skin of her breast.

George stirred, opened his eyes, for a moment not sure where he was, only that something had disturbed him. A touch, a faint familiar scent. Then, as he focused on the paper and wood laid in the grate, waiting only for a match to bring the fire blazing into life, it all came flooding back. Where he was. And all the rest.

His father was in hospital.

His daughter had been suspended from the school he'd chosen with such care—a place apart from the pressures of family, where she could be whoever she wanted to be.

And the scent belonged to Annie Rowland, a woman with lips like the promise of spring who was on the run from something. Someone.

He was three times in trouble, he decided as he raised his hand to his own lips, wiping the back of it hard across them as if he could erase the disturbing thought that while he'd been sleeping Annie had been there. Had kissed him.

He shook his head. That had to be a figment of his imagination.

And yet the image of her kneeling at his feet was so vivid that he stood up abruptly, bumping against the table, sending a mug flying.

He made a grab for it, swearing as hot liquid slopped over the rim, scalding his fingers. Proof that someone had been there in the last minute or two. Someone who wouldn't have left him sleeping in a chair, but would have put her hand on his shoulder. Brushed her fingers across his cheek.

And, if he'd woken, would he have tumbled her in his lap, taken up where they'd left off? Finished what he'd so nearly started earlier that evening when he'd slipped the fake glasses on her nose? When he'd kissed her, wanting her to know that he wasn't fooled by her disguise, that he'd caught her out, only to discover himself snared by a woman who, just hours earlier, he'd dismissed as not worth a second glance.

Kidding himself.

Not that her first impression of him would have been particularly flattering. He'd been sarcastic, angry, torn. Wanting to be anywhere else in the world. Wanting only to be here.

And yet there had been something. A recognition, a dangerous edge, a challenge that had sparked between them from the moment she'd cannoned into his arms, fitting the empty space like a hand coming into a glove.

Damn Xandra for getting him involved, he thought as he carried the mug through to the kitchen and grabbed his jacket from the hook. A woman was a complication he could do without right now. Any woman.

This one…

He caught his breath as he stepped outside. It was already close to freezing and his breath condensed and glowed in the concealed lights that lit the path to the gate and in the security lights that floodlit the garage. But he didn't hurry.

Cold air was exactly what he needed to clear his head and he took his time about checking that everything was safely locked, the alarms switched on before he fetched his holdall from his car.

He did the same inside, checking windows, sliding home bolts, setting the alarm, yawning as the warmth of the house stole over him.

He'd been fighting off sleep for hours, but it was long past time to surrender and, as he pushed open the bedroom door, he kicked off his shoes, pulled his shirt and sweater over his head in one move as he reached the bed, clicked on the bedside light.

And saw Annie's bag open at his feet.

What on earth…?

He straightened, half expecting to see her staring up at him from the pillow. But there was only a ridiculously girlish nightdress—pink with a cartoon rabbit that was saying 'Give me a hug'—that she'd thrown on the bed.

On his bed…

And then it hit him.

His mother had walked into her kitchen and found Annie preparing dinner and she'd leapt to the obvious conclusion that she was with him.

That they were an item. Together. Partners. All those ridiculous expressions used these days to describe a couple who were living together without the blessing of church or state.

He stooped to pick up his shirt and sweater, get out of there, but as he straightened he heard the door open behind him and there she was, reflected in the tall cheval mirror, with only a bath towel wrapped around her like a sarong, her arms full of the clothes she'd been wearing.

She dropped her clothes on the chair. Then, catching sight of her reflection, she pulled a face as she lifted her hands to her hair, using her fingers to push the damp strands off her face, tucking it first behind her ears, then pulling it forward, turning her head first one way, then the other, as if trying to decide what kind of style might suit her.

He'd been given a close-up of that fine bone structure earlier but now, without the distraction of badly cut hair, ugly glasses, he knew without doubt that it was a face he'd seen before.

But where?

Tall, skinny, bones that a camera would love, she had to be a model, he decided, but he didn't have time to think about it. Half hidden in the L, she hadn't seen him and, as she pulled free the tail of a towel that she'd tucked between her breasts, he said, 'I wouldn't do that...'

Practically leaping out of her skin, Annie spun round and her mouth went dry.

George Saxon, wrapped up in a soft shirt and cashmere sweater was a man to turn a woman's head. Now, stripped to the waist, his wide golden shoulders and chest were as bone-meltingly beautiful as a fine Greek bronze.

She swallowed. Managed to croak out, 'Your mother said...' before, realising exactly what his mother must have thought, the words died on her lips and she clutched her towel to her breast as she felt herself blush pink from head to toe. 'Oh...'

George watched, fascinated, as a wave of delicate pink enveloped Annie, not just her face, but her smooth, creamy neck and shoulders, to disappear beneath the towel she was clutching to her breast as she quickly cottoned onto exactly what the mix-up had been.

He knew he shouldn't think about that, but whatever she'd used in her bath smelled as inviting as the promise of a warm spring day and the temptation to unwrap her, see just how far that blush had gone, was almost irresistible.

'Oh, indeed,' he replied, his voice thick, his attempt at briskness failing miserably. 'It's entirely my fault,' he said, trying again. 'I should have explained.'

'She had more important things on her mind.'

'Yes.' Then, 'It's not a problem,' he said, moving to pick up his shoes, but Annie reached out and, with her hand on his arm, stopped him.

'Please. Don't go.'

He barely registered what she said, instead staring at her left hand, white, perfectly manicured nails painted a deep shade of pink against the darker skin of his arm and, when he finally looked up, there were only two things moving in the room. His heart as it pounded against the wall of his chest and the slight rise and fall of Annie's breasts as she breathed a little too fast.

And, as her words finally registered, what had been a simple misunderstanding seemed to become something more. Something that was meant.

One move, that was all it would take, and if she

was looking for a night of forgetfulness in a stranger's arms, he would have said he was her man.

But, deep in his bones, he knew that, despite the disguise, the deception, Annie was not a one-night-stand kind of woman. He, on the other hand, had never been interested in anything else and, taking her hand in his, he held it for a moment, wanting her to know that he wasn't rejecting her but being a friend and discovered that she was trembling.

'What are you running from?'

Unable to speak, she shook her head and, swearing beneath his breath, he put his arm around her, pulled her against him.

'It'll be all right,' he said, holding her close, intensely aware of her breath against his naked chest. Her skin, warm and scented from the bath, against his.

Meaningless words, but they were all he could think of and, far from steady himself as she looked up at him, he stroked the dark smudge under one of her eyes with the pad of his thumb as if he could wipe the shadow away. Make everything better.

'You'll be safe here.'

Her response was no more than a murmur that whispered across his skin and he had to tear himself away from the temptation to go with the moment.

'Sleep well, Annie,' he said and, dropping a kiss on her poor tortured hair, he stepped back, grabbed his shoes and walked swiftly from the room. Closing the door firmly behind him with a snap before he changed his mind.

CHAPTER SEVEN

ANNIE stared at the closed door. 'I don't want to be safe!' she repeated, louder this time.

All her life she'd been kept safe by a grandfather afraid that he'd lose her, as he'd lost his son. She'd been educated at home by tutors, had very few friends—mothers tended to be nervous about inviting her to play when she arrived with a body-guard in tow.

And it hadn't got any better as she got older. The only men her grandfather had allowed within touching distance had known better than to take liberties with the nation's sweetheart. And somehow she'd never managed to get beyond that.

She'd been so sure that George was different.

He'd run out on the family business, had at least one ex-wife, a broken relationship with his teenage daughter. She should have been able to rely on a man with a record like that to take advantage of a damsel in distress.

It wasn't as if she'd screamed when she found him in her bedroom. On the contrary, when she'd turned and seen him she'd known exactly why women lost their heads over totally unsuitable men. Had been more than ready to lose hers. In every sense of the word.

Instead, after a promising start and despite the fact that she was a towel drop away from being naked, he'd kissed her on the top of the head as if she was six years old instead of twenty-six.

How lowering was that?

She looked at the hand with which she'd detained him, used it to tug free the towel, standing defiantly naked. Then, catching sight of herself in the mirror— all skin and bones—she didn't blame him. Who on earth would fall in lust with that? she thought, quickly pulling on the pink nightie to cover herself up.

Pink, cute. With a bunny on the front. Just about perfect for a six-year-old, she thought as she climbed into bed.

Or the oldest virgin in the country.

George woke from a dream in which a large, pink, girl rabbit wearing glasses had him pinned down to the bed, furry paws planted firmly on his chest.

Her familiar blue eyes appealed to him to save her while she murmured softly, over and over, 'I don't want to be safe…' And he knew that in some way they were, for her, one and the same thing.

He sat up with a start, certain that he'd seen those eyes somewhere before. Then he scrubbed his hands over his face to wake himself up properly, telling himself that he'd misheard her. She couldn't possibly have said what he thought she'd said.

It was still pitch dark outside, barely five o'clock, but he swung his legs over the narrow single bed of his boyhood room, not prepared to risk going back to sleep just in case the bunny was still there, lying in wait in his subconscious.

He dressed quickly and, very quietly so as not to disturb anyone, went downstairs and let himself out of the house.

Hetty glanced up from the kitchen scales where she was carefully weighing out flour as Annie walked into the kitchen.

'I'm so sorry,' she apologised. 'I had no idea it was so late.'

As she'd lain alone in the large comfortable bed, certain that once again sleep would elude her, she'd started to make a shopping list in her head. The first thing she was going to buy, she'd decided, was a slinky, sexy nightdress. The kind made for taking off rather than putting on. The last thing she remembered was trying to decide whether it should be black or red.

'I can't remember the last time I slept like that.'

'Well, you must have been tired after your

journey. Can you make yourself breakfast? There are plenty of eggs, bacon…' She made a broad gesture at the collection of ingredients stacked on the kitchen table. 'I find cooking takes my mind off things.'

'A slice of toast will do me,' Annie said. 'And some tea. Can I make a cup for you?'

She smiled. 'That would be lovely. Thank you, dear.'

Annie dropped a couple of slices of bread into the toaster, put on the kettle.

'It's so quiet here,' she said.

'This used to be a farm. Didn't George tell you?' She looked up. 'How did you meet?'

'Actually, Hetty, George and I aren't…' she made a gesture that she hoped would cover the situation '…together.' She swallowed as George's mother, reaching for a bag of sugar, paused, a frown creasing her brow. 'My car broke down yesterday evening and I called the nearest garage. He came and picked me up.'

'George took out the tow-truck?' she asked, astonished.

'Not with any enthusiasm,' she admitted. 'I was going to call a cab to take me to the motel but Xandra asked me to stay.'

'Xandra?' She raised her hand to her mouth. 'You mean…? But I…'

'It's all right. An easy mistake to make and

George was the complete gentleman…' unfortunately '…and retired, leaving me in sole possession of the bedroom. I do hope he wasn't too uncomfortable.'

'He probably used his old bedroom,' she said, pouring the sugar into the scales. 'Pity. It's about time he settled down with a decent woman.'

'I'm sure he'd be much happier with an indecent one.'

His mother laughed. 'No doubt. Maybe that's why he was in such a bad mood when I took him out some tea earlier. I sent Xandra on an errand to keep her out of his way.'

'Oh. I had assumed she was with him. She seems very keen.'

'I know. My husband dotes on her. Let's her do anything she wants.' She sighed. 'Life would have been a great deal easier if George had been a girl. He wouldn't have been so hard. Expected so much…' Hetty sighed, then smiled as Annie handed her a cup of tea. 'Even so, he really shouldn't have let her get so involved with the garage.'

'She would never have stuck at it unless she really wanted to be a motor mechanic,' she said, buttering the toast.

'George told you about that?'

'No, it was Xandra. She's very determined. And I should warn you that she doesn't want to go back to boarding school. She wants to stay here.'

'She already spends most of her holidays with us. Her mother has other interests. Pass me that bowl, will you?'

Annie would have liked to ask about George. What interests kept him away? But that would be invading his privacy and, instead, she handed Hetty a large old-fashioned crockery mixing bowl.

'Are you making a Christmas cake?'

'It's silly really. You can buy such good ones and I don't suppose George—my George—will be able to eat it. The doctor said he needs to lose some weight.'

'Walking is good. For the heart,' she added. Then, sucking melted butter from her thumb, 'Can I do anything to help?'

'You could make a start creaming the sugar and butter, if you like.' She tipped the sugar into the bowl, adding butter she'd already measured and chopped up. 'You'll find a wooden spoon in the drawer.'

There was no fancy electric mixer to make light work of it, but Annie had seen the process often enough as a child to know what she had to do.

'What's the problem with your car?' Hetty asked when she'd spooned the last of the spices into a saucer and everything was measured. 'Will it take long to fix?'

'It's terminal, I'm afraid. George is going to arrange for it to be crushed.'

'But that's—'

Before she could finish, Xandra burst through the door. 'Got them! Oh, hi, Annie.' She dumped the box on one of the chairs. 'I've been up in the attic sorting out the Christmas decs. Now all we need is a tree.'

'Why don't you and Annie take the Land Rover and go and pick one up from the farm?' her grandmother suggested.

'That would be so brilliant.'

Annie blinked at the transformation from last night's moody teen to this childlike enthusiasm.

'But I...'

'What?'

'I really should be going.'

'Where? You're staying for the Christmas market, aren't you? Annie can stay for the weekend, can't she, Gran?'

'It's fine with me.'

'But you don't know me from Adam,' Annie protested. 'Besides, wouldn't you rather go to the farm with your father?'

'You mean the Grinch?'

'That's not fair, Xan,' Hetty said.

'Oh, please. He hates Christmas and we all know why.' Then, 'Come on, Annie, let's go and choose the biggest tree we can find.'

She swallowed. The scent of the newly cut evergreen brought indoors never failed to bring back that terrible Christmas when her parents hadn't come home.

'You will stay?' the girl pressed. 'We could go to the market together. It'll be fun.'

She looked up, ready to explain that she really had to move on, but Hetty, exhaustion in every line of her face, met her gaze with a silent plea that she couldn't ignore.

'Let's go and get the tree and we'll take it from there,' she said.

'Excellent. Can we go now, Gran?'

'I'll be glad to have the place to myself. Not too big,' she called after her, adding a silent, 'Thank you,' to Annie before raising her voice to add, 'We don't want a repeat of last year.' Then, 'Wrap up. It's cold out. There's a scarf on the hook. Gloves in the drawer.'

'What happened last year?' Annie asked Xandra, tucking the ends of her hair into the woolly hat before she hauled herself up behind the wheel of an elderly Land Rover.

'Granddad came home with a ten-foot tree and we couldn't get it through the door. He's really silly about Christmas.'

'Is he? You spend a lot of time with your grandparents?'

She pulled a face. 'We used to have a lovely house with a garden, but my mother took an interior decorating course and caught minimalism, so traded it in for a loft apartment on the Melchester quays. Not the kind of place for a girl with engine oil under her fingernails.'

'There's such a thing as a nail brush,' she pointed out, biting back the *What about your father?* question.

'I suppose, but my mother treats Christmas as a design opportunity. Last year it was silver and white with mauve "accents".' She did the thing with her fingers to indicate the quotes.

'Mauve?' Annie repeated.

'With the tiniest, tiniest white lights.' And, putting on a clipped accent, Xandra said, 'All terribly, terribly tasteful, dahling.' Then, 'Christmas isn't supposed to be tasteful.'

'Isn't it?' Annie asked, sobering as she thought about the Dickens-inspired designer co-ordinated green, red and gold that traditionally decked the halls of King's Lacey for the festive season. 'What is it supposed to be?'

Xandra's response was a broad grin. 'Stick around and see what I've got planned.' Then, with a groan as she saw her father, 'Come on, let's get out of here.'

George had emerged from the workshop and was striding purposefully in their direction and by the time she'd managed to start the cold engine he was at the window and she had no choice but to push it open. He was wearing overalls and there was a smear of grease on his cheek that her fingers itched to wipe away before her lips planted a kiss in that exact spot.

Losing her mind, clearly, she decided, keeping her hands firmly on the steering wheel, her eyes firmly on him, managing a fairly coherent, 'Good morning.' Unable to resist saying, 'I hope you managed to sleep well.'

He lifted an eyebrow, acknowledging the reference to her turning him out of his bed.

'Well enough,' he replied, although he'd apparently had to think about it. 'You?'

'Like a log for the first time in as long as I can remember,' she said gratefully. 'Thank you.'

He nodded. 'You look…rested.' Then, as he wiped his hands on a rag, 'Where are you two off to?'

'We're going to the farm,' she said. 'To buy a tree.'

'Come on, Annie. Let's *go*,' Xandra butted in impatiently.

He put his hand on the open window to keep her where she was. 'Tree?' He frowned.

'A *Christmas* tree? You remember *Christmas*, don't you? Peace on earth, goodwill, tacky decs, bad songs. Terrible presents.'

His jaw tightened. 'I have heard of it.' Then, looking at Annie, 'Have you ever driven a four-wheel drive?'

About to assure him that, despite all evidence to the contrary, she'd not only been taught to drive everything on her grandfather's estate by an ex-police driving instructor, but had been trained in survival driving, she managed to stop herself.

And not simply because mentioning the fact that her grandfather owned an estate seemed like a bad idea.

'Why?' she asked innocently. 'Is it different to driving a car?'

'In other words, no,' he said, opening the door. 'Shift over, I'll take you.'

'Can't you just take me through it?' she suggested. 'I know how busy you are and I've put you to more than enough trouble.'

'You think?' He held her gaze for so long that she was afraid he knew exactly what she was doing. Then, shaking his head, 'It'll be quicker if I run you there.'

'I'm really sorry,' she said as she edged her bottom along the seat. 'It was your mother's idea and she's been so kind. It's the least I can do.'

Xandra was staring straight ahead, rigid with tension.

'Budge up,' she urged.

The girl moved no more than a hand's width and Annie could almost feel the waves of animosity coming off her. Clearly her plan to get father and daughter to bond over the purchase of a Christmas tree wasn't going to be as simple as she'd hoped.

That said, she was a little tense herself as George squashed in beside her, his arm brushing against her as he reached for the gearstick. He glanced at her, asking her with the slightest lift of his eyebrow if she was all right. She gave a barely discernible shrug to indicate that she was fine.

As if.

She was crushed up against the kind of man who would light up any woman's dreams, her cheek against his shoulder, her thigh trembling against the hard muscles of his leg. She could feel every move he made, every breath and even the familiar smell of hot oil from the engine of the aged vehicle couldn't mask the scent of warm male.

It was too noisy to talk but as they came to a halt at a busy roundabout he turned to her.

'You'll have more room if you put your arm on my shoulder,' he said, looking down at her. But for a moment, mesmerised by his sensuous lower lip, close enough to kiss, she didn't, couldn't, move. Then, before she could get a grip, ease her arm free and lay it across those wide shoulders, Xandra abruptly shifted sideways.

'I'm…fine,' she managed as she reluctantly eased herself away from his warmth.

The Christmas tree farm wasn't far and they were soon pulling off the road and into an area cleared for a car park.

Beside it was the seasonal shop in a little chalet decorated with fake snow and strings of fairy lights. In front of it there was a children's ride, a bright red sleigh with Rudolph—complete with flashing nose—and Santa, with his sack of parcels, at the reins.

As soon as they came to a halt, Xandra opened the door and leapt down, not waiting for her or her father, disappearing stiff-legged, stiff-necked into the plantation.

'Are you coming?' Annie paused on the edge of the seat, looking back as she realised that George hadn't moved.

'You know me,' he said, his face expressionless. 'I'm just the driver.'

'I'm sorry.'

'It's not your fault.'

'No. And I am truly grateful to you for stepping in. Xandra wants to decorate the house for your father before he comes home from the hospital.'

Or was it really for him? she wondered.

Despite everything she'd said, he'd said, was Xandra hoping that he'd relent over closing the garage, stay for the holiday? That they'd all have a perfect fairy-tale Christmas together, the kind that proper families had in story books?

Dickens, she thought as she jumped down, had a lot to answer for.

Hitting the uneven ground jarred the ankle she'd wrenched the day before and she gave a little yelp.

And then she moaned.

'What?' George asked.

'Nothing…' She let the word die away as she hung onto the door.

Muttering something that she was clearly not meant to hear, he climbed out and walked round the Land Rover to see for himself.

'It's nothing,' she repeated, letting go of the door with one hand just long enough to wave him away. 'I gave my ankle a bit of a wrench yesterday when I stepped in that pothole and just now, well, the drop was further than I thought…' Enough. Don't overdo it, Annie, she told herself and taking a steadying breath, she straightened herself, touched her toe to the ground. Bravely fought back a wince. 'Give me a minute,' she said with a little gasp. 'I'll be fine.'

'Let me see.'

She didn't have to feign the gasp as he put his hands around her waist and lifted her back up onto the seat, then picked up her left foot, resting her ankle in the palm of his hand.

'It doesn't look swollen,' he said, gently feeling around the bone, the instep and he looked up, slate eyes suddenly filled with suspicion.

'No. I told you. It'll be fine.' She slid down, forcing him back, and began to limp after Xandra.

'Wait!'

'I promised Hetty I'd keep an eye on her,' she said, not looking back. 'Make sure she keeps her ambitions below ceiling height.'

'Oh, for heaven's sake,' he said, closing the door

and coming after her. 'Here,' he said, taking her arms and putting them around his neck. She scarcely had time to react to his irritable command before he'd bent and picked her up. 'Hang on.'

He didn't need to tell her twice and she hung on for dear life, arms around his neck, cheek in the crook of his warm neck as he walked across to the wooden chalet, carried her up the steps and set her down on a chair.

'Stay there and try not to get into any more trouble,' he said, picking up her foot and turning another chair for it to rest on. 'Okay?' his said, his face level with hers.

'Okay,' she said a touch breathlessly.

He nodded. 'Right. I'd better go and make sure Xandra doesn't pick out something that would be more at home in Trafalgar Square.'

'Wait!' she said and, before he could straighten, took his chin in her hand as she searched her pockets for a tissue.

He must have shaved last night after he'd left her, she realised, feeling only the slight rasp of morning stubble against her palm as she reached up and gently wiped the grease off his cheek. Then, because he was looking at her in a way that made her insides melt, she said, 'George Saxon and Son has a reputation to maintain.'

She'd meant to sound brisk, businesslike, matter-of-fact but her voice, trained to deliver a speech to the back of a banqueting hall, for once refused to co-operate and it came out as little more than a whisper.

'And what about Annie Rowland?' he asked, his face expressionless.

'What? I haven't got grease on my face, have I?' she asked, instinctively touching the same place on her own cheek.

'Not grease,' he said, lifting her glasses off her nose and slipping them into the top pocket of his overalls. 'Something far worse.'

'Oh, but—'

He stopped her protest by planting a kiss very firmly on her lips. For a moment she tried to talk through it but then, as the warmth of his lips penetrated the outer chill, heating her through to the bone, a tiny shiver of pleasure rippled through her and she forgot what she was trying to say.

Instead, she clutched at his shoulder, closed her eyes and, oblivious to the woman sitting by the till, she kissed him back. Let slip a tiny mew of disappointment as he drew back and the cold rushed back in.

She opened her eyes and for a moment they just looked at each other before, without another word, he turned and walked out of the door.

The woman behind the counter cleared her throat as, slightly dazed, Annie watched George follow the path his daughter had taken between the trees.

'Are you all right?' she asked.

'I'm not sure,' she said, raising cold fingers to hot lips. 'I'm really not at all sure.'

'Only there are signs warning about the uneven paths,' she said defensively.

'Are there?' She watched George until he disappeared from sight and then turned to look at the woman.

'It says we're not responsible—'

'Oh!' Annie said, finally catching onto the fact that she wasn't referring to the hiccup in her heartbeat, her ragged pulse rate. Or the way George had stolen her glasses before kissing her.

The woman was only concerned about the fact that she'd apparently injured her ankle in their car park and might decide to sue the pants off them.

She shook her head. 'Don't worry about it. I hurt it yesterday,' she said, reassuring her. 'Today was no more than a reminder.'

'Well, that's a relief. You wouldn't believe…' She let it go, smiled, then followed her gaze as she looked along the path that George had taken. 'It's good your man is so caring.'

'Oh, but he isn't…'

Her man.

She'd only met him last night. Barely knew him. And he didn't know her at all. No one who knew her would dare to kiss her the way he'd kissed her.

And yet she'd been closer to him in that short

time than almost any man she'd ever known. She already cared about him in ways she had only dreamed of. And his daughter.

She'd grown up without a father of her own and if she could heal the breach between them she would go home knowing that she'd done something good.

'Can I get you something while you're waiting? Tea? Coffee? Hot chocolate?'

The little wooden chalet was, it seemed, more than simply a place to pay for the trees, the bundles of mistletoe and holly stacked up outside.

There was a little counter for serving hot drinks, cakes and mince pies and the walls were lined with shelves displaying seasonal decorations made by local craftsmen, although she was the only customer for the moment, despite the cars lined up outside. Obviously everyone else was out in the plantation picking out their trees.

Annie ordered a mince pie and a cup of hot chocolate and then, while she was waiting, instead of ignoring the decorations as she usually did, she looked around her, hoping to find something that would amuse Xandra.

There were beautiful handmade candles, charming wooden decorations. All perfectly lovely. All so wonderfully…tasteful.

Outside, a child climbed in the sleigh alongside Santa. His mother put a coin in the machine and it began to move in a motion designed to make over-excited children sick, while it played *Rudolph the Red-Nosed Reindeer*.

Not tasteful at all.

'Here you are.' The woman brought her chocolate and mince pie. 'Would you like the paper?' she asked, offering her one of the red tops. 'Something to look at while you're waiting.'

About to refuse, she changed her mind, deciding to check out the kind of coverage she'd got yesterday. Make sure there was nothing that would rouse the slightest suspicion in an eagle-eyed editor or set alarms bells ringing if anyone in her own office took more than the usual cursory glance.

'Thanks. That would be great.'

A picture of Lydia leaving the Pink Ribbon Lunch had made the front page. With rumours of a wedding, that was inevitable, but the hat, a last-minute special from her favourite designer featuring a Pink Ribbon spangled veil, had successfully blurred her features.

She'd seen so many photographs of herself, her head at just that angle as she'd turned to smile for the cameras, that even she found it hard to believe that it wasn't actually her.

And if Lydia had a bloom that she'd been lacking in recent months, the caption writer had put his own spin on that.

Lady Rose was radiant as she left the Pink Ribbon Lunch yesterday before flying to Bab el Sama for a well-earned break before Christmas at King's Lacey, her family home. The question is, will she be on her own? See page five.

She turned to page five, where there was a double-page spread including a recent picture of her, smiling as she left some event with Rupert. Thankful it was over, no doubt.

There was a huge aerial photograph of Bab el Sama, and another distant shot of the beach taken from the sea, along with many words written by someone who had never been there—no one from the press had ever set foot in the place—speculating on the luxury, the seclusion of a resort that was, apparently, the perfect place for lovers.

Put together the words 'radiant' and 'lovers' and read between the lines…

Yuck.

But, then again, it was only what she'd expected and with luck the possibility would keep the paparazzi fixed to the spot, hoping for a picture that would earn them a fortune.

She smiled. Sorry, chaps, she thought, as she closed the paper, folded it over so that the front page was hidden and put it back on the counter. Then, brimful of goodwill despite rather than because of the season, she said, 'I don't suppose I could persuade you to part with Rudolph, could I?'

'You'd be surprised how many people have asked me that,' she said, 'but we've only got him on hire during December.'

'Pity.'

'Believe me,' she said as the child demanded another ride and the song started up again, 'after the first hundred times, it feels like a lifetime.'

CHAPTER EIGHT

GEORGE followed his daughter down the path to the area where the farmer and his son were harvesting the trees.

The boy, seventeen or eighteen, brawny, good-looking, smiled as he looked up and caught sight of Xandra.

'Can I help?' he asked.

'I need a tree,' she said, with the cool, assessing look that women had been giving men since Adam encountered Eve in the Garden of Eden. 'A big one,' she added, turning away to inspect trees that had already been dug up and netted.

It was a move calculated to draw the boy closer and he followed as if on a string. It was like watching the rerun of an old movie, he thought. She was younger than her mother had been when she'd looked at him like that, but she already had the moves down pat.

'With roots or without?' the boy asked.

'Without,' he replied for her, stepping forward to make his presence felt.

'With,' Xandra countered, not even bothering to look at him. 'I want to plant it in the garden after Christmas.'

'Okay. If you'd like to choose one I'll dig it up for you.'

'What's wrong with those?' George said, nodding at the trees that were ready to go.

'I want to choose my own,' Xandra said.

'And it's best to get it as fresh as possible,' the boy added. Wanting to flex his muscles for a pretty girl. 'I'll get a decent root ball with it and wrap it in sacking for you. That'll give it a better chance.'

'Thanks,' she said before turning, finally, to acknowledge his presence. 'Where's Annie?' she asked, realising that he was on his own.

'She hurt her ankle getting out of the Land Rover. I left her in the shop with her foot up.' Then, in an effort to move things along, he indicated a nicely shaped tree and said, 'What about that one?'

'It's not tall enough.'

Clearly whichever tree he'd chosen was going to be rejected but he pressed on. 'It'll be at least two feet taller once it's out of the ground and in a pot.'

He looked at the boy, who was smart enough to agree with him. 'It's a lovely tree,' he added, but if he hoped to curry favour he was talking to the wrong man. He'd been eighteen once, and this was his daughter.

Xandra shrugged. 'Okay. But I want one for outside as well. A really *big* one.'

About to ask her who was going to put it up, he stopped himself, aware that the boy, if he had anything about him, would leap in with an offer to do it for her.

She'd had sixteen years without him to put up a tree for her. Maybe one really big one would make a bit of a dent in the overdraft.

'No more than ten feet from the ground,' he told the boy and, when she would have objected, 'I won't be able to carry anything bigger than that on the roof of the Land Rover.' Even that would be a push.

Then, beating down the urge to grab her by the arm, drag her back to the shop where he could keep her within sight, he said, 'Don't take too long about choosing it. I want to get Annie back into the warm,' he said, turning to go back to her.

'Is she badly hurt?' She sounded concerned.

'She's putting a brave face on it,' he said, rubbing the flat of his palm over his jaw, where he could still feel the warm touch of her fingers, despite the chill.

It had been the same last night. After leaving her he'd taken a shower, shaved, anything to distance himself from the touch of her hand that had burned like a brand on his arm. Somehow he doubted that even a cold shower would have saved him from the pink bunny.

Now he'd kissed her again, just to shut her up for a moment, he told himself, but this time she'd kissed him back. Yet still he was left with the extraordinary sense that for her it was all brand-new.

How crazy was that? She had to be in her midtwenties at least.

Xandra hesitated, but only for a moment, before turning to the boy. 'Okay, I'm going to trust you to choose the big tree—'

'I know just the one,' he said eagerly. 'A real beauty. You'll love it.' And Xandra bestowed a gracious smile on him before, just a touch of colour darkening her cheekbones, she quickly turned away and swept off up the path.

For a moment they both stood and watched her, each lost for a moment in his own thoughts.

The boy was only seeing Christmas coming early.

His thoughts were darker as he remembered the moment when, not much older than the youth at his side, she'd been put in his arms, the realisation that she was his little girl. The shattering need to protect her. Make her life perfect.

Remembering the beautiful little girl with dark curls who'd run not to him, but to his father for hugs. Who had called Penny's second husband— living in the house he'd paid for—'daddy'.

* * *

Annie looked up as he followed Xandra into the chalet.

'Did you find what you were looking for?' she asked, her eyes narrowing as she looked at him.

'I think I can safely guarantee that our trees will be the best that money can buy.'

She still had her left foot propped up and, ignoring the empty chairs, he picked it up, sat down and placed it on his knee, leaving his hand on the curve between ankle and foot.

It was a slender foot, a slender ankle and there wasn't the slightest sign of a swelling.

'Trees?' she asked.

'A six-footer for inside the house. Something rather more stately for outside.'

'Oh, trees *plural*. You're going to need a ton of tinsel, Xandra,' she said, watching her as she wandered around the shop, checking out what they had to offer.

'I'm working on it,' she said, picking up one of the decorations, then putting it back.

'How's your ankle?' George asked, reclaiming Annie's attention.

'Fine, really,' she assured him, not quite meeting his gaze, adding to his certainty that she had faked the injury. But why?

Could it be that she saw the garage as a sanctuary? Wanted to stay on?

'It was nothing that hot chocolate and a mince

pie couldn't cure,' she assured him, making a move to put it down, but he kept his hand firmly in place.

'Best to keep it up for as long as possible,' he said.

She took her time about answering him, dabbing at the crumbs on the plate in front of her and sucking them off her finger before, finally, lifting her lashes with a look that went straight to his gut.

Was it deliberate? Did she know what she was doing?

Usually, when he looked at a woman, when she looked back, they both knew exactly what they wanted, but Annie wasn't like any woman he'd ever met.

She left him floundering.

'So,' he said quickly, glad he was wearing loose overalls over his trousers so that she couldn't see the disturbing effect she had on him, 'what's your plan for today?'

Her lips parted over perfect teeth but, before she could tell him, Xandra said, 'She's staying with us until after the weekend. Gran asked her,' she added, glaring at him, daring him to offer an argument.

But if his mother had already asked her to stay, why would she—?

Oh. Right.

She'd seen an opportunity to throw him and Xandra together and, instead of seizing the moment, he'd gone in with both feet and made a complete cobblers of it.

'Not that she'd be able to go gallivanting all over the place sightseeing with a dodgy ankle,' she added.

'Honestly,' Annie said, looking at him, her eyes offering him her assurance that if he was unhappy she'd make her excuses and leave, 'it's not that bad.'

'Best not take any chances,' he said, attempting to unravel the curious mixture of elation and dismay he felt at the prospect of her staying on for several more days.

Relief that she wasn't going to walk away, disappear. That he'd never know what happened to her. Who she really was.

Dismay because he wanted to protect her from whatever was out there, threatening her. And that unnerved him.

'I'm having some water,' Xandra said, examining the contents of a glass-fronted fridge. She turned to him. 'Do you want anything?'

To be back at his beach house with nothing on his mind more important than the design of a multi-million-pound software program, a mild flirtation with a pretty woman, he thought, as he reached for his wallet. One with curves and curls and an uncomplicated smile that let you know exactly what was on her mind.

Since that wasn't an option, he said, 'Coffee and—'

'I don't need your money,' she snapped as he offered her a note. Then, perhaps remembering where the money in her own purse had come from, quickly said, 'Black with too much sugar, right?'

'Thanks.'

He'd been about to tell her to buy the angel she'd looked at, but decided against it. She wasn't a little girl he could buy with a doll.

'And?' she added. He must have looked puzzled because she said, 'You said "and".'

'And if you could run to a couple of those mince pies,' he said, 'it would fill a gap. I seem to have missed breakfast.'

'Sugar, fat and caffeine?' She shook her head. 'Tut, tut, tut.' But she turned to the woman behind the counter and said, 'The water for me, a heart attack for George… And what's that, Annie? Hot chocolate? Do you want a top-up?'

'No, I'm good, thanks.'

'Hot chocolate and a mince pie? Have a care, Annie,' he warned her with a grin. 'The food police will be after you too.'

'At least I had a slice of toast before I left the house this morning.'

'Buttered, of course. My father isn't a man to have anything as new-fangled as low-fat spread in the house.'

'Buttered,' she admitted, smiling as she conceded the point. 'But it was unsalted butter.'

'Honestly. What are you two like?' Xandra said disapprovingly. 'You're supposed to be mature adults. I'd get the "breakfast is the most important meal of the day" lecture if I ate like that.'

'Not from me,' he assured her.

'Well, no. Obviously. You'd have to be there.'

'I was,' he reminded her. 'Out of interest, what did you have for breakfast?'

'Gran made us both porridge. I sliced an apple over mine and added a drizzle of maple syrup.'

'Organic, of course.'

'Of course.'

'Well, good for you.' Annie, he noticed, lips pressed together to keep a smile in check, was being very careful to avoid eye contact, this time for all the right reasons. 'Actually,' he continued, 'you seem to have overlooked the fact that there's fruit in the mincemeat.'

Xandra snorted, unimpressed, but she turned away quickly. He was hoping it was so that he wouldn't see that, like Annie, she was trying not to laugh.

He was probably fooling himself, he thought, reaching for the paper lying on the counter to distract himself with the sports headlines on the back page so he wouldn't dwell on how much that hurt.

'Here you are.' Xandra put his coffee and pastries in front of him, then, sipping from the bottle she was holding, wandered over to the window to watch for the arrival of the trees. Or possibly the young man who'd be bringing them.

'It'll take him a while to dig up two big trees,' he warned her.

'Well, I'm sorry to take up so much of your time.' She took the paper from him, pulled out a chair and turned it over and, having glanced at the front page, opened it up. She was using it as a barrier rather than because she was interested in world news, he thought, but after a moment she looked up, stared at Annie, then looked at the paper again.

'Has anyone ever told you how much you look like Lady Rose, Annie?' she asked.

'Who?' she asked, reaching for the paper, but he beat her to it.

'You know.' She made a pair of those irritating quote marks with her fingers. 'The "people's virgin".'

'Who?' he asked.

Xandra leaned over and pointed to a picture of a man and a woman. 'Lady Rose Napier. The nation's sweetheart. She came to Dower House a couple of years ago for prize-giving day. Chauffeur, body-guards, the Warthog genuflecting all over the place.'

Since George paid the school fees, he received

invitations to all school events as a matter of courtesy. Did his best to make all of them.

'I must have missed that one,' he said, realising that Lady Rose was the pampered 'princess' whose wedding plans were the talk of the tabloids.

He looked up from the paper to check the likeness for himself. 'Xandra's right,' he said. 'You do look like her.' Which perhaps explained why she'd seemed vaguely familiar.

'I wish,' Annie said with a slightly shaky laugh. 'I was just reading about her. She's holed up in luxurious seclusion in a palace owned by the Ramal Hamrahn royal family. I could do with some of that.'

'According to this, she's with that old bloke she's going to marry.' Xandra pulled a face. 'I'd rather stay a virgin.'

'I'd rather you did too,' George said.

She glanced at him. 'You're a fine one to talk.'

'Your mother was eighteen,' he protested, then stopped. This was not a conversation he wanted to have with his sixteen-year-old daughter. 'Did you meet her? Lady Rose?'

'In other words, did I win a prize? Sorry, they don't give one for car maintenance.' Then, since that didn't get the intended laugh, 'Lady Rose is nearly as old as Annie. I suppose she must be getting desperate.'

He looked at the picture of the man beside her. 'He's not that old,' he protested.

'He's thirty-nine. It says so right there.'

With his own thirty-sixth birthday in sight, that didn't seem old to him, but when he'd been sixteen it would probably have seemed ancient.

'It also says he's rich. Owns a castle in Scotland, estates in Norfolk and Somerset and is heir to an earldom.'

'I think that cancels out "old",' he countered, looking up from the photograph of the two of them leaving some function together to compare her with Annie.

If you ignored the clothes, the woolly hat pulled down to hide not just her hair but most of her forehead, the likeness was striking.

And Annie had admitted to cutting her hair, borrowing the clothes she was wearing. She'd even talked about security men watching her night and day.

If the evidence that she'd flown to some place called Bab el Sama hadn't been right in front of him, it might have crossed his mind that Annie was Lady Rose Napier.

Assuming, of course, that she really had gone there. But why wouldn't she? It was the ultimate getaway destination. Luxury, privacy.

Why would she swap that for this?

'Rich, smitch,' Xandra said dismissively. 'Lady Rose doesn't need the money. Her father was the Marquess of St Ives and he left her a fortune. And her grandfather is a duke.'

'How do you know all this?'

'Everything she does is news. She's the virgin princess with a heart of gold. An example to us all.'

She clutched at her throat to mime throwing up.

'I'd have thought a woman like that would be fighting off suitors.'

'Yes, well, she's been surrounded by bodyguards all her life, has a posse of photographers in her face wherever she goes and she has a whiter than white image to maintain. She can never let her hair down, kick off and have fun like everyone else, can she?' She thought about it for a moment. 'Actually, you've got to feel just a bit sorry for her.'

'Have you?' he asked, thinking about the way Annie had reached out to him last night. Her whispered 'I don't want to be safe'. 'What about you, Annie?'

'Do I feel sorry for her?' she asked, looking at the picture.

That was what he'd meant, but there was something about the way she was avoiding his eyes that bothered him.

'Would you marry the old guy in the picture?' he pressed.

She looked up then. Straight, direct. 'Not unless I was in love with him.'

'Oh, puh-lease,' Xandra said. Then, taking back the paper, she compared the two pictures and shrugged. 'Maybe she is in love. There was a rumour going around that she was anorexic, but she looks a lot better here. It's a pity, really.'

'What is?' he asked, never taking his eyes off Annie.

It all fitted, he thought.

The timing was right. The poise. He'd even thought that she was acting as if she were royalty when she'd left him to close the tow-truck door behind her. He doubted that Lady Rose Napier, with a chauffeur and bodyguards in attendance, had ever had to do that in her life.

But it had to be coincidence. There was a likeness, it was true, but wasn't everyone supposed to have a double somewhere? And why on earth would a woman with a fortune at her command take off in a rattle bucket car when she could be going first-class all the way to paradise with Mr Big?

'What's a pity?' he repeated sharply.

Xandra gave an awkward little shrug, shook her head, clearly embarrassed, which had to be a first.

'Nothing. It's just that in the earlier picture the likeness is more pronounced.'

When she was thinner? A little less attractive? Was that what his tactless daughter had stopped herself from saying?

'But if Annie worked at it a bit, grew her hair, had the right clothes, make-up, I bet one of those lookalike agencies would snap her up.'

Annie opened her mouth, presumably to protest, but Xandra wasn't finished.

'You'd have to wear high heels,' she went on, getting carried away in her enthusiasm. 'She's really tall. But I bet that if you put on a pound or two you could do it.'

'What about the eyes?' George said, trying to see her not in baggy jeans, a chain store fleece jacket with a woolly hat pulled down to cover her hair, but a designer gown cut low to reveal creamy shoulders, long hair swept up. Her face transformed with make-up. Jewels at her throat. He seemed to get stuck on the shoulders… 'Aren't they the big giveaway?'

'What?' she said, her attention shifting to the sound of a tractor pulling into the car park. She dropped the paper, more interested in what was happening outside. 'Oh, that's not a problem. She could use contacts.'

'Of course she could,' he said, his own attention focused firmly on the woman sitting on the far side of the table. 'So does that appeal as a career move?'

The corner of Annie's mouth lifted in a wry smile. 'You mean if I were a little younger, a little taller, wore a wig, contacts and plenty of make-up?'

'And if you put on a few pounds,' he reminded her. A little weight to fill out the hollows beneath her collarbone. Hollows that matched those of Lady Rose Napier in her evening gown.

'Much more of your mother's meat pie and buttered toast and that won't be a problem,' she replied, the smile a little deeper, but still wry.

'As good a reason to stay as any other,' he suggested. 'As long as you remember to add garlic to the mash.'

'Are you suggesting that I'm scrawny?'

'The trees are here, George.' His daughter impatiently demanded his attention and he pushed back his chair, got to his feet, never taking his eyes off Annie.

'Not if I have any sense,' he replied. 'And you can save the expense of contact lenses. Your eye colour is more than a match for the people's virgin.'

He took her glasses from his pocket and, taking her hand, placed them in her palm, closing her fingers over them, holding them in place as he was held by Annie's vivid gaze.

'They look an awful lot bigger on the trailer than they did growing,' Xandra said, breaking the spell. 'Will they be safe on the roof?'

'Don't worry about it,' he said, telling himself that he was glad of the distraction. 'If it's going to be a problem I'm sure your lovelorn swain will be happy to offer a personal delivery service.'

'My what? Oh, for goodness' sake,' she said, rolling her eyes at him before stomping down the steps and striding across the car park.

'I'd better go and find some rope,' he said, still not moving.

'Is there anything I can do to help?' Annie asked, the glasses still clutched in her hand.

'I think you've done more than enough for one day, Annie. If you don't fancy lookalike work, you could always take up acting.'

'Acting?'

He noted the nervous swallow, the heightened colour that flushed across her cheekbones with relief. Despite his earlier suspicion that she might be a practised con woman, it was clear that, whatever she was hiding, she wasn't a practised liar.

'I don't understand.'

'There's nothing wrong with your ankle,' he said bluntly.

'Oh.' The colour deepened. 'How did you guess?'

'I've rarely encountered one in less perfect condition,' he said, reliving the feel of it beneath his palm. 'In fact, I'm seriously hoping that you'll take Xandra's advice to heart about wearing high heels.'

'I didn't pack any.'

'No? Well, you can't run in high heels, can you?'

'If you hadn't gone all macho over the car—'

'Oh, right. Blame the sucker.'

'It wasn't like that,' she protested. 'I just thought—'

'I know what you thought,' he said curtly, before she could say the words out loud. Determined to crush any foolish notion that throwing him into close proximity with Xandra would produce a cosy father-daughter bond. 'I have no doubt you imagined you were helping, but some relationships can't be fixed.'

No matter how much you might regret that.

'Not without putting a little effort into it,' she came right back at him, her eyes flashing with more than a touch of anger as if he'd lit some personal touchpaper. The air seemed to fizzle with it and he wondered what would have happened if, instead of listening to his head last night and walking away, he'd listened to her.

I don't want to be safe…'

He took a step back, needing to put some space between them, but she wasn't done.

'Don't give up on her, George,' she said, leaning towards him, appealing to him. 'Don't give up on yourself.'

'I'm sure you mean well, Annie, but don't waste your time playing Santa Claus. It's not going to happen.' He pushed the paper towards her. 'You'd be better occupied thinking about your own future than worrying about mine. What you're going to do next week. The money you've got stashed in your underwear isn't going to last very long when you're out there on your own.'

Reminding her that she might have found a temporary sanctuary, but that was all it was.

Reminding himself.

Annie let out a long silent breath as he walked away, but it had more to do with the anger, the pain that had come off him like a blast of ice than fear that he'd seen through her disguise.

Although maybe, she thought, looking down at the glasses in her hand, maybe she should be worrying about that.

She'd assumed that he'd pushed the paper at her so that she could check out her 'double'. Think about the career opportunities it offered. But he hadn't actually said that.

Even with the evidence that she wasn't the 'people's virgin'—and could it be any more lowering than to have her lack of sexual experience pitied by a sixteen-year-old?—on the table in front of her.

She was in Bab el Sama. It said so right there for the whole world to see, yet still he'd handed her back her disguise as if he thought she needed it.

Too late for that, she thought, dropping the glasses into her bag and switching on her cellphone to thumb in a quick text to Lydia.

Tomorrow there would have to be pictures to prove she was there.

'Are you all right, dear?' The woman who'd served them came to clear the table and wipe it down and glanced after George meaningfully.

'I'm fine,' she said, switching off the phone. 'Honestly.'

'Christmas…' she said, sighing as Rudolph started up yet again. 'It's all stress. You wouldn't believe the things I hear. Did you know that there are more marriage break-ups over Christmas than at any other time of year?'

'Really? I'll bear that in mind. Should I ever get married.'

'Oh… You and he aren't…?'

'We only met yesterday, but thank you for caring,' Annie said, stowing her phone and standing up. 'Being ready to listen. That's the true spirit of the season.'

'The Christmas fairy, that's me,' she said with an embarrassed laugh before whisking away the tray.

And nothing wrong with that, Annie thought, before crossing to the window to see how far things had progressed.

One of the trees had already been hoisted onto the roof of the car, but as George and a good-looking boy bent to lift the second, larger tree, Xandra, who had climbed up to lash the first into place, stopped what she was doing and looked down, not at the boy, but at her father.

Full of longing, need, it was a look that she recognised, understood and she forgot her own concerns as her heart went out to the girl.

They'd both lost their parents, but in Xandra's case the situation wasn't irretrievable. Her mother might not be perfect but she'd be home in a few weeks. And George was here right now, bringing the scent of fresh spruce with him as he returned to the chalet to pay for the trees.

For once it didn't bring a lump to her throat, the ache of unbearable memories. This wasn't her Christmas, but Xandra's. A real celebration to share with the grandparents she adored. And with George, if he took his chance and seized the opportunity to change things.

'All done?' she asked.

He gave her a look that suggested she had to be joking. 'This is just the beginning. When we get back I'm going to have to find suitable containers and erect them safely so that they don't topple over if the cat decides to go climbing.'

'Back', not home, she noticed. He never called the house he'd grown up in 'home'.

'Then I'll have to sort out lights and check them to make sure they won't blow all the fuses.'

'Why don't you ask that boy to give you a hand?' she suggested. 'Earn yourself some Brownie points with your daughter.'

'I don't think so,' he said, handing a grubby hand-written docket to the woman behind the till along with some banknotes.

Protective. A good start, she thought.

'You can't keep her wrapped in cotton wool.' At least not without the kind of money that would make Dower House fees look like chicken feed.

'And, even if you could, she wouldn't thank you for it.'

'Nothing new there, then,' he said, slotting the pound coins the woman gave him as change into a charity box on the counter.

They piled back into the car and this time Xandra gave her more room so she wasn't squashed up against George. Just close enough to be tinglingly aware of every movement. For his hand to brush her thigh each time he changed gear.

'We'll need to stop at the garden centre in Longbourne to pick up some bags of compost,' Xandra said carelessly as he paused at the farm gate. 'If the trees are to have a chance of surviving.'

'I don't think—'

'Granddad always plants out the Christmas trees,' she said stubbornly.

'I remember,' he muttered under his breath so that only she heard. Then, raising his voice above the sound of the engine, 'He won't be fit enough to do it this year, Xandra.'

Her eyes widened a little as the reality of her grandfather's heart attack truly hit home, but then she shrugged. 'It's not a problem. I can do it.'

'Damn you!' George banged the steering wheel with the flat of his hand. 'You are just like him, do you know that? Stubborn, pig-headed, deaf to reason…'

Xandra's only response was to switch on the

personal stereo in her jacket pocket and stick in her earplugs.

George didn't say a word and Annie kept her own mouth firmly shut as they pulled into the garden centre car park.

It was one of those out of town places and it had a huge range of house plants that had been forced for the holiday, as well as every kind of seasonal decoration imaginable.

While George disappeared in search of compost, Annie used the time to pick out a dark pink cyclamen for Hetty and Xandra disappeared into the Christmas grotto.

When they met at the till ten minutes later she was half hidden behind an armful of decorations in just about every colour imaginable—none of that colour co-ordination nonsense for her—and wearing a three-foot-long Santa hat.

CHAPTER NINE

ANNIE, desperate to find some way to make George see beyond the defence mechanism that his daughter was using to save herself from the risk of hurt, was so deep in thought as she pushed open the kitchen door with her shoulder that the spicy scent of the Christmas cake baking took her unawares.

A punch to the heart.

Like the fresh, zingy scent of the trees, it evoked only painful memories and the armful of tinsel she was carrying slithered to the floor as she came to a dead stop.

'What's wrong?' George asked, following her in.

She tried to speak, couldn't. Instead, she shook her head and, giving herself time to recover, she bent to scoop up the glittering strands, only to find herself face to face with George as he joined her down at floor level.

'What is it?' he asked quietly as he took the pot plant from her.

'Nothing. It's nothing.' Dredging up a smile—a lady never showed her feelings—she wound a thick gold strand of tinsel around his neck. 'Just blinded by all this glitter,' she said, clutching it to her as she made a move to stand.

He caught her by the wrist, keeping her where she was.

'G-George...' she begged, her voice hoarse with the effort of keeping up the smile.

'You will tell me,' he warned her, his own smile just as broad, just as false as her own as he took a purple strand of tinsel and slowly wrapped it, once, twice around her throat before, his hand still tightly around her wrist, he drew her to her feet.

'Oh, well, there's a picture,' Hetty said, laughing as she caught sight of them. 'Did you buy up their entire stock, Xan?'

'You can never have too much tinsel,' she said as she trailed in with the rest of it.

'Is that right?' She took her coat from the hook and said, 'I'll be off now, if you don't mind, Annie. The cake should be done by one-thirty. I've set the timer. Just stick a skewer in the centre and if it comes out clean you can take it out.' She put on her gloves, found her car keys and picked up a bag laden with treats for the invalid. 'I've made vegetable soup for lunch. Just help yourself.'

'Can I do something about dinner?' Annie asked.

George, giving her a look that suggested she

was kidding herself, said, 'Why don't I get a takeaway?'

'Oh, great!' Xandra said, sorting through the tinsel and finding a heavy strand in shocking pink and throwing it around herself like a boa. 'Can we have Chinese? Please, please, please…'

'Annie?' he asked, turning to her.

'I couldn't think of anything I'd like more,' she said and got a quizzical look for her pains. She ignored it. 'I hope Mr Saxon will be feeling better today, Hetty.'

'Can I come with you?' Xandra asked. 'I could decorate his bed. Cheer him up.'

'I don't think they'll let you do that. Decorations would get in the way if…' Her voice faltered momentarily before she forced a smile. 'And what about this tree you've bought? You can't leave your father to put it up by himself.'

'Trees. We bought two, but they'll wait until the morning.'

'Will they? But if you come with me you'll be stuck in the hospital all day. And, besides, Granddad will want to know why you're home. I don't think it'll do his heart any good if he finds out you've been suspended from school, young lady.'

'He wouldn't care. He thinks Dower House is a total waste of money.'

'Your grandfather always did believe that education is for wimps,' George said. Then, clearly wishing he'd kept his mouth shut, he said, 'Go with your grandmother—'

'George—'

'I'll pick her up when I've finished the Bentley,' he said, glancing at his watch. 'Three o'clock? Be waiting outside. I'm not coming in to fetch you.'

'Congratulations, George,' Annie said when they'd gone. 'You came within a cat's whisker of behaving like a father for a moment, but you managed to rescue the situation before you could be mistaken for anyone who gives a damn.'

Furious with him for missing such a chance, she crossed to the stove, took the lid off the soup and banged it on the side.

'Pass me a bowl if you want some of this,' she said, sticking out a hand.

He put a bowl in it without a word and she filled the ladle with the thick soup, only to find her hand was shaking so much that she couldn't hold it. She dropped it back in the saucepan and George grabbed the bowl before she dropped that too.

'Damn you,' she said, hanging onto the rail that ran along the front of the oven. 'Would it have hurt you so much to spend a few minutes with your father? Have you any idea how lucky you are to have him? Have a mother who cares enough to make your favourite food?'

She turned to face him. He was still wearing the tinsel and he should have looked ridiculous. The truth was that he could have been wearing a pair of glass tree baubles dangling from his ears and Xandra's Santa hat and he'd still melt her bones.

That didn't lessen her anger.

'What did he do to you?' she asked. 'Why do you hate him so much?'

'It's what he didn't do that's the problem, but this isn't about me, is it?'

He reached out, touched her cheek, then held up his fingers so that she could see that they were wet.

'Why are you crying, Annie?'

'For the waste. The stupid waste…' Then, dragging in a deep, shuddering breath, she shook her head and rubbed her palms over her face to dry tears she hadn't been conscious of shedding. 'I'm sorry. You're right. I've no right to shout at you. I know nothing about what happened between you and your father. It's just this time of year. It's just…'

She stalled, unable to even say the word.

'It's just Christmas,' he said. 'I saw the way you reacted when you walked into the kitchen. As if you'd been struck. Spice, nuts, fruit, brandy. It's the quintessential smell of the season. And scent evokes memory as nothing else can.'

She opened her mouth, closed it. Swallowed.

'You think you're alone in hating it?'

She shook her head. Took a long, shuddering breath. Then, realising what he'd said, she looked up.

'Xandra said you hate Christmas. Said she knew why.'

'I came home for Christmas at the end of my first term at university to be met with the news that Penny was pregnant. My father was delighted, in case you're wondering. He thought I'd have to give up all thought of university and join him in the business. He was going to build us a house in the paddock, give me a partnership—'

'And you turned him down.'

'Penny thought, once we were actually married—and believe me, there's nothing like a shotgun wedding to add a little cheer for Christmas—that she could persuade me to change my mind.' He managed a wry smile. 'I've never eaten Christmas cake since.'

She stared at him, then realised that he was joking. Making light of a desperate memory. She wondered just how much pressure—emotional and financial—he'd endured.

'You didn't have to marry her. People don't these days.'

'It was my responsibility. My baby.'

She reached out to him. Touched his big, capable hand. Afraid for him.

If Xandra had inherited just one tenth of his stubborn determination, she feared they were heading for the kind of confrontation that could shatter any hope of reconciliation.

'What happened to you, Annie?' he asked. 'What are you really running away from?'

'Apart from Christmas?'

'There's no escape from that,' he said, 'unless, like Lady Rose Napier, you can borrow a palace from a friend.'

How ironic was that? She'd sent Lydia to a Christmas free zone, while she'd found herself in tinsel land.

'How is it on a Californian beach?' she asked in an attempt to head off the big question.

'Sunny, but it's not the weather, or the decorations or the carols. The trouble with Christmas is that, no matter how high the presents are piled, it shines a light into the empty spaces. Highlights what's missing from your life.' He curved his palm around her cheek. 'What's missing from yours, Annie?'

His touch was warm, his gentle voice coaxing and somehow the words were out before she could stop them.

'My parents. They were killed a week before the holiday. They were away and I was fizzing with excitement, waiting for them to come home so that we could decorate the tree, but they never came.'

There was an infinitesimal pause as he absorbed this information. 'Was it a road accident?'

They had been on a road. Four innocent people who, in the true spirit of Christmas, had been taking aid to a group of desperate people. Food, medicine, clothes, toys even. She'd sent her favourite doll for them to give to some poor homeless, starving child.

She wanted to tell him all that, but she couldn't because then he'd know who she was and she'd have to leave. And she didn't want to leave.

'They were passengers,' she said. 'Two other people with them died, too.' She never forgot them or their families, who went through this same annual nightmare as she did. 'They were buried on the day before Christmas Eve and then everything went on as if nothing had changed. The tree lights were turned on, there were candles in the church on Christmas morning, presents after tea. It was what they would have expected, I was told. Anything else would be letting them down.'

And then there had been the Boxing Day shoot.

She looked up at George. 'Every year it's as if I'm six years old,' she said, trying to make him understand. 'The tree, church, unwrapping presents. Going through the motions, smiling because it's expected and every year that makes me a little bit more—' she clenched her fists, trying to catch the word, but it spilled over, unstoppable '—angry.'

She didn't know where that had come from, but it was as if at that moment a dam had burst and all the pent-up emotion of the last twenty years burst out.

'I hate it,' she said, banging on his chest with her bunched fists. 'Hate the carols...' Bang... 'Hate the lights...' Bang... 'The falseness...' He caught her wrists.

'Is that what you're really running away from, Annie?' he asked, holding her off.

'Yes.' She pulled back, shaking her head as she crumpled against the stove and slid to the floor. 'No...'

George didn't try to coax her up, but kept hold of her hands, going down with her, encouraging her to lean against him so that her cheek was against the hard fabric of his overalls.

'No,' he agreed.

He smelled of engine oil, spruce, some warmer scent that was George himself that mingled to make something new, something that held no bad memories for her, and she let her head fall against his chest.

'You can run away from Christmas, Annie, but you can't escape what it is you hate about it. The bad memories.'

'I thought if I could just get away for a while, see things from a different perspective,' she said after a while, 'I might find a way to deal with it. But you're right. It's nothing to do with the season. It simply shines a light on everything that's wrong in our lives.'

George held her, her hair against his cheek,

thinking about an unhappy little girl who had spent year after year being brave for the adults who clearly hadn't a clue how to cope with her grief. And he wondered whether his daughter's desperate need to decorate every surface for the holiday exposed the emptiness at the heart of her life too.

'We are what circumstances make us,' he said, leaning back. 'My father used to make me work in the garage. Every day, after school, he set me a task that I had to finish before I was allowed to go and get on with my homework.'

He knew she'd turned to look up at him, but he kept staring ahead, remembering how it had been.

Remembering the weeks, months, years when anger had kept him going.

'I learned fast.' He'd had to if he was to defeat his father. 'He set me ever more complex, time-consuming tasks, reasoning that if I failed at school I would have no choice but to stay here, so that he could be George Saxon and not just the "and Son".'

By the time he'd been old enough to work that out, pity him, the battle lines were drawn and there was no going back.

'If I inherited one thing from my old man it was obstinacy. I got up early, worked late. Learned to manage on the minimum of sleep. And when I left for university I was the best mechanic in the garage, including my father. He never forgave me for that.'

Finally he looked down at her, not quite believing that he was sharing his most painful memories with a woman he'd picked up on the side of the road the evening before.

Could scarcely believe that sitting here, on the floor of his mother's kitchen with his arm around her, was the nearest he'd come to peace for as long as he could remember.

'And you still found time for girls?'

'That last summer, before I went up to university, I found time for a lot of things that I'd missed out on.' Life at home might have been unbearable, but there had been compensations. 'The minute I turned eighteen, I got a job at a garage that paid me what I was actually worth.'

'Your poor mother. It must have been as restful as living with two big cats walking stiff-legged around one another, hackles raised.'

He smiled. 'Don't tell me, you were the fly on the wall?'

'I've spent a lot of my life watching people. I can read body language as well as I read English.'

He must have shown a flicker of dismay because she laughed. 'Most body language. There are gaps in my knowledge.'

'What kind of gaps?'

She shook her head. 'Tell me what you did. After you'd turned your back on the "and Son". What paid for the California beach house? The fees for Dower House?'

'I knew two things—software engineering and cars—so I put them together and developed a software application for the motor industry. My father disapproves of computers on principle. Driving, for him, is a question of man and machine—nothing in between. So he never forgave me for that, either.'

'Maybe you have to forgive yourself first,' she said.

Forgive himself?

For a moment his brain floundered with the concept, but only for a moment. Annie was looking up at him, smiling a little as if she knew something he didn't. The tears she'd shed had added a sparkle to her eyes and as her lips parted to reveal a glimpse of perfect teeth he forgot what she'd said, knew only that he wanted to kiss her, was trembling with the need to kiss her in a way he hadn't since he was eighteen years old and Penny Lomax had made a man of him.

'Who are you?' he demanded, but as she opened her mouth to answer him he covered it with his hand.

'No. Don't tell me. I don't want to know.'

He didn't want her to tell him anything that would stop him from kissing her, from doing what he'd wanted to do ever since she'd stumbled into him and her scent had taken up residence in his head.

Fluent in body language, she knew exactly what

he was thinking and didn't wait, but reached up and pulled him down to her, coming up to meet him with a raw to-hell-and-back kiss that said only one thing.

I want you. I need you.

Her other hand, clutching at his shoulder, her nails digging through the heavy material of his overalls, proclaimed the urgency of that need.

The heat of it shuddered through him, igniting a flame that would have taken an ice-cold shower to cool. Sitting by a solid-fuel stove, they didn't stand a chance, even if he'd wanted one, he thought, tugging her shirt free of her jeans and reaching inside it to unhook the fastening of her bra. He half expected a bundle of twenty-pound notes to cascade out of it but, as he slid his hand inside it, it was filled with nothing more than a small, firm breast.

She moaned into his mouth, tearing at the studs on his overalls, her touch electric as she pushed up the T-shirt he was wearing beneath it before drawing back a little to look up at him, her eyes shining like hot sapphires, silently asking permission to touch him.

He shrugged his arms out of his overalls, pulled off the T-shirt he was wearing beneath it and fell back against the thick rag rug that had lain in that spot for as long as he could remember.

'Help yourself,' he said, grinning as he offered himself up to her.

Her fingers stopped a tantalising hair's breadth from his skin.

'What can I do?'

Do?

'Anything…' he began, then caught his breath as her fingertips made contact with his chest. 'Anything that feels good,' he managed, through a throat apparently stuffed with cobwebs. 'Good for you,' he added and he nearly lost it as they trailed down his chest, her long nails grazing the hollow of his stomach.

For a moment, as she straightened, he thought she'd changed her mind, but she caught the hem of her sweater and pulled it, shirt and bra over her head and discarded them impatiently. Her long body was taut, strong, her breasts were high, firm, beautiful and her eyes widened in shock and a shiver ran through her body as he touched a nipple.

'You like that?' he asked.

She made an unintelligible sound that was pure delight and, seizing her around the waist, he lifted her so that she straddled his body, wanting her to know that he liked it too. To feel his heat, know what she was doing to him. Had been doing to him since the moment she'd pitched into his arms.

For a moment she didn't move, then, with the tiniest of sighs, she bent to lay her lips against his stomach and this time the moan came from him.

'You like that?' she asked mischievously, looking up with the smile of a child who'd just been given the freedom of a sweet shop. Then he was the one catching his breath as she leaned forward to touch her lips to his, her breasts brushing his chest. He wanted to crush her to him, overwhelm her, cut short the teasing foreplay, but some things were too good to rush and this was going to be very good indeed.

As she took her lips on a slow trail of moist kisses over his chin, down his throat, he held her in the very lightest of touches, his hands doing no more than rest against her ribcage, giving her control, all the time, all the freedom she wanted to explore his body, knowing that his time would come.

Little feathers of silky hair brushed against his skin, a subtle counterpoint to her tongue probing the hollows beneath his shoulders, to the satiny feel of her skin as his hands slid lower over her back, exploring the curve of her waist, learning the shape of her body.

Annie was drowning in pure sensation. The gentle touch of George's hands as he caressed her back, her waist, slipping beneath the loose waist of her jeans to cup her bottom in his hands, holding her close so that she could feel the power of his need as she kissed and licked and nibbled at his chest, the hollow of his stomach. Came against the barrier of clothes.

Her lips were hot, swollen against his skin and every cell in her body was thrumming with power. For the first time in her life she felt totally alive, warm, vital. This ache in her womb, this need was the essence of life, of being a woman and she wanted him. Wanted all of him.

'Touch me,' she whispered as she pulled at the next stud.

Begging or commanding?

It didn't matter. He'd told her she could do anything that felt good. And this felt...

He released the button at the waist of her jeans, pushed jeans, underwear over her hips.

There were no words to describe what this felt like. All she could manage was his name.

'George...'

And then her body shattered.

George caught her, held her as she collapsed against him, kissing her shoulder, nuzzling his chin against her hair as she recovered, trying not to think about the look in her eyes, an appeal for something unknown, in that moment before she'd dissolved into his arms.

Because he knew where he'd see it before.

He murmured her name and when she looked up, her eyes filled with tears, he knew it was true. She was the 'people's virgin'.

'Will I get sent to the Tower for that?' he asked.

'Not by me,' she assured him, laughing shakily.

Damn it, she was crying with gratitude.

She sniffed. Brushed the tears from her cheeks with the palm of her hand, lifted damp lashes and finally realised that he wasn't laughing with her.

'What?' she asked. 'What did I do?'

He didn't answer and he saw the exact moment when she realised that she answered not to the lie she'd told him when she'd sworn that Annie was her real name, but to Lady Rose.

'Rose*anne*,' she said. 'My name is Rose*anne*. I was named for my grandmother but my mother thought I was entitled to a name of my own so she called me Annie.'

Did she think that was all that mattered? That she hadn't actually lied about that.

Then, when he didn't answer, 'Does it matter?'

He picked up the clothes she'd discarded and thrust them at her.

'George?'

For a long moment she didn't take them but continued to look at him, those dangerous eyes pleading with him.

All his senses were vibrating with the feel of her, her touch, the musky scent of her most intimate being. They were urging him to say that it didn't matter a damn before reaching out to take what she was offering him. Pretend that nothing mattered but this moment.

The shattering sound of the timer announcing that the cake was done saved them both.

'Clearly it does,' she said, snatching her clothes from his hand, standing up, turning her back on him as she pulled them on.

'You used me,' he said to her back. 'You're on a quest to lose your virginity before you settle for the guy with the castle.'

'If that's what you think then there's nothing more to say. Pass me the oven gloves,' she said, sticking out a hand as she opened the oven door.

He got up, passed her the thickly padded gloves, then pulled the overalls back on, fastening the studs with shaking fingers while, still with her back to him, she tested the cake.

'Is it done?'

'As if you care,' she replied, still not looking at him but turning the cake out over the rack his mother had left out. When the cake didn't fall out she gave it a shake, catching her breath as the hot tin touched the pale skin of her inner arm.

'You have to leave it to cool for a few minutes,' he said, taking her hand, turning it to look at the red mark.

'I get cookery lessons too?'

'Simple physics,' he said, not bothering to ask her if it hurt, just grabbing her hand and taking her to the sink, where he turned on the cold tap, holding the burn beneath the running water.

It was icy-cold and he knew that would hurt as much as the burn but she clamped her jaws together. Schooled from the age of six not to show pain, she'd saved her tears for him.

It had taken the new, shocking pleasure of a

man's intimate touch to break down that reserve, reduce her to weeping for herself.

'Who is she?' he asked, not wanting to think about how that made him feel. Feeling would destroy him. 'The girl in the photograph.'

'Lydia,' she said.

'The friend who lent you her car? But she—'

'Looks just like me? Type "Lady Rose" and "lookalike" into your search engine and you can book her next time you want "Lady Rose Napier" to grace your party.'

'Why would I want a copy…?'

He managed to stop himself but she finished for him. 'Why would you want a copy when you rejected the real thing?'

She was shaking, he realised. Or maybe it was him.

'She's a professional lookalike?'

'Since she was fifteen years old. Her mother made her a copy of the outfit I was wearing on my sixteenth birthday and someone took a picture and sent it to the local newspaper. It's not a full-time job for her, of course, but the manager of the supermarket where she works is very good about juggling her shifts.'

'You paid a girl who works in a supermarket to take your place?'

'No. She wouldn't take any money. We met by chance one day and there was a connection.'

'I'll bet there was. Do you really trust her not to

sell her story to the tabloids the minute she gets home?'

She looked up at him. 'Do you know something, George? I don't really care. I wanted to escape and she was willing to take my place so that I could disappear without raising a hue and cry. Once I go back I don't care who knows.'

'But how on earth will she carry it off? It's one thing turning up at a party where everyone knows you're not the real thing, but something like this...' Words failed him.

'There's no one at Bab el Sama who knows me. I insisted on going there on my own.'

'But if you wanted a break, surely—'

'I wanted a break from being me, George. From my grandfather's unspoken expectations. I wanted to be ordinary. Just be...myself.'

'How is that?' he asked, gently dabbing her arm dry.

'I can't feel a thing.'

He nodded. 'I've got a car to fix,' he said, tossing the towel aside, wishing he could say the same.

He walked from the room while he still could.

CHAPTER TEN

ANNIE, weak to her bones, leaned against the sink. What had she done, said, to give herself away?

A tear trickled onto her cheek and as she palmed it away she knew. He'd responded to her not as a national institution but as a woman and she'd wept with the joy of it. Ironic, really, when she'd spent her entire life keeping her emotions under wraps.

Tears were private things.

Before the cameras you kept your dignity, looked the world in the eye.

But with a lover you could be yourself. Utterly, completely…

A long shivering sigh escaped her but the years of training stood her in good stead. She took a deep breath, straightened, told herself that George had every right to be angry.

What man, on discovering that what he'd imagined was a quick tumble in the metaphorical hay had the potential to make him front-page news, wouldn't be absolutely livid?

She might be inexperienced, but she wasn't naïve.

Sex exposed two people in a way that nothing else could. It wasn't the nakedness, but the stripping away of pretence that took it beyond the purely physical. Without total honesty it was a sham, a lie.

She knew how she'd feel if he'd lied to her about his identity. But he'd laid it all out while she hadn't even been honest about the way her parents had died.

She had abused his trust in the most fundamental way and now she would have to leave. First, though, she carefully turned out the cake and left it to cool. Washed the cake tin. Put away the soup bowls.

Straightened the rag rug.

When all trace of her presence had been erased, she went upstairs and threw everything into her bag. Then, because she couldn't leave without saying goodbye to Xandra, she walked along the hall, opening doors, searching for her room, and found herself standing in the doorway of the room in which George Saxon had grown up.

The cashmere sweater he'd been wearing the day before was draped over the wooden chair. She touched it, then picked it up, hugging it to her as she looked around at what had been his boyhood room.

It was sparse by modern standards, with none of the high-tech appliances that were the essential requirements of the average teen's life. Just a narrow bed with an old-fashioned quilt, a small scarred table he'd used as a desk and a bookcase. She knelt to run her fingers over the spines of the books he'd held, read. Physics, maths, computer languages.

The car maintenance manuals seemed out of place, but keeping ahead of his father must have required more than manual dexterity, although personally she'd have given him a starred A for that.

She stood up, holding the sweater to her face for a moment, yearning to pull it over her head and walk away with it. Instead, she refolded it and laid it back on the chair before leaving the room, closing the door behind her.

Xandra's room was next door. Large, comfortable, a total contrast to her father's childhood room, it was obvious that she spent a lot of time with her grandparents.

She had a small colour television, an expensive laptop, although the girlish embroidered bed cover was somewhat at odds with the posters of racing drivers rather than pop stars that decorated the walls.

There was paper and a pen on the writing desk and a note to Mrs Warburton ready for the post.

She picked up the pen, then put it down again. What could she say? She couldn't tell her the truth and she couldn't bear to write a lie. Better to leave George to make whatever excuses he thought best.

Downstairs, she'd looked up the number of a taxi firm and made the call. She'd catch a bus or a train; it didn't matter where to, so long as it was leaving Maybridge.

'It's a busy time of the day,' the dispatcher warned her. 'It'll be half an hour before we can pick you up.'

'That will be fine,' she said. It wasn't, but if it was a busy time she'd get the same response from anyone else. As she replaced the receiver, the cat found her legs and she bent to pick it up, ruffling it behind the ear as she carried it into the study to wait in the chair where George had fallen asleep the night before. Self-indulgently resting her head in the place where his had been.

The cat settled on her lap, purring contentedly and she closed her eyes for a moment, letting herself rerun images of George's body, his face as he'd looked at her, the taste of his skin, his lips, the way he'd touched her. Fixing it like a film in her memory so that she would be able to take it out and run it like a video when she needed to remind herself what it was like to just let go.

'Annie!'

She woke with a start as the cat dug its claws into her legs before fleeing.

It took her a moment for her head to clear, to

focus on George standing in the doorway. 'Sorry, I must have fallen asleep. Is my taxi here?'

'Were you going to leave without a word?' he demanded.

'What word did you expect? I can't stay here, George. Not now you know who I am.'

He didn't bother to deny it. 'Where are you going?'

'That's none of your business.'

'You think?' He moved so swiftly that she didn't have time to do more than think about moving before his hands were on either side of her, pinning her in the chair. 'Do you really believe I'm going to let the nation's sweetheart wander off into the wild blue yonder by herself with a fistful of money stuffed down her bra?'

He was close enough that she could see the vein throbbing at his temple, the tiny sparks of hot anger that were firing the lead grey of his eyes, turning it molten.

'I don't think you have a choice.'

'Think again, Your Ladyship. I've got a whole heap of options open to me, while you've got just two. One, you stay here where I know you're safe. Two, I take you home to your grandfather, His Grace the Duke of Oldfield. Take your pick.'

'You've been checking up on me?'

'You're not the only one with a fancy Internet cellphone.'

Obviously he had. Searched for her on the Net instead of asking. Maybe he thought that was the only way to get straight answers. Her fault.

'And if I don't fancy either of those options?' she asked, refusing to be browbeaten into capitulation. 'You said you had a whole heap?'

'I could ring around the tabloids and tell them what you've been doing for the last twenty-four hours.'

'You wouldn't do that.' He'd hesitated for a fraction of a second before he'd spoken and instinctively she lifted her hand to his face. His cold cheek warmed to her touch. His eyes darkened. 'You wouldn't betray me, George.'

'Try me,' he said, abruptly straightening, taking a step back, putting himself out of reach. Pulling the shutters down, just as he had with Xandra. 'Anything could happen to you out there. Use a little of your famous empathy to consider how I'd feel if anything did.'

'I'm not your responsibility.'

'You can't absolve me of that. I know who you are. That changes everything.'

'I'm sorry,' she said.

'Prove it.'

'By going home or staying here until the seventeenth?'

'The seventeenth?' He looked hunted, as if the prospect of a whole week of her company appalled him, but he said, 'If that's your time frame, then yes. Take your pick.'

'It's a long time to put up with a stranger.' And a long time to spend with a man who despised you. 'If you let me go I'll be careful,' she promised.

'Would that be reversing-into-a-farm-gate-in-the-dark careful?'

'I'll use public transport.'

'That's supposed to reassure me? You stay here or you go home,' he said. 'It's not open for discussion.'

'What would you say to your mother if I stayed?'

'She's got more important things to worry about. This is just between us,' he warned. 'As far as Xandra and my mother are concerned, you're Annie Rowland. Is that understood?'

'You guessed who I was,' she pointed out.

'I don't think they're ever going to see you quite the way I did.'

'No?' She felt a tremor deep within her at the memory of just how he'd seen her. Remembered how powerful she'd felt as he'd looked at her, touched her. As she'd touched him. She wanted that again. Wanted him… 'If I stay, George,' she asked softly, 'will you finish what you started?'

He opened his mouth, then shut it again sharply. Shook his head.

No. Faced with her image, he was just like everyone else. Being the nation's virgin was, apparently, the world's biggest turn-off.

'It's just sex, George,' she said, hoping that she could provoke him, disgust him sufficiently so that he would let her go.

'If it's just sex, Annie, I'm sure Rupert Devenish would be happy to do you the favour. Put it on the top of your Christmas wish list. Or does he have to wait until he puts a ring on your finger? Were you simply looking for something a little more earthy than His Lordship before you settle for the coronet?'

If he'd actually hit her the shock couldn't have been more brutal. It wasn't the suggestion that she was on the loose looking for a bit of rough. It was the fact that he thought she'd marry for position, the castle, the estates, that drove through her heart like a dagger. And maybe the fear that, in desperation, six months, a year from now she might settle for the chance to be a mother.

Picking up the phone, admitting what she'd done and waiting for a car to take her home would, she knew without doubt, be the first step.

It took her a moment to gather herself, find her voice. 'I'd better go and pay the taxi.'

'It's done.'

'What?' Then, realising what he meant, 'You sent it away without waiting for my answer?'

'He's busy. You owe me twenty pounds, by the way.'

'A little more than that, surely? There's the call-out charge, towing me back to the garage, the time you spent on the car.' She looked up enquiringly when he didn't answer. 'Or shall I ask Xandra to prepare the invoice for that?'

'Forget it,' he said. 'The garage is closed. And forget the taxi fare too.'

'What about board and lodging? Or do you expect me to work for my keep?'

'You are my daughter's guest,' he said, glancing at his watch. 'And right now we have to go and pick her up.'

'We?'

'You don't imagine I'm going to leave you here on your own?'

She thought about arguing with him for all of a second before she said, 'I'll get my coat.'

Two minutes later she was wrapped in the soft leather of the sports car that had been parked on the garage forecourt and heading towards Maybridge General.

They exchanged barely two words as the car ate up the miles but, when he pulled into the pick-up bay a couple of minutes before three, Annie said, 'There's a parking space over there.'

'It's nearly three. Xandra will be here any minute.'

She didn't say a word.

'Are you suggesting that she won't?'

'I'm suggesting that she'll make you go and get

her, so you might as well make a virtue out of a necessity.'

'I could send you.'

'You could. But then you'd have to come and get me too. Always supposing I don't take the opportunity to leave by another entrance.'

'Without your bag?'

'I could replace everything in it in ten minutes.'

'A thousand pounds won't go far if you're travelling by public transport. Staying at hotels.'

Again she said nothing.

'There's more? How much?'

'You'll have to search me to discover that,' she said, glancing at him. 'I won't resist.'

His hands tightened on the steering wheel, the knuckles turning white.

'Go and visit your father. It would make your mother happy, make Xandra happy. And me. It would make me very happy.'

'And why would I give a damn whether you're happy or not?'

He was so stubborn. He knew it was the right thing to do, wanted to build bridges with his daughter, but pride kept him from taking that first step. She'd just have to give him a little push.

'Because, if you don't, George, I'll be the one calling the tabloids to tell them that Lady Rose isn't in Bab el Sama but holed up at Saxon's Garage. With her lover.'

'Lover!'

'Why spoil a good story by telling the truth?' she said. 'They certainly won't.'

'You wouldn't do that.'

Exactly what she'd said when he'd threatened her.

'Within an hour of our return from the hospital there'll be television crews, photographers and half the press pack on your doorstep.'

'They wouldn't believe you. They've seen you get on a plane.'

'So what? You were bluffing?'

'Of course I was bluffing!'

He cared, she thought. Cared enough.

So did she.

'Take your pick, George. Visit your father or let me go.'

George dragged both hands through his hair. 'I can't. Please, Annie, you must see that. If anything happened to you—'

'You'd never forgive yourself? Oh, dear. That is unfortunate because, you see, I'm not bluffing. And I know those journalists well enough to convince them I'm not some fantasist sending them on a wild-goose chase.' She held her breath. Would he believe her? After what seemed like the longest moment in history, he glared at her, then pulled over into the empty space she'd pointed out. Cut the engine.

'This isn't going to work,' he said, releasing his seat belt, climbing out. 'Whatever it is you think you're doing.' She jumped as he vented his frustration on the car door, but made no move to get out, forcing him to walk around to the passenger door and open it for her.

George watched as she swung her long legs over the sill, stood up and, without a word, walked towards the entrance of the hospital.

'You know that's a dead giveaway too,' he said when he caught up with her. 'Modern independent women can usually manage a car door.'

'If you insist on acting as my bodyguard, George, I'll insist on treating you like one.'

'Remind me why they call you the nation's sweetheart?' he said.

'Sweetheart, angel, virgin.' She stopped without warning and looked at him, a tiny frown wrinkling her smooth forehead. '*Am* I still the people's virgin?' she asked, her clear voice carrying down the corridor. 'Technically?'

'Annie!' He grabbed her elbow in an attempt to hurry her past a couple of nurses who'd turned to stare. 'What the hell do you think you're doing?'

'Behaving badly?' she offered, staying stubbornly put. 'It's a new experience for me and I'm rather enjoying it. But you didn't answer my question. Am I—'

'Don't say another word,' he snapped. He didn't

want to talk about it. Or think about it. Fat chance. He hadn't been able to think about anything else all afternoon and while his head was saying no, absolutely no, a thousand times no, his body was refusing to listen. 'It's this way.'

But it wasn't. His father had improved sufficiently to be moved out of the cardiac suite and into a small ward. Xandra was sitting cross-legged on the bed, Santa hat perched on her head, while his father occupied an armchair beside it. He was laughing at something she'd said and it was obvious that they were on the same wavelength, despite the generation gap. That they liked one another. Were friends. Everything that he and his father were not. Everything that he and his daughter were not.

They both froze as they saw him.

'I was just coming,' Xandra said, immediately defensive.

'No problem,' he lied. 'We were a bit early.'

'Is this Annie?' his father asked, looking beyond him. 'Xandra's been telling me all about you.'

'Oh, dear…' she stepped forward, hand extended—a scene reminiscent of every news clip he'd ever seen of a royal hospital visit '…I don't like the sound of that!' Then, 'How d'you do, Mr Saxon?'

'I do very well, thank you,' he said. 'Certainly well enough to get out of here.'

'I'm glad to hear it.'

George wondered how many times she'd done

that. Visited a total stranger in hospital, completely at ease, sure of her welcome.

'Xandra is a tonic,' he said. Then, finally turning to grudgingly acknowledge him, 'You've managed to drag yourself into the garage, I see.'

'Mike is picking up the Bentley in an hour.'

The nod his father managed was as close as he'd ever come to a thank you and he thought that was it, but he said, 'We've been looking after his cars ever since he started the business. I'm glad we didn't let him down.' And then he looked up. 'Thanks, son.'

The words were barely audible but he'd said them and it was George's turn to be lost for words.

It was Annie who broke the silence. 'Where's Hetty?'

'She went to the shop to get Granddad an evening paper,' Xandra said, watching them both.

'You could die of boredom in here,' his father said, with considerably more force in his voice than the day before. 'I don't care what that doctor says, I'm going home tomorrow.'

'Dad…' he protested.

'Your mother will take care of me,' he said stubbornly, the brief moment of rapport already history.

Annie's hand grabbed his before he let slip his first response, which was to tell him not to be so selfish.

'We'll all take care of you,' Xandra said quickly, looking at him, her eyes pleading with him to say that it would be all right. As if what he said actually mattered.

They were all taking tiny steps here and for a moment he clung to Annie's hand as if to a lifeline. She squeezed his fingers, encouraging him to take the risk, throw his heart into the ring.

'If that's what you want,' he said, 'I'm sure we'll manage. Especially since Annie is staying on for a while to help out.'

'Really?' Xandra grinned. 'Great. You can help me put up the decorations.'

'Thank you,' Annie said, but she was looking at him. 'I'd like that.' Then, turning to his father, 'But you really must listen to the doctor, Mr Saxon. If you come home too soon, you'll be back in here for Christmas.'

His father regarded her thoughtfully. Then, taking note of the way their hands were interlinked and apparently putting one and one together and making a pair, he smiled with satisfaction. 'Maybe you're right, Annie. I don't suppose another day or two will kill me.'

Setting himself up for yet another disappointment that he'd get the blame for, George thought, and removing his hand from hers, he said, 'We'd better go, Xandra. Mike is coming for the car at four.'

She bounced off the bed, gave her granddad a hug. Then, transferring the Santa hat from her own head to his, she said, 'Behave yourself. And don't let Gran stay so late tonight. She was too tired to eat last night.'

'Really?' He shook his head. 'Silly woman. I'll make sure she leaves early.'

'Thanks for thinking about your gran,' he said as they headed for the car.

'She can't bear to leave him there on his own.' She turned to Annie. 'They absolutely dote on one another, you know. It's really sweet.' Then, taking advantage of his approval, she said, 'Can you drop me off in town? I'll catch the bus home.'

'I thought we'd decided that you're grounded.'

'Oh, absolutely,' she said. 'But this isn't for me. We've only got indoor lights. I'll have to get some new ones for the outside tree.' Then, 'Annie could come with me if you like. Just to make sure I don't have any fun.'

'Actually, I could do with a run at the shops,' Annie said before he could voice his objection to the idea of Lady Roseanne Napier, her underwear stuffed with cash and about as street-smart as a newborn lamb, let loose in the Christmas crowds with only a teenager for protection. 'I came away with the bare minimum.'

Oh, no...

The look in her eye told him she knew exactly what he was thinking.

'I'll do my absolute best to make sure that neither

of us have any fun,' she assured him. 'Although I can't positively guarantee it.'

Xandra's face lit up. Annie did that to people, he thought. Lit them up. His mother, his father, his daughter. They all responded to that effortless charm, the natural warmth she exuded, but he'd done a lot more than just light up.

He'd lit up, overloaded, blown every fuse in his brain as he'd surrendered, had let down a barrier he'd been building against the world ever since the day when, years younger than Xandra, he'd understood that he was on his own.

Only now, when he knew that any kind of relationship between them was impossible, did he understand just how exposed he'd left himself.

Keeping his distance emotionally from this woman who was so far out of his orbit that he might as well be on Mars was now an absolute necessity. As was keeping her safe. But forbidding her to leave the house wasn't an option either.

'It's Friday so the shops will be open late, won't they?' he asked.

'I suppose.'

'In that case, if you're prepared to wait until after Mike's collected the Bentley, I'll take you both into town. We could pick up the takeaway on the way home.'

It sounded reasonable but he wasn't looking at Annie, knowing that she'd have raised that eyebrow a fraction, telling him that she was winning this stand-off hands down, instead concentrating on his daughter, willing her to say yes.

'You want to come shopping with us?' She sounded doubtful.

'Same deal as always,' he replied. 'I drive, you do the hard work.'

'That means you're going to have to carry your own bags to the car,' Annie said. 'Obviously, as a lady of rather more advanced years, I will expect him to carry mine.' She laid the lightest emphasis on the word 'lady'. She tilted an eyebrow at him. Taunting him. No, teasing him. 'Do you have a problem with that, George?'

'I can live with it,' he said, refusing to meet her gaze, afraid he might just break down and laugh. He was too angry with her to laugh. Too angry with himself for wanting to wrap his arms around her, hold her, kiss her, beg her never to leave because most of all he wanted her.

'What a hero,' she said gently. 'And the three of us could put up those trees while we're waiting.'

And right there and then, knowing that Christmas brought her a world of pain, he thought his heart might break that she would do that for his daughter. For him.

CHAPTER ELEVEN

THREE hours later, the car parked, her arm tucked firmly in George's—it was clear he wasn't going to let her stray from his side—Annie stood in the centre of Maybridge. There were lights everywhere and a brass band was playing Christmas carols as crowds of shoppers searched out presents for their loved ones.

Somewhere, in her subconscious, she knew this was how Christmas was meant to be, but now she was touching it, feeling it as she was jostled by shoppers laden with bags, excited children who'd spotted 'Santa' in a mock-up sleigh, collecting for a local charity. Noisy, joyful, it was a world away from Christmas as she knew it.

'What do you need?' George asked.

This. This normality. This man, she thought, as she looked up at him and for a moment the carols, the lights faded.

'Annie?'

This moment, she thought, refusing to think about next week.

'Just a few basic essentials. Underwear, another pair of jeans—these are a bit big,' she said, tugging at the waist. 'Nothing fancy.'

'I know just the place,' Xandra said. She paused at the entrance to a large store, glanced at her father. 'You might want to give this a miss.'

'If you think you can scare me away with threats of female undergarments, think again.'

'You are so embarrassing.'

'I understood it was a parent's duty to embarrass their offspring,' he replied, unmoved.

'Oh, please! I'll wait here,' she said, taking out her cellphone, her thumb already busy texting before she reached the nearest bench.

'I won't be long,' Annie said, then, realising that he wasn't going to let her out of his sight, proceeded to test his assertion. Faced with the choice between six-packs of pants in plain white, mixed colours or patterned, she asked him to choose.

He took all three packs and dropped them in the basket, lips firmly sealed.

She tried on jeans while he stood guard at the changing room door, modelling them for him. By the time they reached the socks he'd had enough and, after looking down at her feet, he gathered up a pair of each before she could tease him further.

'Spoilsport,' she said.

'You'd better believe it,' he said.

She added a sweater and three tops to the basket and then queued up to pay.

'That was fun,' she said, handing the bags to George and waving to Xandra before obediently slipping her hand through the elbow he'd stuck out. 'What now?'

'Food?' he suggested, heading for a van from which the tantalising smell of frying onions was wafting. 'Who fancies a hot dog?'

'Not for me,' Xandra said, backing away. 'I need some shampoo. Can I get you anything, Annie?'

'Please.' By the time she'd given Xandra some money, George had a halfeaten hot dog in one hand. 'Are they good?'

'You've never had one?' He shook his head. 'Stupid question.'

He ordered two. 'I missed lunch,' he said, catching her look as he sucked mustard from his thumb.

'Me too,' she said, holding his gaze as she took one of them from him.

He looked away first, which wasn't as pleasing as it should have been and, taking the only comfort on offer, she bit deep into the bun, reminding herself that she was in search of new experiences.

Who knew when she'd share another hot dog moment with a seriously sexy man?

It must have been the fumes of the mustard

hitting the back of her throat that brought tears to her eyes, making her choke.

'Better?' George asked, helpfully thumping her back. Leaving his hand there.

'Not much,' she said, dropping the remains of the hot dog in the bin. 'It's been quite a day for new experiences.'

He removed his hand as if burned. 'What's keeping Xandra?'

She sighed. 'She said she'd meet us by the Christmas tree in the square.'

All the trees that surrounded the square had white lights threaded through their bare branches, creating a fairyland arena for the seasonal ice rink that had been created in the central plaza and throwing the huge Christmas tree, ablaze with colour, into vivid contrast.

But it wasn't the figures on the ice or the lights that brought George to an abrupt halt. It was the sight of his daughter, sitting on a bench, much too close to the boy from the Christmas tree farm.

'The damned lights were just an excuse to come into town and meet him,' he declared but, as he surged forward, Annie stepped in front of him, a hand on his chest.

'They could have met by chance.'

He looked at her. 'Do you really believe that?'

'Does it matter? She chose to wait and come into town with you.'

'She wanted to come on her own.'

'Oh, for heaven's sake, I could shake you!' She took a deep breath, then, slowly, talking to him as if he were a child, she said, 'Don't you understand? Xandra got herself suspended from school deliberately. Mrs Warburton would have let her go and visit her grandfather in hospital, but she didn't want an afternoon off school. She wanted to be with you.'

'That's ridiculous,' he said. He took another step but Annie didn't budge. 'I tried,' he said. 'It's not easy from the other side of the Atlantic, but I've tried and tried to be a father—I even applied for joint custody.'

'The Family Court turned you down?'

'Penny told them that she would be confused. She was already that. Calling her new husband Daddy, ignoring me. Wouldn't come and see me in London when I was here on business. Wouldn't come to the States, even when I offered the theme park incentive.'

'She doesn't want theme parks,' she said. 'She wants you.'

'But—'

'Not in America, not in London, but here.'

He spread his arms, indicating that she'd got what she wanted.

'That's just the beginning. She's not going to make it easy for you. She'll test you and test you.

Keep pushing you away to see how resilient you are. Whether you love her enough to stay.'

'She knows I love her,' he protested. 'I've given her everything she's ever wanted. Ever asked for.'

'Except yourself. She wants you, here, in her life. Not some Santa figure with a bottomless cheque book, but a father. She's afraid that you've only come to close down the garage, tidy up the loose ends, and she's desperately afraid that this time when you leave you'll never come back.'

'How can you know that?' he demanded, not wanting to believe it.

'Because I tested everyone. Not with tears or tantrums, I just withheld myself. Made nannies, governesses, teachers, even my grandfather prove that they weren't going to go away and never come back, the way my parents had.'

'I came back.'

'How often? Once a year? Twice?' She put her hands on his shoulders, forced him to look at her. 'How much do you want to be a father?' she demanded. 'Final answer.'

'Enough not to turn a blind eye to hot-wiring cars or making secret plans to meet up with boys.'

'Right answer,' she said, with a smile that made the lights seem dim. 'Come on, let's go and say hello.'

'Hello?' he said, staying put. 'That's it?'

'It's a start.'

'But—'

Annie felt for him. She could see that he wanted to go over there and grab that boy by the throat, demand that he never come near his precious little girl.

'Open your eyes, open your ears, George. Listen to what she's telling you. She wants you to be part of her life but you're going to have to accept that she's a young woman.'

George tore his gaze from his daughter and looked at her advocate. Passionate. Caring.

'You're not talking about her,' he said. 'You're talking about yourself.'

She didn't answer. She didn't have to. It was obvious. When she was six years old her life had changed for ever. At sixteen she'd become a national icon and had never had the freedom to meet a boy in town. Test herself. Make mistakes.

She knew everything. And nothing. But it was the everything that was important.

'Okay,' he said, 'let's go and say hello.'

'And?' she said, still pushing him.

'And what?'

'And ask him if he likes Chinese food,' she said.

He took a deep breath. 'Let's go and say hello. And ask him if he likes Chinese food.'

'You ask him while I get the skates,' she said, straightening, taking a step back. 'What size do you take?'

'Skates?' He groaned. 'Please tell me you're kidding.'

'I've only got a week. Less. I'm not missing out on a single opportunity.'

'Couldn't you just wait until you go home?' he asked. 'Get your personal assistant to call some Olympic champion to give you a twirl around the ice?'

'I could,' she agreed, 'but I wouldn't be that self-indulgent.' He was being facetious, she knew. He'd briefly let down his guard and now he was using sarcasm to keep her at a distance. No deal. If he wanted her distant, he was going to have to let her go. 'And, anyway, where would the fun be in that?'

'You're saying that you'd rather go out there and be pushed, shoved, fall over, make a fool of yourself in public?'

'Exactly like everyone else,' she said, 'but I don't need you to hold my hand. If you'd rather watch from the sidelines I'd quite understand.'

George growled with frustration.

She was an enigma. A woman of supreme confidence who was at home with the powerful and the most vulnerable. Touchingly innocent and yet old beyond her years. Clear-sighted when it came to other people's problems, but lost in the maze of her own confusion.

On the surface she had everything. She had only

to express a wish for it to be granted. Any wish except one. The privacy to be herself.

He regarded her—her eyes were shining with a look of anticipation that he'd seen before—and for a moment he forgot to breathe as he revised the number of impossible items on her wish list to two.

The second should have been tailor-made for a man who had made a life's work of the no-strings-attached, mutually enjoyable sexual encounter. It was the perfect scenario. A beautiful woman who would, in the reverse of the Cinderella story, on the seventeenth of December change back into a princess.

But Annie had, from the first moment she'd turned that penetrating gaze full on him, set about turning his life upside down.

Within twenty-four hours of meeting her he was beginning to forge a shaky relationship with his daughter, was talking to his father and found himself thinking all kinds of impossible things both before and after breakfast.

And accepting one irrefutable truth.

If he made love to Annie, he would never be able to let her go.

But she wasn't Annie Rowland. She was Lady Roseanne Napier and, no matter what her eyes were telling him, they both knew that she could never stay.

'Well?' she demanded impatiently.

'Have you ever been on ice skates?' he asked.

'No, but they're all doing it,' she said, turning to look at the figures moving with varying stages of competence across the ice. 'How hard can it be?'

'They all had someone to hold their hand when they did it for the first time.'

Skating he could do. Holding her hand, knowing that he would have to let go, would be harder, but a few days of being ordinary would be his gift to her. Something for her to look back on with pleasure. For him to remember for ever.

She looked back at him, hesitated.

'What are you waiting for?' he asked. 'Let's go and get those boots. Just don't complain to me when you can't move in the morning.'

'What about Xandra?' she asked. 'That boy?'

He glanced at them, sitting on the bench talking, laughing.

'They can take care of the bags.'

Annie felt the pain a lot sooner than the next morning. She'd spent more time in close contact with the ice than gliding across it—would have spent more but for George—and had been laughing too much to waste time or breath complaining about it.

George was laughing too as he lifted her back onto her feet for the umpteenth time. 'Hold onto my shoulders,' he said as he steadied her, hands on her waist, then grabbed her more tightly as her feet began to slide from beneath her again. Too late. They both went down.

'Have you had enough of this?' he asked, his smile fading as, ignoring the skaters swirling around them, he focused his entire attention on giving her exactly what she wanted. 'Or do you want to give it one more try?'

One more, a hundred times more wouldn't be enough, Annie knew. She wanted a lifetime of George Saxon's strong arms about her, holding her, supporting her. A lifetime of him laughing at her, with her.

'Aren't we supposed to be shopping for lights?' she said, looking away.

Xandra and her new boyfriend were leaning on the rail watching them. 'Pathetic,' she called out, laughing at the pair of them. 'Give it up.'

'She might have a point,' Annie said, turning back to George.

'She hasn't the first idea,' he said, his expression intent, his lips kissing close. And neither of them were talking about ice skating.

While the skaters whirled around them, in their small space on the ice the world seemed to stand still as they drank in each other. Every moment.

'Come on,' Xandra called. 'Dan knows a great place to buy lights.'

Annie scrambled to her feet and, for the first time since she'd stepped onto the ice, her feet were doing what they were supposed to as she glided gracefully to the edge of the rink with George a heartbeat behind her.

'Dan?' he said.

'Dan Cartwright.' The boy stuck out his hand. 'We met this morning, sir. At the farm.'

'I remember,' George said, taking it.

The boy didn't actually wince but he swallowed hard.

'I'm Annie,' she said, holding out her own hand so that George was forced to relinquish his grip. 'Shall we go and look at these lights?'

The tree lights were just the start. They piled icicle lights for the eaves, curtain lights for the walls, rope lights for the fence into their trolley. And then Annie spotted a life-size reindeer-driven sleigh with Santa himself at the reins and refused to leave without it.

'We won't be able to get it into the car,' George protested.

'Dan's got a motorbike,' Xandra said. 'He's got a spare helmet so I could go home on the back of that.'

'No,' he replied without hesitation. 'You can't.'

'In fact,' she said, carrying on as if he hadn't spoken, 'when I go to Maybridge High I'll need some transport. You had a motorbike, didn't you?'

Yes, he'd had a bike, but that was different. She was a… 'If you want to go to Maybridge High I'll drive you there myself,' he snapped back.

There was a pause, no longer than a heartbeat, while the reality of what he'd said sank in.

He would drive her. Be here. Change his life for her...

'Oh, *please*!' She rolled her eyes. 'How pathetic would I look? Besides, Dan said he'd teach me to ride.'

'I've never been on a motorbike,' Annie cut in before he could respond. 'Why don't I go with Dan?' Then, 'Actually, I'd love a lesson too.'

'No one is going on the back of Dan's bike!' he exploded. 'And if anyone is going to teach anyone to ride anything, it will be me!'

'Brilliant,' Xandra said, then, just as he realised that he'd been stitched up like a kipper, she nudged him with her shoulder and said, 'Thanks, Dad.'

Dad...

He looked at Annie. She had her hand to her mouth, confirmation that he hadn't misheard, hadn't got it wrong, but something amazing had just happened and he had to swallow twice before he could manage, 'We could come and pick up the sleigh tomorrow in the four-wheel drive.'

'Great. I can get my hair cut at the same time.'

'Whatever you want, Annie,' he replied, and meant it. 'Now, shall we get out of here and pick up some food? Dan? Chinese?'

* * *

'Well?' Annie asked, giving a twirl so that George, who'd been waiting for her in a coffee shop opposite the hairdresser, could fully appreciate the stylish elfin cut that now framed her face. 'What do you think?'

'It doesn't matter what I think,' he replied. 'The question is, are you happy?'

'Absolutely,' she said. 'I love it. Even better, no one in there even suggested I looked like…anyone else.'

'A result, then. Although when you reappear in public sporting your new look, they might just wonder.'

'They might wonder, but I've got the pictures to prove I'm in Bab el Sama,' she said, indicating a newspaper left by one of the café's patrons. 'Actually, that's the one downside. Poor Lydia doesn't get a choice in the matter. She's going to have to have her hair cut whether she wants to or not.'

'It goes with the job, but if it worries you buy her a wig for Christmas,' he suggested.

'You're not just a pretty face,' she said, slipping her arm in his. 'Now, let's take a look at this Christmas market.'

'Really? What happened to hating Christmas?'

'Not this Christmas,' she said as they wandered amongst the little stalls decorated with lights and fake snow, admiring the handmade gifts and decorations. 'The new memories I've made will make this a Christmas I will always cherish.'

'That makes two of us,' he said.

They drank gingerbread lattes to warm themselves, tasted tiny samples of every kind of food, bought some of it, then stopped at a stall selling silly seasonal headgear.

'I have to have one of those,' Annie said and George picked up an angel headband which he settled carefully on her head.

'Uh-uh. The angel is on holiday.' She pulled it off and replaced it with one bearing sprigs of mistletoe that lit up and flashed enticingly. 'Let's give this one a test run,' she teased, closing her eyes and tilting her face to invite a kiss.

His cold lips barely brushed her cheek and, about to pull it off, ask the stallholder if he had something a little more effective, something in George's eyes stopped her. Not the warning to behave that she anticipated, but the mute appeal of a man for whom one more kiss would be one too many. An admission that while he'd walked away from temptation it had not been easy. That he was on a knife-edge.

'Perfect!' she exclaimed brightly as she turned swiftly away to check the rest of the stall. 'This for you, I think,' she said, choosing a Santa hat. She wanted to put it on him, just as he'd put on the angel headband. Pull it down over his ears, cradle his dear face, kiss him so thoroughly that he'd fall.

Yesterday she might have done. Yesterday he'd been this sexy, gorgeous man who'd turned her on, lit her up like the Christmas tree in the square. Today, with one look, she knew that one kiss was never going to be enough. Understood what he'd known instinctively. That walking away after anything more would tear her in two.

So she simply handed him the hat and left him to pay for it, stepping quickly away to look at a stall selling handmade jewellery. Giving them both space to take a breath, put back the smiles, continue as if the world hadn't just shifted on its axis.

She chose a pair of pretty snowman earrings for Xandra, a snowflake brooch for Hetty, a holly tie-tack for George's father and had them put in little gift bags. Just something to thank them for accepting her as she was—no trappings, just ordinary Annie.

She didn't buy anything for George.

She'd already given him her heart.

'All done?' he asked, joining her, and she nodded but, as they were leaving, she spotted the same angels that had been on sale at the Christmas tree farm and stopped. 'I have to have one of those,' she said.

'You're really getting into the Christmas thing,' he said, taking the bag while she paid for the angel.

She shook her head. 'It's for the tree at King's Lacey. A discordant note of simplicity amongst the ornate designer perfection to remind me...' She faltered and, when he didn't press her, she said, 'Let's go home.'

George gave the reindeer a final tug to test the fixing, making sure that it was secure.

'Switch it on,' he called down. 'Let's see if it works.' He was leaving it as long as possible before he was forced to climb down. He felt safer up here on the roof, as far from Annie as he could get.

He'd known a week would be hard, he just hadn't realised how hard. How hard he'd fallen.

He'd never believed in love at first sight and yet from the first moment he'd set eyes on her it had been there, a magnetic pull. Each day, hour, minute he spent in her company was drawing him closer to her. And the nearer he got, the harder it was going to be to break away.

She understood, he knew. Had been careful to keep her distance since that moment at the market when she'd lifted her face for a kiss—he'd kissed her before without invitation, after all—and he hadn't been able to do it. Not kiss her and let her go.

She'd urged him to get involved with the renovation of Xandra's car, build on the new start they'd made—not that he'd needed much encouragement. The moment when she'd called him 'Dad' had been a turning point. There was a long way to go, but he was here for the long haul and he'd spent a lot of time on the phone to Chicago, reorganising his life. But that had still left a lot of time to be together.

Time when she got into trouble trying to cook and needed a taster and he'd stayed to help.

Time around the table when, even when they weren't alone, somehow there was a silent connection, something that grew stronger each day.

Time for quiet moments by the fire when his mother and Xandra were at the hospital. Not saying much. Not touching. Just looking up and seeing her curled up in the chair opposite. Being together.

Perfect moments that had felt like coming home.

'Xandra should do the official switch on,' she called back. 'It was all her idea.'

'This is just a test run. She can do it properly later, when it's dark.'

'Okay…' She put her hand on the switch, then said, 'It gives me great pleasure to light up the Saxon family home this Christmas. God bless it and all who live in it.'

She threw the switch and the lights came on, twinkling faintly in the bright winter sunlight.

'It's going to look fabulous when it gets dark,' Annie said, shading her eyes as she looked up at him. 'You've done an amazing job with Santa. He looks as if he's just touched down on the roof.'

There was no putting it off and he climbed down the scaffold tower. 'I suspect I've broken at least half a dozen town planning laws,' he said. 'It'll be a distraction for passing motorists and in all probability an air traffic hazard. And, as for cheering up my father when he gets home, he'll undoubtedly have a relapse at the prospect of the electricity bill when he sees it.'

'Phooey.'

He looked at her. 'Phooey? What kind of language is that for the daughter of a marquess?'

'Completely inappropriate,' she admitted, looking right back at him, and they both knew that he was reminding her that time was running out. 'Annie Rowland, on the other hand, can say phooey as much as she wants. So… Phooey,' she said, clinging to these final hours. Then, turning back to the house, 'Besides, you won't be able to see it from the road. Well, apart from Santa up there on the roof. And the rest of the lights are energy efficient, so a very merry eco-friendly Christmas to you.'

'I'll bet you don't have one of those on the roof of your stately home,' he said a touch desperately. Reminding himself that she wasn't Annie Rowland, that this was a little fantasy she was living. When the metaphorical clock struck midnight she would turn back into Lady Rose and drive off in a limo with chauffeur and bodyguard in attendance, return to the waiting Viscount and the life she was born to.

'They did have another one in the shop,' she said, turning those stunning blue eyes on him. 'Do you think they'd deliver it to King's Lacey?'

'If you were prepared to pay the carriage, I imagine they'd deliver it to the moon, but what would your grandfather say?'

'I've no idea, but the estate children would love it. In fact, I might see if I can hire a Rudolph the Red-Nosed Reindeer sleigh ride for the Christmas party.'

'You have a party?'

'Of course. It's expected. A party for the local children, with Santa in attendance with presents for everyone. The tenant farmers in for drinks on Christmas Eve and then, on Christmas Day, my grandfather and I sit in state in the dining room for lunch before exchanging perfectly wrapped gifts. The only thing that's missing is conversation because, rather than say the wrong thing, we say nothing at all.'

'I find it hard to imagine you tiptoeing around anyone's feelings. You certainly don't tiptoe around mine.'

'I know.' She smiled at him. 'You can't imagine how relaxing that is.'

'So why do you put up with it year after year?' he demanded, suddenly angry, not with her grandfather but with her for enduring it rather than changing it.

'Duty?' she said. 'And my grandfather is all the

family I have.' Then, in a clear attempt to change the subject, 'What about you, George? Are you really going to stay on?'

'You suspect I might be pining for my beach bum existence?'

'That would be George Saxon, the beach bum who designed a series of computer programs that helps to reduce wear and tear on combustion engines?' He waited, knowing that she had something on her mind. 'Who's since designed a dozen applications that have made him so much money he never has to work again?'

'Does Rupert Devenish work for a living?' he asked.

'Rupert runs his estates. Holds directorships in numerous companies. Works for charity. He's not idle.'

'It's no wonder the press are so excited,' he said, wishing he hadn't started this. 'You sound like the perfect match.'

The colour drained from her face but, without missing a beat, she said, 'Don't we?' Then, briskly, 'Okay. The lights are done and we've just got time for that motorcycle lesson you promised me before your father gets home from the hospital.'

'For that we'd need a motorcycle,' he pointed out thankfully. 'I thought perhaps, this year, I might break with tradition and, instead of a bank transfer, I'd let Xandra choose her own present. No prizes for guessing what she'll choose.'

It was meant to distract her and it did.

'It'll be a cheap Christmas, then. The only bike she wants is yours.'

'Mine?'

'The one in the barn?'

George glanced at the stone long-barn, all that remained of the original farm buildings. Over the years it had served as a stable, a depository for tack, garden tools and every item of transportation he'd ever owned since his first trike, then crossed to the door and pushed it open.

'What is it?' she asked as he stared at a familiar tarpaulin.

'Nothing,' he said. 'History. A heap of rust.' But, unable to help himself, he pulled back the tarpaulin to reveal the motorbike he'd bought on his sixteenth birthday.

It wasn't a classic. Nothing like the high-powered one he rode in California, but he'd saved every last penny of money he'd earned or been given for birthdays, Christmas, to buy it and it had represented freedom, independence. He'd ridden it home from Cambridge that first Christmas, high on his new life, full of everything he'd done and seen.

Four weeks later, when it was time to return to his studies, Penny had refused to ride on the back because of the baby and they'd taken the train.

CHAPTER TWELVE

'I DON'T see any rust,' Annie said.

'No.'

The bike had been sitting in the barn for fifteen years and for fifteen years someone had lavished care on it, keeping it polished, oiled, ready to kick-start and go.

There was only one someone who could have done that—his father—and he slammed his fist against the leather saddle, understanding exactly how angry, how *helpless* Annie had felt as she'd lashed out at him.

He wanted to smash something. Roar at the waste of it, the stupidity.

'Why didn't he say? Why didn't he tell me?'

'That he loved you? Missed you?'

Annie reached out for him and, wrapping her arms around him, she held him as he'd held her. And he clung to her because she understood as no one else could. Clung to her, wanting never to let her go.

In the end it was Annie who made the move, leaning back a little, laying warm lips against his cold cheek for just a moment, before turning to the bike.

'Will it start?' she asked.

He didn't care about the damn bike. He only cared about her but, just as he'd kept his distance in the last few days, protecting himself as much as her, now she was the one wearing an aura of untouchability.

Standing a little straighter, a little taller, even wearing a woolly hat and gloves, he had no doubt he was looking not at Annie Rowland, but Lady Rose.

And still he wanted to crush her to him, kiss her, do what she'd asked of him and make her so entirely his that she could never go back.

And that, he discovered, was the difference between lust and love.

When you loved someone your heart overrode desire.

'There's only one way to find out,' he said, unhooking a helmet from the wall. He wiped off a layer of dust with his sleeve and handed it to her, unhooked a second one for himself, then pulled the bike off its stand and wheeled it out into the yard.

It felt smaller than he remembered as he slung a leg over the saddle, kicked it into life, but his hands fitted the worn places on the handlebars and the familiar throb of the engine as he sat astride the bike seemed to jump-start something inside him.

Or maybe it was Annie, grinning at him in pure delight. Somehow the two seemed inextricably connected. Part of each other, part of him. Pulling on the helmet, he grinned back and said, 'Well, what are you waiting for? Let's go for a ride.'

She didn't need a second invitation, but climbed on behind him.

'Hold tight,' he warned and, as he took off, she hung on for dear life, her arms around his waist, her body glued to his.

It was beyond exhilarating. The nearness to everything, the road racing beneath them, the closeness, the trust, their two bodies working as one as they leaned into the bends of the winding country roads. It was as if they were one and when, far too soon, they raced back into the garage forecourt, he seemed to know instinctively the exact moment to ease back, turn, put out his foot as they came to a halt in front of the barn door.

Coming home, exactly as he had done countless times in the past.

For a moment the engine continued to throb, then everything went quiet. It was only then, when she tried to move, dismount, that Annie realised that she was not just breathless, light-headed but apparently boneless.

'Oh,' she said stupidly, clinging to George as he

helped her off the bike and her legs buckled beneath her. He removed her helmet as if she were a child. 'Oh, good grief, that was—'

George didn't wait to hear what she thought—he knew. Despite the fact that she was so far out of his reach that she might as well be on Mars, that in a few days she would walk away, taking his heart with her, and he would have to smile and pretend he didn't care. Knowing that each touch, each kiss, would intensify the pain of losing her, he kissed her anyway.

He kissed her not to test her probity, not as a prelude to the kind of intimacy that had overtaken them in the kitchen.

It was a kiss without an agenda, one that would endure in his memory and maybe, on the days when Annie felt alone, in hers. A kiss given with a whole heart.

And that was as new for him as it was for her.

That she responded with all the passion of a woman who knew it would be their last made it all the more heartbreaking. Finally, breathlessly, she broke away.

'No,' she said, backing rapidly away, tears streaming down her face. 'I can't do this to you.' Then she turned and ran into the house.

'Annie!'

George's desperate cry still ringing in her ears, Annie raced up the stairs and by the time he caught up with her she had her cellphone in one hand, calling up the taxi firm while she emptied a drawer. She'd never wear any of the clothes again, but she'd bought them with George and they held precious memories.

She'd crammed a lifetime of ordinary experiences into a few days. She'd laughed more than she had in her entire life. She'd loved more. And been loved by Hetty, Xandra, called 'lass' by George senior, which she recognised as a mark of acceptance. While George…

George had made it his purpose in life to give her what she most wanted—to be ordinary—even while taking the utmost care to keep a physical distance between them.

And then he'd found the bike and, overwhelmed by what that meant, for a precious moment he'd let down his guard. It was then, when he'd kissed her in a way that made her feel like the woman she wanted to be, when tearing herself away from him had been beyond bearing—

'What the hell are you doing?' he demanded, bursting into the room, taking the cellphone from her and breaking the connection.

'Leaving,' she said, taking it from him and hitting Redial, throwing the clothes into her bag. 'Now. I should never have stayed.'

George Saxon had a real life, a family who wanted him and nothing on earth would allow her to inflict even the smallest part of her life on them.

Somewhere, deep down, she'd hoped that they would be able to remain friends. That she could, once in a while, call him, talk to him. But, if she'd learned one thing this week, it was that for someone you truly loved you would sacrifice anything, even love itself.

Forget Thursday. She couldn't wait until then. She had to leave now. Tonight. Never look back.

George stood there, watching her fling her clothes into a bag and feeling more helpless than he had in his entire life. He said her name, as if that would somehow keep her from leaving. 'Annie.'

She looked up.

'I love you.'

The hand holding the phone fell to her side. She opened her mouth, took a breath, shook her head. 'You don't know me.'

'I know what makes you laugh,' he said, lifting a hand to her face, wiping his fingers across the tears that were running unchecked down her face. 'I know what makes you cry.'

She didn't deny it, just shivered as he put his arms around her, drew her close, resting his own cheek against her pale hair.

'I know how your skin feels beneath my hands,' he continued, more to himself than to her. 'The taste of your mouth. The way your eyes look when I touch you. I know that you're kind, generous, caring, intuitive, smart.' He looked down at her. 'I know that, no matter what I say, you'll go home. What I'm asking is—will you come back?'

'This isn't a fairy-tale, George. Will you call me a taxi? Please?'

There was a note of desperation in that final please, but she'd given him his answer and there didn't seem a lot to say after that.

His mother and Xandra had gone shopping before going to the hospital to collect his father and he left a note on the kitchen table, explaining that a family emergency had called Annie home.

'How long will it be?' she asked when she followed him downstairs. 'The taxi.'

'There's no taxi. The deal was always that I'd take you home.'

She didn't argue, just surrendered her bag, got into his car. Neither of them said another word until they reached the motorway, when she looked at him.

'What?' he asked.

'No…'

'Spit it out.'

'It's Lydia's car. Could you… Would you find a replacement?' She took a paper bag out of the big shoulder bag she carried everywhere, placed it in the glove compartment. 'There should be enough.'

'Just how much money were you carrying around with you?' he demanded.

'Don't you mean where did I have it all stashed?'

His knuckles whitened as his hands tightened on the steering wheel.

'Will you do it?'

'Don't you have some little man who does that kind of thing for you?' Then, 'Oh, no. My mistake. You can't ask anyone at home. You wouldn't be allowed out on your own for the rest of your life if your grandfather found out what you did.'

'Red would be good, if you could manage it,' she said, her voice even, controlled. Holding everything in. 'I've left her address with the money.'

'Roadworthy. Red. Is that it?'

'I'd like her to have it before Christmas.'

'Do you want me to put on the Santa hat, climb on her roof and push it down the chimney?' He banged the flat of his hand against the steering wheel. 'I could start hating Christmas all over again.'

Annie could understand why he was angry. There were a thousand things she wanted to say, but nothing that would help either of them.

'If there's any money left, will you give it to some local charity?'

'Anonymously, of course. That's it? All debts paid?'

No. Not by a long shot but there was one thing she could do. 'Would you like me to speak to Mrs Warburton? At Dower House. In case Xandra changes her mind about going back.'

'She won't be returning to boarding school.'

'Her mother might not take the same view,' she pointed out.

'Her mother lost her vote when she switched off her cellphone.'

'Yes, well, I'm sure she'll be happier living with you and her grandparents.'

He shook his head. 'I left home when I was eighteen, Annie. I'm not about to move back in with my parents. What about you?'

'What about me?'

'Are you going to go home and grovel to your grandfather for being a bad girl?' he asked, driven by helpless anger into goading her. 'Beg his forgiveness and promise never to do it again?'

'George—'

'Go on playing the part that he wrote for you when you were six years old?'

'Wrote for me?'

'Isn't that what he did?' He'd read her story on the Net, wanting to know everything about her. 'From the moment you stepped into the limelight. Isn't he the one pushing the wedding bells story?'

She didn't answer.

'I saw that photograph of the two of you together on the day it was first published. Your mouth was smiling, but your eyes… You looked hunted.'

He saw the slip road for a motorway service station and took it. Pulling into the car park, he turned on her. 'You told Xandra that you'd only marry Rupert Devenish if you loved him. Do you?'

'George… Don't do this.'

'Do you?'

'No…' The word was hoarse, barely audible. 'Before I met you…'

'Before you met me—what?'

'I might have been that desperate.'

She was no more than a dark shape against the lights. He couldn't see her face or read her expression and that made it easier. One look from those tender blue eyes and he'd be lost.

'What do you want, Annie?' he asked, fighting the urge to just take her in his arms, tell her that it would be all right, that he would make it so. But he knew that this was something she had to do for herself.

She opened her mouth. Closed it again.

'Don't think about it,' he said a touch desperately, wanting to shake her. 'Just speak. Say the first thing that comes into your head. What do you really want?'

'I want to be the person I would have been if my parents had lived,' she blurted out. Then gave a little gasp, as if she hadn't known what she was going to say. 'A doctor,' she said. 'I was going to be a doctor, like my mother.'

That was it? Something so simple?

'So what stopped you?' he asked.

'It was impossible. You must see that.'

'I see only a woman who had a dream but not the courage to fight for it. A quitter.'

'You don't understand—'

'Oh, I understand.' He understood that if she went back like this, afraid to admit even to herself what she wanted, she'd never break free. She'd forced him to take a look at his life, to straighten it out, and now, because he loved her, he was going to fight for her whether she liked it or not. 'I understand that you were enjoying being the nation's sweetheart a little bit too much to give it up,' he said, twisting the knife, goading her, wanting her to kick out, fight back. 'Being on the front page all the time. Everyone telling you how wonderful you were, how brave…'

Her eyes flared in the lights of a passing car and he knew he'd done it. That if she'd had the room to swing her arm she might have slapped him and he'd have welcomed it, but he didn't let up.

'If you'd wanted to be a doctor, Annie, you'd have been one. I'm not saying it would have been easy, but you're not short of determination. What you wanted was your mother,' he said, 'and being her was the closest you could get.'

'No!' There was the longest pause. 'Yes…' And then, with something that was almost a laugh, 'Instead, I became my father. Good works, duty. Everything by the book.' She looked at him. 'Until he met my mother.'

'She was a bad influence?'

'That depends on your point of view. Without her, he'd have been like my grandfather, like Rupert. But my mother came from another world and she stirred his social conscience. Together they used his money, his contacts, his influence to help change the world.' In the darkness he heard her swallow. 'That's why they were targeted, killed. Because they were the kind of people whose death mattered enough to make headlines.'

She didn't say that her grandfather had blamed her mother for that. She didn't have to. But it explained why he'd kept her so close, so protected. Not just from unnamed threats, but so that she wouldn't meet someone like him. Someone who would take her away, as her mother had taken his son, and, from disliking the man on principle, he found himself pitying him.

But it was Annie who mattered.

'You're not a copy of anyone,' he told her fiercely. 'You encompass the best of both of them. Your father's *noblesse oblige*, your mother's special ability to reach out to those in need, her genuine empathy for people in trouble. You make the front page so often because people reach for it. Your smile lights up their day.'

As it lit up his life.

'But—'

'I've seen you in action. You're not acting. That's all you, straight from the heart, but you have to take charge of your life. Hold onto what's good. Walk away from the rest.'

'You make it sound so easy.'

'Nothing worthwhile is ever easy. I've no doubt you'll meet resistance. The "just leave it to us" response. Like punching marshmallow. It's easy to get sucked in. I'm a designer, so I hire the best in the business to run my company.' He smiled, even though she couldn't see his face. 'The difference between us is that I can fire anyone who doesn't do it the way I want it done.'

'I can't fire my grandfather.'

'No. Family you have for life. You told me to talk to my father—actually, you blackmailed me into it. Now I'm going to return the favour. Talk to him, tell him what you want.'

'Or?'

He shrugged, knowing that he didn't need to say the words.

'You're bluffing again.'

'You want to bet?'

There was the briefest pause before she said, 'No.'

'Good call.'

'Hungry?' he asked.

'Surprisingly, yes,' she said.

'Then here comes another new experience for you. The motorway service station.'

* * *

'You're going to keep the garage open to specialise in vintage cars?' Annie asked once they were seated with their trays containing pre-wrapped sandwiches and coffee and, because he'd made his point, he was filling her in on his own plans. 'Will Xandra go for that?'

'I mentioned it when we were working on the Austin yesterday.' George stirred sugar into his coffee, smiling at the memory of Xandra forgetting herself enough to fling her arms around him. 'She knows it's a good niche market. I'll start looking for a manager, staff, in the New Year.'

'So, if you're not going to live with your parents, where will you live?'

'I'm not going to move. They are. I'll buy the farm—'

'Farm?'

'There are just over five hundred acres still let to tenants. Not quite an estate, no park gates, but it's good arable land. I'm going to build a bungalow in the paddock for my parents, something easy to manage.'

'And you'll live in the house.'

The way she said that made him look up. 'It needs some work and I'll have to find a housekeeper, but that's the plan.'

'What about your business?'

'I'll have to make regular trips to Chicago, but I'll turn the barn into an office. Anything I could do in California, I can do here.'

'Everything in one place. The work-life balance achieved. Your extended family around you.'

'You like the idea?'

Annie sighed. 'I'm deeply envious. I totally fell in love with the farmhouse. But won't you miss your place on the beach?'

'There'll be time for that too. Maybe next time you want a break you should give me a call. We could catch up on those motorbike lessons.'

She shook her head. 'I'm not going to run away again, George.'

'No?'

She swallowed. 'No. Open, upfront. The trouble is that when you've used publicity you can't just turn it off, expect the media to back off just because it's no longer convenient. I come with a lot of baggage.'

He heard what she said. Something more. It was the sound of a woman taking a tentative step away from the past. Coming towards him.

'You'll just have to keep your top on when we're on the beach then,' he replied casually.

For a moment the world seemed to hold its breath.

Then she replied, 'And keep the curtains drawn when we're inside.'

'Actually, taking photographs through the window would be an invasion of privacy.'

'You think they'd care?' she said, faltering.

'If we were married it wouldn't be a story.'

'I never thought of that.'

And suddenly they were talking about a life. The possibility of a future.

'What about Xandra? You've just got your life together.'

'Nothing worthwhile is ever easy, Annie. I've fought for everything I've got. Worked hours that would have raised the eyebrows of a Victorian mill owner. Say the word and I'd fight the world for you.'

'I have to learn to fight my own battles, George.'

His only answer was to take a little white box from his pocket.

'I was going to give you this before you left. A conversation starter at the Christmas dinner table. Something to make you smile.' He handed it to her. 'When you're ready to try life on Mars, wear them to some dress-up gala and I'll come and spring you.'

She looked up at him, then opened the box. Nestling in cotton wool were a pair of earrings that matched the mistletoe headband. She removed the studs from her ears and replaced them with the earrings. Clicked the tiny switch to set the lights twinkling.

'Are they working?' she asked.

By way of reply, he leaned forward, took her chin in his hand and kissed her, hard. Then he switched them off.

'That's it,' he said. 'Next time I do that it's for keeps.'

He drove, without haste but sooner, rather than the later he would have wished for, they reached the village of Lacey Parva. Annie directed him to the entrance to her grandfather's estate but as they cleared a bend there were dozens of cars, vans, even a TV truck parked along the side of the road.

'Don't stop,' she said, ducking down as he slowed in the narrow lane and everyone turned to look. 'Drive on,' she muttered, scrabbling in her bag for her cellphone.

She switched it on, scrolled the news channels. Used that word she'd learned.

'What?' he asked.

'Lydia's missing,' she said, desperately checking her texts. Her voicemail. 'The world thinks I've been kidnapped.'

'Have you?'

She shook her head. 'No. She's left a message to say that there's nothing to worry about.'

'I'm glad to hear it. So, is there another way into the estate?'

'A dozen, but they'll have them all staked out. Just keep going. I'll show you where you can drop me off. I'll walk to the house.'

'Drop… You expect me to leave you by the side of the road?'

'It's all going to come out, George. If I can get to the house, the PR team can cobble together some story. There's no need for you to be involved.'

'That's it? One setback and you're going to run for cover?'

'You don't understand—'

'I understand,' he replied, his jaw so rigid that he thought it might break. Mars? Who did he think he'd been kidding? He was so far out on a limb here that Pluto was out of sight. 'But you don't actually have a say in the matter. I'm taking you home through the front gates,' he said, swinging into a lay-by and turning back in the direction of the house. 'It's not open to negotiation, so if being seen with me is going to be difficult, then buckle up. It's going to be a bumpy ride.'

'Stop!' she demanded. 'Stop right here.'

And that, apparently, was all it took. 'Damn you, Annie,' he said as he brought the car to a halt, eyes front, his hands gripping the steering wheel. 'I thought for a minute that we had something. A future.'

'So did I. So what just happened?' she demanded.

She was angry with him?

He risked a glance at her, felt a surge of hope, but this wasn't the time to pussyfoot around, it was time for plain speaking.

'Reality? Life?' he offered. 'I'm an ordinary man, Annie, from ordinary people. Yeoman stock. Farmers. Mechanics. Why would you want a Saxon when you should have a prince?'

'Ordinary,' she repeated. 'It wasn't dukes or barons that made this country great. It was hard-working, purposeful, good people like your family. *Extraordinary*, every one of you.'

She reached out, took his hand from the wheel, held it in hers.

'I love you, George Saxon, and I would be the proudest woman in Britain to be seen on every front page in the world with you, but this is going to be a media feeding frenzy. I simply wanted to protect you, protect your family from the fallout of my pathetic lack of courage. I should have talked to my grandfather years ago. I won't let another night pass without telling him what I want.'

'What do you want, Annie?'

'You. A house filled with little Saxons. Xandra. Your parents. You…'

'You've got me, angel. The rest comes included.' And he lifted the hand holding his, kissed it. 'As for the hounds at the gate, maybe the answer is to give them a bigger story than you disappearing for a week.'

'Oh? What story did you have in mind?'

He smiled. 'Switch those earrings on and I'll show you.'

They could have spent the entire evening parked up in the wood but there were people to call, explanations to be made and they spent the next fifteen minutes making phone calls.

'What did your family say?' Annie asked.

'My mother is thrilled. My father said I don't deserve you. Xandra said, "Cool". Yours?'

'My grandfather is so relieved that I could have announced I was marrying a Martian,' she said.

'Then all we have to do is tell the world. Ready?'

'Ready.'

He kissed her once more, then drove slowly up to the gates of King's Lacey.

Cameramen surged forward as a policeman came to the window.

'Lady Roseanne Napier,' he said. 'George Saxon. We're expected.'

He peered in. 'Lady Rose! You're a sight for sore eyes. We've all been worried sick.'

'Just a misunderstanding, Michael. We'll make a statement for the press and then, hopefully, you can go home.'

'No rush, madam,' he said, opening the door for her, waving the press back. 'The overtime comes in handy at this time of year.'

There was a volley of flashes as she stepped from the car. 'Lady Rose! Who was the man in Bab el Sama, Lady Rose?'

'I'm afraid I've no idea,' she said, holding out a hand as George joined her. 'I haven't left England all week. And this is the only man in my life,' she said, turning to him. Smiling only for him. 'George Saxon. The man I love. The man I'm going to marry.'

For a moment they could have heard a pin drop. Then they lit up the night with their cameras as George lifted her hand to kiss it.

It was a photograph that went around the world.

Daily Chronicle, 10th June

FAMILY WEDDING FOR LADY ROSE

Lady Roseanne Napier was married yesterday to billionaire businessman, Mr George Saxon, in the private chapel on her grandfather's estate at King's Lacey.

Miss Alexandra Saxon, the groom's daughter by an earlier marriage, attended the bride, along with children from her grandfather's estate.

The wedding and reception were a quiet family affair, despite a bidding war from gossip magazines who offered a million pounds to charity for the privilege of covering the affair.

The groom made a counter bid, pledging five million to charity if the media left them in peace to enjoy their special day with their family and friends, something we were happy to do.

This photograph of the couple, released to the press by the happy couple, is copyrighted to

Susanne House and that charity will benefit from its publication.

We understand that the couple will honeymoon in the United States.

* * * * *

A CHRISTMAS TRADITION

Some years ago, when I'd taken my Christmas cards to the post and felt slightly sick when I realised just how much money I'd spent mailing greetings to every corner of the world, I made a decision that in the future I would send my greetings via the Internet and give the money saved to charity; a far greener, and much more lasting way of wishing the world a Merry Christmas and Happy New Year.

Since then, Third World communities have benefited from, amongst other things, a camel, a trained midwife and a goat, but cards are a hard habit to give up. There are always some truly special people you want to reach out to. Some very senior aunts. Faraway friends. People who have done something special for you during the year whom you want to thank with a special wish. For those two or three dozen people we make our own cards.

This isn't one of those 'craft' things. We don't sit down with paper and ribbons and glue—no one would thank me for anything I made like that. Instead my husband and I go through the photographs taken on trips throughout the year and pick out some moment we really want to share with friends and family.

A mist-shrouded castle, autumn woods, a favourite beach.

Last year we went to Bruges, and whilst there John took a photograph of Michelangelo's beautiful 'Madonna and Child' in the Church of Our Lady. As we looked through the photographs we'd taken through the year the image leapt out as the perfect subject for our card.

It's not just a question of printing a few cards, though. We spend a lot of time together choosing a card that works best with the image—gloss, silk, matt. Then there's the font style and colour, the words. It's truly a joint effort until that point, but once all the details have been decided I leave it to John to work his magic with the computer. My job is to write the envelopes, stick on the stamps, walk across to the box to post them.

It has, in a very short time, become a special Christmas tradition. One that sits happily alongside the cards I post on my website and blog. And beside the Oxfam catalogue from which I choose my Christmas card to the world.

A joyful Christmas and a peaceful New Year to you all.

Liz

UNDER THE BOSS'S MISTLETOE

BY
JESSICA HART

First published in Great Britain 2009
Harlequin Mills & Boon Limited,
Eton House, 18-24 Paradise Road, Richmond, Surrey TW9 1SR

© Jessica Hart 2009

ISBN: 978 0 263 86977 4

Set in Times Roman 12½ on 14 pt
02-1109-55514

Harlequin Mills & Boon policy is to use papers that are natural, renewable and recyclable products and made from wood grown in sustainable forests. The logging and manufacturing process conform to the legal environmental regulations of the country of origin.

Printed and bound in Spain
by Litografia Rosés, S.A., Barcelona

Jessica Hart was born in West Africa, and has suffered from itchy feet ever since—travelling and working around the world in a wide variety of interesting but very lowly jobs, all of which have provided inspiration on which to draw when it comes to the settings and plots of her stories. Now she lives a rather more settled existence in York, where she has been able to pursue her interest in history, although she still yearns sometimes for wider horizons. If you'd like to know more about Jessica, visit her website www.jessicahart.co.uk

PROLOGUE

'I WANT a word with you!'

Cassie almost fell down the steps in her hurry to catch Jake before he zoomed off like the coward he was. The stumble did nothing to improve her temper as she stormed over to where he had just got onto his motorbike.

He had been about to put on his helmet, but he paused at the sound of her voice. In his battered leathers, he looked as dark and mean as the machine he sat astride. There was a dangerous edge to Jake Trevelyan that Cassie normally found deeply unnerving, but today she was too angry to be intimidated.

'You broke Rupert's nose!' she said furiously.

Jake observed her approach through narrowed eyes. The estate manager's ungainly daughter had a wild mane of curls, a round, quirky face and a mouth that showed promise of an interesting woman to come. Right now, though, she was still only seventeen, and reminded him of an exuberant puppy about to fall over its paws.

Not such a friendly puppy today, he observed. The normally dreamy brown eyes were flashing with temper. It wasn't too hard to guess what had her all riled up; she must have just been to see her precious Rupert.

'Not quite such a pretty boy today, is he?' he grinned.

Cassie's fists clenched. 'I'd like to break *your* nose,' she said and Jake laughed mockingly.

'Have a go,' he offered.

'And give you the excuse to beat me up as well? I don't think so.'

'I didn't beat Rupert up,' said Jake dismissively. 'Is that what he told you?'

'I've just seen him. He looks *awful*.'

Cassie heard the crack in her voice and pressed her lips together in a fierce, straight line before she could humiliate herself utterly by bursting into tears.

She had been so happy, she had had to keep pinching herself. For as long as she could remember she had dreamed of Rupert, and now he was hers—or he had been. It was only three days since the ball, and he was in a vicious temper, which he'd taken out on her. It was all spoilt now.

And it was all Jake Trevelyan's fault.

'He's going to bring assault charges against you,'

she told Jake, hoping to shock him, but he only looked contemptuous.

'So Sir Ian has just been telling me.'

Cassie had never understood why Sir Ian had so much time for a thug like Jake, especially now that he had beaten up his own nephew!

The Trevelyans were notorious in Portrevick for their shady dealings, and the only member of the family who had ever appeared to hold down a job at all was Jake's mother, who had cleaned for Sir Ian until her untimely death a couple of years ago. Jake himself had long had a reputation as a troublemaker. He was four years older than Cassie, and she couldn't remember a time when his dark, surly presence hadn't made him the kind of boy you crossed the road to avoid.

It was a pity she hadn't remembered that at the Allantide Ball.

Now Cassie glared at him, astonished by her own bravery. 'But then, I suppose the thought of prison wouldn't bother you,' she said. 'It's something of a family tradition, isn't it?'

Something unpleasant flared in Jake's eyes, and she took an involuntary step backwards, wondering a little too late whether she might have gone too far. There was a suppressed anger about him that should have warned her not to provoke him. She wouldn't put it past him to take out all that simmering resentment on her the way he so clearly had on

Rupert, but in the end he only looked at her with dislike.

'What do you want, Miss Not-So-Goody Two Shoes?'

Cassie took a deep breath. 'I want to know why you hit Rupert.'

'Why does it matter?'

'Rupert said it was over me.' She bit her lip. 'He wouldn't tell me exactly what.'

Jake laughed shortly. 'No, I bet he wouldn't!'

'Was it…was it because of what happened at the Allantide Ball?'

'When you offered yourself to me on a plate?' he said, and her face flamed.

'I was just talking,' she protested, although she knew she had been doing more than that.

'You don't wear a dress like that just to *talk*,' said Jake.

Cassie's cheeks were as scarlet as the dress she had bought as part of a desperate strategy to convince Rupert that she had grown up.

Her parents had been aghast when they had seen it, and Cassie herself had been half-horrified, half-thrilled by how it had made her look. The colour was lovely—a deep, rich red—but it was made of cheap Lycra that had clung embarrassingly to every curve. Cut daringly short, it had such a low neckline that Cassie had had to keep tugging at it to stop herself spilling out. She cringed to think how fat and tarty she must have looked next to all those cool, skinny blondes dressed in black.

On the other hand, it had worked.

Rupert had definitely noticed her when she'd arrived, and that had given her the confidence to put Plan B into action. 'You need to make him jealous,' her best friend Tina had said. 'Make him realise that you're not just his for the taking—even if you are.'

Emboldened by Rupert's reaction, Cassie had smiled coolly and sashayed up to Jake instead. To this day, she didn't know where she had found the nerve to do it; he had been on his own for once, and watching the proceedings with a cynical air.

The Allantide Ball was a local tradition revived by Sir Ian, who had been obsessed by Cornish folklore. Less a formal ball than a big party, it was held in the Hall every year on 31st October, when the rest of the country was celebrating Hallowe'en, and everyone in Portrevick went, the one occasion when social divisions were put aside.

In theory, if not in practice.

Jake's expression had not been encouraging, but Cassie had flirted with him anyway. Or she had thought she was flirting. In retrospect, her heavy-handed attempts to bat her lashes and look sultry must have been laughable, but at the time she had been quite pleased with herself.

'OK, maybe I was flirting,' she conceded. 'That was no reason to…to…'

'To kiss you?' said Jake. 'But how else were you to make Rupert jealous? That *was* the whole point of the exercise, wasn't it?'

Taking Cassie's expression as an answer, he settled back into the saddle and regarded her with a mocking smile that made her want to slap him. 'It was a good strategy,' he congratulated her. 'Rupert Branscombe Fox is the kind of jerk who's only interested in what someone else has got. I'll bet even as a small boy he only ever wanted to play with someone else's toys. It was very astute of you to notice that.'

'I didn't.'

She had just wanted Rupert to notice her. Was that so bad? And he had. It had worked perfectly.

She just hadn't counted on Jake taking her flirtation so seriously. He had taken her by the hand and pulled her outside. Catching a glimpse of Rupert watching her, Cassie had been delighted at first. She'd been expecting a kiss, but not the kiss that she got.

It had begun with cool assurance—and, really, that would have been fine—but then something had changed. The coolness had become warmth, and then it had become heat, and then, worst of all, there had been a terrifying sweetness to it. Cassie had felt as if she were standing in a river with the sand rushing away beneath her feet, sucking her down into something wild and uncontrollable.

She'd been terrified and exhilarated at the same time, and when Jake had let her go at last she had been shaking.

It wasn't even as if she liked Jake. He was the exact opposite of Rupert, who was the embodiment of a dream. Secretly, Cassie thought of them as Beauty and the Beast. Not that Jake was ugly, exactly, but he had dark, beaky features, a bitter mouth and angry eyes, while Rupert was all golden charm, like a prince in a fairy tale.

'Much good it'll do you,' Jake was saying, reading her expression without difficulty. 'You're wasting your time. Rupert's never going to bother with a nice girl like you.'

'Well, that's where you're wrong,' said Cassie, stung. 'Maybe I *did* want to make him notice me, but it worked, didn't it?'

'You're not asking me to believe that you're Rupert's latest girlfriend?'

Cassie lifted her chin. 'Believe what you want,' she said. 'It happens to be true.'

But Jake only laughed. 'Having sex with Rupert doesn't make you his girlfriend, as you'll soon find out,' he said. He reached for his helmet again. 'You need to grow up, Cassie. You've wandered around with your head in the clouds ever since you were a little kid, and it looks like you're still living in a fantasy world. It's time you woke up to reality!'

'You're just jealous of Rupert!' Cassie accused him, her voice shaking with fury.

'Because of you?' Jake raised his dark brows contemptuously. 'I don't think so!'

'Because he's handsome and charming and rich and Sir Ian's nephew, while you're just…just…' Too angry and humiliated to be cautious, she was practically toe to toe with him by now. 'Just an *animal*.'

And that was when Jake really did lose the temper he had been hanging onto by a thread all day. His hands shot out and yanked Cassie towards him so hard that she fell against him. Luckily his bike was still on its stand, or they would both have fallen over.

'So you think I'm jealous of Rupert, do you?' he snarled, shoving his hands into the mass of curls. 'Well, maybe I am.'

He brought his mouth down on hers in a hard, punishing kiss that had her squirming in protest, her palms jammed against his leather jacket, until abruptly the pressure softened.

His lips didn't leave hers, but he shifted slightly so that he could draw her more comfortably against him as he sat astride the bike. The fierce grip on her hair had loosened, and now her curls were twined around his fingers as the kiss grew seductively insistent.

Cassie's heart was pounding with that same mixture of fear and excitement, and she could feel herself losing her footing again. A surge of unfamiliar feeling was rapidly uncoiling inside her, so fast in fact that it was scaring her; her fingers curled instinctively into his leather jacket to anchor herself.

And then—the bit that would make her cringe for years afterwards—somehow she actually found herself leaning into him to kiss him back.

That was the point at which Jake let her go so abruptly that she stumbled back against the handlebars.

'How dare you?' Cassie managed, drawing a shaking hand across her mouth as she tried to leap away from the bike, only to find that her cardigan was caught up in the handlebars. Desperately, she tried to disentangle herself. 'I never want to see you again!'

'Don't worry, you won't have to.' Infuriatingly casual, Jake leant forward to pull the sleeve free; she practically fell back in her haste to put some distance between them. 'I'm leaving today. You stick to your fantasy life, Cassie,' he told her as she huddled into her cardigan, hugging her arms together. 'I'm getting out of here.'

And with that, he calmly fastened his helmet, kicked the bike off its stand and into gear and roared off down the long drive—leaving Cassie staring after him, her heart tumbling with shock and humiliation and the memory of a deep, dark, dangerous excitement.

CHAPTER ONE

Ten years later

'JAKE Trevelyan?' Cassie repeated blankly. 'Are you sure?'

'I wrote his name down. Where is it?' Joss hunted through the mess on her desk and produced a scrap of paper. 'Here—Jake Trevelyan,' she read. 'Somebody in Portrevick—isn't that where you grew up?—recommended us.'

Puzzled, Cassie dropped into the chair at her own desk. It felt very strange, hearing Jake's name after all this time. She could still picture him with terrifying clarity, sitting astride that mean-looking machine, an angry young man with hard hands and a bitter smile. The memory of that kiss still had the power to make her toes curl inside her shoes.

'He's getting married?'

'Why else would he get in touch with a wedding planner?'

'I just can't imagine it.' The Jake Trevelyan Cassie had known wasn't the type to settle down.

'Luckily for us, he obviously can.' Joss turned back to her computer. 'He sounded keen, anyway, so I said you'd go round this afternoon.'

'Me?' Cassie looked at her boss in dismay. 'You always meet the clients first.'

'I can't today. I've got a meeting with the accountant, which I'm not looking forward to at all. Besides, he knows you.'

'Yes, but he hates me!' She told Joss about that last encounter outside Portrevick Hall. 'And what's his fiancée going to think? I wouldn't want to plan my wedding with someone who'd kissed my bridegroom.'

'Teenage kisses don't count.' Joss waved them aside. 'It was ten years ago. Chances are, he won't even remember.'

Cassie wasn't sure if that would make her feel better or worse. She would just as soon Jake didn't remember the gawky teenager who had thrown herself at him at the Allantide Ball, but what girl wanted to know that she was utterly forgettable?

'Anyway, if he didn't like you, why ring up and ask to speak to you?' Joss asked reasonably. 'We can't afford to let a possible client slip through our fingers, Cassie. You know how tight things are at the moment. This is our best chance of new work in weeks, and if it means being embarrassed then I'm afraid you're going to have to be embarrassed,' she warned. 'Otherwise, I'm really not sure how much longer I'm going to be able to keep you on.'

Which was how Cassie came to stand outside a gleaming office-building that afternoon. Its windows reflected a bright September sky, and she had to crane her neck to look up to the top. Jake Trevelyan had done well for himself if he worked somewhere like this, she thought, impressed in spite of herself.

Better than she had, that was for sure, thought Cassie, remembering Avalon's chaotic office above the Chinese takeaway. Not that she minded. She had only been working for Joss a few months and she loved it. Wedding planning was far and away the best job she had ever had—Cassie had had a few, it had to be admitted—and she would do whatever it took to hang on to it. She couldn't bear to admit to her family of super-achievers that she was out of work.

Again.

'Oh, *darling*!' her mother would sigh with disappointment, while her father would frown and remind her that she should have gone to university like her elder sister and her two brothers, all of whom had high-flying careers.

No, she had to keep this job, Cassie resolved, and if that meant facing Jake Trevelyan again then that was what she would do.

Squaring her shoulders, she tugged her jacket into place and headed up the marble steps.

Worms were squirming in the pit of her stomach but she did her best to ignore them. It was stupid to be nervous about seeing Jake again. She wasn't a dreamy seventeen-year-old any longer. She was twenty-seven, and holding down a demanding job. People might not think that being a wedding planner was much of a career, but it required tact, diplomacy and formidable organizational-skills. If she could organise a wedding— well, help Joss organise one—she could deal with Jake Trevelyan.

A glimpse of herself in the mirrored windows re-assured her. Luckily, she had dressed smartly to visit a luxurious hotel which one of their clients had chosen as a venue that morning. The teal-green jacket and narrow skirt gave her a sharp, professional image, Cassie decided, eyeing her reflection. Together with the slim briefcase, it made for an impressive look.

Misleading, but impressive. She hardly recognised herself, so with any luck Jake Trevelyan wouldn't recognise her either.

Her only regret was the shoes. It wasn't that they didn't look fabulous—the teal suede with a black stripe was perfect with the suit—but she wasn't used to walking on quite such high heels, and the lobby floor had an alarmingly, glossy sheen to it. It was a relief to get across to the reception desk without mishap.

'I'm looking for a company called Primordia,' she said, glancing down at the address Joss had scribbled down. 'Can you tell me which floor it's on?'

The receptionist lifted immaculate brows. 'This *is* Primordia,' she said.

'What, the whole building?' Cassie's jaw sagged as she stared around the soaring lobby, taking in the impressive artwork on the walls and the ranks of gleaming lifts with their lights going up, up, up...

'Apparently he's boss of some outfit called Primordia,' Joss had said casually when she'd tossed the address across the desk.

This didn't look like an 'outfit' to Cassie. It looked like a solid, blue-chip company exuding wealth and prestige. Suddenly her suit didn't seem quite so smart.

'Um, I'm looking for someone called Jake Trevelyan,' she told the receptionist. 'I'm not sure which department he's in.'

The receptionist's brows climbed higher. 'Mr Trevelyan, our Chief Executive? Is he expecting you?'

Chief Executive? Cassie swallowed. 'I think so.'

The receptionist turned away to murmur into the phone while Cassie stood, fingering the buttons on her jacket nervously. Jake Trevelyan, bad boy of Portrevick, Chief Executive of all this?

Blimey.

An intimidatingly quiet lift took her up to the Chief Executive's suite. It was like stepping into a different world. Everything was new and of cutting-edge design, and blanketed with the hush that only serious money can buy.

It was a very long way from Portrevick.

Cassie was still half-convinced that there must be some mistake, but no. There was an elegant PA, who was obviously expecting her, and who escorted her into an impressively swish office.

'Mr Trevelyan won't be a minute,' she said.

Mr Trevelyan! Cassie thought of the surly tearaway she had known and tried not to goggle. She hoped Jake—sorry, *Mr Trevelyan*—didn't remember her flirting with him in that tacky dress or telling him that she never wanted to see him again. It wasn't exactly the best basis on which to build a winning client-relationship.

On the other hand, he was the one who had asked to see her. Surely he wouldn't have done that if he had any memory of those disastrous kisses? Joss must be right; he had probably forgotten them completely. And, even if he hadn't, he was unlikely to mention that he had kissed her in front of his fiancée, wasn't he? He would be just as anxious as her to pretend that that had never happened.

Reassured, Cassie pinned on a bright smile as his PA opened a door into an even swisher office than the first. 'Cassandra Grey,' the woman announced.

It was a huge room, with glass walls on two sides that offered a spectacular view down the Thames to the Houses of Parliament and the London Eye.

Not that Cassie took in the view. She had eyes only for Jake, who was getting up from behind his desk and buttoning his jacket as he came round to greet her.

Her first thought was that he had grown into a surprisingly attractive man.

Ten years ago he had been a wiry young man, with turbulent eyes and a dangerous edge that had always left her tongue-tied and nervous around him. He was dark still, and there were traces of the difficult boy he had been in his face, but he had grown into the once-beaky features, and the surliness had metamorphosed into a forcefulness that was literally breathtaking. At least, Cassie presumed that was why she was having trouble dragging enough oxygen into her lungs all of a sudden.

He might not actually be taller, but he seemed it—taller, tougher, more solid somehow. And the mouth that had once been twisted into a sneer was now set in a cool, self-contained line.

Cassie was forced to revise her first thought. He wasn't attractive; he was *gorgeous*.

Well. Who would have thought it?

His fiancée was a lucky woman.

Keeping her smile firmly in place, she took a step

towards him with her hand outstretched. 'Hel…' she began, but that was as far as she got. Her ankle tipped over on the unfamiliar heels and the next moment her shoes seemed to be hopelessly entangled. Before Cassie knew what was happening, she found herself pitching forward with a squawk of dismay as her briefcase thudded to the floor.

She would have landed flat on her face next to it if a pair of hard hands hadn't grabbed her arms. Cassie had no idea how Jake got there in time to catch her, but she ended up sprawling against him and clutching instinctively at his jacket.

Just as she had clutched at his leather jacket ten years ago when he had kissed her.

'Hello, Cassie,' he said.

Mortified, Cassie struggled to find her balance. Why, why, *why*, was she so clumsy?

Her face was squashed against his jacket, and with an odd, detached part of her brain she registered that he smelt wonderful, of expensive shirts, clean, male skin and a faint tang of aftershave. His body was rock-solid, and for a treacherous moment Cassie was tempted to cling to the blissful illusion of steadiness and safety.

Possibly not a good move, if she wanted to impress him with her new-found professionalism. Or very tactful, given that he was a newly engaged man.

With an effort, Cassie pulled herself away from

the comfort of that broad chest. 'I'm so sorry,' she managed.

Jake set her on her feet but kept hold of her upper arms until he was sure she was steady. 'Are you all right?'

His hands felt hard and strong through the sleeves of her jacket, and he held her just as he had done that other day.

Cassie couldn't help staring. It was strangely dislocating to look into his face and see a cool stranger overlaying the angry young man he had been then. This time the resentment in the dark-blue eyes had been replaced by a gleam of amusement, although it was impossible to tell whether he was remembering that kiss, too, or was simply entertained by her unconventional arrival.

Cassie's cheeks burned. 'I'm fine,' she said, stepping out of his grip.

Jake bent to pick up the briefcase and handed it back to her. 'Shall we sit down?' he suggested, gesturing towards two luxurious leather sofas. 'Given those shoes, it might be safer!'

Willing her flaming colour to fade, Cassie subsided onto a sofa and swallowed as she set the briefcase on the low table. 'I don't normally throw myself into the client's arms when we first meet,' she said with a nervous smile.

The corner of Jake's mouth quivered in an unnervingly attractive way. 'It's always good to make a spectacular entrance. But then, you always did have a certain style,' he added.

Cassie rather suspected that last comment was sarcastic; she had always been hopelessly clumsy.

She sighed. 'I was rather hoping you wouldn't recognise me,' she confessed.

Jake looked across the table at her. She was perched on the edge of the sofa, looking hot and ruffled, her round, sweet face flushed, and brown eyes bright with mortification.

The wild curls he remembered had been cut into a more manageable style, and she had slimmed down and smartened up. Remarkably so, in fact. When he had looked up to see her in the doorway, she had seemed a vividly pretty stranger, and he had felt a strange sensation in the pit of his stomach.

Then she had tripped and pitched into his arms, and Jake wasn't sure if he was disappointed or relieved to find out that she hadn't changed that much after all.

The feel of her was startlingly familiar, which was odd, given that he had only held her twice before. But he had caught her, and all at once it was as if he had been back at that last Allantide Ball. He could still see Cassie as she sashayed up to him in that tight red dress, teetering on heels almost as ridiculous as the ones she was wearing now, and suddenly all grown-up. That was the first time he had noticed her lush mouth, and wondered about the woman she would become.

That mouth was still the same, Jake thought, remembering its warmth, its innocence, remembering how unprepared he had been for the piercing sweetness that just for a moment had held them in its grip.

Now here she was again, sitting there and watching him with a wary expression in the big brown eyes. Not recognise her?

Jake smiled. 'Not a chance,' he said.

Oh dear. That wasn't what she had wanted to hear at all. Almost reluctantly, Cassie met the dark-blue gaze and felt her skin prickle at the amusement she read there. It was obvious that Jake remembered the gawky teenager she had been all too well. Those kisses might have been shattering for her, but for him they must have been just part of her gaucheness and lack of sophistication.

She lifted her chin. 'It's a long time ago,' she said. 'I didn't think you'd remember me.'

Jake met her eyes blandly. 'You'd be surprised what I remember,' he said, and the memory of the Allantide Ball was suddenly shimmering between them. He didn't have to say anything. Cassie just knew that he was remembering her hopeless attempts to flirt, and her clumsy, mortifyingly eager response to his kiss, and a tide of heat seemed to sweep up from her toes.

She jerked her eyes away. 'So,' she began, but all at once her voice was so high and thin that she had to clear her throat and start again. 'So…' Oh God, now she sounded positively gravelly! 'What took you back to Portrevick?' She managed to find something approaching a normal pitch at last. As far as she knew, Jake had left the village that awful day he had kissed her on his motorbike and had never been back.

Jake's expression sobered. 'Sir Ian's death,' he said.

'Oh yes, I was so sorry when I heard about that,' said Cassie, latching on to what she hoped would be a safe subject. 'He was such a lovely man,' she remembered sadly. 'Mum and Dad went back for the funeral, but one of our clients was getting married that day so I was on duty.'

The door opened at that point and Jake's PA came in with a tray of coffee which she set on the table between them. She poured two cups and made a discreet exit. Why could *she* never be that quiet and efficient? Cassie wondered, admiring the other woman's style.

Jake passed one of the cups to her, and she accepted it gingerly. It was made of the finest porcelain, and she couldn't help comparing it to the chipped mugs she and Joss used to drink endless cups of tea in the office.

'I had to go and see Sir Ian's solicitor on Friday,'

Jake said, pushing the milk jug towards her. 'I stayed in the pub at Portrevick, and your name was mentioned in connection with weddings. One of your old friends—Tina?—said that you were in the business.'

'*Did* she?' Cassie made a mental note to ring Tina the moment she left and demand to know why she hadn't told her that Jake Trevelyan had reappeared. It wasn't as if Tina didn't know all about that devastating kiss at the Allantide Ball, although Cassie had never told anyone about the second one.

Jake raised his eyes a little at her tone, and she hastened to make amends. Perhaps she had sounded rather vengeful, there. 'I mean, yes, that's right,' she said, helping herself to milk but managing to slop most of it into the saucer.

Now the cup was going to drip all over everything. With an inward sigh, Cassie hunted around in her bag for a tissue to mop up the mess. 'I am.'

That sounded a bit too bald, didn't it? *You're supposed to be selling yourself here,* Cassie reminded herself, but she was distracted by the need to dispose of the sodden tissue now. She couldn't just leave it in the saucer. It looked disgusting, and so unprofessional.

'In the wedding business, that is,' she added, losing track of where she had begun. Helplessly, she looked around for a bin, but of course there was nothing so prosaic in Jake's office.

It was immaculate, she noticed for the first time. Everything was squeaky clean, and the desk was clear except for a telephone and a very small, very expensive-looking computer. Ten years ago, Jake would only have been in an office like this to pinch the electronic equipment, she thought, wondering how on earth the rebel Jake, with his battered leathers and his bike, had made it to this exclusive, perfectly controlled space.

She could see Jake eyeing the tissue askance. Obviously any kind of mess offended him now, which was a shame, given that she was banking her entire future on being able to work closely with him and his fiancée for the next few months. Cassie belonged to the creative school of organising, the one that miraculously produced order out of chaos at the very last minute, although no one, least of all her, ever knew quite how it happened.

Unable to think of anything else do with it, Cassie quickly shoved the tissue back into her bag, where it would no doubt fester with all the other crumbs, chocolate wrappers, pen lids and blunt emery-boards that she never got round to clearing out. She would have to remember to be careful next time she put her hand in there.

Jake's expression was faintly disgusted, but he offered her the plate of biscuits. Cassie eyed them longingly. She was starving, but she knew better than to take one. The next thing, there would be biscuit crumbs everywhere, and her professional image had taken enough of a battering as it was this afternoon.

'No thank you,' she said politely, deciding to skip the coffee as well. At this rate she would just spill it all over herself and, worse, Jake's pristine leather sofa.

Leaning forward, Jake added milk to his own coffee without spilling so much as a drop. He stirred it briskly, tapped the spoon on the side of the cup, set it in the saucer and looked up at Cassie. The dark-blue eyes were very direct, and in spite of her determination to stay cool Cassie's pulse gave an alarming jolt.

'Well, shall we get down to business?' he suggested.

'Good idea.' Delighted to leave the past and all its embarrassing associations behind, Cassie leapt into action.

This was it. Her whole career—well, her job, Cassie amended to herself. She didn't have a career so much as a haphazard series of unrelated jobs. Anyway, *everything* depended on how she sold herself now.

Reaching for her briefcase, she unzipped it with a flourish, dug out a brochure and handed it to Jake. 'This will give you some idea of what we do,' she said in her best professional voice. It was odd that his fiancée wasn't here. Joss always aimed her pitch at the bride-to-be; she would just have to make the best of it, Cassie supposed.

'Of course, we offer a bespoke service, so we really start with what *you* want.' She hesitated. 'We usually discuss what you'd like with both members of the couple,' she added delicately. 'Will your fiancée be joining us?'

Jake had been flicking through the brochure, but at that he glanced up. 'Fiancée?'

'The bride generally has a good idea about what kind of wedding she wants,' Cassie explained. 'In our experience, grooms tend to be less concerned with the nitty-gritty of the organisation.'

'I think there may be some misunderstanding,' said Jake, frowning. 'I'm not engaged.'

Cassie's face fell ludicrously. 'Not…? You're not getting married?' she said, hoping against hope that she had misheard.

'No.'

Then how was she to hold on to her job? Cassie wondered wildly. 'So you don't need help planning a wedding?' she asked, just to make sure, and Jake let the brochure drop onto the table with a slap of finality.

'No.'

'But…' Cassie was struggling to understand how it could all have gone so wrong before she had even started. 'Why did you get in touch?'

'When Tina told me that you were in the wedding

business I was under the impression that you managed a venue. I hadn't appreciated that you were involved with planning the weddings themselves.'

'Well, we *deal* with venues, of course,' said Cassie, desperate to hold on to something. 'We help couples with every aspect of the wedding and honeymoon.' She launched into her spiel, but Jake cut her off before she could really get going.

'I'm really looking for someone who can advise on what's involved in converting a house into a wedding venue. I'm sorry,' he said, making to get to his feet. 'It looks as if I've been wasting your time.'

Cassie wasn't ready to give up yet. 'We do that too,' she said quickly.

'What, waste time?'

'Set up wedding venues,' she said, refusing to rise to the bait, and meeting his eyes so guilelessly that Jake was fairly sure that she was lying. 'Between us, Joss and I have a lot of experience of using venues, and we know exactly what's required. Where is the house?' she asked quickly, before he could draw the conversation to a close.

'I'm thinking about the Hall,' he relented.

'The Hall?' Cassie repeated blankly. 'Portrevick Hall?'

'Exactly.'

'But…isn't it Rupert's now?'

'No,' said Jake. 'Sir Ian left the estate in trust and I'm the trustee.'

Cassie stared at him, her career crisis momentarily forgotten. *'You?'* she said incredulously.

He smiled grimly at her expression. 'Yes, me.'

'What about Rupert?' she asked, too surprised for tact.

'Sir Ian's money was left in trust for him. He hasn't proved the steadiest of characters, as you may know.'

Cassie did know. Rupert's picture was regularly in the gossip columns. There was a certain irony in the fact that Jake was now the wealthy, successful one while Rupert had a reputation as a hellraiser, albeit a very glamorous one. He seemed to get by largely on charm and those dazzling good looks.

She forced her attention back to Jake, who was still talking. 'Sir Ian was concerned that, if he left him the money outright, Rupert would just squander it the way he has already squandered his inheritance from his parents.'

'It just seems unfair,' she said tentatively. 'Rupert is Sir Ian's nephew, after all. I'm sure he expected to inherit Portrevick Hall.'

'I'm sure he did too,' said Jake in a dry voice. 'Rupert's been borrowing heavily on exactly that expectation for the last few years now. That's why Sir Ian put the estate into a trust. He was afraid

Rupert would simply sell it off to the highest bidder otherwise.'

'But why make *you* the trustee?' said Cassie without thinking.

'It's not a position I angled for, I can assure you,' Jake said with a certain astringency. 'But I owe Sir Ian a lot, so I had to agree when he asked me. I assumed there would be plenty of time for him to change his mind, and he probably did the same. He was only in his sixties, and he'd had no history of heart problems. If only he'd lived longer…'

Restlessly, Jake pushed away his coffee cup and got to his feet. There was no point in 'if only's. 'Anyway, the fact remains that I'm stuck with responsibility for the house now. I promised Sir Ian that I would make sure the estate remained intact. He couldn't bear the thought of the Hall being broken up into flats, or holiday houses built in the grounds.

'Obviously, I need to fulfil his wishes, but I can't leave a house like that standing empty. It needs to be used and maintained, and somehow I've got to find a way for it to pay for itself.'

Coming to a halt by the window, Jake frowned unseeingly at the view while he remembered his problem. 'When I was down at Portrevick last week, sorting out things with the solicitor, she suggested that it might make a suitable wedding-venue. It seemed like an idea worth pursuing. I happened to mention it in the pub that night, and that's how your name came up. But, judging by your brochure, your company is more concerned with the weddings themselves rather than running the venues.'

'Normally, yes,' said Cassie, not so engrossed in the story of Sir Ian's extraordinary will that she had forgotten that her new-found career with Avalon was on the line. 'But the management of a venue is closely related to what we do, and in fact this is an area we're looking at moving into,' she added fluently. She would have to remember to tell Joss that they were diversifying. 'Clearly, we have considerable experience of dealing with various venues, so we're in a position to know exactly what facilities they need to offer.'

'Hmm.' Jake sounded unconvinced. He turned from the window to study Cassie, sitting alert and eager on the sofa. 'All right, you know the Hall. Given your *considerable experience*, what would you think of it as a wedding venue?'

'It would be perfect,' said Cassie, ignoring his sarcasm. 'It's a beautiful old house with a wonderful location on the coast. It would be hard to imagine anywhere more romantic! I should think couples all over the South West would be queuing up to get married there.'

Jake came back to sit opposite her once more. He drummed his fingers absently on the table, obviously thinking. 'It's encouraging that you think it would make a popular venue, anyway,' he said at last.

'Yes, I do,' said Cassie eagerly, sensing that Jake might be buying her spur-of-the-moment career shift into project management.

She leant forward persuasively. 'I'm sure Sir Ian would approve of the idea,' she went on. 'He loved people, didn't he? I bet he would have liked to see the Hall used for weddings. They're such happy occasions.'

'If you say so,' said Jake, clearly unconvinced.

He studied Cassie with a faint frown, wondering if he was mad to even consider taking her advice. She had always been a dreamer, he remembered, and the curly hair and dimple gave her a warm, sweet but slightly dishevelled air that completely contradicted the businesslike suit and the stylish, totally impractical shoes.

There was something chaotic about Cassie, Jake decided. Even sitting still, she gave the alarming impression that she was on the verge of knocking something over or making a mess. Good grief, the girl couldn't even manage walking into a room without falling over her own shoes! Having spent the last few years cultivating a careful sense of order and control, Jake found the aura of unpredictability Cassie exuded faintly disturbing.

He had a strong suspicion, too, that Cassie's experience of managing a venue was no wider than his own. She was clearly desperate for work, and would say whatever she thought he wanted to hear.

If he had any sense, he would close the meeting right now.

CHAPTER TWO

ON THE other hand…

On the other hand, Jake reminded himself, Sir Ian had been fond of her, and the fact that she knew the Hall was an undoubted advantage.

He could at least give her the chance to convince him that she knew what she was talking about. For old times' sake, thought Jake, looking at Cassie's mouth.

'So what would need to be done to make the Hall a venue?' he asked abruptly. 'Presumably we'd have to get a licence?'

'Absolutely,' said Cassie with more confidence than she was feeling. 'I imagine it would need quite a bit of refurbishment, too. You can charge a substantial fee for the hire of the venue, but in return couples will expect everything to be perfect. All the major rooms would have to be completely redecorated, and anything shabby or dingy replaced.'

Cassie was making it up as she went along, but

she was banking on the fact that Jake knew less than she did about what weddings involved. Besides, how difficult could it be? She couldn't let a little thing like not knowing what she was talking about stop her, not when the alternative was losing her job and having to admit to her family that she had failed again.

'Naturally you would have to set it up so that everything is laid on,' she went on, rather enjoying the authoritative note in her own voice. She would convince *herself* at this rate! 'You need to think about catering, flowers, music; whatever a bride and groom could possibly want. They're paying a lot of money for their big day, so you've got to make it very special for them.

'Some people like to make all the arrangements themselves,' she told Jake, who was listening with a kind of horrified fascination. 'But if you want the Hall to be successful you'll have to make it possible for them to hand over all the arrangements to the staff and not think about anything. That means being prepared to cater for every whim, as well as different kinds of weddings. It might just be a reception, or it might be the wedding itself, and that could include all sorts of different faiths, as well as civil partnerships.'

Cassie was really getting into her stride now. 'Then you need to think about what other facilities you're going to provide,' she said, impressing herself with her own fluency. Who would have thought she could come out with this stuff off the top of her head? All those weddings she had attended over the past few months must have paid off.

'The bride and groom will want somewhere to change, at the very least, or they might want to take over the whole house for a wedding party. You'll need new kitchens too. Loos, obviously. And, of course, you'll have to think about finding staff and making contacts with local caterers, florists, photographers and so on.

'There's marketing and publicity to consider as well,' she pointed out. 'Eventually, you'll be able to rely on word of mouth, but it'll be important until you're established.'

Jake was looking appalled. 'I didn't realise it was such a business,' he admitted. 'You mean it's not enough to clear the great hall for dancing and lay on a few white tablecloths?'

'I'm afraid not.'

There was a long pause. Jake's mouth was turned down, and Cassie could see him rethinking the whole idea.

Oh God, what if she had put him off? She bit her lip. That was what you got for showing off.

You always go a bit too far. How many times when she had been growing up had her mother said that to her? Cassie could practically hear her saying it now.

Anxiously, she watched Jake's face. It was impossible to tell what he was thinking.

'We're talking about a substantial investment,' he said slowly at last, and Cassie let out a long breath she hadn't known she was holding.

'Yes, but it'll be worth it,' she said, trying to disguise her relief. 'Weddings are big business. If you aim for the top end of the market, the house will more than pay for itself.'

Jake was still not entirely convinced. 'It's a lot to think about.'

'Not if you let us oversee everything for you,' said Cassie, marvelling at her own nerve. 'We could manage the whole project and set it up until it's ready to hand over to a permanent manager.'

It was a brilliant idea, even if she said so herself. She couldn't think why Joss hadn't thought of going into venue management before.

Jake was watching her with an indecipherable expression. Cassie lifted her chin and tried to look confident, half-expecting him to accuse her—accurately—of bluffing, but in the end he just asked how they structured their fees.

'I'd have to discuss that with Joss when we've got a clearer idea of exactly what needs to be done,' said Cassie evasively. Joss was much harder-headed when it came to money and always dealt with the financial side of things.

'OK.' Jake made up his mind abruptly. 'Let me have a detailed proposal and I'll consider it.'

'Great.' Cassie's relief was rapidly being overtaken by panic. What on earth had she committed herself to?

'So, what next?'

Yes, what next, Cassie? Cassie gulped. 'I think I need to take another look at the Hall and draw up a list of work required,' she improvised.

Fortunately, this seemed to be the right thing to say. Jake nodded. 'That makes sense. Can you come to Cornwall on Thursday? I've got to go back myself to see the solicitor, so we could drive down together if that suits you.'

It didn't, but Cassie knew better than to say so. Having bluffed this far, she couldn't give up now. A seven-hour car journey with Jake Trevelyan wasn't her idea of a fun day, but if she could pull off a contract it would be worth it.

'Of course,' she said, relaxing enough to pick up her coffee at last, and promptly splashing it over her skirt. She brushed the drops away hastily, hoping that Jake hadn't noticed. 'I can be ready to leave whenever you are.'

Jake watched Cassie practically fall out of the door, struggling with a weekend case on wheels, a motley collection of plastic carrier-bags and a handbag that kept slipping down her arm. With a sigh, he got out of the car to help her. He was double parked outside her office, and had hoped for a quick getaway, but clearly that wasn't going to happen.

He hadn't made many mistakes in the last ten years, but Jake had a nasty feeling that appointing Cassie to manage the transformation of Portrevick Hall into a wedding venue might be one of them. He had been secretly impressed by the fluent way she had talked about weddings, and by the way she had seemed to know exactly what was involved, but at the same time her lack of experience was obvious. And yet she had fixed him with those big, brown eyes and distracted him with that mouth, and before Jake had quite known what he was doing he had agreed to give her the job.

He must have been mad, he decided as he took the case from her. Cassie had to be the least organised organiser he had ever met. *Look at her*, laden with carrier bags, the wayward brown curls blowing around face, her cardigan all twisted under the weight of her handbag!

She was a mess, Jake thought disapprovingly. She was casually dressed in a mishmash of colourful garments that appeared to be thrown together without any thought for neatness or elegance. Yes, she had grown into a surprisingly pretty girl, but she could do with some of Natasha's poise and sophistication.

He stashed the carrier bags in the boot with the

case. 'What on earth do you need all this stuff for?' he demanded. 'We're only going for a couple of nights.'

'Most of it's Tina's. She came to London months ago and left half her clothes behind, so I'm taking them back to her. She's invited me to stay with her,' Cassie added.

Jake was sleeping at the Hall, and he'd suggested that Cassie stay there as well, but Cassie couldn't help thinking it all seemed a bit intimate. True, the Hall had bedrooms to spare, but they would still be sleeping in the same place, bumping into each other on the way to the bathroom, wandering into the kitchen in their PJs to make tea in the morning... No; Cassie wasn't ready to meet Jake without her make-up on yet.

'I thought I might as well stay for the weekend, since I'm down there,' she went on, talking over the roof of the car as she made her way round to the passenger door. 'I haven't seen Tina for ages. I might talk to some local contractors on Monday, too, and then come back on the train.'

Cassie knew that she was talking too much, but the prospect of the long journey in Jake's company was making her stupidly jittery. She had been fine until he'd appeared. Joss had given her unqualified approval to the plan, and Cassie had been enjoying dizzying fantasies about her new career in project management.

It had been a strange experience, seeing Jake again, and she'd been left disorientated by the way he looked familiar but behaved like a total stranger. In some ways, that made it easier to dissassociate him from the Jake she had known in the past. This Jake was less menacing than the old one, for sure. The surliness and resentment had been replaced by steely control, but it was somehow just as intimidating.

But at least she had the possibility of a job, Cassie reminded herself sternly as she got into the car. She had to concentrate on that, and not on the unnerving prospect of being shut up in a car with Jake Trevelyan. He had come straight from his office and was still wearing his suit, but, having slammed the boot shut, he took off his jacket, loosened his tie and rolled up his shirt sleeves before getting back into the driver's seat.

'Right,' he said briskly, switching on the ignition. 'Let's go.'

It was a big, luxuriously comfortable car with swish leather seats, but Cassie felt cramped and uneasy as she pulled on the seatbelt. It wouldn't have been so bad if Jake wasn't just *there*, only inches away, filling the whole car with his dark, forceful presence, using up all the available oxygen so that she had to open the window to drag in a breath.

'There's air conditioning,' said Jake, using the electric controls on his side to close it again.

Air conditioning. Right. So how come it was so hard to breathe?

'I was half-expecting you to turn up on a motorbike,' she said chattily, to conceal her nervousness.

'It's just as well I didn't, with all those bags you've brought along with you.' Jake checked his mirror, indicated and pulled out into the traffic.

'I always fancied the idea of riding pillion,' said Cassie.

'I don't think you'd fancy it all the way down to Cornwall,' Jake said, dampening her. 'You'll be much more comfortable in a car.'

Under normal circumstances, maybe, but Cassie couldn't imagine anything less comfortable than being shut up with him in a confined space for seven hours. They had barely left Fulham, but the car seemed to have shrunk already, and she was desperately aware of Jake beside her. Her eyes kept snagging on his hands, strong and competent on the steering wheel, and she would find herself remembering how they had felt on her arms as he had yanked her towards him.

Turning her head to remove them from her vision, Cassie found herself looking awkwardly out of the side window, but that was hard on her neck. Before she knew it, her eyes were skittering back to Jake's side of the car, to the line of his cheek, the corner of his mouth and the faint prickle of stubble under his jaw where he had wrenched impatiently at his tie to loosen it.

She could see the pulse beating steadily in his throat, and for one bizarre moment let herself imagine what it would be like to lean across and press her lips to it. Then she imagined Jake jerking away in horror and losing control of the car, which would crash into that newsagent's, and then the police would come and she would have to make a statement: *I'm sorry, officer, I was just overcome by an uncontrollable urge to kiss Jake Trevelyan.*

It would be in all the papers, and in no time at all the news would reach the Portrevick Arms, where they would all snigger. Village memories were long. No one would have forgotten what a fool she had made of herself over Rupert, and they would shake their heads and tell each other that Cassandra Grey never had been able to keep her hands off a man...

Cassie's heart was thumping just at the thought of it, and she jerked her head back to the side, ignoring the protest of her neck muscles.

Comfortable? Hah!

'Besides,' Jake went on as Cassie offered up thanks that he hadn't spent the last ten years learning to read minds, 'I haven't got a motorbike any more. I've left my biking days behind me.'

It would have been impossible to imagine Jake without that mean-looking bike years ago in Portrevick.

'You've changed,' said Cassie.

'I sincerely hope so,' said Jake.

Why couldn't she have changed that much? Cassie wondered enviously. If she had, she could be svelte and sophisticated, with a successful career behind her, instead of muddling along feeling most of the time much as she had at seventeen. She might look different, but deep down she felt just the same as she had done then. How had Jake done it?

'What have you been doing for the past ten years?' she asked him curiously.

'I've been in the States for most of them. I got myself a degree, and then did an MBA at Harvard.'

'*Really?*' said Cassie, impressed. In all the years she had wondered where Jake Trevelyan was and what he was doing, she had never considered that he might be at university. She had imagined him surfing, perhaps, or running a bar on some beach somewhere, or possibly making shady deals astride his motorbike—but *Harvard*? Even her father would be impressed by that.

'I had no idea,' she said.

Jake shrugged. 'I was lucky. I went to work for a smallish firm in Seattle, just as it was poised for expansion. It was an exciting time, and it gave me a lot of valuable experience. That company was at the forefront of digital technology, and Primordia is in the same field, which put me in a good position when they were looking for a new Chief Executive, although it took some negotiation to get me back to London.'

'Didn't you want to come back?'

'Not particularly. But they made me an offer even I couldn't refuse.'

'You were head-hunted?' said Cassie, trying to imagine a company going out of its way to recruit her. *Cassandra Grey's just the person we want for this job*, they would say. *How can we tempt her?*

Nope, she couldn't do it.

Jake obviously took the whole business for granted. 'That's how it works.' He pulled up at a red light and glanced at Cassie. 'What about you? How long have you been with Avalon?'

'Just since the beginning of the year. Before that I was a receptionist,' she said. 'I did a couple of stints in retail, a bit of temping, a bit of waitressing…'

She sighed. 'Not a very impressive career, as my father is always pointing out. I'm a huge disappointment to my parents. The others have all done really well. They all went to Cambridge. Liz is a doctor, Tom's an architect and even Jack is a lawyer now. They're all grown-ups, and I'm just the family problem.'

Cassie had intended the words to sound humorous, but was uneasily aware they had come out rather flat. Rather as if she didn't think it was such a funny joke after all. 'They're always ringing each other up and wondering what to do about Cassie.'

But that was all going to change, she reminded

herself. This could be the start of a whole new career. She was going to turn Portrevick Hall into a model venue. Celebrities would be queuing up to get married there. After a year or two, they wouldn't even have to advertise. Just mentioning that a wedding would be at Portrevick Hall would mean that it would be the last word in style and elegance.

Cassandra Grey? they would say. *Isn't she the one who made Portrevick Hall a byword for chic and exclusive?* She would get tired of calls from the head-hunters. *Not again*, she would sigh. *When are you people going to get the message that I don't want to commit to one job?* Because, of course, by then she would be a consultant. She had always fancied the thought of being one of those.

Cassie settled herself more comfortably in her seat, liking the way this fantasy was going. All those smart hotels in London would be constantly ringing her up and begging her to come and sort out their events facilities—and probably not just in London, now she came to think of it. She would have an international reputation.

Yes, she'd get tired of jetting off to New York and Dubai and Sydney. Cassie smiled to herself. Liz, Tom and Jack would still be ringing each other up, but instead of worrying about her they would be complaining about how humdrum their sensible careers seemed in comparison with her glamorous life. *I'm sick of Cassie telling me she'd really just like a few days at home doing nothing*, Liz would grumble.

'And what's Cassie going to do about herself?' asked Jake, breaking rudely into her dream.

'I'm going to do what I'm doing,' she told him firmly. 'I love working for Joss at Avalon. It's the best job I've ever had, and I'll do anything to keep it.'

Even pretending to understand about project management, she added mentally.

'What does a wedding planner *do* all day?'

'It could be anything,' she said. 'I might book string quartets, or find exactly the right shade of ribbon, or source an unusual cake-topper. I love the variety. I can be helping a bride to choose her dress one minute, and sorting out accommodation for the wedding party the next. And then, of course, I get to go to all the weddings.'

Jake made a face. He couldn't think of anything worse. 'It sounds hellish,' he said frankly. 'Don't you get bored?'

'Never,' said Cassie. 'I love weddings. I cry every time—I do!' she insisted when he looked at her in disbelief.

'Why? These people are clients, not friends.'

'They feel like friends by the time we've spent months together planning the wedding,' she retorted. 'But it doesn't matter whether I know the bride and groom or not. I always want to cry when I walk past Chelsea register office and see people on the steps after they've got married. I love seeing everyone so happy. A wedding is such a *hopeful* occasion.'

'In spite of all the evidence to the contrary,' said Jake astringently. 'How many of those weddings you're snivelling at this year will end in divorce by the end of the next? Talk about the triumph of hope over experience!'

'But that's exactly why weddings are so moving,' said Cassie. 'They're about people choosing to love each other. Lots of people get married more than once. They know how difficult marriage can be, but they still want to make that commitment. I think it's wonderful,' she added defiantly. 'What have you got against marriage, anyway?'

'I've got nothing against marriage,' said Jake. 'It's all the expense and fuss of weddings that I find pointless. It seems to me that marriage is a serious business, and you should approach it in a serious way, not muddle it all up with big dresses, flowers, cakes and whatever else goes on at weddings these days.'

'Weddings are meant to be a celebration,' she reminded him. 'What do you want the bride and groom to do instead—sit down and complete a checklist?'

'At least then they would know they were compatible.'

Cassie rolled her eyes. 'So what would be on your checklist?'

'I'd want to know that the woman I was marrying was intelligent, and sensible…and confident,' Jake decided. 'More importantly, I'd need to be sure that we shared the same goals, that we both had the same attitude to success in our careers…and sex, of course…and to little things like tidiness that can put the kybosh on a relationship quicker than anything else.'

'You don't ask for much, do you?' said Cassie tartly, reflecting that she wouldn't get many ticks on Jake's checklist. In fact, if he had set out to describe her exact opposite, he could hardly have done a better job. 'Clever, confident, successful and tidy. Where are you going to find a paragon like that?'

'I already have,' said Jake.

Oh.

'Oh,' said Cassie, unaccountably put out. 'What's her name?'

'Natasha. We've been together six months.'

'So why haven't you married her if she's so perfect?' Try as she might, Cassie couldn't keep the snippiness from her voice.

'We just haven't got round to talking about it,' said Jake. 'I think it would be a good move, though. It makes sense.'

'Makes sense?' echoed Cassie in disbelief. 'You should get married because you're in love, not because it *makes sense*!'

'In my book, committing yourself to someone for

life because you're in love is what *doesn't* make sense,' he retorted.

Crikey, whatever happened to romance? Cassie shook her head. 'Well, if you ever decide that doing a checklist together isn't quite enough, remember that Avalon can help you plan your wedding.'

'I'll bear it in mind,' he said. 'I imagine Natasha would like a wedding of some kind, but she's a very successful solicitor, so she wouldn't have the time to organise much herself.'

Of course, Natasha *would* be a successful solicitor, Cassie thought, having taken a dislike to his perfect girlfriend without ever having met her. She was tempted to say that Natasha would no doubt be too busy being marvellous to have time to bother with anything as inconsequential as a wedding, but remembered in time that Avalon's business relied on brides being too busy to do everything themselves.

Besides, it might sound as if she was jealous of Natasha.

Which was nonsense, of course.

'I certainly wouldn't know where to start,' Jake went on. 'Weddings are unfamiliar territory to me.'

'You must have been to loads of weddings, mustn't you?'

'Very few,' he said. 'In fact, only a couple. I lived in the States until last year, so I missed out on various family weddings.'

'I don't know how you managed to avoid them,'

said Cassie. 'All my friends seem have got married in the last year or so. There was a time when it felt as if I was going to a wedding every other weekend, and that was just people I knew! It was as if it was catching. Suddenly everyone was married.'

'Everyone except you?'

'That's what it feels like, anyway,' she said with little sigh.

'Why not you? You're obviously not averse to the idea of getting married.'

'I just haven't found the right guy, I suppose.' Cassie sighed again. 'I've had boyfriends, of course, but none of them have had that special something.'

Jake slanted a sardonic glance at her. 'Don't tell me you're still holding out for Rupert Branscombe Fox?'

'Of course not,' she said, flushing with embarrassment at the memory of the massive crush she had had on Rupert.

Not that she could really blame herself. What seventeen-year-old girl could be expected to resist that lethal combination of good looks and glamour? And Rupert could be extraordinarily charming when he wanted to be. He wasn't so charming when he didn't, of course, as Cassie had discovered even before Jake had kissed her.

Whoops; she didn't want to be thinking about that kiss, did she?

Too late.

Cassie tried the looking-out-of-the window thing again, but London was a blur, and she was back outside the Hall again, being yanked against Jake again. She could smell the leather of his jacket, feel the hardness of his body and the unforgiving steel of the motorbike.

In spite of Cassie's increasingly desperate efforts to keep her eyes on the interminable houses lining the road, they kept sliding round to Jake's profile. The traffic was heavy and he was concentrating on driving, so she gave in and let them skitter over the angular planes of his face to the corner of his mouth, at which point her heart started thumping and thudding alarmingly.

It was ten years later. Jake had changed completely. The leather jacket had gone, the bike had gone.

But that mouth was still exactly the same.

That mouth… She knew what it felt like. She knew how it tasted. She knew just how warm and sure those firm lips could be. Jake was an austere stranger beside her now, but she had *kissed* him. The memory was so vivid and so disorientating that Cassie felt quite giddy for a moment.

She swallowed. 'I had a major crush on Rupert, but it was just a teenage thing. Remember what a gawk I was?' she said, removing her gaze firmly back to the road. 'I have this fantasy that if I bumped into Rupert now he wouldn't recognise me.'

'I recognised you,' Jake pointed out unhelpfully.

'Yes, well, that's the thing about fantasies,' Cassie retorted in a tart voice. 'They're not real. I'm never likely to meet Rupert again. He lives in a different world, and the closest I get to him is seeing his picture in a celebrity magazine with some incredibly beautiful woman on his arm. Even if by some remote chance I did meet him I know he wouldn't even *notice* me, let along recognise me.'

'Why not?'

'Oh, I'm much too ordinary for the likes of Rupert,' said Cassie with a sigh. 'You were right about that, anyway.'

Jake looked taken aback. 'When did I ever say you were ordinary?'

'You know when.' She flashed him an accusing glance. 'After the Allentide Ball.' *After you kissed me.* 'Before you punched Rupert on the nose. I gather you took it upon yourself to tell Rupert I wasn't nearly sophisticated enough for him.'

It still rankled after all these years.

'You weren't,' said Jake.

'Then why were you fighting?'

'Not because Rupert leapt to defend your sophistication and readiness to embark on a torrid affair, if that's what you were thinking!'

'He said you'd been offensive,' said Cassie.

'Did he?' said Jake with a certain grimness.

It was typical of Rupert to have twisted the truth, he thought. He had been sitting at the bar, having a quiet drink, when Rupert had strolled in with his usual tame audience. Jake had found Rupert's arrogance difficult to deal with at the best of times, and that night certainly hadn't been one of those.

Jake often wondered how his life would have turned out if he hadn't been in a particularly bad temper that night. The raw, piercing sweetness of Cassie's kiss at the Allentide ball had caught him unawares, and it didn't help that she had so patently been using him to attract Rupert's attention. Jake had been left feeling edgy, and furious with himself for expecting that it could have been any different and caring one way or the other.

And then Rupert had been there, showing off as usual. He'd been boasting about having had the estate manager's ungainly daughter, and making the others laugh. Jake's hand had clenched around his glass. He might not have liked being used, but Cassie was very young. She hadn't deserved to have her first experience of sex made the subject of pub banter.

Rupert had gone on and on, enjoying his audience, and Jake had finally had enough. He'd set down his glass very deliberately and risen to his feet to face Rupert. There had been a chorus of taunting, 'Ooohs' when he'd told him to leave

Cassie alone, but he'd at least had the satisfaction of wiping the smirks off all their faces.

Especially Rupert's. Jake smiled ferociously as he remembered how he had released years of pent-up resentment. The moment his fist had connected with Rupert's nose had been a sweet one, and worth being banned from the village pub for. If it hadn't been for that fight, Rupert wouldn't have talked about assault charges, news of the fight wouldn't have reached Sir Ian's ears, and he wouldn't be where he was now.

Oh yes; it had definitely been worth it.

CHAPTER THREE

'It's my word against Rupert's, I suppose, but I can tell you, I was never offensive about you,' he said to Cassie. 'And being ordinary isn't the same thing as not being sophisticated. Believe me, you've never struck me as ordinary!'

'But I am,' said Cassie glumly. 'Or I am compared to Rupert, anyway. He's just so glamorous. Even you'd have to admit that.'

Jake's snort suggested he wasn't prepared to admit anything of the kind.

Of course, he'd never had any time for Rupert. Cassie supposed she could understand it. Rupert might be handsome, but even at the height of her crush she had recognised that arrogance in him as well. At the time, she had thought that it just added to his air of glamour.

The truth was that she still had a soft spot for Rupert, so good-looking and so badly behaved. In another age, he would have been a rake, ravishing women left, right and centre. Cassie could just see him in breeches and ruffles, smiling that irresistible smile, and breaking hearts without a flicker of shame.

Not the kind of man you would want to marry, perhaps, but very attractive all the same.

Cassie sighed a little wistfully. 'Rupert could be very charming,' she tried to explain, not that Jake was likely to be convinced.

They had barely got going on the motorway, and already overhead gantries were flashing messages about queues ahead. Muttering in frustration, he eased his foot up from the accelerator.

'What's so charming about squandering an inheritance from your parents and then sponging off your uncle?' he demanded irritably. 'Sir Ian got tired of bailing him out in the end, but he did what he could to encourage Rupert to settle down. He left his fortune to Rupert in trust until he's forty, in the hope that by then he'll have come to his senses.'

'*Forty?*' Cassie gasped. Rupert was only in his early thirties, like Jake, and eight years would be an eternity to wait when you had a lifestyle like Rupert's. 'That's awful,' she said without thinking. 'What's he going to do?'

'He could always try getting a job like the rest of us,' said Jake astringently 'Or, if he really can't bring himself to do anything as sordid as earning his own living, he can always get married. Sir Ian specified that the trust money could be released if Rupert gets married and settles down. He can't just marry anyone to get his hands on the money, though. He'll have to convince me as trustee that it's a real marriage and his wife a sensible woman before I'll release the funds.'

'Gosh, Rupert must have been livid when he found out!'

'He wasn't too happy,' Jake agreed with masterly understatement. 'He tried to contest the will, and when he didn't get anywhere with that he suggested we try and discuss things in a "civilised" way—which I gather meant me ignoring Sir Ian's wishes and handing the estate over to him to do with as he pleased.

'I was prepared to be civilised, of course. I invited him round for a drink, and it was just like old times,' he went on ironically. 'Rupert was arrogant and patronising, and I wanted to break his nose again!'

'You didn't!'

'No,' admitted Jake. 'But I don't know what would have happened if Natasha hadn't been there.'

'What did she make of Rupert?'

'She thought he was shallow.'

'I bet she thought he was gorgeous too,' said Cassie with a provocative look, and Jake pokered up and looked down his nose.

'Natasha is much too sensible to judge people on their appearances,' he said stiffly.

Of course she was. Cassie rolled her eyes as they overtook a van that was hogging the middle lane, startling the driver, who gave a grimace that was well out of Jake's field of vision. The van moved smartly into the slow lane.

'So how come she got involved with you if she's so sensible?' she asked, forgetting for a moment that Jake was an important client.

'We get on very well,' said Jake austerely.

'What does getting on very well mean, exactly?'

Ahead, there was a flurry of red lights as cars braked, and Jake moved smoothly into the middle lane. 'It means we're very compatible,' he said.

And they were. Natasha was everything he admired in a woman. She was very attractive—beautiful, in fact—and clear-thinking. She didn't constantly demand emotional reassurance the way his previous girlfriends had. She was focused on her own career, and understood if he had to work late, as he often did. She never made a fuss.

And she was classy. That was a large part of her appeal, Jake was prepared to admit. Years ago in Portrevick, Natasha wouldn't have looked at him twice, but when he walked into a party with her on his arm now he knew that he had arrived. She was everything Jake had never known when he was growing up. She had the assurance that came from a life of wealth and privilege, and every time Jake looked at her she reassured him that he had left Portrevick and the past behind him at last.

He didn't feel like telling Cassie all of that, though.

The traffic had slowed to a crawl and Jake shifted gear. 'I hope this is just sheer weight of traffic,' he said. 'I don't want to spend any more time on the road than we have to.'

Nor did Cassie. She wriggled in her seat. Quite apart from anything else, she was starving. Afraid that she would be late, she hadn't had time for breakfast that morning, and her stomach was gurgling ominously. She was hoping Jake would stop for petrol at some point, but at this rate they'd be lucky to get to a service station for supper, let alone lunch.

The lines of cars were inching forward in a staggered pattern. Sometimes the lane on their left would have a spurt of movement, only to grind to a halt as the supposed fast-lane speeded up, and then it would be the middle lane's turn. They kept passing or being passed by the same cars, and Cassie was beginning to recognise the occupants.

An expensive saloon on their left was creeping ahead of them once more. Covertly, Cassie studied the driver and passenger, both of whom were staring grimly ahead and not talking.

'I bet they've had a row,' she said.

'Who?'

'The couple on our left in the blue car.' Cassie pointed discreetly. 'Have a look when we go past. I can't decide whether she left the top off the toothpaste again, or whether she's incredibly possessive and sulking because he just had a text from his secretary.'

Jake cast her an incredulous glance. 'What's wrong with getting a text from your secretary?'

'She thinks he's having an affair with her,' said Cassie, barely pausing to consider. 'She insists on answering his phone while he's driving. Of course the text was completely bland, just confirming some meeting or something, but she just *knows* that it's a code.'

It was their lane's turn to move. Against his better judgement, Jake found himself glancing left as they passed. Cassie was right; the people both looked hatched-faced.

'They could be going to visit the in-laws,' he suggested, drawn into the fantasy in spite of himself.

Cassie took another look. 'You might be right,' she allowed. 'Her parents?'

'His, I think. She's got a face like concrete, so she's doing something she doesn't want to do. They don't really approve of her.'

'Hey, you're good at this!' Cassie laughed and swivelled back to watch the traffic. 'Now, who have we got here?' They were passing a hatchback driven by an elderly man who was clutching onto the wheel for dear life. Beside him, a tiny old lady was talking. 'Grandparents off to visit their daughter,' she said instantly. 'Too easy.'

'Perhaps they've been having a wild affair and are running away together,' said Jake, tongue in cheek.

'I like the way you're thinking, but they look way too comfortable together for that. I bet she's been talking for hours and he hasn't heard a word.'

'Can't imagine what that feels like,' murmured Jake, and she shot him a look.

'I wonder what they think about us?' she mused.

'I doubt very much that anyone else is thinking about us at all.'

'We must look like any other couple heading out of town for a long weekend,' said Cassie, ignoring him.

Perhaps that was why it felt so intimate sitting here beside him. If they were a couple, she could rest her hand on Jake's thigh. She could unwrap a toffee and pop it in his mouth without thinking. She could put her feet up on the dashboard and choose some music, and they could argue about which was the best route. She could nag him about stopping for something to eat.

But of course she couldn't do any of that. Especially not laying a hand on his leg.

She turned her attention firmly back to the other

cars. 'Ooh, now…' she said, spying a single middle-aged man looking harassed at the wheel of his car, and instantly wove a complicated story about the double life he was leading, naming both wives, all five children and even the hamster with barely a pause for breath.

Jake shook his head. He tried to imagine Natasha speculating about the occupants of the other cars, and couldn't do it. She would think it childish. As it was, thought Jake.

On the other hand, this traffic jam was a lot less tedious than others he had sat in. Cassie's expression was animated, and he was very aware of her beside him. She had pushed back the seat as far as it would go, and her legs, in vivid blue tights, were stretched out before her. Her mobile face was alight with humour, her hands in constant motion. Jake had a jumbled impression of colour and warmth tugging at the edges of his vision the whole time. It was very distracting.

Now she was pulling faces at a little boy in the back seat of the car beside them. He crossed his eyes and stuck out his tongue, while Cassie stuck her thumbs in her ears and waggled her fingers in response.

Jake was torn between exasperation and amusement. He didn't know where Cassie got her idea that she was ordinary. There was absolutely nothing ordinary about her that he could see.

He glanced at the clock as they inched forward. It was a bad sign that they were hitting heavy traffic this early. It wasn't even midday, and already they seemed to have been travelling for ever.

Cassie had fallen silent at last. Bizarrely, Jake almost missed her ridiculous stories. Suddenly there was a curdled growl that startled him out of his distraction. He glanced at Cassie in surprise and she blushed and folded her arms over her stomach.

'Sorry, that was me,' she apologised. 'I didn't have time for breakfast.'

How embarrassing! Cassie was mortified. Natasha's stomach would never even murmur. At least Jake seemed prepared to cope with the problem.

'We'll stop and get something to eat when we get out of this,' he promised, but it was another twenty minutes before the blockage cleared, miraculously and for no apparent reason, and he could put his foot down.

To Cassie's disappointment they didn't stop at the first service-station they came to, or even the second. 'We need to get as far on our way as we can,' Jake said, but as her stomach became increasingly vocal he eventually relented as they came up to the third.

After a drizzly summer, the sun had finally come out for September. 'Let's sit outside,' Cassie suggested when they had bought coffee and sandwiches. 'We should make the most of the sun while we've got it.'

They found a wooden table in a sunny spot, away from the ceaseless growl of the motorway. Cassie turned sideways so that she could straddle the bench, and turned her face up to the sun.

'I love September,' she said. 'It still feels like the start of a new school year. I want to sharpen my pencils and write my name at the front of a blank exercise-book.'

Perhaps that was why she was so excited about transforming Portrevick Hall into a wedding venue, Cassie thought as she unwrapped her sandwich. It was a whole new project, her chance to draw a line under all her past muddles and mistakes and start afresh. She was determined not to mess up this time.

'It's great to get out of London too,' she went on indistinctly through a mouthful of egg mayonnaise. 'I'm really looking forward to seeing Portrevick again, too. I haven't been back since my parents moved away, but the place where you grow up always feels like home, doesn't it?'

'No,' said Jake.

'Really?' Cassie was brushing egg from her skirt, but at that she looked up at him in surprise. 'Don't you miss it at all?'

'I miss the sea sometimes,' he said after a

moment. 'But Portrevick? No. It's not such a romantic place to live when there's never any money, and the moment there's trouble the police are at your door wanting you to account for where you've been and what you've been doing.'

Jake could hear the bitterness seeping into his voice in spite of every effort to keep it neutral. Cassie had no idea. She had grown up in a solid, cosy house in a solid, cosy, middle-class family. They might have lived in the same place, but they had inhabited different worlds.

Miss it? He had spent ten years trying to put Portrevick behind him.

'You must have family still there, though, mustn't you?' said Cassie. There had always been lots of Trevelyans in Portrevick, all of them reputedly skirting around the edges of the law.

'Not in Portrevick,' said Jake. 'There's no work in a village like that any more.' And there were richer pickings in places like Newquay or Penzance, he thought dryly. 'They've all moved away, so there's no one to go back for. If it wasn't for Sir Ian and the trust, I'd be happy never to see Portrevick again. And once I've sorted out something for the Hall I'll be leaving and I won't ever be going back.'

Cassie was having trouble keeping the filling in her sandwich. The egg kept oozing out of the baguette and dropping everywhere. Why hadn't she chosen a nice, neat sandwich like Jake's ham and cheese? He was managing to eat his without any mess at all.

She eyed him under her lashes as she licked her finger and gathered up some of the crumbs that were scattered on her side of the table. Jake had always been such a cool figure in her memories of Portrevick that it had never occurred to her to wonder how happy he had been.

He hadn't seemed unhappy. In Cassie's mind, he had always flirted with danger, roaring around on his motorbike or surfing in the roughest seas. She could still see him, sleek and dark as a seal in his wetsuit, riding the surf, his body leaning and bending in tune with the rolling wave.

It was hard to believe it was the same man as the one who sat across the table from her now, contained and controlled, eating his sandwich methodically. What had happened to that fierce, reckless boy?

Abandoning her sandwich for a moment, Cassie took a sip of coffee. 'If you feel like that about Portrevick, why did you agree to be Sir Ian's trustee?'

'Because I owed him.'

Jake had finished his own sandwich and brushed the crumbs from his fingers. 'It was Sir Ian that got me out of Portrevick,' he told her. 'He was always good to my mother, and after she died he let me earn

some money by doing odd jobs for him. He was
from a different world, but I liked him. He was the
only person in the village who'd talk to you as if he
was really interested in what you had to say. I was
just a difficult kid from a problem family, but I never
once had the feeling that Sir Ian was looking down
on me.'

Unlike his nephew, Jake added to himself.
Rupert got up every morning, looked in the mirror
and found himself perfect. From the dizzying
heights of his pedestal, how could he do anything
but look down on lesser mortals? A boy from a
dubious family and without the benefit of private
schooling... Well, clearly Jake ought to be grateful
that Rupert had ever noticed him at all.

'Sir Ian was lovely,' Cassie was agreeing. 'I know
he was a bit eccentric, but he always made you feel
that you were the one person he really wanted to
see.'

Jake nodded. He had felt that, too. 'I saw him the
day after that fight with Rupert,' he went on.
'Rupert was all set to press assault charges against
me, but Sir Ian said he would persuade him to drop
them. In return, he told me I should leave
Portrevick. He said that if I stayed I would never
shake off my family's reputation. There would be
other fights, other brushes with the police. I'd drift
over the line the way my father had done and end
up in prison.'

Turning the beaker between his hands, Jake looked broodingly down into his coffee, remembering the conversation. Sir Ian hadn't pulled his punches. 'You're a bright lad,' he had said. 'But you're in danger of wasting all the potential you've got. You're eaten up with resentment, you're a troublemaker and you take stupid risks. If you're not careful, you'll end up in prison too. You can make a new life for yourself if you want it, but you're going to have to work for it. Are you prepared to do that?'

Jake could still feel that churning sense of elation at the prospect of escape, all mixed up with what had felt like a shameful nervousness about leaving everything familiar behind. There had been anger and resentment, too, mostly with Rupert, but also with Cassie, whose clumsy attempt to make Rupert jealous had precipitated the fight, and the offer that would change his life if he was brave enough to take it.

'The upshot was that Sir Ian said that he would sponsor me through university if I wanted the chance to start afresh somewhere new,' he told Cassie. 'It was an extraordinarily generous offer,' he said. 'It was my chance to escape from Portrevick, and I took it. I walked out of the Hall and didn't look back.'

'Was that when…?' Cassie stopped, realising too late where the question was leading, and a smile touched Jake's mouth.

'When you accosted me on my bike?' he suggested.

Cassie could feel herself turning pink, but she could hardly pretend now that she didn't remember that kiss. 'I seem to remember it was *you* who accosted *me*, wasn't it?' she said with as much dignity as she could, and Jake's smile deepened.

'I was provoked,' he excused himself.

'*Provoked?*' Cassie sat up straight, embarrassment forgotten in outrage. 'I did *not* provoke you!'

'You certainly did,' said Jake coolly. 'I wasn't in the mood to listen to you defending Rupert. He asked for that punch, and it was only because he was all set to report me to the police that Sir Ian suggested I leave Portrevick.

'That turned out to be the best thing that could have happened to me,' he allowed. 'And I'm grateful in retrospect. But it didn't feel like that at the time. It felt as if Rupert could behave as badly as he liked and that silver spoon would stay firmly stuck in his mouth. I knew nobody would ever suggest that *Rupert* should leave everything he'd ever known and work for his living. I was angry, excited and confused, and I'm afraid you got in the way.'

He paused and looked straight at Cassie, the dark-blue eyes gleaming with unmistakable amusement. 'If it's any comfort, that kiss was my last memory of Portrevick.'

That kiss... The memory of it shimmered between them, so vividly that for one jangling moment it was as if they were kissing again, as if his fingers were still twined in her hair, her lips still parting as she melted into him, that wicked excitement still tumbling along her veins.

With an effort, Cassie dragged her gaze away and buried her burning face in her coffee cup. 'Nice to know that I was memorable,' she muttered.

'You were certainly that,' said Jake.

'Yes, well, it was all a long time ago.' Cassie cleared her throat and cast around for something, anything, to change the subject. 'I'd no idea Sir Ian helped you like that,' she managed at last, seizing on the first thing she could think of. 'We all assumed you'd just taken off to avoid the assault charges.'

'That doesn't surprise me. Portrevick was always ready to think the worst of me,' said Jake, gathering up the debris of their lunch. 'Sir Ian wasn't the type to boast about his generosity, but I kept in touch all the time, and as soon as I was in a position to do so I offered to repay all the money he'd spent on my education. He flatly refused to take it, but he did say there was one thing I could do for him, and that was when he asked me to be his executor and the trustee. He asked me if I would make sure that the Portrevick estate stayed intact. You know how much he loved the Hall.'

Cassie nodded. 'Yes, he did.'

'I can't say I liked the idea of taking on a complicated trust, and I knew how much Rupert would resent me, but I owed Sir Ian too much to refuse. So,' said Jake, 'that's why we're driving down this motorway. That's why I want to get the Hall established as a venue. Once it's up and running, and self-supporting, I'll feel as if I've paid my debt to him at last. I'll have done what Sir Ian asked me to do, and then I really can put Portrevick and the past behind me once and for all.'

He drained his coffee and shoved the sandwich wrappers inside the empty cup. 'Have you finished? We've still got a long way to go, so let's hit the road again.'

Cassie studied Portrevick Hall with affection as she cut across the grounds to the sweep of gravel at its imposing entrance. A rambling manor-house dating back to the middle ages, it had grown organically as succeeding generations had added a wing here, a turret there. The result was a muddle of architectural styles that time had blended into a harmonious if faintly dilapidated whole, with crumbling terraces looking out over what had once been landscaped gardens.

It was charming from any angle, Cassie decided, and would make a wonderful backdrop for wedding photos.

Her feet crunched on the gravel as she walked up to the front door and pulled the ancient bell, deliberately avoiding looking at where Jake had sat astride his motorbike that day. She wouldn't have been at all surprised to see the outline of her feet still scorched into the stones.

Don't think about it, she told herself sternly. She was supposed to be impressing Jake with her professionalism, and she was going to have to try a lot harder today after babbling on in the car yesterday. Jake had dropped her at Tina's and driven off with barely a goodbye, and Cassie didn't blame him. He must have been sick of listening to her inane chatter for seven hours.

So today she was going to concentrate on being cool, calm and competent.

Which was easily said but harder to remember, when Jake opened the door and her heart gave a sickening lurch . He was wearing jeans and a blue Guernsey with the sleeves pushed above his wrists; without the business suit he looked younger and more approachable.

And very attractive.

'Come in,' he said. 'I was just making coffee. Do you want some?'

'Thanks.' Cassie followed him down a long, stone-flagged corridor to the Hall's vast kitchen. Without those unsettling blue eyes on her face, she could admire his lean figure and easy stride.

'Quite a looker now, isn't he?' Tina had said when they were catching up over a bottle of wine the night before. 'And rich too, I hear. You should go for it, Cassie. You always did have a bit of a thing for him.'

'No, I didn't!' said Cassie, ruffled. A thing for Jake Trevelyan? The very idea!

'Remember that Allantide Ball…?' Tina winked. 'I'm sure Jake does. Do you think you could be in with a chance?'

'No,' said Cassie, and then was horrified to hear how glum she sounded about it. 'I mean, no,' she tried again brightly. 'He's already got a perfect girl-friend.'

'Shame,' said Tina.

And the worst thing was that a tiny bit of Cassie was thinking the same thing as she watched Jake making the coffee.

Which was very unprofessional of her.

Giving herself a mental slap, Cassie pulled out her Netbook and made a show of looking around the kitchen. They might as well get down to business straight away.

'The kitchen will need replacing as a priority,' she said. 'You couldn't do professional catering in here. There's plenty of space, which is good, but it needs gutting and proper catering equipment installed.'

Jake could see that made sense. 'Get some quotes.' He nodded.

Cassie tapped in 'kitchen—get quotes' and felt efficient.

'We should start with the great hall and see how much work needs to be done there,' she went on, encouraged. 'That's the obvious place for wedding ceremonies.'

'Fine by me,' said Jake, handing her a mug. 'Let's take our coffee with us.'

The great hall had been the heart of the medieval house, but its stone walls had been panelled in the seventeenth century, and a grand wooden-staircase now swept down from a gallery on the first floor. At one end, a vast fireplace dominated an entire wall, and there was a dais at the other.

'Perfect for the high table,' said Cassie, pointing at it with her mug. Netbook under one arm, coffee clutched in her other hand, she turned slowly, imagining the space filled with people. 'They'll love this,' she enthused. 'I can see it being really popular for winter weddings.

'I always dreamed about having a Christmas wedding here,' she confided to Jake, who was also looking around, but with a lot less enthusiasm. 'There was going to be a fire burning, an enormous Christmas tree with lights, candles everywhere… Outside it would be cold and dark, but in here it would be warm and cosy.'

Funny how she could remember that fantasy so vividly after all this time. In her dream, Cassie was up there on the dais, looking beautiful and elegant—naturally—with Rupert, who gazed tenderly down at her. Her family were gathered round, bursting with pride in her, and Sir Ian was there, too, beaming with delight.

Cassie sighed.

'Anyway, I think it could look wonderful, don't you?'

Jake's mouth turned down as he studied the hall. 'Not really. It looks pretty dingy and gloomy to me.'

'That's because it's been empty for a while, and it needs a good clean. You've got to use your imagination,' said Cassie. Perching on an immense wooden trestle-table, she laid the Netbook down and sipped at her own coffee. It was cool in the hall, and she was glad of the warmth.

'It wouldn't be so different from the Allantide Ball,' she said. 'Remember how Sir Ian used to decorate it with candles and apples and it looked really inviting?'

Then she wished that she hadn't mentioned the Allantide Ball. In spite of herself, her eyes flickered to where Jake had been standing that night. She had been over by the stairs when she had spotted him. She could retrace her route across the floor, aware of the dark-blue eyes watching her approach, and a sharp little frisson shivered down her spine just as it had ten years ago.

And over there was the door leading out to the terrace… Cassie remembered the mixture of panic and excitement as Jake had taken her hand and led her out into the dark. She could still feel his hard hands on her, still feel her heart jerking frantically, and her blood still pounded at the devastating sureness of his lips.

Swallowing, she risked a glance at Jake and found her gaze snared on his. He was watching her with a faint, mocking smile, and although nothing was said she knew—she just *knew*—that he was remembering that kiss, too. The very air seemed to be jangling with the memory of that wretched ball, and Cassie wrenched her eyes away. What on earth had possessed her to mention it?

She sipped her coffee, trying desperately to think of something to say to break the awkward silence, and show Jake that she hadn't forgotten that she was here to do a job.

'What would you think about holding an Allantide Ball this year?' she said, starting slowly but gathering pace as she realised that the idea, born of desperation, might not be such a bad one after all. 'As a kind of memorial to Sir Ian? It would be good publicity.'

'No one would come,' said Jake. 'I'm not exactly popular in Portrevick. I went into the pub the last time I came down and there was dead silence when I walked in. I felt about as welcome as a cup of cold sick.'

Cassie had gathered something of that from Tina. Apparently there was much speculation in the village about Sir Ian's will, and the general feeling was that Jake had somehow pulled a fast one for his own nefarious purposes, in keeping with the Trevelyan tradition.

'That's because they don't know the truth,' she said. 'Inviting everyone to the ball for Sir Ian and explaining what you're planning for the Hall would make them see that you're not just out to make a quick buck. You need the locals on your side if the wedding venue is to be a success,' she went on persuasively. 'I think this would be a great way to kick things off.'

CHAPTER FOUR

'I'm DAMNED if I'm going to waste my time sucking up to Portrevick,' said Jake, a mulish look about his mouth..

'You won't have to. I'll do it for you,' said Cassie soothingly. 'You won't need to do anything but turn up on 31st October, put on a tux and be civil for two or three hours. You can manage that, can't you?'

'I suppose so,' he said grudgingly.

'It'll be worth it when you can walk away and know the Hall is established as part of the community and has local support,' she encouraged him. 'If you want to fulfil Sir Ian's wishes, then this is the best way you can go about it.'

Jake looked at her; she was sitting on the old table and swinging her legs. She was a vibrant figure in the gloomy hall with her bright cardigan, bright face and bright, unruly hair. She didn't look sensible, but he had a feeling that what she had said just might be.

'It's not long to Allantide,' he pointed out. 'You'll never get contractors in that quickly.'

'We will if you're prepared to pay for it,' said Cassie, gaining confidence with every word. 'We've got six weeks. If we aimed to have the great hall redecorated by then, it would give us a real incentive to get things moving.'

Narrowing her eyes, she pictured the hall decorated and full of people. 'It's not as if any major structural work is required. It just needs cleaning up a bit.'

She flicked open her Netbook and began typing notes to herself. This was good. There had been a nasty little wobble there when she'd remembered the time they had kissed, but she was feeling under control again now. Cool, calm, competent; wasn't that how she was supposed to be?

OK, maybe she wasn't *calm*, exactly—not with the unsettling feeling that seemed to fizz under her skin whenever she looked at Jake—but at least she was giving a good impression of competence for once.

'The more I think about it, the more I like the idea,' she said. 'We can use the ball to start spreading the word that the Hall can be hired for special occasions. We'll invite the local paper here to take some pictures…oh! And we can have some photos done for a website too, so people can see how fabulous the great hall can look. We can hardly put a picture up of it looking the way it does now, can we?'

'Website?' said Jake, a little taken aback at how quickly her plans seemed to be developing.

'You've got to have a website,' Cassie said as if stating the obvious. 'In fact, we should think about that right away. We can't afford to leave it until all the work's been done, or we'll miss out on another year.'

Fired with enthusiasm, she snapped the Netbook closed and jumped off the table. 'Come on, let's look at the other rooms.'

She dragged Jake round the entire house, looking into every room and getting more and more excited as she went.

'You know, I really think this could be fantastic,' she said when they ended up on the terraces outside. She gestured expansively. 'You've got everything: a wonderfully old and romantic place for ceremonies, enough space for big parties, plenty of bedrooms…

'We don't need to do them all at once,' she reassured Jake, who had been mentally calculating how much all these grand plans were going to cost. 'At first, we just need somewhere the bride can get ready, but eventually we could offer rooms for the whole wedding-party.'

'Maybe,' said Jake, unwilling to commit himself too far at this stage. He wanted the Hall to become self-sufficient so he didn't need to think about it any more, but it was becoming evident as Cassie outlined her ideas that it was going to prove a lot more expensive than he had first anticipated.

'And the best thing is, there's no major structural work required yet,' she went on. 'We just need to think about the initial refurbishment for now.'

She pointed over towards the fine nineteenth-century stable block with older barns beyond. 'Eventually you could have more than one wedding at a time. The barns would be great for an informal wedding.'

Her face was alight with enthusiasm, and Jake found himself thinking that perhaps giving Cassie the contract might not be such a big mistake after all.

Last night, he had bitterly regretted that he had ever taken the advice to contact her. Cassie had talked all the way down the motorway, barely drawing breath for seven whole hours. She had an extraordinarily vivid imagination and was, Jake had to admit, very funny at times. But she was much too distracting. He had been exasperated by the way she kept tugging at the edge of his vision when he should have been concentrating on the road.

Now he was changing his mind again. Perhaps Cassie wasn't as coolly professional as the people he normally did business with, but she seemed to know what she was talking about. Her speech was refreshingly free of business jargon, and she had a warmth and an enthusiasm that might in the end get the job done faster than one of his marketing team, however sound their grasp of financial imperatives or strategic analysis.

She was leaning on the terrace wall, looking out over garden, her hands resting on the crumbling coping-stones. In profile, her lashes were long and tilting, the edge of her mouth a dreamy curve. The sunlight glinted on her brown curls—except that brown was too dull a word for her hair, Jake realised. Funny how he had never noticed what a beautiful colour it was before, a shade somewhere between auburn and chestnut with hints of honey and gold.

Unaware of his gaze, Cassie was following her own train of thought. 'I've just had a great idea!' she said, turning to him, and Jake looked quickly away. 'I've got contacts with a couple of wedding magazines. Maybe I could get them to do a story about how we're turning the Hall into the ultimate wedding venue? It would be fantastic promotion and get people talking about it. We could even start taking some advance bookings… What do you think?'

'I think I'm going to leave it all up to you,' said Jake slowly.

'*Really?*' The big brown eyes lit with excitement.

'Yes,' he said, making up his mind. He doubted that he would find anyone else as committed to the project, even if he had the time to find them. 'We can agree the fees when we get back to London, but in the meantime I'd like you to go ahead, make whatever decisions you need and get work started as soon as possible.'

'Er…it's me.' Cassie made a face at the phone. *Excellent, Cassie.* Stuttering and stumbling was always a good way to impress an important client with your professionalism. 'Cassie… Cassandra Grey,' she added, just in case Jake knew anyone else who went to pieces at the sound of his voice.

'Yes, so my PA said when she put you through,' said Jake with an edge of impatience.

'Oh yes, I suppose she did. Um, well, I just thought I'd let you know how things are going at the Hall.'

'Yes?'

His voice was clipped, and Cassie bit her lip, furious with herself for irritating him before she had even started. Why was she being so moronic? Everything was working out just as she'd planned, and she had been feeling really pleased with herself. Ringing Jake with an update hadn't seemed like a big deal when she had picked up the phone two minutes ago, but the minute he had barked his name her insides had jerked themselves into a knot of nerves.

He sounded so distant that she was tempted to

put the phone down, but that would be even sillier. Besides, she needed his OK on a number of matters.

'We've been making progress,' she told him brightly.

'Yes?' he said again, and her heart sank. She had hoped they had reached a kind of understanding at the Hall. Jake had certainly seemed more approachable then, but he was obviously in a vile mood now—which didn't bode well for the idea she wanted to put to him.

She cleared her throat. 'There are one or two things I need to talk to you about,' she said. 'Are you free for lunch at all this week?'

'Is it important?'

What did he think—that she wanted to take him out for the pleasure of his company? Wisely, Cassie held her tongue.

'It is, rather.'

There was an exasperated sigh at the other end of the phone, and she imagined him checking his electronic organiser. 'Does it have to be this week?'

Clearly, he couldn't wait to see her again. 'The sooner the better, really,' said Cassie.

More tsking. 'Lunch might be tricky,' he said after a moment. 'Could we make it dinner instead?'

Oh, great. And there she had been feeling nervous at the prospect of an hour's lunch. 'Er, yes. Of course.'

'What about tomorrow?'

'Fine. I'll book a table,' said Cassie quickly, just so he knew that it was a business dinner and that she would be picking up the tab. Not that there was any question of a date. She hesitated. 'As it's dinner, would Natasha like to join us?' she asked delicately.

There was a pause. 'Not tomorrow,' said Jake curtly.

'Oh, that's a pity,' said Cassie, although actually she was rather glad. She didn't fancy spending a whole evening being compared to the perfect Natasha, and besides she couldn't help feeling that her idea would be better put to Jake alone in the first instance.

They arranged to meet at Giovanni's, an Italian restaurant just round the corner from Avalon's office, where she and Joss were regulars. There was no way Cassie's expense account could rise to the kind of restaurants Jake was no doubt accustomed to, but the food at Giovanni's was good and the ambience cheerful, and in the end Cassie decided that it was better to stick to the unpretentious.

It was only when she arrived the following evening that she began to wonder if it had been such a good idea. Giovanni treated her and Joss like daughters, and the brides-to-be they took there were invariably delighted by him, but Cassie had a feeling Jake would be less charmed.

Still, it was too late to change now. Cassie hurried along the street, her heels clicking on the pavement. Anxious not to make it look as if she were expecting some kind of date, but wanting to make an effort for their now most-important client, she had dithered too long about what to wear. Eventually she had decided on a sleeveless dress with a little cardigan and her favourite suede boots, but they had proved to be a mistake, too. Fabulous as they were, it was hard to walk very fast in them.

Jake, of course, hadn't even had the decency to be a few minutes late and was waiting for her outside Giovanni's, looking dark, lean and remote. His suit was immaculately tailored, his expression shuttered. Oh God, now he was cross with her for not being on time.

Cassie's heart sank further. It didn't look as if the evening was getting off to a good start.

'I'm *so* sorry,' she said breathlessly as she clicked up on her heels. 'I hope you haven't been waiting long?'

'A couple of minutes, that's all. I was early.'

The dark gaze rested on her face and Cassie saw herself in his eyes, red-faced and puffing, her hair all anyhow. So much for cool professionalism. She had been so proud of herself recently, too, and had vowed that it would be the start of a whole new image.

'Well, let's go in.' Flustered, she reached for the

door, intending to stand back and usher Jake through, but Jake was too quick for her. He reached an arm behind her and held the door, leaving Cassie no option but to go ahead of him. It was that or an unseemly tussle, but as it was she was left looking like the little woman rather than the cool, capable businesswoman she wanted to be.

No, *not* a good start.

Giovanni spied her across the restaurant and came sailing over to greet her, his arms out-stretched.

'Cassie! *Bella!*' His kissed her soundly on both cheeks before holding her away from him. 'You're looking too thin,' he scolded her, the way he always did, before turning his beady gaze on Jake. 'And who is this?' he asked interestedly. 'It's about time you brought a man here!'

'Mr Trevelyan is a *client*, Giovanni,' said Cassie hastily.

'Shame!' he whispered to her, plucking a couple of menus from the bar. 'He looks your type, I think.'

Cassie opened her mouth to protest that Jake was most certainly *not* her type, but realised just in time that she could hardly embark on an argument with Jake right there. She would just have to hope that he hadn't heard. He hadn't recoiled in horror, anyway. In fact, he didn't seem to be paying them much attention at all, which was a little irritating in one way, but a big relief in another.

So she contented herself with crossing her eyes and giving Giovanni a warning glare, which he ignored completely as he gestured them towards a table tucked away in a little alcove where a candle flickered invitingly. It looked warm and intimate, and perfect for lovers.

'My best table for you,' he said, handing them the menus with a flourish. 'Nice and quiet so you can talk to your *client*,' he added to Cassie with an outrageous wink.

At least the dim lighting hid her scarlet cheeks. Cassie was mortified. 'Did I mention Joss and I were thinking of taking our clients to the Thai restaurant next door in future?' she muttered, but Giovanni only laughed.

'I will bring you some wine and Roberto will take your order and then, don't worry, you can be quite alone…' Chuckling to himself, he surged off to the kitchen, leaving a little pool of silence behind him.

Cassie unfolded her napkin. 'I'm sorry about that,' she said awkwardly after a moment. 'He's quite a character.'

'So I gather,' said Jake.

'I mean, he's lovely, but he does go a bit far sometimes. We bring a lot of clients here, but it's usually at lunchtime, and they're usually brides, so it's become a bit of a standing joke that I never come with a boyfriend.'

She trailed off, horribly aware that she was babbling. Jake was making her nervous. There was a tightness to him tonight, a grim set to his mouth, and an air of suppressed anger. Surely it wasn't anything she had done, was it? Everything had been going so well down in Portrevick. Had he heard something?

'Er, well, anyway… We're supposed to be talking about the Hall,' she said brightly.

Jake seemed to focus on her properly for the first time. 'You said you had made some progress?'

'I have.' Cassie told him about the contractors she had engaged. A small army of them was already hard at work. 'They're mostly cleaners,' she explained. 'There's so much wood in the great hall that it doesn't need much decorating—although they're repainting the roof—but the walls, the floor and the fireplace need a thorough clean and polish. It's all well in hand for the Allantide Ball.'

'Good,' said Jake absently. Cassie wondered if he had even been listening. He was frowning down at a knife he was spinning beneath one finger.

'I've also been in touch with various local caterers, florists, photographers and so on, and started to draw up a directory of our own.'

'It all sounds very promising,' said Jake as Giovanni's nephew appeared with a carafe of wine. Less expansive than his uncle, or perhaps just more sensitive to Jake's grim expression, he took their orders with the minimum of fuss.

'You've been busy,' Jake added to Cassie, folding the menu and handing it back to the waiter.

Well, at least he had been listening. She had wondered there for a minute. 'There's lots to do, but I'm enjoying it.'

Jake reached for the carafe, but, mindful that she was supposed to be the host, Cassie got there first, and he watched without comment as she filled two glasses. She didn't know about Jake, but she certainly needed one!

She drew a breath. 'I've been thinking about a promotion, too.'

If only Jake was in a more amenable mood, she thought. It was going to be tricky enough breaking the news of the deal she had made with *Wedding Belles* as it was. She took a sip of wine to fortify herself. 'Do you remember me saying it might be worth contacting a couple of magazines in case they wanted to run a piece about setting up the Hall as a venue?' she began cautiously.

'Vaguely.'

It was hardly the most encouraging of responses, but Cassie ploughed on anyway. 'Well, I did that, and one of them is very keen on the idea.'

There was a pause. Jake could see that she was waiting for him to say something, although he wasn't sure what. 'OK,' he said.

'But they want a bit more of a human-interest angle.'

'Human interest?'

'Yes, you know, to personalise the story? So it's not just the story of how the building is being prepared, it's also about a couple preparing to get married there. The readers love real-life stories,' Cassie hurried on. 'The editor of *Wedding Belles*—that's the magazine—wants to follow a couple who are going to be married there. So the article will be illustrated with pictures of them choosing the flowers, planning menus, trying on wedding dresses and all that kind of thing.'

'But we haven't got any couples yet,' Jake objected. 'Surely the whole point of promoting the Hall like this is to *find* someone who wants to get married there?'

'Quite,' said Cassie, relieved that he at least could see the point of the article. 'We haven't got any punters yet, but we *have* got you and Natasha…' She trailed off, hoping that Jake would get where this was all going.

He had gone very still. 'What about me and Natasha?'

'OK, I *may* have stretched the truth a little bit here,' Cassie acknowledged, and took the final hurdle in a rush. 'But the editor was so keen on the idea that I told her that you were getting married at the Hall at Christmas.'

'What?'

Jake's voice was like a lash, and carried right

across the restaurant. Diners on nearby tables turned to look at them in surprise, and behind Jake at the bar Giovanni clutched a hand to his heart with an exaggerated expression of sympathy for her.

Cassie glowered at him and turned deliberately back to Jake. She had been afraid he might react like that.

'I know it's a cheek,' she said, holding up her hands in a placatory gesture. 'But I really do think it would be great publicity for the Hall. And you don't have to go through with it if Natasha doesn't want to get married there. They'll only want pictures of a few set occasions, so I don't see any reason why we shouldn't set up a few shots and create a story for them.'

Jake was looking grimly discouraging, so she hurried on before he could give her a flat no. 'We don't need to tell them that it isn't actually the dress Natasha is going to wear, or those aren't really the flowers she'd choose,' she reassured him. 'You and Natasha would just be models, if you like, showing what a wonderful wedding-venue the Hall will be. I know you're both busy, but it shouldn't take up too much time. Just a few hours every now and then to have your photos taken.

'It would be a really effective way to promote the Hall,' Cassie went on when there was still no response from Jake. There was an edge of desperation in her voice by now. It had taken ages to get the editor of *Wedding Belles* to agree to feature Portrevick Hall, and it was only the promise of the human interest lent by the owner himself getting married there—another little stretching of the truth—that had swung it for her.

'You did say you wanted the venue to be self-sustaining as soon as possible,' she reminded him. '*Wedding Belles* is really popular with brides-to-be around the country, and its circulation figures are amazing. If they run a feature about the Hall, we'll have couples queuing up to book it, and you'll be able to hand the whole place over to a manager much sooner than you thought.'

Jake drank some wine, then put down his glass. 'There's just one problem,' he said.

'Just one?' said Cassie, trying to lighten the atmosphere. 'That doesn't sound too bad!'

He didn't smile back. 'Unfortunately it's quite a major one,' he said. 'I'm afraid Natasha isn't around to model anything any more. She's left me.'

Cassie put down her glass so abruptly, wine sloshed onto the tablecloth. 'Natasha's *left* you?'

'So it seems.'

'But…but…' Cassie was floundering. It was the last thing she had expected to hear. 'God, I'm so sorry! I had no idea…' No wonder Jake was looking so grim! 'When did all this happen?'

'When I got back from Cornwall.' Jake reached

across with his napkin and mopped up the wine Cassie had spilt before she made even more of a mess. 'Natasha was waiting for me with her case packed. She said she was sorry, but she had met someone else and fallen madly in love with him.'

His first reaction had been one of surprise at her words. Natasha had never been the type to do anything *madly*. One of the things he had always liked about her was her calm, rational approach to everything, and now it seemed as if she was just as illogical and emotional as, well, as Cassie.

'How awful for you.' Cassie's round face was puckered with sympathy. 'How long had it been going on?'

'Hardly any time. She said he'd literally swept her off her feet. I'll bet he did,' Jake added grimly. 'He's had plenty of practice.'

'Gosh, he's not a friend of yours, is he?' That would make it twice as humiliating for him.

'A friend?' Jake gave a short, mirthless laugh. 'Hardly! Rupert Branscombe Fox is no friend of mine.'

'*Rupert?*' Cassie's eyes were out on stalks. Crikey, this was like something out of a soap opera! 'But how on earth did Natasha meet Rupert?'

'It was my own fault,' said Jake. Funnily enough, now that he'd started talking, he didn't feel too bad. He'd been so angry before that he could barely bite out a word. 'I invited Rupert round to discuss the trust at home, and Natasha was there. I didn't think she was that impressed with him at the time.'

Cassie remembered now. Perfect Natasha had decided that Rupert was shallow—or that was what she had said, anyway.

'What changed her mind?'

'Rupert did. He deliberately set out to seduce Natasha to get at me.' Jake's expression was set. 'I can't believe she fell for it,' he said, sounding genuinely baffled. 'I thought she was too sensible to have her head turned by Rupert's very superficial attraction. I can't understand it at all.'

Cassie could. Even as a boy, Rupert had been extraordinarily good-looking, and if he had turned the full battery of his sex appeal on Natasha he must have been well nigh irresistible. Perhaps Natasha had been tired of being told how admirably sensible she was.

But poor Jake. How hurt and angry he must have been!

'Rupert's very…charming,' she said lamely.

Jake tossed back his wine and poured himself another glass. 'He's *using* Natasha. I can't believe she can't see it for herself!'

'Maybe he's fallen in love with her,' Cassie suggested

'Love?' Jake snorted. 'Rupert doesn't love anyone but himself.'

'You don't *know* that—'

'Sure I do,' he interrupted her. 'Rupert was kind enough to explain it to me. Natasha was perfect for his purposes, he said. He was furious and humiliated by the trust Sir Ian had set up, and he's chosen to blame me for it. Breaking up my relationship with Natasha was doubly sweet. It hurt me, and it gives him access to the trust money, or so he thinks. He claims he's going to marry her because I won't have any grounds for arguing that Natasha isn't a sensible woman, as specified by Sir Ian. He was quite sure I would understand, *old chap*.'

Ouch. Cassie grimaced at the savagery in Jake's voice. She didn't blame him for being angry. She could practically hear Rupert's light, cut-glass tones, and could just imagine what effect they would have had on Jake.

'What are you going to do?'

'Well, I'm certainly not handing over the money yet. Natasha deserves better than to be married for such a cynical reason. The moment Rupert's got his hands on the money, he'll dump her like the proverbial ton of bricks,' said Jake. 'He's still got to prove to me that he's settled down, and I'll believe that when I see it!'

Under the circumstances, it was generous of him to still think about Natasha, Cassie thought. He must love her, even if she had proved to be not quite as perfect as he had believed.

Cassie pushed her glass around, making patterns

on the tablecloth. It would be quite something to be loved by someone like Jake, who didn't give up on you even when you made a terrible mistake. She wondered if Natasha would realise that once the first thrill of being with Rupert wore off.

As it inevitably would. Cassie wasn't a fool, whatever her family thought. She had long ago realised that Rupert's appeal lay largely in the fact that he was out of reach. He was so impossibly handsome, so extraordinarily charming, so unbelievably glamorous, that you couldn't imagine doing anything ordinary with him. He was the kind of man you dreamed of having a mad, passionate affair with, not the kind of man you lived with and loved every day.

Not like Jake.

Cassie's fingers stilled on the glass. Where had *that* thought come from?

Looking up from her wine, she studied him across the table. Lost in his own thoughts, he was broodingly turning a fork on the tablecloth, his own head bent and the dark, stormy eyes hidden. She could see the angular planes of his face, the jut of his nose, the set of his mouth, and all at once it was as if she had never seen him before.

There was a solidity and a control to him, she realised, disconcerted to realise that she could imagine living with him in a way she had never been able to with Rupert. Bumping into Rupert again had been one of her favourite fantasies for years, but in her dreams they were never doing anything ordinary. They were *getting* married, not *being* married. They were going to Paris or sitting on a yacht in the Caribbean, not having breakfast or watching television or emptying the dishwasher.

How strange that she could picture Jake in her flat, could see him coming in from work, taking off his jacket, loosening his tie, reaching for her with a smile…

A strange shiver snaked its way down her spine. It was just Jake, she reminded herself. But he was so immediate, so real, so *there*, that his presence felt like a hand against her skin, and all at once she was struggling to drag enough oxygen into her lungs.

And then he looked up, the dark-blue eyes locked with hers, and she forgot to breathe at all.

'Spaghetti carbonara.'

Cassie actually jumped as Giovanni deposited a steaming plate in front of her.

'And fettucine *all'arrabiata* for your client!'

She barely noticed Giovanni's jovial winks and nods of encouragement as he fussed around with pepper and parmesan. How long had she been staring into Jake's eyes, unable to look away? A second? Ten? Ten *minutes*? She hoped it was the first, but it was impossible to tell. She felt oddly jarred, and her heart was knocking erratically against her ribs.

She was terrified in case Jake was able to read her thoughts in her eyes. Of course, she would have known if he had, because he would look absolutely horrified. He probably couldn't think of anything worse than going home to her in an untidy flat every night.

Why was *that* a depressing thought?

CHAPTER FIVE

AND why was she even *thinking* about it? Cassie asked herself crossly as she picked up her fork. Disappointed by her lack of response, Giovanni had taken himself off at last. Jake was obviously still in love with the not-quite-so-perfect Natasha, who had had her sensible head turned by Rupert.

Twirling spaghetti in her spoon, she forced her mind back to the conversation. 'I'm really sorry,' she said when Giovanni had left. 'If it's any comfort, I don't imagine Rupert will be easy to live with. Perhaps Natasha will change her mind.'

'That's what I'm hoping,' said Jake.

That wasn't quite what Cassie had been hoping to hear. *I wouldn't take her back if she grovelled from here to Friday* was more what she had had in mind.

She sighed inwardly. Stop being so silly, she told herself.

'In the meantime, I'll go back to *Wedding Belles*

and tell them that we'd still like a feature on the Hall, but we can't manage the human-interest angle.'

Jake's gaze sharpened. 'I thought you said they wouldn't do a piece without that?'

'No, well, it's not the end of the world. We can find other ways of promoting the Hall.'

'They won't reach the same market, though?'

'Probably not.'

Jake brooded, stirring his fork mindlessly around in the fettucine. 'To hell with it!' he said explosively after a while and looked up at Cassie, who regarded him warily. 'I'm damned if I'm going to let Rupert mess up my plans for the Hall, too. He's made enough trouble! I say we go ahead with it anyway.'

'We can't do much about it without Natasha,' she reminded him reluctantly.

'Unless…' Jake trailed off, staring at Cassie as if seeing her properly for the first time.

She stared back, more than a little unnerved. 'What?'

'Did you tell this editor Natasha's name?'

'No, I didn't go into details. I just said the owner of the Hall was getting married.'

'So I don't really need Natasha—I just need a fiancée?'

'Well, yes, but—'

'So why don't I marry you?'

There was a rushing sound in Cassie's ears. She

went hot, then cold, then hot again. 'Me?' she squeaked. 'You don't want to marry me!'

'Of course I don't,' said Jake, recoiling. 'God, no! But you said yourself that it doesn't have to be a real engagement. If all we need is to have a few photographs taken, why shouldn't you be the bride-to-be?'

'Well, because—because—' Cassie stuttered, groping for all the glaringly obvious reasons why she couldn't, and bizarrely unable to think of any. 'Because everyone would know it wasn't true.'

'You just said you didn't give the magazine any names.'

'I wasn't thinking of them. I was thinking of all the people who know perfectly well we're not engaged.'

'Who's going to know?'

'Anyone who sees the article,' she said, exasperated, but Jake only looked down his nose.

'I don't know anyone who's likely to read *Wedding Belles*,' he said.

Cassie glared at him. 'It's not just about you, though, is it? I know masses of people who read it for one reason or another, and if one of my friends gets whiff of the fact that I'm apparently engaged without telling anyone I'll never hear the end of it!'

Jake couldn't see the problem. 'The article won't be published until next year,' he said dismissively. 'We can worry about what we tell people then.

Rupert will never stick with Natasha for more than a few weeks, so there'll be no reason not to tell everyone the truth then. We'll say it was just a marketing exercise.'

'And what about when the *Wedding Belles* photographer comes down to take pictures of us supposedly planning our wedding at the Hall?' asked Cassie, picking up her spoon and fork once more. 'It'll be all over Portrevick in no time. You know what the village is like. We'd never be able to keep it secret. Rupert's got some fancy weekend place in St Ives; what's the betting he'll hear about it?'

'What if he does? It wouldn't do him any harm to think that I'm not inconsolable.'

'No, but if he gets wind of the fact that you're just pretending…' Cassie trailed off and Jake nodded.

'You're right,' he said. 'Rupert wouldn't hesitate to make trouble for me in whatever way he could.' He looked across the table at Cassie. 'In that case, let's make it true,' he said.

She stared at him. 'What do you mean?'

'Let's make it a real engagement,' he said, as if it were the most obvious thing in the world. 'Or, at least, not a secret one,' he amended. 'We can tell everybody who needs to know, and do the photographs for the article quite openly. We'll know it's not a real engagement, but we don't have to tell anyone else that.'

Let's make it a real engagement. Cassie was

furious with herself for the way her heart had jumped at his words, in spite of the fact that only a matter of minutes ago he had been recoiling in horror at the very idea. 'Nobody would believe it,' she said flatly.

'Why not?'

'Come on, Jake. I'm hardly your type, am I? Are you really going to ask people to believe you took one look at me and fell in love with me? They'd know it wasn't true.'

'Oh, I don't know.' Jake studied her over the rim of his glass. It was warm in the restaurant, and she had shrugged off the silky cardigan, leaving her shoulders bare. She was a warm, glowing figure in the candlelight. 'I can think of more unlikely scenarios,' he said.

His gaze flustered Cassie, and she tore her eyes away to concentrate fiercely on twisting spaghetti around her fork. 'Sure,' she said. 'And when was this supposed to have happened?'

'How about when you walked into my office and fell into my arms?'

Cassie felt her colour rising at the memory. 'And you thought, "I've been waiting all my life for someone clumsy to come along"?'

'Perhaps I've had a thing about you since I kissed you at the Allantide Ball,' Jake suggested. 'Perhaps I've been waiting ten years to find you again.'

It was clear that he was being flippant, but there

was an undercurrent of *something* in his voice. Cassie did everything she could to stop herself looking up to meet his eyes again, but it was hopeless. Something stronger than her was dragging her gaze up from the fork to lock with Jake's. She could almost hear the click as it snapped into place.

His eyes were dark and unreadable in the candle-light, but still her heart began that silly pattering again, while her pulse throbbed alarmingly.

She swallowed. 'I don't think that sounds very likely either.'

'Well, then, we'll tell it exactly as it was,' said Jake, sounding infuriatingly normal. How come *his* heart wasn't lurching all over the place at the very thought of falling in love with her? He clearly wasn't having any trouble breathing, either.

'We met when you came to discuss developing the Hall as a wedding venue. Then we drove down to Portrevick together.'

'And on the way we fell madly in love and agreed to get married right away?' said Cassie, who had managed to look away again at last.

Jake shrugged away her scorn. 'You're the one who believes in that kind of thing,' he reminded her. 'If we say that's what happened, why would anyone believe it wasn't true?'

'I can't believe you're making it all sound so reasonable,' she protested.

How had they got to this point? It was as if the whole evening had been turned on its head. When she arrived, she had been cock-a-hoop at the idea of the magazine feature, and her only concern had been how to convince Jake to go for it. Now it was Jake talking her into an engagement just to make sure the article went ahead. How had that happened?

'Look, it makes sense.' Jake was clearly losing patience. 'You're the ideal person to feature in the article. You know all about weddings. You'll be able to say all the right things and make sure the Hall comes out of it looking beautiful.'

'That's true, I suppose.' Cassie looked at the fork she had laden so carefully with spaghetti and put it down. She had lost her appetite. 'But what about you?' she said hesitantly.

'What about me?'

'Won't you find it very difficult?'

'It might be a bit of a struggle to look interested in table decorations,' said Jake. 'But I expect I can manage if it's just one or two photo sessions. I won't be required to do much else, will I?'

'I wasn't thinking about that,' said Cassie. 'I was thinking about what it would be like for you to have to pretend to be happy with me when I know how you must be feeling about Natasha. I'd be devastated if it was me.'

'At least I won't look it,' said Jake, wondering how he did feel.

Angry, humiliated—yes. But *devastated*? Jake didn't think so. His overwhelming feeling, he decided, was one of disappointment in Natasha. He had been attracted by her beauty, of course, but just as much he had liked her intelligence and composure. He couldn't believe that she would lose her head over someone like Rupert, of all people.

Jake remembered telling Cassie how well he and Natasha were matched. Natasha was perfect, he had told her. And she had been. She had never irritated or distracted him the way Cassie did, for instance. She was everything he needed in a woman.

More than that, when he looked at Natasha, Jake had felt as if he had left Portrevick behind him once and for all. With a beautiful, accomplished, sexy, successful woman like Natasha on his arm, he'd been able to believe that he had made it at last.

And then Rupert Branscombe Fox had lifted his little finger and she had gone.

Jake's jaw tightened and he stared down at the wine he was swirling in his glass. Rupert's condescension could still reduce him to a state of seething resentment. Rupert in return would never forgive him for humiliating him in that stupid fight, or for being the one his uncle had entrusted with his not-inconsiderable fortune.

'Rupert wants me to be devastated,' he told Cassie. 'He wants me to feel humiliated and heartbroken. He wants me to have to tell everyone that my beautiful girlfriend has dumped me for him. I've got no intention of giving him that satisfaction.'

Jake set down his glass and looked directly at Cassie. 'You asked if I'd find it difficult to pretend to be in love with you instead of Natasha—the answer is that it wouldn't be half as hard as losing face with Rupert. I'd do anything rather than do that. I'm sorry about Natasha, but this isn't about her. It's between Rupert and me.'

'Getting engaged to me would make it look as if Rupert had done you a favour by taking Natasha off your hands,' said Cassie slowly. She knew that Jake and Rupert had never got on, but she hadn't realised the rivalry between them was still so bitter.

'Exactly,' said Jake. 'You'd be helping me to save face, and that would mean a lot to me. I'm not proud. I'll beg if you want me to.'

'I don't know.' Cassie fingered the wax dribbling down the candle uncertainly. 'If we're pretending to be engaged in Portrevick, word's bound to get back to my parents. What are they going to think if they find out I'm apparently marrying you and haven't told them?'

Jake shrugged. 'Tell them the truth, then. What does it matter if they know? They're not going to rush off to *Wedding Belles* to tell the editor their daughter is telling a big fib, are they?'

'No, but they might rush to tell Liz and my

brothers that I've got myself in a stupid mess again,' said Cassie, who could imagine the conversation all too clearly: *why can Cassie never do anything properly? When is she going to grow up and get a proper job that doesn't involve silly pretences?*

'I'm sick of being the family failure,' she told Jake. 'I wanted to show them that I could be successful too. That was why I so pleased when you gave us the contract to turn the Hall into a wedding venue. I rang my parents and told them I had a real career at last.'

She squeezed a piece of wax between her fingers, remembering the warm glow of her parents' approval. 'I don't want to tell them my great new job involves pretending to be in love with you.'

'Do you want to tell them you've lost your great new job because you weren't prepared to do whatever it took to make it work?'

Cassie dropped the wax and sat back in her chair. 'Isn't that blackmail?' she said dubiously, and Jake sighed impatiently.

'It's telling you to hurry up and make a decision,' he said. 'Look, if it's such a problem, say we really *are* engaged, then when we've finished with all the photos you can tell them you've changed your mind and dumped me. If they remember me at all, I'm sure they'll be delighted to hear it,' he finished in an arid voice.

Cassie turned it over in her mind. It might work. Of course, the best scenario would be that her family never got to hear about her supposed engagement at all, but if they did get a whiff of it she could always pretend that Jake had swept her off her feet. It was only three months to Christmas. She could easily find excuses not to take him home in that time.

Tina might be a little harder to fool, especially as she was on the spot in Portrevick, but there was no reason why she shouldn't tell her old friend the truth. Tina could be trusted to keep it to herself—and besides they might need her to pretend to be the bridesmaid.

Anyway, it didn't sound as if she had a choice. Cassie wasn't entirely sure whether Jake was serious about making the engagement a condition of the contract, but she wasn't prepared to push him on it. He had been hurt by Natasha, humiliated by Rupert, and was clearly in no mood to compromise.

And really, would it be so bad? Cassie asked herself. The article had been her idea to start with, and she still believed it would be just what they needed to kick-start promotion for the Hall. Of course, she hadn't reckoned on taking such a prominent role herself, but Jake was right. She would be able to decorate the Hall exactly as she wanted without having to take Natasha's wishes into account. She could recreate her dream wedding for the article.

Cassie felt a flicker of excitement at the prospect. It might be fun.

It wasn't as if they were planning on doing anything illegal or immoral, after all. A mock engagement would save Jake's face, ensure a lucrative contract and her job at Avalon, if not a whole new career. Why was she even hesitating?

'All right,' she said abruptly. 'I'll do it. But, if we're going to pretend to be engaged, we're going to have to do it properly,' she warned him. 'That means that when the photographer is around you'll have to be there and be prepared to look suitably besotted.'

'Don't you think I can do that?'

Jake reached across the table for her hands, taking Cassie by surprise. 'I'm sure you can,' she said, flustered, trying to tug them free, but he tightened his grip.

'I can do whatever you need me to,' he said, turning her hands over and lifting first one palm and then the other to his mouth to kiss.

Cassie felt the touch of his lips like a shock reverberating down to her toes, and she sucked in a shuddering breath.

'See?' Jake said softly, without letting go of her hands. '*I* can do it. More to the point,' he said, 'can you?'

The challenge hung between them, flickering in the candlelight.

Cassie swallowed hard. It was hard to think straight with his warm, strong fingers clasping hers, and the feel of his lips scorched onto her palms, but she retained enough sanity to know that the last thing she needed was to let him know how his touch affected her.

He had recoiled at the very idea of marrying her. *Of course I don't*, he had said. Cassie suspected that Jake had been more hurt by Natasha's betrayal than he was letting on. This was partly to be his revenge on her, partly a game, a pretence, a strategy to save his face and solve the problem of his unwanted responsibility for the Hall. That was all.

Which was fine. All she had to do was treat it like a game too, and remember that her strategy was to turn the Hall into the most sought-after wedding venue in the South West. She would prove to her family that she was not just a dreamer, but could be just as successful in her chosen field as they were in theirs.

So she drew her hands from Jake's and laid them instead on either side of his face. 'Of course I can, darling,' she said, shivering at the prickle of the rough male skin beneath her fingers, and she leant forward across the table to brush a kiss against his mouth.

She felt Jake stiffen in surprise, and, although a

panic-stricken part of her was screaming at her to sit back and laugh it off as a joke, another more persuasive part was noting that his lips were warm and firm and that they fitted her own perfectly, as if their mouths had been made for each other.

It felt so good to kiss him, to touch him, that Cassie pushed the panicky thoughts aside and let her lips linger on his. But that was a mistake, of course. Beneath hers, his mouth curved into a smile, and the next moment she felt his hand slide beneath her hair to hold her head still, and he began kissing her back.

And then they were kissing each other, their lips parting, their tongues twining, teasing, and Cassie murmured deep in her throat, smiling too even as she kissed him again, lost in the dizzying rush of heat and the terrifying sense of rightness.

Afterwards, she never had any idea how long that kiss had lasted. But when they broke apart at last she was thudding from the tips of her hair to her toenails, and Giovanni was standing by the table wearing a broad smile.

'Client, huh?' he said to her with a wink, but it was Jake who answered.

'Not any more,' he said. 'We just got engaged.'

Cassie tossed and turned half the night, reliving that kiss. She had gone too far, just like her mother always said she did. A brief peck on the lips would have been enough to make her point, and she could have gone back to being businesslike—but, oh no! She had had to push it. She had had to *kiss* him.

She mustn't let herself get carried away like that again, Cassie told herself sternly. This was just a pretence, and she mustn't forget it. On the other hand, her job might have depended on pretending to be engaged to a man with wet lips and clammy hands. As it was, well, she might as well enjoy the perks, mightn't she?

So she was in high good humour when she bounced into the office the next morning. She had never been engaged before. OK, she wasn't *really* engaged, and she probably ought to be feeling more cross about having been effectively blackmailed into it, but at least it meant that she didn't have any choice in the matter. If anyone—for example her super-achieving family—ever asked her how she came to do such a crazy thing, she could hold up her hands and say, 'Hey, I was forced into it.'

Or perhaps it would be better to put a more positive spin on it. She didn't want to look like a victim. She could narrow her eyes, look serious and explain that she was someone who was prepared to do anything—anything!—to get the job done.

'Well, I hope you know what you're doing,' said Joss doubtfully when Cassie tried this line on her. Joss, like Tina, had to know the truth. 'This Jake

Trevelyan is a tough character. It was bad enough negotiating the terms of the contract with him!

'Don't get me wrong,' she said as Cassie's face fell. 'I'm delighted about the contract. But I'd hate to think you got hurt trying to save Avalon. I just think you should be careful about getting too involved with someone like that.'

'I'll be fine,' said Cassie buoyantly. 'Anyway, I'm not *involved* with Jake,' she said, firmly pushing the memory of last night's kiss away. 'Pretending to be engaged is simply a way to promote Portrevick Hall as a wedding venue. I'm just doing my job.'

She was still in a breezy mood when she rang Jake at his office later that morning.

'Hi!' she said when his PA put her through. 'It's me. Your brand-new fiancée,' she added, just in case he needed his memory jogging.

'Hello,' said Jake. He sounded cool and businesslike, and it was hard to believe that it was only a matter of hours since his lips had been warm and sure against hers.

'I think you mean "hello, *darling*", don't you?' Cassie prompted. 'We're engaged, remember?'

Jake sighed. 'Hello, *darling*,' he said ironically.

'OK, the darling is good, but you might want to work on your tone,' said Cassie, enjoying herself. 'You know? A bit lower, a bit warmer…a bit more like you're counting the seconds until you can see me again!'

'Darling,' Jake repeated obediently, and this time his voice was deep and warm and held a hint of a smile. Cassie's heart skipped just a little, even though she knew he was just pretending.

'Very good,' she approved.

'It's not that it's not wonderful to hear from you,' he said, reverting to his usual sardonic tone. 'But I've got a meeting in five minutes.'

'I won't keep you,' she promised. 'I just thought I'd tell you that I've spoken to *Wedding Belles* and broken the news that I'm the bride-to-be. I made up some story about being too shy to admit it before. I'm not sure if they believed me, but they're not asking too many questions, which is a relief.'

'Presumably they don't really care as long as they get a decent story.'

'Yes, that's right.' Cassie could feel his impatience to get off the phone. Just as well they weren't really engaged, or she *would* have been hurt. 'Anyway, we're committed now.'

'So what happens next?' asked Jake without much interest. Cassie imagined him scrolling through his emails while he listened to her with half an ear.

But she could do businesslike, too. 'I was just coming to that,' she said. 'It turns out that *Wedding Belles* is hosting a wedding fair at some fancy hotel this weekend. The opening party is on Friday night, and they want us to go. Apparently they're inviting all the couples who are going to be featured in the magazine next year, and we're getting a special preview of the show.'

She could practically see Jake grimacing at the idea. 'Do we have to go?'

'Yes, we do,' said Cassie briskly. 'This is the first part of the story. The photographer will be there, and we'll meet the editor, so we'll have to be on our best behaviour.

'Besides,' she said, 'the theme of the fair is Winter Wonderland Weddings, so we'll be able to pick up some ideas. Joss and I always go to the shows, but I've never been to the preview or the party before. It should be great.'

'What goes on at a wedding show?' Jake asked, not at all sure that he was going to like the answer.

'Oh, they're fantastic,' Cassie assured him. 'There's everything you could ever need to plan a wedding under one roof. It doesn't matter if you're looking for a chocolate fountain or a tiara: you'll find someone who specialises in providing just what you want for every stage of getting married, from the engagement party to the honeymoon. Oh, and there's always a fashion show too. We don't want to miss that.'

'A fashion show,' Jake echoed dryly. 'Fabulous!'

'It'll be fun,' Cassie told him.

Jake thought that it sounded as much fun as sticking pins in his eyes, but he was the one who had insisted that they go ahead with the article, so he could hardly quibble now.

Since the hotel was almost exactly halfway between their offices, they agreed to meet in the lobby at six-thirty on the Friday.

'OK, I'd better go,' said Cassie in the same brisk tone. About to switch off the phone, she paused. 'Oh, nearly forgot,' she said, and cooed, *'Love you!'* in an exaggeratedly saccharine voice before spoiling the effect by laughing.

Jake put the phone down and sat looking at it for a long moment, her gurgling laugh echoing in his ears. Then he smiled unwillingly, shook his head, and pushed back his chair to go to his meeting, where everyone would be sane and sensible and dressed in shades of grey.

Jake looked at his watch as Cassie came tumbling into the hotel's ornate lobby through the revolving door. 'You're late,' he said.

'I know, I know, I'm sorry,' she panted, struggling out of her coat. 'I spent all afternoon trying to track down a carriage for one of our clients. It wouldn't be a problem, except that she wants four horses—all white, naturally—and the carriage has to be purple to fit the colour theme. Oh, and did I mention she wants it for next weekend? I finally found someone who was prepared to paint the carriage, but by the time we'd negotiated how much it would all cost it was nearly six…'

Still talking, she managed to get rid of her coat and checked it into the cloakroom, which gave Jake a chance to get his breathing back under control. It had got ridiculously muddled up at the sight of Cassie spilling through the doors, her cheeks pink, her eyes bright and brown, and the wild curls even more tousled than usual. She was like a crisp autumn breeze, swirling into the stultifyingly grand lobby, freshening the air and sharpening his senses. For a moment there Jake had forgotten whether he was supposed to be breathing in or breathing out.

How had he come up with a crazy idea like pretending to be engaged to her? Jake had spent the day wondering if Giovanni's wine had gone to his head. It wasn't the plan that bothered him, it was Cassie. It was that aura of turbulence that always seemed to be whirling around her, that sense that everything might tip into chaos at any moment. Jake, whose life now was built on rigorous order and control, found it deeply unsettling.

If only she could be more like Natasha, who was always calm, always neat, always predictable.

Except when she was running off with Rupert, of course.

The memory of Rupert was enough to make Jake's jaw tighten with resolve. He might not like muddle and chaos, but he disliked Rupert more. He mustn't lose his nerve about the plan now, he told himself. It made perfect sense. Pretending to be engaged to Cassie would deprive Rupert of his triumph and achieve his most pressing objective, which was to get the Hall up and running. If a little pretence was required for the purposes of promotion, well, Jake could handle that.

It wasn't as if anyone in London would ever know anything about it, either, he reassured himself. No; everything would be fine.

It had been fine until that damned kiss.

Natasha's defection had been a blow to his pride, true, but he'd had a plan. Life had been back under control. And then Cassie had leant forward in the candlelight, that dimple deepening enticingly as she smiled. *Darling*, she had called him, and then she had kissed him.

The moment her lips had touched his, control had gone out the window. Jake had forgotten everything but warmth, softness and searing, seductive sweetness. He'd forgotten Rupert, forgotten Natasha, forgotten the *plan*.

It had taken him all day to remember what was important and get himself back under control, and all Cassie had had to do was appear and he'd lost it all over again.

He was being ridiculous, Jake told himself savagely. It was just Cassie. He looked at her as she tucked the cloakroom ticket away in her bag. She was wearing loose trousers and a fine-knit top with a wide belt. She looked really quite stylish for once, although nothing like as elegant as Natasha would have seemed in exactly the same outfit.

She was just a girl. Pretty, yes—in fact, much prettier than she seemed at first glance—but a bit messy, a bit clumsy, a bit disorganised. Nothing special, in fact. Not the kind of girl you got yourself into a state about, that was for sure.

CHAPTER SIX

'YOU'RE looking very fierce,' Cassie commented, hoisting her bag back onto her shoulder. 'You're supposed to be deliriously happy at the prospect of spending an evening with me planning our special day together!'

She saw his mouth turn down at the corners. 'Look, this was your idea,' she reminded him. 'The editor of *Wedding Belles* is going to be in there. If you want to promote the Hall, you're going to have to convince her the way you convinced me the other night.'

Jake raised his brows. 'What, I have to kiss her?'

'You're not taking this seriously,' said Cassie. 'All you've got to do is look affectionate and not as if you can't decide whether to fire me or shoot me!'

She was right, Jake thought. He was the one who had insisted on doing this. He bared his teeth in a smile. 'Better?'

'A bit,' she allowed, glancing around for signs to the wedding fair. A notice board pointed them down to the lower floor. 'Come on, then,' she said. 'Let's go and find the party.'

'Shouldn't we hold hands?' suggested Jake.

'Er, yes, we probably should. Good idea.'

Cassie tried to sound casual, but she was desperately aware of the dry warmth of his palm and the firm fingers closing around hers. He had lovely hands, big, strong and safe, the kind of hands that could catch you if you were falling, the kind of hands that wouldn't let you go.

She was being fanciful, Cassie told herself as they made their way downstairs, where they found the party already in full swing. She wasn't falling anywhere, not even off her heels, and Jake would be only too keen to let her go as soon as possible.

The editor of *Wedding Belles* was greeting arrivals at the door, but they managed to brush through the introductions without rousing any suspicions, and were disgorged into the party. A passing waiter offered them champagne and Cassie accepted thankfully. Holding Jake's hand was making her jittery and self-conscious, and it was the perfect excuse to drop it and grab a glass from the tray.

Amazing how a gulp of champagne could make you feel better, she thought, looking around her and trying not to notice how tingly and somehow empty her hand felt now. She switched the glass to give it something to hold.

'We'd better try and circulate,' she murmured.

They were standing next to another couple, who introduced themselves after a few banalities as Mark and Michelle; it soon turned out that it was Michelle who did all the talking.

'We're getting married in April,' she told Cassie and Jake. 'Aren't we, Mark?'

Mark opened his mouth to agree but she was already sweeping on. 'We've been planning the wedding for two years. We got engaged on a cruise, so our theme is the sea.'

'Theme?'

'The theme of the wedding.' Michelle looked at Jake as if he were stupid. 'Blue is our main colour, of course, so all our favours will be blue, and we're having blue sashes on the chair covers. We had waves on the invitations, didn't we, Mark? And we're naming all the tables after different seas,' she finished triumphantly.

'Who are you putting in the Bermuda Triangle?' asked Jake, and Cassie nudged him.

'That sounds lovely,' she said quickly. 'Have you decided on a dress yet?'

Michelle had, of course, and described it at length. Then she went on to tell them about their matching stationery, the wedding website, the special, blue fascinators she had sourced for her five bridesmaids, the first dance they were practising already, and the personalised shells that she was trying to track down as place settings.

Her monologue was punctuated with requests for confirmation from Mark, although the poor man never got a chance even to agree. Michelle had a spreadsheet she was using to keep track of her budget, and kept all the paperwork to do with the wedding in a colour-coded filing system.

Weddings were Cassie's business, and she wouldn't have minded listening to Michelle drone on if she hadn't been aware that Jake was glazing over beside her.

'We're having a Christmas wedding,' she interrupted brightly at last.

'I think you mean a Christmas *theme*, don't you?' muttered Jake.

'We're getting married this Christmas, actually,' Cassie hurried on, trying not to giggle.

'Really? So, not long to go!' Michelle looked from one to the other. 'You must be excited!'

'I'm beside myself,' Jake agreed, deadpan.

'Don't mind him,' said Cassie, taking his arm and leaning into him. 'He's thrilled, really—especially since we found him a Regency-buck outfit.' She smiled winsomely up at him. 'You're going to look *soooo* gorgeous in those breeches!'

She turned back to Michelle. 'We're going for the Mr Darcy look, you know? But he's worried he won't be able to tie his cravat properly.'

'I'm sure you can get instructions on the Internet,' said Michelle, completely missing Jake's expression at the very thought of a cravat. 'So, are you going for a Regency dress as well?' she asked Cassie.

'I haven't got it yet,' Cassie admitted.

'You're getting married at Christmas and you haven't got your *dress*?' Michelle fell back in horror. 'You're leaving it very late!'

'Maybe I'll find something here tonight. Perhaps you're right; I could go for a period look and wear a bonnet.' She pretended to muse.

'A muff's very nice at a Christmas wedding,' offered Michelle.

That was when Cassie made the mistake of catching Jake's eye. 'Now, there's a thought,' he said, and waggled his eyebrows at her. It would have been fine if she hadn't just lifted her glass to her lips to hide her smile, and at that she spluttered champagne all down the front of her top and started choking.

Jake patted her none too gently on the back. 'Here, let's go and find you a glass of water,' he said, taking her by the arm and bearing her off with barely time for a goodbye to Michelle and the silent Mark.

'Look, my top is all stained,' Cassie complained, brushing champagne from her cleavage. 'And it's all your fault for making me laugh!'

'*My* fault? I wasn't the one who started on the Regency bucks!' said Jake. He had his hand on her back and was steering her firmly to the other side of the room. 'I couldn't stand it any longer. Poor Mark looked like he had lost the will to live, and I don't blame him. And what the hell is a "favour" anyway?'

'It's a little thank-you gift for your guests. It usually goes on the table as a memento of the day that they can take away.'

Jake snorted. 'Well, the only favour *I* want is for you to get me out of here!'

'We can't go yet,' said Cassie. 'We've only just arrived. Besides, they haven't opened the show. I think there are going to be some speeches first.'

Putting her empty glass down on a passing tray she took another one and turned to see who else they could talk to. Fortunately, the next couple they met was less obsessed with weddings than Michelle

'We're only here for the champagne,' Kevin said.

'And for the draw,' said Victoria. 'First prize is a weekend in Paris as a break from the stress of planning a wedding, but the others sound worth winning too. Everyone here tonight is in with a chance.'

'Paris sounds lovely,' Cassie said wistfully, imagining strolling around Montmartre hand in hand with Jake. Then she caught herself up. What was she thinking? They weren't lovers. There would be no one to see them in Paris. Why would they be holding hands?

She forced a smile. 'Not that I ever win anything. Oh, I take that back,' she said. 'I once won a jar of pickled onions in the tombola at the village fête.'

Victoria laughed. 'Well, it looks as if you've won yourself a gorgeous guy,' she said with a meaningful glance at Jake, who was talking to Kevin about a new sports channel.

'Yes,' said Cassie, stifling a little sigh.

'Isn't it the best feeling when you find the right guy?'

Cassie looked at Jake, deep in blokey conversation with Kevin. She remembered the feel of his hand holding hers, the devastating sureness of his lips. 'Yes,' she said in a hollow voice.

'I'd almost given up on men,' Victoria confided. 'I thought it was never going to happen for me. Then I walked into work one day, and there he was! The moment I saw him, I knew he was the one.'

She showed Cassie her engagement ring. 'Every time I look at it, I feel so happy I want to cry,' she said.

Kevin obviously caught the end of her sentence as he broke off his conversation with Jake. 'Oh no, not the "I'm so happy I could cry" line again?' he said, rolling his eyes, but he put his arm around Victoria and pulled her close. 'Do you get that one?' he asked Jake.

'Not yet,' said Jake.

There was a tiny pause, when it suddenly seemed glaringly obvious that they weren't touching with the easy affection Kevin and Victoria showed, but then he slid his hand beneath Cassie's hair and rested it at the nape of her neck.

'You don't want to cry, do you?'

Actually, right then, Cassie did. Her throat had tightened painfully, watching Victoria and Kevin so obviously in love, and now the warm, comforting weight of Jake's hand on her neck only made her eyes sting with tears. She blinked them firmly away and mustered a smile. 'I probably *would* cry with happiness if I had a lovely ring like Victoria's!' She pretended to joke.

'Hasn't he bought you a ring yet?' Victoria tutted.

'We haven't been engaged very long.' Cassie excused him, and then sucked in a breath as Jake caressed the nape of her neck.

'Besides,' he said. 'I'm waiting to find something really special for her.'

The more couples they talked to, the more wistful Cassie felt. The others were all so happy, so much in love, so excited about their weddings; the happier they were together, the more conscious she was that she and Jake were just pretending.

'Doesn't it make you feel a bit sad?' she asked him when they found themselves alone for a moment.

'Sad? No. Why?'

'Oh, I suppose I'm just envious,' she said with a sigh. 'Everyone else here is in love, and we're just promoting the Hall.'

Over Jake's shoulder, she could see a couple laughing together. Unaware that anyone was watching them, the girl hugged her fiancé's arm and lifted her face naturally for his kiss. They looked so comfortable together that Cassie's heart twisted and she jerked her eyes back to Jake.

'It must be even worse for you,' she said, and he lifted his brows.

'For me?'

'You might have been here with Natasha,' Cassie said. 'It's never easy, seeing everyone else all loved up when your own relationship has just fallen apart.'

And she ought to know, she thought glumly. Her relationships had a nasty habit of crashing and burning after a few weeks, and she had almost given up on meeting someone she could fall in love with, someone who would love her back.

'I can't imagine Natasha here,' said Jake, looking around him with a derisive expression. 'We didn't have that kind of relationship. If we had decided to get married, she wouldn't have had much time for all of this.'

'All of what?'

'All this lovey-dovey stuff isn't a good basis for a strong marriage.'

He had given her that line before, Cassie remembered. She didn't buy it any more this time round. 'I would have thought love was the *only* real basis for a marriage,' she said.

'I don't agree with you,' said Jake coolly. 'Love is too random. It's a hit and miss affair, and even if you do get a hit it soon runs out of steam. How many times have you seen friends wild for their new partner, only to end up complaining about how they never put the top back on the toothpaste barely weeks later?'

All too often in her own case, thought Cassie.

'It doesn't always run out of steam,' she said. 'Sometimes it gets stronger. OK, the red-hot passion may not last, but it can change into something better, something that *will* last. When you love someone completely, you accept their little quirks as part of who they are. You certainly don't throw away a good relationship because they squeeze the toothpaste in the middle instead of rolling up the ends neatly!'

'Are you talking from your own experience?' asked Jake, and she lifted her chin.

'Not personally, no,' she said with dignity. 'But I've seen plenty of other relationships where both partners learn to compromise because they love each other. It *can* work.'

'Not often enough.' Jake shook his head. 'Marriage is too serious a business to be left to love,' he said. 'It should be about shared interests, shared goals, about practicalities and the things that can't change. If you can add in sexual attraction as well, *then* you've got yourself a winning formula.'

'You can't reduce love to a formula, Jake.'

'What else is it?'

'It's—it's finding someone who makes your heart beat faster. Someone who makes your senses tingle.'

Hang on, that sounded alarmingly like the way Jake made her feel, Cassie realised uncomfortably.

'Someone who makes the sun shine brighter.' She hurried on into unfamiliar territory. Jake didn't do that, did he?

'That's just chemical attraction,' said Jake dismissively.

'It isn't chemistry that makes someone the first person you want to talk to in the morning and the last person you want to see at night,' Cassie said hotly. 'The person who believes in you, however bad things are, who will take you in their arms and make you feel that you've found a safe harbour.'

Her voice cracked a little. She had never found that person, but she wasn't giving up on the belief that he was out there somewhere, whatever Jake Trevelyan said. 'It's got nothing to do with chemistry,' she said, recovering.

'And how long does that feeling last?' Jake countered. He gestured around the room with his head. 'How many of these loving couples are going to feel like that a year from now, let alone in ten years, twenty years? Relying on how you feel is too random a way to choose a partner for life. Call it a formula, if you like, but if you're interested in the long haul you're better off sticking to what you know works.'

'The formula didn't work for you and Natasha, though, did it?' Cassie retorted without thinking.

There was a short, not entirely pleasant silence. 'No,' Jake said just as she opened her mouth to apologise. 'The formula isn't foolproof, sure. But if you find someone who fits your specifications I'd say your chances of a successful marriage are much greater than investing all your happiness in someone you don't really know.'

'Well,' said Cassie, draining her glass of champagne defiantly. 'I couldn't disagree with you more. It looks as if we're completely incompatible on that front, anyway. It's just as well we're not really getting married!'

'Just as well,' Jake agreed dryly.

At the front of the room, a microphone was spluttering into life. The editor of *Wedding Belles* was up on the little stage, making a speech and announcing the winners of the prize draw to much ooh-ing and aah-ing from the crowd. The happy couple who had won the trip to Paris was called up and had their photo taken, beaming from ear to ear.

It gave Cassie a chance to get a grip. There was a time, when they'd been chatting to other couples, when it had felt quite normal being with Jake. It had felt more than normal, in fact. It had felt strangely right to have him at her side, talking, laughing, being able to catch his eye and know that he would find the same comments amusing. For a while there, she had forgotten how different they were.

But the conversation just now had reminded her. Jake, it seemed, had a completely different idea of love. He was looking for someone who fitted his specifications the way Natasha had.

The way *she* never would. Cassie didn't need to ask what kind of woman Jake wanted. She was fairly sure the answer wouldn't be someone scatty, messy or with a poor time-keeping record. No, he would be looking for someone poised, quiet, elegant. Someone who would slot into the carefully controlled life he seemed to have built for himself since he'd left Portrevick.

And why is that a problem, Cassie?

It wasn't; Cassie answered her own question firmly. It wasn't as if she wanted a man like Jake either. Control freaks weren't her style. It didn't matter that they were completely incompatible. It wasn't as if they were actually having a relationship. This was just a pretence, and the less seriously they both took it the better.

Clutching their tickets to Paris, the winners of the first prize were leaving the stage, and more prizes were announced. Cassie was getting tired of clapping politely, and her thoughts were wandering so much that when she heard their own names called she hadn't even heard what they had won.

Perhaps her luck was changing at last, she thought buoyantly.

She dug Jake in the ribs with her elbow. 'Come on. We're on. Don't forget to smile!'

Together they climbed the stage; Cassie accepted a voucher from the editor, and they posed obediently for the camera.

'A bit closer,' called the photographer, and after the tiniest of hesitations Jake put his arm around Cassie, who had little choice but to snuggle in to his lean, hard body.

'Perfect,' said the photographer, and for a dangerous moment there it *felt* perfect too. Jake was warm and solid, and his arm was very strong. It felt wonderfully safe, being held hard against him, and Cassie found herself wishing that he would hold her like that for ever.

The moment the shot was taken, she straightened and pushed the treacherous thought aside, cross with herself. There was no point in thinking like that. Hadn't she just decided that they were incompatible?

'What have we won?' Jake asked out of the corner of his mouth as they left the stage and the next winners were called up.

Cassie opened the envelope and started to laugh. 'It's vouchers for a his 'n' hers day at a luxury spa, including treatments.'

'Treatments?' he asked nervously. 'What sort of treatments?'

'Oh, you know, pedicures, massages, waxing.'

Jake paled. '*Waxing*?'

'I believe a certain wax is very popular with men nowadays,' said Cassie naughtily, enjoying his expression of horror. 'You want to look your best for our wedding photos, don't you?'

'Not if it involves wax of any kind *anywhere*!'

'Oh well, if you're going to be such a baby…'

'Why don't we just give the voucher to someone else?'

'We can't do that. *Wedding Belles* might want photos of us enjoying our prize for the article.'

'If they think they're getting a photo of me having any hairs ripped out, they've got another think coming!' said Jake firmly.

'Don't worry; I'm sure we can find you something less painful,' Cassie soothed him as she flicked through the brochure that had come with the voucher. 'Maybe you could have a facial—or, I know, a seaweed wrap! That wouldn't hurt.'

Jake was looking aghast. 'A *wrap*?' Then he caught Cassie's dancing brown eyes, realised that she was teasing and relaxed into a laugh. 'If you *dare* book me in for anything like that, Cassie…!'

'What, and risk you cancelling our contract? No way—although it would be almost worth it to see your face.'

It was a good thing they had had that discussion about love earlier, Cassie decided. She had been in danger of forgetting that theirs wasn't a real relationship for a while, but now that she'd remembered she could relax and enjoy herself again.

She tucked her hand into his arm. 'Worry not,' she said. 'I wouldn't do anything like that to you.'

'So, can we go now?'

'Go? We haven't even started yet!' Cassie pointed to where a set of doors was swinging apart to revel a huge ballroom crammed with stalls. 'The show's just opened, and we've got a whole winter-wonderland of weddings to explore…'

'Have you got a moment?'

'Jake!' Cassie looked up in astonishment as he appeared in the doorway. It was the following Tuesday, and she was sitting on the office floor surrounded by fabric samples. She scrambled to her feet, ridiculously breathless. 'What on earth are you doing here?'

He was looking uncharacteristically hesitant. 'I wanted to ask a favour. In the circumstances, it seemed only fair that I should come to you, but I can go away if you're busy.'

'No, no. It's fine.' Cassie swept a pile of magazines off a chair. 'Sit down. I'm sorry it's all such a mess.'

She grimaced, looking at the office through

Jake's eyes. They really ought to tidy up some time. Every surface was piled high with magazines, fabric books, photographs, brochures, and samples of everything you could think of from thank-you cards to lip salves to artificial flowers. A wedding dress in a protective bag hung from a door, and the walls were covered with photos of all the weddings Avalon had planned. It was a colourful, cheerfully chaotic place, but, coming from his immaculately cool and contemporary office, Jake was unlikely to be impressed.

'Coffee?' she offered, and then wished she hadn't. They only had chipped mugs, and the milk was probably off.

'No. Thank you.'

Phew. Cassie lifted a pile of cake-design brochures off another chair and sat down. A favour, he had said. 'So, what can I do for you?'

She was rather proud of how normal she sounded, not at all as if her heart was bouncing around in her ribcage and interfering ludicrously with her breathing. She was disconcerted, in fact, by how pleased she was to see Jake.

In the end, they had had a good time at the wedding fair, and the weekend had seemed, well, a bit *empty* without him. Jake had said goodnight as they parted, but hadn't mentioned meeting again. Why would he? It was her job to get things going at the Hall, and she had that well in hand. They would need to arrange a photo session at some point, but the Hall wasn't ready for that yet.

As it was, the week stretched drearily ahead. Cassie had even caught herself wondering if she could invent an excuse to call him, and had had to give herself a stern talking-to, reminding herself about key words like 'contract', 'professionalism', and 'incompatibility'.

Jake seemed to be having trouble deciding where to start. 'Remember that voucher we won on Friday?' he said at last.

He had taken so long that Cassie had begun to worry that he was about to give her bad news. Relief made her laugh. 'Look, there's no need to worry,' she assured him, relaxing. 'I won't book anything.'

'It's not that.' Jake wanted to get to his feet, but the office was so crowded with stuff that there was nowhere to step, let alone pace. How on earth did Cassie manage to work in all this clutter?

He brought his attention back to the matter in hand. 'It turns out that one of the accountants at Primordia is getting married next year, and she was at the *Wedding Belles* party.'

'Ah,' said Cassie, seeing where this was going at last.

'I didn't recognise her, but she thought she recognised me, apparently, and when our names were announced as winners of that bloody voucher that just confirmed it. So she trotted in to work yesterday and mentioned to someone she worked with in finance that I was engaged.'

'And word went round faster than you can say "seaweed wrap"?'

Jake nodded heavily. 'That's about it. The next thing I know, Ruth, my communications director, is congratulating me and saying I must bring you to some fund-raising event we're sponsoring on Thursday.' He sighed. 'I can't believe how quickly it's all got out of hand. I didn't think anyone in London would need to know about our so-called engagement,' he confessed. 'I obviously didn't think things through properly.'

'You weren't to know anyone from work would be at the wedding fair,' Cassie pointed out consolingly.

'No.' Jake brooded, trying to work out where it had all gone wrong. He wasn't used to his plans going awry. He spent so much of his life keeping things under rigid control; this was way out of his comfort zone.

'Perhaps I should have laughed it off when Ruth first mentioned it,' he said. 'But it seemed humiliating to admit that my engagement was just a marketing exercise. Ruth knew Natasha, too. She would have felt sorry for me.'

He didn't need to tell Cassie how much he would have hated that.

'The upshot is that I let her believe that you and I really were engaged,' he went on, looking directly at Cassie. 'I'm sorry about this, but I wondered if you would mind putting on an appearance at this do on Thursday, and any other similar events in the next couple of months?' He took a breath. 'If you don't want to do it, I'll understand, of course.'

'What, no more blackmail?' said Cassie, brown eyes dancing.

Jake set his teeth. 'No. This wasn't part of our agreement. I'm just asking you to help me.'

'Of course I will,' said Cassie, regretting now that she'd teased him. He so obviously hated the whole situation. 'It'll be fine. Honestly, I don't mind.'

'It's not likely to be a big deal,' Jake said. 'Just a couple of outings.'

'There you go, then. No problem.'

'Well…thank you.'

Jake was taken aback by how relieved he was, and he had a nasty feeling it wasn't just because Cassie was prepared to save his face at work. It was barely two weeks since she had—literally—tripped back into his life, and already she had changed things more than Natasha had in six months.

That wedding fair on Friday…Jake had thought about it all weekend. Cassie had dragged him round every stall. She had tried on tiaras and sampled cupcakes. She had sighed over shoes and chatted to other brides-to-be about make-up and hen parties and how to keep children entertained at a reception.

It should have been Jake's worst nightmare, but oddly he'd found that he was enjoying himself. He'd liked watching Cassie's animated face as she talked and waved her arms around, her intent expression as she'd studied the dizzying array of goods and services on offer, and the way she'd licked her fingers after trying a piece of fruit at the chocolate fountain.

They had wrangled over table decorations, pretended to choose a honeymoon destination, dodged behind stalls to avoid Michelle and the ever-silent Mark, and generally laughed more than Jake could remember since... Well, he couldn't remember the last time he had laughed like that. And all the time he had been aware of Cassie, of her bright face and her warm smile, and the memory of her kiss was like a hum underneath his skin.

So when Ruth had congratulated him on his engagement, instead of quietly admitting that it was all a mistake he had imagined seeing Cassie again, and he had found himself playing along.

It was only after Ruth had gone that he'd realised how much he had taken it for granted that Cassie would agree. He had blackmailed her into this charade, for goodness' sake! That didn't happen to nice middle-class girls like her. Jake wouldn't have blamed her if she had told him to stuff his pretence.

After all, it wasn't as if she could like being with him. They'd got on well enough at the wedding fair, but in lots of ways being there had just pointed out the differences between them. Cassie was ridiculously romantic, he was rigidly practical. She was warm, vibrant and spontaneous, he was cool and controlled. The only thing they could agree on was that they were completely incompatible.

Jake had told himself he would deserve the humiliation of admitting to Ruth that he had lied if Cassie didn't agree.

But she had agreed. 'It'll be fine,' she had said easily, and Jake had felt his heart lift.

'Thank you,' he said again.

'When do you want me?'

Now. I want you now. Unbidden, the words hovered on the tip of Jake's tongue. He clamped his lips together, aghast at how close he had come to opening his mouth and letting them spill out without any idea of where the thought had come from.

Cassie misunderstood his silence. A blush unfurled in her cheeks. 'On Thursday, I mean.'

'Can you come to my office at six?' said Jake, recovering. 'The reception starts at half past. We may as well go together and look like a proper couple.'

CHAPTER SEVEN

'DON'T say anything!' Unbuttoning her coat, Cassie collapsed onto one of the sofas in Jake's office. 'I was so determined I was going to be on time for once, but it's really not my fault this time,' she told him. 'I've been stuck on the tube for *forty* minutes!' She groaned at the memory. 'Some problem with the signals, they said. I thought I was never going to get here.'

Jake didn't sit down. He needed a few moments to readjust. Had he actually been worrying about her? He had certainly started looking at his watch a good half-hour before she was even due to arrive, and as the minutes ticked past six o'clock he had looked more and more frequently.

And now she was here, lying on the sofa in a pose of exaggerated exhaustion, looking extraordinarily vivid. Her coat had fallen open to reveal a party dress. Jake had an impression of a vibrant blue colour, and some kind of satiny material, but all he really noticed was that it was rucked up over

Cassie's knees, and in spite of himself his eyes travelled over the legs sprawled over the leather. His mouth dried. Had Cassie always had those spectacular legs? Surely he would have noticed if she had?

Clearing his throat, Jake made himself look away. 'If you're too tired, we can always give the party a miss.'

'Absolutely not.' Cassie sat up. 'How can we convince everyone we're engaged if we don't turn up? I'm fine,' she said, pushing back her hair.

Getting to her feet, she crossed to the window, and looked down at the street below. The traffic was nose to tail, the pavements choked with umbrellas, everyone anxious to get home or heading for the nearest pub. Thousands of people, all with somewhere to go and something to do, even in the rain. She loved London like this, busy, purposeful and pulsating with energy.

Jake was reaching for his coat when he stopped. 'Oh, I nearly forgot…' He patted his jacket and pulled a small jewellery-box from the inside pocket. 'You'd better have this.'

Cassie turned from window. 'What is it?'

'Open it.'

Jake handed the box to Cassie, who opened it almost fearfully and found herself staring down at a ring set with three large square-cut rubies separated by two dazzling diamonds.

'Oh…' she said on a long breath.

Watching her face, Jake found himself rushing into speech. 'I remembered how all the other brides at the wedding fair had a ring,' he said. 'I thought you needed one for tonight. It would be odd if we'd got as far as announcing our engagement and you didn't have one. Do you like it?' he finished abruptly.

Cassie raised her eyes from the ring to look directly into his, and Jake felt as if a great fist was squeezing his heart. 'It's beautiful,' she said.

'Perhaps I should have gone down on one knee.' He tried to joke in a weak attempt to disguise his relief. He didn't want to admit even to himself how long he had spent choosing the damn thing, or how determined he had been to find exactly the right ring for her.

The brown eyes flickered and dropped again to the ring. 'There's no need for that,' she said. 'It's just a prop.'

A prop he had spent a whole afternoon agonising over. 'Yes,' said Jake.

Cassie pulled the ring out of the velvet and slipped it onto her finger. She couldn't help imagining what it would have been like if this was a real engagement ring, if Jake had bought it for her because he loved her.

She swallowed the tightness from her throat. 'It's really lovely,' she told him. 'It must have been terribly expensive. Will you be able to take it back when this is all over?' she said, just to reassure him that she hadn't forgotten that they were just pretending.

Jake was shrugging himself into his coat. 'I expect so,' he said.

'I'll take great care of it,' Cassie promised, overwhelmed by the feel of the ring on her finger.

She had never worn anything remotely as beautiful or as valuable, and the thought that Jake had chosen it for her made the breath snare again in her throat. He could have picked out a plain diamond, which would have done the job just as well, but instead he had bought *this*.

'It's gorgeous,' she said, turning her hand so that the gems flashed in the light. 'Look what a beautiful warm glow it has.'

Jake didn't need to look. The glowing warmth was the reason he had bought the ring. It had reminded him of her.

'Does it fit?' he asked.

'It's a tiny bit loose, maybe,' said Cassie, turning the ring on her finger. 'But it'll be fine just for a couple of evenings. How on earth did you know what size to get?'

'One of the assistants in the shop had hands about the same size as yours.'

Cassie didn't think Jake had ever noticed her hands. The thought that he had felt like a tiny shiver deep inside her.

'Well…thank you,' she said.

An awkward silence fell. If it had been anyone else, Cassie wouldn't have hesitated to kiss him. Just on the cheek, of course; it was the obvious way to thank him for choosing such a lovely ring for her to wear, even if only temporarily.

But Jake had stepped back after giving her the box, and now he wasn't close enough for her to give him a quick hug or brush her cheek against his. She would have had to walk across to him, and that would have made too much of a big deal of it, wouldn't it? It wasn't as if he had given her the ring because he loved her. He had agreed that it was just a prop.

Jake put an end to her dithering by looking at his watch. 'We'd better go,' he said. 'We're late.'

Outside, it was still raining. The tyres of the passing cars hissed on the wet tarmac, and the pavements gleamed with puddles. Cassie huddled into her coat. It was only the middle of September, but the temperature had dropped over the last few days, and there was an unmistakable smell of autumn in the air.

'Where are we going?' she asked.

'The Strand,' said Jake, and her face fell.

'That's miles!'

'It's too far for you to walk in those shoes, certainly,' he said, nodding down at them.

'What shall we do? We'll never get a taxi in this weather.'

The words were barely out of Cassie's mouth when Jake put two fingers in his mouth and produced a piercing whistle that had a taxi heading in the opposite direction, turning instantly and ignoring the blare of horns to cut right across the traffic and pull up in front of them.

'Well, that was annoying,' said Cassie as Jake opened the door with a mocking bow. 'But a relief too,' she decided, sinking back into the seat and fastening her seatbelt.

'The Savoy,' Jake told the taxi driver, and sat back beside her. 'Why don't you wear something more sensible on your feet?' he said, half-relieved to find something to irritate him again. He scowled at her shoes. 'Look at them—they're ridiculous!'

'They're not ridiculous!' Stung, Cassie stuck her legs straight out in front of her so she could admire her shoes. Perhaps the heels weren't *that* practical, but she loved the sling backs, and the cute, peep-toe effect, and the hot pink was a fabulous colour. 'They're party shoes. I couldn't wear sensible shoes with a party dress, now, could I? That really *would* be ridiculous!'

Jake wished she'd put her legs down. They were distracting him. *She* was distracting him.

He had to keep reminding himself that this was Cassie. He'd known her as an eager child, as an ungainly adolescent. She had never been cool, clever or graceful, or any of the things he admired in a girl.

She was an unstable force, chaotic and uncontrollable.

And now that force was bouncing uncontrollably around in his carefully constructed life.

Jake didn't like it one little bit. He had spent ten years fighting his way to the top, ten years making sure he never had to go back to Portrevick. He had changed himself quite deliberately. He had had enough of being the child wearing cast-offs, the troublemaker, the one who made eyebrows twitch suspiciously whenever he walked along the street. He had made himself cool, focused, guarded. Invulnerable.

Until Rupert Branscombe Fox had cracked his defences by taking Natasha from him, and Cassie had kicked them down completely the moment she'd laid her mouth against his.

Dragging his eyes from Cassie's legs, Jake made himself look out of the window. They were driving along the Embankment, and the Thames gleamed grey and oily in the rain, but he didn't see the river. He saw Cassie—her eyes dark and glowing in candlelight. Cassie perched on the table at Portrevick Hall, swinging her legs. Cassie laughing as she tried on a fancy tiara. Cassie looking down at the ring on her finger.

He was disturbingly aware of her warm, bright presence on the other side of the taxi. Her perfume was already achingly familiar. When had that happened? His careful life seemed to be unravelling by the minute, and Jake didn't like the feeling at all.

Completely unaware of the desperate trend of his thoughts, Cassie was patting her hair, trying to smooth it into some kind of shape. Jake's hands itched to do it for her, to slide into the soft curls, the way they had in the restaurant before that buffoon Giovanni had interrupted them. He imagined twisting its silkiness around his fingers, tucking it neatly behind her delicate ears, and then he could let his hands drift down her throat, let his lips follow…

'Is this it?' said Cassie, leaning forward to peer through the window as the taxi drew up outside the hotel, and Jake had to unscramble his thoughts enough to pay the taxi driver.

At least he had a few minutes to pull himself together while Cassie disappeared into a cloakroom to leave her coat and check her make-up. Adjusting the knot of his tie, he made himself think of something other than Cassie and the strange, disturbing way she made him feel. He remembered Portrevick instead, and the grim house where he had grown up. That was always a good way to remind himself of the importance of control. He thought about his mother's worn face, and the long, silent bus rides to visit his father in prison.

And then he thought about Rupert's supercilious

smile and his jaw tightened. If it wasn't for Rupert, he wouldn't be in this mess. If it wasn't for Rupert, he and Natasha could have posed for a few photographs for this damned article and that would have been that. If it wasn't for Rupert, he would never have kissed Cassie, and he wouldn't be standing here now, unable to shake the feel of her, the taste of her, the scent of her from his mind.

Jake gave his tie a final wrench and looked at his watch. What the hell was Cassie doing in there? He was just getting ready to storm into the Ladies and drag her out when she appeared, smoothing down her dress. It was short and simply cut, and held up with tiny spaghetti-straps that left her shoulders bare. The colour—less a blue than a purple, he could see now—was so vivid that it dazzled the eye—or maybe that was just Cassie, Jake thought as the breath leaked from his lungs. She looked warm, lush, bright and unbelievably sexy. As she walked towards him he couldn't help remembering another time, ten years ago, when she had walked towards him in a different dress.

Cassie was smiling as she walked towards him, but as she got closer and her eyes met that dark, deep-blue gaze she faltered and the smile evaporated from her face. All at once, the air seemed to close around them, sealing them into an invisible bubble and sucking the air out of her lungs. The babble and laughter from Reception inside the big doors faded, and there was just Jake, watching her with unfathomable eyes, and a silence that stretched and twanged with the memory of how it had felt to kiss him.

Suddenly ridiculously shy, she struggled to think of something to say. Something other than 'kiss me again', anyway. 'How do I look?' was the best she could do.

'Very nice,' said Jake.

He couldn't have said anything better to break the tension, thought Cassie gratefully. 'No,' she told him, rolling her eyes. 'Not "very nice". You're in love with me, remember? Tell me I look beautiful or gorgeous or sexy—anything but *very nice!*'

'Maybe I won't say anything at all,' said Jake. 'Maybe I'll just do this instead.' And, putting his hands to her waist, he drew her to him and kissed her.

His lips were warm and persuasive, and wickedly exciting. Afterwards, Cassie thought that she should have resisted somehow, but at the time it felt so utterly natural that she melted into him without even a token protest. Her hands spread over his broad chest, and she parted her lips with a tiny murmur low in her throat.

It wasn't a long kiss, but it was a very thorough one, and Cassie's knees were weak when Jake let her go.

'Sometimes actions speak louder than words,' he said.

From somewhere, Cassie produced a smile. It felt a little unsteady, but at least it was a smile. At least she could pretend that her heart wasn't thudding, that her bones hadn't dissolved, and that her arms weren't aching to cling to him. That she didn't desperately, desperately want him to kiss her again.

'That's better,' she said, astonished at how steady her voice sounded. 'See how convincing you can be when you try?'

'Let's hope we can convince everyone else too,' said Jake. 'Ready?'

Of course she wasn't ready! How could he kiss her like that and then expect her to calmly swan into a party and act like a chief executive's fiancée—whatever one of those was like?

But she had agreed, and to make some feeble excuse now would just make it look as if she had been thrown into confusion by a meaningless kiss. Even if she had, Cassie didn't want Jake to know it.

She drew a deep breath. 'Ready,' she said.

Jake kept a hand at the small of her back as they made their way through the crowd. Cassie was intensely aware of it, and even when he dropped his arm she could feel its warmth like a tingling imprint on her skin burnt through the fabric of her dress.

She was nervous at first, but Jake seemed to know a lot of people there, and everyone was very friendly. There was quite a bit of interest when he introduced her as his fiancée, and Cassie wondered how many of them had known Natasha. It soon became clear, in fact, that they should have prepared their story more carefully.

'So, where did you pop up from, Cassie?' someone asked, and Jake put an arm around her waist.

'We knew each other years ago,' he said. 'We met up again recently.'

'Oh, so you've found your first love again? How sweet!'

'Well, not really,' said Jake, just as Cassie said,

'Yes. Jake was the first boy who ever kissed me.'

There was a tiny silence. 'Jake wasn't in love with me.' Cassie rose to the occasion magnificently. 'But I had a thing about him for years. Didn't I?' she said to Jake, but he was looking so baffled that she swept on, feeling rather like Michelle at the wedding fair. 'Anyway, the moment we met up again, it just clicked.'

She chattered on, inventing an entire love-affair while Jake watched her distractedly. He had been completely thrown by that kiss out there in the lobby. What had possessed him to kiss her like that? But she had looked so warm and enticing, he couldn't help himself. Now he could still taste the soft lips that had parted in surprise, still feel her body melting into his.

As the party wore on, Jake was achingly aware of Cassie by his side, a vibrant, glowing figure chatting animatedly to whoever they met. She was behaving beautifully—much better than him, anyway, Jake thought. *Look at her*, showing off her ring, turning a laughing face to his, leaning into him as if it was the most natural thing in the world for her to be here with him.

It was obvious that everyone found her so charming that Jake began to feel almost resentful. He didn't want Cassie to be able to play her role so well. He wanted her to be as disconcerted by him as he was by her.

She seemed to be managing perfectly well on her own, so he joined a neighbouring group in the hope that a little distance would help. But it was almost impossible to concentrate on chit-chat when he could feel Cassie somewhere behind him, not touching him, not talking to him, not even looking at him, but her presence as immediate as if she had laid a hand against his bare skin.

Jake finished his champagne in a gulp and looked around for a fresh glass, only to find himself face to face with the two people he least wanted to see. They saw him at the same time. Natasha looked appalled, Rupert predictably amused.

'Well, well, look who's here,' said Rupert. 'We'd no idea you'd be here too, Jake—but it's inevitable we had to meet some time, I suppose. Much best to get the first meeting over in civilised surroundings, I can't help feeling. After all, we're a little old for pistols at dawn, don't you think?'

Jake ignored that. 'Rupert,' he acknowledged him curtly. 'And Natasha.' It was odd, he thought, how much of a stranger she seemed already. 'How are you?'

'I'm fine,' she said, but Jake didn't think that she was looking her best. She was still beautiful, of course, but after Cassie she seemed a bit muted. She had none of Cassie's vitality, none of her warmth. It was hard to remember now how bitter he had felt at losing her.

Rupert put his arm around her. 'We've just been talking about getting married, haven't we, darling?' The question was for Natasha, but the words were aimed squarely at Jake. Rupert's smile was slyly triumphant. 'It's an awkward situation, knowing how much Natasha meant to you, but we hope you'll be pleased for us.'

'Or are you just hoping that I'll end the trust?' Jake asked.

'I believe marriage to a sensible woman *was* the condition—and Natasha is certainly that, aren't you, sweetheart?'

'Settling down was also a condition,' said Jake. 'When you've been married a year or so, I'll consider it.'

There was an unpleasant silence. Jake and

Rupert eyed each other with acute dislike, and Jake found himself longing for Cassie. He could hardly go and drag her away from the conversation she was having just because he was confronting Rupert and Natasha on his own.

But suddenly there she was anyway, almost as if she'd sensed that he needed her, touching his rigid back, tucking her hand into his arm. Jake felt something unlock inside his chest.

Cassie studied Natasha. She was very lovely, with immaculate, silvery-blonde hair, green eyes, flawless skin, and intimidatingly well-groomed. From her perfect eyebrows to the tips of her beautifully manicured nails, Natasha was a model of elegance and restraint. She was wearing a simple top and silk trousers, but the combination of subdued neutrals and striking jewellery was wonderful.

'Classy' was the only word Cassie could think of to describe her, and her heart sank. Next to Natasha, she felt like a garish lump.

Why hadn't she thought to wear black or elegant neutral colours like every other woman here? Cassie wondered miserably. She should have known this would be a sophisticated party. She looked ludicrously out of place in her vivid, purple dress and pink shoes. No wonder Jake had been distracted since they'd come in. He must be horribly embarrassed by her. He was used to being with

Natasha, who fitted into this world in a way she never could.

How awful for Jake, to come face to face with the woman he loved on the arm of a man he hated, and to realise just what he had lost. Cassie had sensed his sudden tension somehow, and had turned to see him with Rupert and a woman she had known instantly was Natasha. His shoulders were set rigidly, and his back when she had touched it to let him know that she was there had been as stiff and as unyielding as a plank.

Well, she might not be Natasha, but she was here, and she could help him through this awkward meeting if nothing else.

Forcing a smile, Cassie turned her attention to Rupert. Even if she hadn't seen his photo in the papers over the years, she would have recognised him. He was still astonishingly good-looking, with golden hair, chiselled features and mesmerising blue eyes. It was only when you looked a little closer that you could see the lines of dissipation around his eyes.

And the faint bump in his nose where it had been broken.

Cassie hoped Jake could see it, too.

'Hello, Rupert,' she said pleasantly.

Rupert looked at her, arrested. 'Do we know each other?'

'We used to,' said Cassie. 'Portrevick?' she

prompted him. 'Cassie Grey? My father was Sir Ian's estate manager.'

'Good God, *Cassie*! I do remember now, but I would never have recognised you.' Rupert's eyes ran over her appreciatively. 'Well, well, well,' he drawled, evidently remembering how she had looked the last time he'd seen her. 'Who would have thought it? You look absolutely gorgeous! How lovely to see you, darling.' Taking his arm from around Natasha, he kissed her warmly on both cheeks.

The force of his charm was hard to resist, but Cassie felt Jake stiffen, and she made herself step back. 'How are you, Rupert?'

'All the better for seeing you,' he said, eyeing her with lazy appreciation. 'Where have you been hiding yourself all these years?'

How odd, thought Cassie. Here she was with Rupert, who hadn't recognised her, and was doing a very good impression of being bowled over by her looks. It was just like her fantasy.

But in her fantasy she hadn't been aware of Jake beside her, dark and rigid with hostility. She could see a muscle twitching in his jaw. He must be hating this.

'Growing up,' she said, and for the first time realised that it was true. She could look at Rupert and see that he was just a handsome face, a teenage fantasy, but not a man you could ever build a real relationship with. Had Natasha come to realise that as well? Cassie wondered. It seemed to her that the other woman's eyes were on Jake rather than Rupert, and when Cassie took Jake's hand Natasha's gaze sharpened unmistakably.

Jake's fingers closed hard around hers. 'Cassie, this is Natasha.' He introduced her stiffly.

Natasha smiled, although it looked as if it was a bit of an effort. 'You've obviously met before,' she said.

'We all grew up together in Cornwall,' said Cassie cheerfully. 'I was madly in love with Rupert for years.' She laughed. 'You know how intense adolescent love is? I promise you, I adored him.'

'You mean you don't any more?' said Rupert with mock disappointment, and with one of his patented smiles guaranteed to make a girl go weak at the knees.

Ten years ago, Cassie would have dissolved in a puddle at a smile like that. This time her knees stayed strangely steady. 'Not since I discovered what real love is,' she said, smiling at Jake, who looked straight back into her eyes; for a second the two of them were quite alone.

And then her knees *did* wobble.

Rupert's brows shot up. 'You and Jake...? How very unlikely!' His voice was light and mocking, but Cassie refused to be fazed.

'That's what we thought, didn't we, darling?'

she said to Jake, and to her relief he managed to unclench his jaw at last.

'We thought we were completely different,' he agreed. 'And it turns out that we are made for each other.'

'What do your parents think about that?' Rupert asked Cassie smoothly. 'The Greys and the Trevelyans used to move in rather different social circles, as I remember.'

Cassie lifted her chin. 'They're delighted,' she told him. 'They're coming back to Portrevick for the wedding,' she added, and heard Natasha's sharp intake of breath.

'Wedding?'

'We're getting married at Christmas.' Cassie held out her hand to show her the ring, and then wished she hadn't. Her nail polish was bright-pink and chipped, and looked slatternly compared to Natasha's perfect French manicure. She pulled her hand back quickly.

'Engaged?' said Rupert. 'That's very sudden, isn't it?'

'It must seem that way to other people,' said Cassie, annoyed by his mocking expression. Anyone would think he didn't believe them. 'But to me it feels as if I've been waiting all my life to find Jake again.'

Slipping an arm around his waist, she leant adoringly into him. 'I can't believe how lucky I am. I always thought about him, but I never dreamt we would bump into each other again, and as soon as we did…bang! That was it, wasn't it, darling?'

'It was,' said Jake. 'It's enough to make you believe in fate. Cassie came along just when I needed her. I should thank you,' he said to Rupert and Natasha. 'I didn't think so at the time, I must admit, but you both did me a huge favour. If it hadn't been for you, I might never have found Cassie again.'

'So pleased to have been of help,' said Rupert a little tightly.

Natasha managed a bleak smile. 'Christmas is very soon. I thought you didn't believe in rushing into things,' she said to Jake.

'I didn't until I met Cassie. But I know I want to spend the rest of my life with her, so there doesn't seem much point in waiting.'

Cassie saw the stricken look in Natasha's eyes and for a moment felt sorry for her. But only for a moment. Natasha had hurt Jake. She had left him for Rupert, but it was clear she wasn't at all happy to see him with someone else. It wouldn't do her any harm to think about just what she had thrown away, Cassie decided.

'It's going to be a bit of a rush to get everything organised in time,' she said, with another adoring look at Jake. 'But you're all for it, aren't you?'

'Absolutely,' he said, and a smile creased his

eyes as he looked back at her. 'I'm just worried about where I'm going to get that Regency-buck outfit.'

'Regency buck?' echoed Rupert with a contemptuous look as Cassie smothered a giggle, and Jake met his eyes squarely.

'Cassie has always had a Mr Darcy fantasy. If she wants me in a cravat, I'll wear one,' he lied. 'Actually, Rupert, you might be able to give me a few tips about how to wear one. You look like the kind of man who knows his way around a cravat.'

Rupert's eyes narrowed dangerously. Clearly he couldn't decide whether Jake was joking about what he was wearing, but he knew a snide attack when he heard one. 'I'm afraid not, old chap,' he said. 'Natasha, there's Fiona—didn't you want to have a word with her? We'd better move on. Congratulations, and it was *marvellous* to see you again, Cassie.'

He produced a card as if by magic and handed it to her, as Natasha nodded to them both and headed off as if grateful to escape. 'We should meet up and talk about old times,' he said caressingly in her ear as he kissed her goodbye. 'I know Jake works all hours, but, as you're so in love, I'm sure he trusts you off the leash! Why don't you give me a ring some time?'

Cassie looked after him, fingering the card. By rights she should have been thrilled. Rupert

Branscombe Fox wanted her to ring him! He was as devastatingly attractive as ever, but she couldn't shake the feeling that he had only shown an interest in her to rile Jake. Years ago, Jake had pointed out that Rupert was only interested in girls who belonged to someone else, and it seemed as if he hadn't changed very much. He had taken Natasha from Jake. Did he really think he could seduce her away, too?

She glanced at Jake, who was wearing a shuttered expression. 'Don't worry,' she said, 'I'm not going to ring him.'

His face closed even further. 'It's up to you,' he said abruptly. 'We're not really engaged. Keep the card, and you can call Rupert when all this is over.'

Cassie stared at him, hurt. She had forgotten about the pretence for a while, but clearly Jake hadn't. Then she remembered how difficult it must have been for him to pretend, with Natasha looking so beautiful with Rupert, and she felt guilty for not realising how embarrassing it would be for him if he suspected that there was a danger of her taking this all too seriously.

She tucked the card away in her bag. 'Maybe I will,' she said.

CHAPTER EIGHT

'It's coming on well, isn't it?' Cassie watched anxiously as Jake looked around the great hall. She badly wanted him to be impressed with the progress they had made, but to his eyes it must still look a bit of a mess.

'That scaffolding will come down as soon as the decorators have finished that last bit of ceiling,' she said. 'And then the sheets will come up so you can see the floor. That still needs to be cleaned, but the fireplace and the windows have been done—see?—and they've made a good start on the panelling, too.'

Cassie had a nasty feeling that she was babbling, but she was feeling ridiculously nervous. This was the first time she'd seen Jake since the reception at the Savoy. It had been a busy couple of weeks, most of which she had spent running up and down between London and Portrevick so that she could keep an eye on the work at the Hall. But there had still been rather too much time to think about Jake and remember how it had felt when he had kissed her.

To wonder if he would ever kiss her again.

Not that there seemed much chance of that. Jake hadn't asked her to appear as his fiancée again. She had obviously been much too crass. Cassie felt hot all over whenever she thought about how garish she had looked that evening. She must have stuck out like a tart at a vicar's tea-party. It wasn't surprising that Jake wasn't keen to repeat the experience. He only had to look at her next to Natasha's immaculate elegance to realise just how unconvincing a fiancée she made.

Their only contact since then had been by email. Cassie sent long, chatty messages about what was happening at the Hall, and Jake sent terse acknowledgements. She couldn't help wishing that he would show a little more interest. Email was convenient, but she wanted to hear his voice. She needed to know what he thought about the decisions she was making. It was lonely doing it all on her own.

But that was what he was paying her for, Cassie had to keep reminding herself. What was the point in a consultant you had to encourage the whole time, after all? Still, she had thought that they had more than a strictly businesslike relationship. They had laughed together. They had pretended to be in love.

They had *kissed*.

Whenever she thought about those kisses—and it was far too often—Cassie's heart would start to slam against her ribs. The memory of Jake's mouth—the feel of it, the taste of it—uncoiled like a serpent inside her, shivering along her veins and stirring up her blood.

It was stupid.

It was embarrassing.

It was pointless.

Time and again, Cassie reminded herself that Jake only cared about saving face with Rupert. The engagement was a tactic, that was all, one that had the added advantage of promoting the Hall so that he could rid himself of an unwanted responsibility. He hated Portrevick and all it represented. Once the Hall was up and running as a wedding venue, he would settle their fee and that would be that. She had to keep things strictly professional.

That didn't stop her heart lurching whenever she saw an email from him in her inbox, or sinking just a little when she read the brief message. It didn't stop her hoping that he would come down at the weekend, or being ridiculously disappointed when he decided to stay in London instead.

But he was here now. Cassie had—rather cleverly, she thought—arranged with *Wedding Belles* that they would supply photos themselves rather than have the magazine send a photographer all the way from London to Cornwall. It would be cheaper for the magazine, and much more convenient for them.

Tina's boyfriend was a photographer, Cassie had explained to Jake in one of her many emails. He and Tina were in on the secret, and Cassie had organised for him to take some photographs to illustrate the article. They needed some shots of the two of them apparently working on the renovation of the Hall and preparing for the wedding together, Cassie had told Jake. Could he come to Cornwall that weekend?

He would come down on Saturday, Jake had agreed, and Cassie had been jittery all day while she'd waited for him to arrive. She had changed three times that morning, and hours before there was any chance that he would turn up she would jump every time she heard a car. It was impossible to concentrate on anything, and even the most prosaic of conversations had her trailing off in mid-sentence or unable to make a decision about whether she wanted a cup of tea or not.

'What on earth is the matter with you this morning?' Tina had asked with a searching look.

'Nothing,' Cassie had said quickly. 'I'm just thinking about how much there is to do. I might as well go up to the Hall now, in fact. There's plenty to be getting on with. When Jake arrives, can you tell him I'm up there already?' she'd added casually, as if she wasn't counting the minutes until she saw him again.

She'd given herself a good talking-to as she walked up to the Hall. She'd hauled out all those well-worn arguments about being cool and professional, and concentrating on making the Hall a success, and had been so stern that she'd been feeling quite composed when she'd heard Jake's car crunching on the gravel outside.

So it had been unnerving to discover that all he had to do was walk in, looking lean and dark and forceful, for the air to evaporate from her lungs in a great whoosh. How could she think coolly and professionally when every cell in her body was jumping up and down in excitement at the mere sight of him?

Cassie swallowed and made herself shut up.

Jake was still inspecting the hall. 'It looks much better than it did,' he agreed. 'Are we still on target to have this room ready for the Allantide Ball? We're in October already,' he reminded her.

'It's only the fourth,' said Cassie. 'That gives us nearly a month until Hallowe'en. It'll be fine.'

It'll be fine. That was what she always said. Jake wasn't sure whether he envied Cassie her relaxed attitude or disapproved of it. There was so much about Cassie that made him feel unsure, he realised. Like the way he hadn't known whether he was looking forward to seeing her again or dreading it.

Jake didn't like feeling unsure, and that was how Cassie made him feel all the time. Ever since he had met her again, he seemed to have lost the control he had fought so hard to achieve.

Take that reception at the Savoy, when he had been so distracted by her that he had hardly been able to string two words together. Having to stand and watch Rupert kissing Cassie goodbye and slipping her his card had left Jake consumed by such fury that it was all he'd been able to do to stop himself from breaking Rupert's nose again. He'd had to remind himself that Cassie was probably delighted. She had told him herself of how she had dreamed of Rupert for years.

And, when it came down to it, she wasn't actually his fiancée, was she? Why was that so hard to remember?

Hating the feeling of things being out of his control, Jake had retreated into himself. He would focus on work. Work had got him where he was today, and it would see him through this odd, uncertain patch.

He had been glad when Cassie had said that she was going down to Portrevick. It had felt like his chance to get some order back into his life—but the strange thing was that he had missed her. Her message about the photographs Tina's boyfriend had agreed to take had pitched him back into confusion again, but he hadn't been able to think of an excuse not to come, and then he had despised himself for needing an excuse. What was wrong with him? It was only Cassie.

Now he was here, and so glad to see her his throat felt tight and uncomfortable. At least she was dressed more practically today, in jeans and a soft red jumper, but he had forgotten what a bright, vibrant figure she was. It was like looking at the sun. Even when you dragged your eyes away, her image was burned onto your vision.

Jake cleared his throat. 'So, what's happening about these photos?'

'Oh, yes. Well, it's not a big deal. Rob is just going to take a few pictures of us inspecting the work here, maybe pretending to look as if we're making lists or looking at fabric samples. The idea is to have some "before and after" shots, but we don't need many now. We'll have to pull out the stops for the supposed "wedding" photos, but we'll do those after the Allantide Ball, when the great hall is finished and we can decorate it as if for Christmas.' Cassie looked at him a little nervously. 'Is that OK?'

'I suppose so,' said Jake. 'I can't say I'm looking forward to it, but we're committed now. We may as well get it over and done with.'

'Tina and Rob said they'd be here at five.' Cassie glanced at her watch. 'It's only three now. Do you want me to ring them and get them to come earlier?'

'What I'd really like is to stretch my legs,' said Jake. His gaze dropped to Cassie's feet. 'Those look like sensible shoes for once. Can you walk in them?'

Outside it was cool and blustery, and the sea was a sullen grey. It heaved itself at the rocks, smashing in a froth of white spray as they walked along the cliff tops. The coastal path was narrow, and the buffeting wind made conversation difficult, so they walked in silence—but it wasn't an uncomfortable one.

When at length they dropped down onto the long curve of beach, they were sheltered from the worst of the wind. Although Cassie's curls were still blown crazily around her head, it felt peaceful in comparison with the rugged cliffs.

'This was a good idea,' she said as they walked side by side along the tide line, their heads bent against the breeze and their hands thrust into their jacket pockets.

'It's good to get out of the car,' Jake agreed. 'Good to get out of London,' he added slowly, realising for the first time in years that it was true. He had been feeling restless and uneasy, but now, with the waves crashing relentlessly onto the shore, the wind in his hair and Cassie beside him, he had the strangest feeling of coming home. 'It's been… busy,' he finished, although the truth was that he had deliberately created work for himself so that he didn't have time to think.

'Has anyone said any more about our engagement?' Cassie asked after a moment.

'Nobody seems to talk about anything else,' said Jake. 'My staff are giving me grief that I haven't introduced you, and you've been specifically included in endless invitations to drinks and dinner and God knows what else. I'm running out of excuses.'

'I don't mind going,' said Cassie. 'But you probably don't want me to,' she added quickly. 'I know I don't exactly fit in.'

Jake stopped to stare at her. 'What do you mean?'

'I was so out of place at that reception,' she reminded him. 'I know I looked crass and ridiculous compared to everybody else there. It must have been really embarrassing for you.'

'I wasn't embarrassed,' he said. 'I was proud of you. You didn't look crass. You looked wonderful. Nobody could take their eyes off you. Do you have any idea of how refreshing you were?'

'Really?' she stammered, colouring with pleasure.

Jake began walking again. 'You ought to have more confidence in yourself,' he told her. 'You might not have a profession, but you've got social skills coming out your ears, and they're worth as much as any qualification. Look at what you've achieved down here.'

'I haven't really done anything,' said Cassie. 'The contractors are doing all the work.'

'They wouldn't be doing it if it wasn't for you. You had the idea; you're getting them all organised. It's time you stopped thinking of yourself as such a failure, Cassie.'

'Easy to say,' she said with a sigh. 'But it's hard when you've spent years being the under-achiever in the family. Social skills are all very well, but it's not that difficult to chat at a party.'

'It's difficult for me,' Jake pointed out. 'I never learnt how to talk easily to people. There were no parties when I was growing up, and precious little conversation at all. We didn't do birthdays or Christmas or celebrating.'

He walked with his eyes on the sand, remembering. 'My mother did her best, but there was never enough money, and she was constantly scrimping to put food on the table. She was a hard worker. She didn't just clean for Sir Ian, but at the pub and several other houses in the village. When she came home at night she was so tired she just wanted to sit in front of the television. I don't blame her,' he said. 'She had little enough pleasure in her life.'

And how much pleasure had there been for a little boy? Cassie wondered. Starved of attention, brought up in a joyless home without even Christmas to look forward to, it was no wonder he had grown up wild.

'It was hard for her trying to manage on her own,' Jake went on. 'I barely remember my father being at home. He was sent to prison when I was six. After he was released, he came home for a couple of weeks, but nobody in Portrevick was going to employ him. He went off to London to find a job, he said, and we never heard from him again.'

'I'm sorry,' said Cassie quietly, thinking of how far Jake had come since then. From village tearaway to chief executive in ten years was a spectacular achievement, and he had done it without any of the support she, her brothers and sister had taken for granted from their own parents. 'I can't imagine life without my dad,' she said. Her father might be a bit stuffy, but at least he was always there.

'You're lucky,' Jake agreed. 'I used to wish that I could have a father at home like everyone else, but maybe if he had been around I would have ended up following in his footsteps. As it was, I inherited his entrepreneurial spirit, but decided to stick to the right side of the law. But it was touch and go,' he added honestly. 'I was getting out of control. When you've got no money, no family life and no future, it feels like there's nothing to lose.

'Sir Ian's offer came just in time,' he said. 'It made me realise that I could have a future after all, and how close I'd come to throwing it away. I knew then that if I was going to escape I had to get myself under control. I built myself a rigid structure for my life. I worked and I focused and I got out of Portrevick and the mess my life had become, thanks to Sir Ian.'

He glanced at Cassie. 'But there wasn't much time along the way to learn about social niceties. You said you felt out of place at that reception, but you belonged much more than I did. I'm the real outsider in those situations. It's one of the reasons I was so drawn to Natasha,' he admitted. 'She fits in perfectly. I could go anywhere with her and be sure that she would know exactly what to do and what to say. It sounds pathetic, but I felt safe with her,' said Jake with a sheepish look.

'But you look so confident!' Cassie said, unable to put a lack of confidence together with her image of Jake, who had always been the coolest guy around. 'You were always leader of the pack.'

'In Portrevick, and the pack was a pretty disreputable one,' said Jake. 'And I can talk business with anyone. It's a different story in a smart social setting, like that reception, where you're supposed to know exactly how to address Lord This and Lady That, how to hold your knife and fork properly, and chit-chat about nothing I know anything about.

'You could do it,' he told Cassie. 'You chatted away without a problem, but I can't do that. It makes me feel…inadequate,' he confessed. 'It's one of the reasons I resent Rupert so much, I suppose. He's colossally arrogant and not particularly bright, but he can sail into a social situation and charm the pants off everyone. Look at what he was like with you,' said Jake bitterly. 'All over you like a rash, and never mind that you're supposed to be my fiancée and I'm standing right there.'

'I think it's just an automatic reflex with Rupert,' said Cassie, hugging this hint of jealousy to her. 'He flirts with every woman he meets.'

'Does he give them all his number and tell them to call him?'

'Probably,' she said. 'And most of them no doubt will ring him. But I'm not going to. I've thrown his card away.'

Jake felt a tightness in his chest loosen. 'Good,' he said, and when he looked sideways at Cassie their eyes snagged as if on barbed wire. Without being aware of it, their steps faltered and they stopped.

Cassie was intensely aware of the dull boom of the waves crashing into the shallows, of the familiar tang of salt on the air, and the screech of a lone gull circling above. The wind blew her hair around her face and she held it back with one hand as she finally managed to tear her eyes from Jake's.

He looked different down here on the beach, more relaxed, as if the rigid control that gripped him in London had loosened. She was glad that he had told her more about his past. It sounded as if his childhood had been much bleaker than she had realised, and she understood a little better now why

he had been so insistent on a formula for relationships. If you had no experience of an open, loving
relationship like her parents', fixing on a partner
who shared your practical approach must seem a
much better bet than putting your trust in turbulent
emotions that couldn't be pinned down or analysed.

It was sad, though. In spite of herself, Cassie
sighed.

Beside her, Jake was watching the wet-suited
figures bobbing out in the swell. Even at this time
of year there were surfers here. Portrevick was a
popular surfing beach, and lifeguards kept a careful
eye from a vehicle parked between the two flags
that marked the safe area.

Following his gaze, Cassie saw one of the surfers
paddling furiously to pick up a big wave just before
it crested. He rose agilely on his board, riding the
wave as it powered inland, until the curling foam
overtook him and broke over him, sending him
tumbling gracefully into the water.

'Why don't you surf any more?' she asked him
abruptly.

'I can't.'

'But you were so good at it,' Cassie protested.
'You were always in the water. I used to watch you
from up there,' she said, pointing up to the dunes.
'You were easily the best.'

Jake's mouth twisted. 'I loved it,' he said. 'It was
the only time I felt really free. When things got too

bad at home, I'd come down here. When you're out there, just you and the sea, you feel like you can do anything. There's nothing like the exhilaration you get from riding a big wave, being part of the sea and its power…' He trailed off, remembering.

'Then why not do it again?'

'Because…' Jake started and then stopped, wondering how to explain. 'Because surfing is part of who I was when I was here. I don't want to be that boy any more. When I left Portrevick, I cut off all associations with what I'd been. I wanted to change.'

'Is that why you gave up riding a motorbike too?'

He nodded. 'Maybe it's not very rational, but there's part of me that thinks the surfing, the bike, the risks I used to take, all of those were bound up with being reckless, being wild and out of control. It felt as if the freedom they gave me was the price I had to pay to get out of Portrevick and start again.'

'But you've changed,' said Cassie. 'Taking out a surf board or riding a motorbike isn't going to change you back.'

'What if it does?' countered Jake, who had obviously been through this many times before. 'What if I remember how good it felt out there? I'm afraid that, if I let go even for a moment, I might slide back and lose everything I've worked so hard for. I can't risk that. My whole life has been about leaving Portrevick behind.'

He was never going back, Jake vowed. No matter if here, by the sea, was the only place he ever felt truly at home. He had escaped, and the only way was forward.

'It seems a shame,' said Cassie. 'You can't wipe out the past. That wild boy is still part of who you are now.'

'That's what I'm afraid of,' said Jake.

Who was she to talk, anyway? Cassie asked herself as they turned and walked slowly back along beach. She didn't want to be the gauche adolescent she had been, either. Perhaps if she could put her past behind her as firmly as Jake had she too could be driven and successful, instead of muddling along, living down her family's expectations.

Tina and Rob were waiting for them back at the Hall, and Rob took a series of photos. 'Detailed shots are best,' Tina said authoritatively. 'I've been looking through a few bridal magazines, and that's what the readers want to see. A close up of a table decoration, or your shoes or something, so they can think, "ooh, I'd like something like that".'

'What about a close up of the engagement ring, in that case?' Jake suggested.

'That's a brilliant idea. Why aren't you wearing it, Cassie?'

'It feels all wrong to wear it all the time,' said Cassie, taking the box out of her bag and slipping the ring onto her finger. 'It's not as if it's a real engagement ring.' Unaware of her wistful expression, she turned her hand to make the jewels flash. 'It's just a prop.'

'Some prop,' said Tina, admiring it. 'It's absolutely gorgeous—and perfect for you, Cassie.'

'It's beautiful, isn't it?' Cassie's eyes were still on the ring. 'Jake chose it.'

Tina's sharp gaze flicked from her friend's face to Jake, who was watching Cassie. 'Did he now?'

Cassie was glad they had had that talk on the beach. Things were much easier between them after that, and they were able to chat quite comfortably when Jake gave her a lift back to London the next day.

She understood a little more why he was so determined to leave his old life behind him, and could admire the way he had transformed himself—but a little part of Cassie was sad too. Their conversation had underlined yet again how very different they were. She wished Jake could let go just a little bit, just enough to let him want someone a little muddled, a little messy.

A little bit like her, in fact.

Oh yes, and how likely is that? Cassie asked herself. Jake was used to a woman like Natasha, who was beautiful and clever and fit perfectly into his new life. Why on earth would he want to 'let go' for *her*? The best she could hope for was to be a friend.

And that was what she would be, Cassie decided. After the photo session, she had persuaded Jake to come to the pub with her, Tina and Rob. He had been reluctant at first, remembering the less-than-warm welcome he had had on previous occasions, but this time it was different. Cassie had made sure that Portrevick knew the truth about Sir Ian's will, and word had got round about the Allantide Ball too. She was determined to see Jake accepted back in the village, whether he liked it or not.

So the drive back to London was fine. Or, sort of fine. It was comfortable in one way, and deeply uncomfortable in another. A friend would enjoy Jake's company, and that was what she did. A friend would ask him about his time in the States and about his job, and chat away about nothing really. A friend would make him laugh.

But a true friend *wouldn't* spend her whole time having to drag her eyes away from his mouth. She wouldn't have to clutch her hands together to stop them straying over to his thigh. She wouldn't drift off into a lovely fantasy, where Jake would pull off the road and rip out her seatbelt in a frenzy, unable to keep his hands off her a moment longer.

'Quick—where's the nearest Travelodge?' he would say—except a motel was a bit tacky, wasn't it? Cassie rewound the fantasy a short way and tried a new script. 'Let's get off the main road and find a charming pub with a Michelin-starred restaurant and a four-poster bed upstairs,' she tried instead.

Yes, that was more like it, she decided, almost purring in anticipation. There would be a roaring fire and they would sit thigh-to-thigh in front of it with a bottle of wine…then Jake would take her hand and lead her up some rickety stairs to their bedroom. He'd close the door and smile as he drew her down onto the bed, unbuttoning her blouse and kissing his way down her throat at the same time.

'I've been thinking about this for weeks,' he would murmur, his lips hot against her skin, his hands sliding wickedly over her. 'I'm crazy about you.'

'I love you too,' she would sigh.

'Did you mean what you said?' said Jake, startling her out of her fantasy at just the wrong point.

'What?' Cassie jerked upright, her blood pounding. Good grief, she hadn't been dreaming aloud, had she? 'No! I mean…when? What did I say?'

'On the beach yesterday. You said you wouldn't mind coming along to various events as my fiancée again?'

Cassie fanned herself with relief. 'Oh…no, of course not.' Willing her booming pulse to subside, she pulled at her collar in an attempt to cool herself.

She had got a bit carried away there. *I love you too.* What on earth was that about? She wasn't in love with Jake. What a ridiculous idea. She just... found him very attractive.

Yes, that was all it was.

On the other hand, friendly was all she was supposed to be, she reminded herself sternly. 'I'm always up for a party.'

Keep it light, Cassie had told herself. But it didn't stop her spending hours searching for the definitive little black dress when Jake rang and asked if she could come to a drinks party later that week.

She should have spared herself the effort. Jake hated it. 'It's boring,' he said when Cassie presented herself with a twirl and made the mistake of asking what he thought. 'Why didn't you buy a red one? Or a green one? Anything but black!'

Cassie was crestfallen. 'I thought you'd like it if I wore what everyone else was wearing,' she said. 'I didn't want to stand out.'

'I like you as you are,' said Jake.

When Cassie thought about it afterwards, she realised that it was actually quite a nice thing for him to say, but the words were delivered in such a grumpy, un-lover-like tone that at the time she was rather miffed. She had thought she looked really smart for once.

She didn't bother dressing up for the day at the

spa. To Jake's horror, *Wedding Belles* had decided to send a photographer along to take a picture of them enjoying their prize, so Cassie had to hurriedly arrange a day when they could make the most of the voucher. Jake was furious when he heard that he had to take a day off work.

'It'll be good for you,' Cassie told him. 'You need to relax. I'll book some treatments.'

'There had better not be any seaweed involved,' warned Jake as they signed in to the spa, which promised them 'utter serenity'…'a time out of time'.

'Don't worry,' said Cassie. 'I knew you didn't like the idea of seaweed, so you're going to be smeared in mud from the Dead Sea, and then wrapped in cling film instead.'

'What?'

She rolled her eyes and laughed at his aghast expression. 'Oh, don't panic. You're just getting a back massage. It'll help you unwind.'

Jake was deeply uncomfortable about the thought of a massage at all, but in the end it wasn't too bad. He couldn't say he found the spa a relaxing experience, though. There was nothing relaxing about spending an entire day with Cassie, dressed only in a swimming costume and a fluffy robe which she cast off frequently as she dragged him between steam rooms, saunas and an admittedly fabulous pool.

How could he relax when Cassie was just *there*,

almost naked? Jake couldn't take his eyes off her body. She wasn't as slender or as perfectly formed as Natasha, but she had long, strong legs and she was enticingly curved. She looked so *touchable*, thought Jake, his mouth dry.

He had to keep dragging his eyes back to her face as she sat on the edge of the pool, dangling her legs in the water, or stretched out on the pine slats in the sauna, chatting unconcernedly. The photographer took a snap of them in their robes, and Jake had a feeling that he was going to look cross-eyed with the effort of keeping his hands off that lush, glowing body.

Utter serenity? Utter something else entirely, in Jake's book!

He told himself that it would be a relief when Cassie went back to Portrevick to prepare for the Allantide Ball. But as soon as she had gone he missed her. It was almost as if he was getting used to her colourful, chaotic presence; as if a day without seeing her walk towards him on a pair of ridiculously unsuitable shoes, or hearing her laugh on the end of the phone, was somehow dull and monochrome. Cassie enthused by email from Portrevick:

Wait till you see the great hall! It's looking fab. As soon as ball is over, will redecorate as if for a Christmas wedding and Rob is all teed up to come and take some photos of us. Will send them to *Wedding Belles* in January, and then it'll all be over, you'll be glad to know! Cxxx

Jake spent a long time looking at those three kisses. Kiss, kiss, kiss. What kind of kisses did she mean? Brief, meaningless, peck-on-the-cheek kisses? Or the kind of kisses that made your heart thunder and your head reel? The kind of kisses you couldn't bear to stop, but were never enough? She had added,

P.S., We're having an evening wedding (just so you know!) so don't forget your tuxedo!

But all Jake saw was 'it'll all be over'. He wasn't sure that he wanted it to be over, and not being sure threw him into turmoil. For ten years now he *had* been sure. He had known exactly what he needed to do. Now Cassie had thrown all that into question with three little kisses.

CHAPTER NINE

'WHAT do you think?' Cassie gestured around the great hall, and Jake turned slowly, staring at the transformation she had wrought.

From the ceiling hung a mass of paper lanterns, gold, red, russet and orange, their autumn colours investing the great hall with a vivid warmth. Everywhere else in the country rooms were being decorated with pumpkins, ghoulies and ghosties for Hallowe'en, but here in Portrevick Hall there were candles in every stone niche and great bowls piled high with Allan apples, just as there had been in Sir Ian's time.

Outside, it was cold and damp. Fallen leaves were lying in great drifts and the air held an unmistakable edge, with the promise of winter blowing in from the sea, but inside the Hall was warm and inviting.

'It looks wonderful,' said Jake sincerely. He couldn't believe how Cassie had transformed the

Hall in such a short time. He couldn't quite put his finger on what she had done. It was as if she had waved a wand and brought the old house to life again. 'You've done an amazing job,' he told her.

Cassie coloured with pleasure. 'I'm glad you like it. I think it'll look good in the photos. The local paper are sending someone to cover the ball, and they're going to mention the fact that the Hall is being developed as a venue—so that should get us some coverage locally, at least.

'Oh, by the way,' she said, carefully casual, 'word has got out about our supposed engagement, so I thought I'd better move into the Hall with you. It's not as if we're short of bedrooms here, and it might look a bit odd if I was engaged to you but still staying chastely with Tina.'

'Fine,' said Jake, too heartily. The idea of Cassie moving in with him was like a shot of adrenalin. He knew quite well that she wouldn't be sharing a bedroom with him, but still there was a moment when the blood roared in his ears and he felt quite lightheaded. 'Good idea.'

He cleared his throat, wondering how to get off the subject of bedrooms. 'How many people are you expecting tonight?' he asked Cassie.

'I'm not sure. Probably about a hundred and fifty or so,' she guessed. 'More or less the same as usual. Everyone I've spoken to in the village has said they're coming.'

She didn't add that she suspected that most of them were curious to see Jake again. 'I've put notices up in the local pubs, the way Sir Ian used to do, so we may have some people from round about, too.'

Jake ran his finger around his collar. 'I'm not sure how I feel about confronting so much of my past in one fell swoop,' he admitted.

'It'll be fine.' Cassie laid a hand on his arm, her brown eyes warm. 'Everyone knows the truth about Sir Ian's will. They're prepared to accept you for how you are now.'

Jake didn't believe that for a moment, but he was too proud to admit that he was dreading the evening ahead. 'What time are they all coming?'

'Seven o'clock.' Cassie looked at the old clock still ticking steadily after all these years. 'We'd better get changed.'

'I hope you're not wearing that black dress again,' said Jake as they moved towards the stairs.

'No,' she said. 'You made such a fuss about that, I thought I'd wear a red one this time.'

'A red one?' Jake paused with one foot on the first step. 'Like the one you wore to the last Allantide Ball?'

Their eyes met, and the memory of how they had kissed that evening shimmered in the air so vividly that Cassie could almost reach out and touch it. A tinge of colour crept into her cheeks. 'I hope this one is a little more classy.'

'Shame,' said Jake lightly. 'Does that mean you're not going to flirt with me again?'

'I might do,' said Cassie, equally lightly, but the moment the words were out she wanted to call them back. If she was going to flirt with Jake, was she going to kiss him too? The question seemed to reverberate in the sudden silence: *did flirting mean kissing…kissing…kissing?*

She swallowed and set off up the stairs. 'Only if I have time—and nothing better to do, of course.' She tried to joke her way out of it.

'Of course,' Jake agreed dryly.

'Use this bathroom here,' he said, leading her down a long, draughty corridor. He pointed at a door. 'It's the warmest, and the only one with halfway decent plumbing.'

Cassie tried to calm her galloping pulse as she showered and changed into the dress she had bought after Jake had so summarily rejected her foray into black elegance. This one was a lovely cherry-red, and the slinky fabric draped beautifully over her curves and fell to her ankles. It had a halter neck and a daringly low back. Her mother would have taken one look at it and told her that she would catch her death and should cover up with a cardigan, but Cassie wasn't cold at all. The thought of Jake in the shower just down the hall was keeping her nicely heated, thank you.

She leant towards the mirror to put on her make-up, but her hand wasn't quite steady; she kept remembering the look in Jake's eyes when he'd asked if she was going to flirt with him the way she had ten years ago.

She was no good at this 'just being friends' thing, Cassie decided. A friend would have treated his question as a joke. Had she done that? No, she had given him a smouldering look under her lashes. *I might do*, she had said.

Cassie cringed at the memory. Good grief, why hadn't she just offered herself on a plate while she was at it? She would have to try harder to be cool, she decided. But she couldn't stop the treacherous excitement flickering along her veins and simmering under her skin as she slid the ruby ring onto her finger, took a deep breath and went to find Jake.

He was still in his room, but the door was open. Cassie knocked lightly. 'Ready?' she asked.

'Nearly.' Jake was fastening his cuffs, a black bow-tie hanging loose around his neck. Glancing up from his wrists, he did a double take as he saw her standing in the doorway, vibrant and glowing in the stunning red dress.

For a moment, he couldn't say anything. 'You look…incredible,' he said, feeling like a stuttering schoolboy.

'Thank you.'

Mouth dry, Jake turned away. 'I'll be with you in a second,' he managed, marvelling at how normal he sounded. 'I just have to do something about this damned tie.' He stood in front of the mirror and lifted his chin, grimacing in frustration as he attempted to tie it with fingers that felt thick and unwieldy. 'I hate these things,' he scowled.

'Here, let me do it.' Cassie stopped hovering in the doorway to come and push his hands away from the mess he was making with the tie. 'I deal with these all the time at weddings. Stand still.'

Jake stood rigidly, staring stolidly ahead. He was excruciatingly aware of her standing so close to him. He could smell her warm, clean skin, and the fresh scent of her shampoo drifted enticingly from her soft curls, as if beckoning him to bury his face in them.

In spite of himself, his gaze flickered down. Cassie's expression was intent, a faint pucker between her brows as she concentrated on the tie with deft fingers. He could see her dark lashes, the sweet curve of her cheek, and he had to clench his fists to stop himself reaching for her.

'OK, that'll do.' Cassie gave the tie a final pat and stood back. And made the fatal mistake of looking into his eyes.

The dark-blue depths seemed to suck her in, making the floor unsteady beneath her feet, and her mind reeled. Cassie could feel herself swaying back towards him, pulled as if by an invisible magnet, and her hands were actually lifting to reach for him when Jake stepped abruptly back.

'Thank you,' he said hoarsely, and cleared his throat. 'That looks very professional.'

Cassie's pulse was booming in her ears. She moistened her lips. 'I should go down—see if the caterers need a hand.'

She practically ran down the stairs. Oh God, one more second there and she would have flung herself at him! It had taken all her concentration to fasten that tie when every instinct had been shrieking at her to rip it off him, to undo his buttons, to pull the shirt out of his trousers and press her lips to his bare chest. To run her hands feverishly over him, to reach for his belt, to drag him down onto the floor there and then. What if Jake had seen it in her eyes?

Well, what if he had? Cassie slowed as she reached the bottom of the staircase. It wasn't as if either of them had any commitments. They were both single, both unattached. Why *not* act on the attraction that had jarred the air between them just now?

Because Jake had felt it too, Cassie was sure.

The prospect set a warm thrill quivering deep inside her. It grew steadily, spilling heat through her as she helped a tense Jake greet the first arrivals, until she felt as if she were burning with it.

Cassie was convinced everyone must be able to see the naked desire in her face, but if they could nobody commented. There was much oohing and aahing about the decorations instead, and undisguised curiosity about Jake and their apparent engagement, of course. But nobody seemed to think that there was anything odd about the feverish heat that must surely be radiating out of every pore.

She kept an anxious eye on Jake, knowing how much he had been dreading the evening. He might not think he could do social chit-chat, but it seemed to Cassie that he was managing fine. Only a muscle jumping in his cheek betrayed his tension. She had felt him taut beside her at the beginning, but as he relaxed gradually Cassie left him to it. Standing next to him was too tempting, and it wouldn't do to jump him right in front of everyone.

Smiling and chatting easily, she moved around the Hall. Having grown up in Portrevick, she knew almost everyone there, and they all wanted to know about her parents, brothers and sister. Normally, Cassie would have been very conscious of how unimpressive her own achievements were compared to the rest of the family's, but tonight she was too aware of Jake to care. She talked about how Liz juggled her family and her career, about Jack's promotion, about the award Tom had won—but her attention was on Jake, who was looking guarded, but obviously making an effort for the village that had rejected him.

Cassie was talking to one of her mother's old bridge friends when she became aware of a stir by the main door, and she looked over to see

Rupert and Natasha stroll in, looking impossibly glamorous. Her first reaction was one of fury—that they should turn up, tonight of all nights, to make the ball even more difficult for Jake than it needed to be.

Jake had his back to the door and hadn't seen them yet. Cassie excused herself and hurried over to intercept Rupert and Natasha. 'I'm surprised to see you here,' she said, although she was more surprised at how irritated she was by Rupert's ostentatiously warm greeting.

'I saw the ball advertised, and thought we would drop in for old times' sake,' said Rupert. 'After all, Sir Ian *was* my uncle.' He looked nostalgically around the great hall. 'Besides, I wanted Natasha to see the house where I grew up.'

'You only came for part of the summer holidays,' Cassie pointed out, knowing that what Rupert really wanted to do was flaunt Natasha in front of Jake and remind him of his humiliation.

'Now, why do I get the impression you're not pleased to see me, Cassie?' Rupert smiled and leant closer. 'Or is it possible that you're not pleased to see Natasha?' he murmured in her ear.

Natasha, looking cool and lovely, was standing a little apart, her green eyes wandering around the great hall. She might have been admiring the architecture, but Cassie was sure that she was searching for Jake, and her lips tightened.

'Oh, dear, I suppose it was a bit tactless of us to come,' Rupert went on with mock regret. 'Jake did adore her so, and you can see why. She's perfection, isn't she?'

'She's very beautiful,' Cassie said shortly, thinking that that really was tactless of Rupert. As Jake's fiancée, she was hardly likely to want to hear about how much he had loved another woman, was she? 'But looks aren't everything, Rupert. Jake's in love with me now.'

'Is he?' Rupert's smile broadened as he looked down into Cassie's face. 'You don't think there could be a little touch of the rebound going on? Or even, dare I say it, a little face-saving, hmm? He did get together with you very quickly after Natasha left, after all.'

Cassie met his amused blue eyes as steadily as she could. Rupert might be extraordinarily handsome, but he wasn't stupid. 'Think what you want, Rupert,' she said as she turned on her heel. 'Jake loves me and I love him.'

She heard the words fall from her lips, and the truth hit her like a splash of cold water in her face: she *did* love Jake. Why hadn't she realised it before? It had snuck up on her without her realising.

Trembling as if she had had a shock, Cassie looked around for Jake and caught a glimpse of him through the crowd, standing almost exactly where he had been standing ten years ago. He was momentarily alone, looking dark and formidable, and the sight of him was like a great vise squeezing her entrails.

Cassie knew why she hadn't wanted to see the truth. It was impossible that a man like Jake could love her back. Rupert was right, of course. Jake had adored Natasha. He had told her so himself, hadn't he? If he had indeed felt the…*something* fizzing between them, Cassie was fairly sure that he would think of it as no more than a physical attraction.

Well, that might be enough, Cassie told herself as she wove her way through the chattering groups towards him, very aware of Rupert's mocking gaze following her. She would convince him that what was between her and Jake was real—even if it wasn't—and, if that meant seducing Jake, so much the better.

She wouldn't fool herself that it could last for ever, but she could at least make the most of the time she did have with him. She could save Jake's face and assuage the terrible need that was thudding and thumping in the pit of her belly at the same time.

So she smiled at Jake and ran her hand lightly down the sleeve of his dinner jacket, hoping if nothing else to distract him from the fact that Natasha and Rupert were here. 'I thought I'd come and see if my flirting technique is any better than ten years ago.'

Amusement bracketed his mouth, but his eyes were hot and dark as they ran over her. 'The thing about wearing a dress like that is that you don't need to flirt. You don't need to say anything at all. You just need to stand there and look like that.'

Cassie swallowed. 'Gosh, you're much better at flirting than I am!'

'You haven't even started yet,' Jake pointed out. 'I'm waiting for you to do your worst. Get those eyelashes batting!' The dark-blue gaze came up to meet hers, and their smiles faded in unison. 'Come on—flirt with me, Cassie,' he said softly, and her breath snared in her throat.

Her heart, which had been pounding away like mad, had decelerated suddenly to a painful slam, so slow that she was afraid that it might stop altogether.

'I…can't,' she whispered, unable to tear her eyes from his, and Jake lifted a gentle hand to run a finger down her cheek, searing her skin with its caress.

'Shall we skip the flirting, then?' His voice was very deep and very low. 'Shall we just go straight to the kissing?'

Unable to speak, Cassie nodded dumbly. She had forgotten Rupert, forgotten Natasha, forgotten that they were surrounded by the whole of Portrevick. As far as she was concerned, they could sink right down onto the stone flags together and make love right there. But Jake, more aware of everyone around them, took her hand and pulled her out along the corridor and onto the side terrace, just as he had done ten years ago.

Like then, it was cold and drizzly, but neither of them noticed. The door banged behind them, and Jake was already sliding his fingers into Cassie's hair the way he had fantasised about doing for so long. His mouth came down hungrily on hers and they kissed fiercely, almost desperately.

Cassie grabbed his shirt, holding on to it for dear life; suppressed excitement was unleashed by the touch of his lips and rocketed through her so powerfully that she could have sworn she felt her feet leave the ground.

God, it felt so good to be kissing him! He tasted wonderful, he felt wonderful, so hard, so strong, so gloriously, solidly male. She slid her arms around him to pull him tighter, her pulse roaring in her ears, as Jake backed her into the wall, his hands moving possessively, insistently, over her, making her dress ruck and slither, smoothing warm hands down her bare back.

'I've wanted this for weeks,' he whispered unevenly in her ear, when they broke for breath.

'I think I've wanted it for ten years,' she said, equally shaky.

'Liar,' Jake laughed softly, but his mouth was drifting down her throat, making her gasp and arch her head to one side. 'You wanted Rupert.'

It was hard to think clearly with his lips teasing their way along her jaw and his fingers tracing wicked patterns on her skin. 'I don't want Rupert now,' she managed raggedly, clutching her hands in his dark hair. 'I want *you*.'

Jake lifted his head at that and took her face between his hands, looking deep into her eyes. 'Are you sure, Cassie?'

'Oh yes,' she said, reaching for him again. 'I'm quite sure.'

Cassie drew a long, shuddering sigh of sheer pleasure and snuggled closer into Jake. Her head was on his shoulder, and his arm was around her, warm and strong, holding her securely as they waited for their heart rates to subside and their breathing to steady. She suspected Jake had fallen asleep, but her blood was still fizzing with a strange mixture of peace and exhilaration. She could feel herself glowing, radiating, shimmering with such contentment that she was surprised she wasn't lighting the dark room. Plug her in and she could power a chandelier, if not a city full of street lights. They could keep her as an emergency back-up for the energy crisis. Who needed a nuclear power-station when all Jake had to do was make love to her like that?

Somehow they had got themselves from the terrace to Jake's room. Cassie had no idea whether anyone had seen them and she didn't care. Nothing had mattered but Jake: the feel of him, the taste of him, the sureness of his hands, the delicious drift of his lips, the hard possession of his body.

Cassie felt giddy just thinking about that heady blur of sensation. They had lost all sense of time, of place. Nothing had existed except touch— *there…there…yes, there…yes, yes*—need so powerful that it hurt, and excitement that spun like a dervish, faster and faster, terrifyingly faster, until they lost control of it and it shattered in a burst of heart-stopping glory.

Downstairs, Cassie could hear the muted sounds of the Allantide Ball still in full swing without them, and felt sanity creeping back. It wasn't entirely welcome, she realised, and wondered if Rupert was still down there.

And Natasha.

What was it Rupert had said? *A little touch of the rebound going on? Jake did adore her so.*

He had. Cassie remembered him telling her about Natasha the first time they had driven down here together. *She's perfect,* he had said. She was everything he'd ever wanted.

Which made her just someone to catch him on the rebound.

Cassie sighed and stroked the broad chest she was resting so comfortably against. What did she have to offer, after all? Look at her, the failure of her family. She wasn't beautiful, wasn't successful, wasn't accomplished, wasn't calm and sensible. She couldn't begin to compare with Natasha.

On the other hand, she was here, lying next to Jake, and Natasha wasn't.

She would have to keep her fantasies firmly under control for once, Cassie vowed. There was no point in getting carried away like she usually did. She wasn't Jake's dream, and she never would be. Best to face it now.

But she didn't have to think about the future yet. She had the here and now. Cassie rested her palm over Jake's heart and felt it beating steadily. For now that was enough.

'We'd better get on.' Cassie sighed and stretched reluctantly. November had dawned dark and dank, and she would have loved to stay snuggled up to Jake's warm, solid body all day. 'There's lots to do.'

Lazily, Jake slid his hand from the curve of her hip to her breast, and she caught her breath at the heart-stopping intimacy of the gesture. 'Like what?' he asked, pulling her closer.

'Like getting married,' she reminded him, and laughed as he froze for a moment. 'I can't believe you've forgotten that Tina and Rob are coming tonight for another photo session!'

'I've had other things on my mind,' said Jake, rolling her beneath him, lips hot and wicked against her breast, making her arch beneath his hands. 'More important things—like reminding you what you've been waiting ten years for…'

Here and now, Cassie told herself as desire flooded her. Jake was right. What was more important than that?

It was much later when she finally forced herself out of bed, and nearly had a fit when she saw the time. 'There's so much to do!'

Fortunately the caterers had cleared up most of the debris from the party the night before, but they still had to take down the Allantide decorations and make the great hall look as if it was Christmas instead.

'Why don't we leave it until it *is* Christmas?' asked Jake as Cassie ran around putting up fairy lights and piling pine cones into bowls.

'Because I was trying to get everything over as soon as possible,' she said. 'I thought it made sense to do all the photos at once. Rob said he took some good ones last night, which we can use on the website, and I've arranged for him to come back tonight since you'd be down here anyway. I didn't think you'd want to come down more than you had to.'

'I don't mind,' said Jake, who couldn't quite remember now why he had been so resistant to the idea. He couldn't remember much about anything this morning except how warm, sweet and exciting Cassie had been the night before.

He felt as if he were walking along the edge of a cliff, knowing that a false step would send him tumbling out of control. Jake wasn't sure how he had got himself there, but he couldn't turn round and go back now. He had to keep going and not look down to see how far it was to fall.

They hadn't talked about the future at all, and Jake was glad. He had a feeling that even thinking about a future that accommodated Cassie, and the chaos she took with her wherever she went, would send his careful life slipping over the edge of that cliff.

The sensible thing, of course, would have been to remember that before he had made love to her. But he was here now, and Cassie's bright presence was lighting up the great hall. He could be sensible again when he got back to London.

'If we left it until December, you could have a Christmas tree,' he pointed out.

Cassie hesitated, picturing a tall tree in the corner by the staircase. 'It would look lovely,' she admitted. 'But everything else is ready now. I've got my dress on loan, as it's just going to be used for photographs, and Rob and Tina are all sorted too. We might as well go ahead,' she decided reluctantly. A Christmas tree would have been the perfect finishing touch.

She was setting a round table as if for a reception, and Jake was astounded by the detail. She seemed to have thought of everything, from carefully designed place-card holders to tiny Christmas puddings on each plate. A stunning dried-flower arrangement with oranges and berries in the centre of the table held candles, wine glasses were filled with white rose-petals, and silver crackers added a festive touch.

'How on earth did you think of all this?' he asked. He would have thrown on a tablecloth, and might have risen to a candle or two, but that was where his inspiration would have run out.

'Oh, it was easy,' said Cassie, straightening the last cracker and standing back to survey the table with satisfaction. 'This is my job, remember? Besides, all I had to do in this case was act out a fantasy I've had for years,' she went on cheerfully. 'I always wanted a Christmas wedding, and in my fantasy it was here at the Hall, so I didn't really have to think of anything. I knew exactly what I wanted.'

Of course, in her fantasy Rupert would probably have been the groom, Jake thought jealously.

Cassie was chattering on. 'Naturally, there would be lots more tables if this was a real wedding. I'm hoping Rob will be able to take some pictures of us that will give the impression that hundreds of guests are milling around in the background. We'll feel complete prats, I know, but it's all in a good cause, and if Rob can get some good shots of details the Hall should look wonderful in that article.'

Ah yes, the article. Jake had almost forgotten why they were doing this.

'It does look surprisingly Christmassy,' he said, looking around. He wasn't sure how Cassie had done it. There were no snowmen or reindeer, no Santa Claus climbing down the chimney. Instead she had created a subtle effect with colour and light.

'Wait till we've lit the fire and the candles,' said Cassie. 'I've made some mince pies too, and some mulled wine to offer our guests as they come in from the cold. Rob can take a still-life shot and then we might as well enjoy them to get us in the mood.'

'All you need is some mistletoe,' said Jake.

'It's too early, unfortunately, but don't think I haven't tried to get some!'

'Let's pretend it's hanging right here,' he said, pointing above their heads and drawing Cassie to him with his other arm. 'Then I can kiss you right underneath it.'

Dizzy with delight, Cassie melted in to him and wound her arms around his neck to kiss him back.

'When are Tina and Rob coming?' Jake's voice was thick as he nuzzled her throat, making her shiver with anticipation.

Cassie opened her mouth, but before she could say anything the old-fashioned door-bell jangled.

Jake sighed. 'Now?'

'I'm afraid so.'

Tina gasped at the transformation Cassie had

wrought on the great hall. 'It feels like Christmas already! I can feel a carol coming on… O come, all ye faithful,' she warbled tunelessly.

They left Rob taking photos of the table and decorations while they went to change. Tina had bought a black-evening dress, which they had decided would be suitable for a bridesmaid, and she helped Cassie into the borrowed wedding-dress. Made of satin and organza, it was fitted underneath with a floaty outer layer that was fixed at the waist with a diamond detail.

'Oh Cassie, you look beautiful,' Tina said tearfully as she fastened a simple tiara into Cassie's hair. The curls didn't lend themselves to a sophisticated up-do, and in the end Cassie had decided to leave her hair as it was and save on the expense of a hairdresser.

'Hey, I'm not really getting married,' she reminded Tina, but her expression was wistful as she studied her reflection. It was her dream dress, and it was impossible not to wish that she was wearing it for real.

Jake waited in the great hall with Rob as she and Tina headed down the grand staircase. Without the bother of make-up, it hadn't taken him long to change into his tuxedo again. He stood at the bottom of the stairs watching Cassie coming down, and looking so devastating. Her knees felt weak and her mind spun with the longing to throw herself into his arms.

And then she almost did as she missed a step and lurched to one side. She would have fallen if Tina hadn't grabbed her and hauled her upright. 'God, you're such a klutz, Cassie,' her friend scolded. 'It won't make much of a photo with you lying at the bottom of the stairs with a broken neck!'

Then Cassie was all fingers and thumbs as she attempted to pin a white-rose buttonhole on Jake. 'I'll do it,' he said in the end, and she turned away to pick up the bouquet she had ordered, only to fumble that too. Jake caught it just before it hit the ground, and shook his head. 'You're hopeless,' he said, but he was smiling.

Get a grip, Cassie, she told herself sternly.

'So, what's the idea?' said Tina, getting down to business. 'Are you having the wedding here too?'

'No, just the reception,' said Cassie who had managed to pull herself together. 'We've been married in Portrevick church, and we've just arrived in a horse and carriage.'

Jake made a face. 'A car would be much more sensible. It's a steep hill up from the village.'

'Yes, well, this is a fantasy,' said Cassie a little crossly. 'Who wants a sensible fantasy? It was a horse and carriage,' she insisted. 'A *white* horse, in fact. Or possibly two.'

'OK,' said Rob, breaking into the discussion. 'I've taken as many details as I can. Let's have the bride and groom looking into each other's eyes.'

He posed them by some candles Cassie had lit, and while he fiddled with his camera Cassie adjusted Jake's bow tie. 'You look very nice,' she said approvingly.

'And you look beautiful,' said Jake.

A jolt had shot through him as he had looked up to see her coming down the staircase, and he was feeling jarred, as if it was still reverberating through him. The dress was white and elegantly floaty. She looked glamorous and sexy and, yes, beautiful.

And then she had stumbled, and he hadn't been able to resist smiling, pleased to see that it was Cassie after all and not some elegant stranger.

Unable to resist touching her, he ran his hands up her bare arms. 'It's Christmas Eve. Weren't you a bit chilly in that carriage?' he said, trying to lighten the atmosphere, trying to loosen whatever it was that had taken such a tight grip on his heart when he had looked up to see Cassie as a bride.

'I had a *faux* fur stole to wear when we came out of the church,' she explained.

'And a muff, I hope?' said Jake, remembering Michelle at the wedding fair, and they both started to laugh at the same time.

They had forgotten Tina and Rob, who was snapping away. They had forgotten the article, forgotten why they were dressed up as a bride and groom. They had forgotten everything except the warmth and the laughter—then somehow they weren't laughing any more, but were staring hungrily at each other.

'That's great,' called Rob from behind his camera. 'Now, what about a…?'

He tailed off, realising that Cassie and Jake weren't even listening.

'A kiss,' he finished, but they were already there. Cassie was locked in Jake's arms, and they were kissing in a way that would have raised a few eyebrows at a real wedding, where kisses for the camera were usually sweet and chaste. There was nothing sweet or chaste about this kiss.

Rob looked at Tina, who rolled her eyes. 'Guys? *Guys!*' she shouted, startling Jake and Cassie apart at last. 'You're embarrassing Rob,' she said with a grin as they looked at her with identically disorientated expressions. 'These photos are supposed to be for a brides' magazine, not something they keep on the top shelf! They don't want pictures of the wedding night, just a sweet little peck on the lips so the readers can all go "aah".'

'Sorry, yes, I suppose we got a bit carried away,' said Cassie, flustered.

'A bit? We didn't know where to look, did we, Rob?'

'It must have been all the time shut up in that carriage,' muttered Jake, alarmed at how easily he lost control the moment he laid hands on Cassie.

They posed for a whole ream of photographs; but at last Rob decided that he had enough. 'I'll send you the link so that you can look at them online,' he told Cassie. 'And then you can pick a selection of the best to send to *Wedding Belles* after Christmas.'

Jake couldn't wait for Rob and Tina to be gone. He closed the door after them with relief and turned back to Cassie, who was blowing out the candles.

'Now, where was that mistletoe again?' he said, and she beckoned him over so that she could put her arms around his neck and kiss him.

'Right here,' she said.

CHAPTER TEN

'I've got to go back to London this afternoon,' said Jake the next morning as they lay in bed. Realising how reluctant he was to go sent him teetering perilously on the edge of that sheer drop again, though, and he shied away from the thought. He smoothed the curls back from Cassie's face. 'Do you want a lift?'

Keep it light, he told himself. Offering a lift back to London wasn't the same as suggesting that she move in with him, have his baby or anything that smacked remotely of commitment. It was just saving a train fare.

'I can't,' sighed Cassie. 'I promised to meet one of the contractors tomorrow to talk about electrics. Now that the hall is done, we need to start work on the kitchens and bathrooms. There's still a long way to go before we can open as a venue. I really need to stay another couple of days.'

Jake was horrified by how disappointed he was

at the prospect of three nights without her, but perhaps a few days apart wasn't a bad thing. It would give him a chance to get himself under control and start thinking clearly again. He wasn't himself when Cassie was right there, warm, soft and desperately distracting. It was too easy to lose control, too easy to forget what he risked by letting go of his careful, ordered life.

So when Cassie said that she would be back in London on Wednesday he made himself hold back. He didn't offer to meet her at the station, take her out to dinner or take her back to his apartment to see how she looked amongst his furniture, the way he really wanted to do. 'Give me a ring when you're back,' was all he said.

Right. Not 'I'll miss you'. Not 'I love you'. Not even 'I'll call you', thought Cassie. But what had she expected? Jake was a careful man nowadays. He might have made love to her with a heart-stopping tenderness and passion, but he wasn't about to rush into a relationship with her.

And quite right too, Cassie reminded herself. She had decided that the here and now was enough for her, and it was obviously enough for Jake as well. So she smiled as she kissed him goodbye after lunch and waved him off to London.

She ought to be happy, she thought as she went back inside and began the dreary task of taking down the Christmas decorations. She had had the most wonderful weekend. OK, so Jake hadn't said that he wanted to see her again, but he hadn't said that he *didn't* want to, either. He couldn't have made love to her like that if he didn't feel anything, could he?

They had all the photos they needed for the article, so there was no real need for him to come down to Portrevick again. But he might need her to be his fiancée again in London. It would look suspicious if they broke off their supposed engagement just yet. They had agreed that they would keep the pretence going until after Christmas, and that was still weeks away, Cassie reassured herself. It was only the beginning of November. Anything could happen in that time.

Just because Jake hadn't talked about the future didn't mean they couldn't have one.

Still, Cassie couldn't help feeling bereft now that he had gone. She wandered disconsolately around the great hall, taking down the fairy lights and dismantling the table she had laid so carefully the day before.

When the bell jangled, she hurried to open the massive front door, relieved at the distraction. She hoped it would be Tina, who had promised to come and give her a lift back to the village. A good chat with her old friend was just what she needed. But when she threw the door open wide, the smile was wiped from her face. It wasn't Tina who stood there.

It was Natasha.

'Oh!'

Natasha smiled a little hesitantly. 'Hi,' she said.

'I'm afraid Jake isn't here,' said Cassie, unable to think of any other reason Natasha would be here on her own. 'He's gone back to London.'

'Actually, it was you I was hoping to see. Have you got a moment?'

The last person Cassie wanted to talk to right then was Natasha, but she couldn't think of a polite way to refuse. 'Sure,' she said reluctantly, and stood back. 'Come in.'

Gracefully, Natasha stepped into the hall. Swathed in a fabulous cream cashmere pashmina, she stood looking beautiful and making everything around her seem faintly shabby in comparison.

Including Cassie.

There was an awkward silence. 'Would you like some tea?' Cassie found herself asking to her own disgust.

'That would be nice, thank you.'

'We'll go to the kitchen. It's warmer there.'

Cursing her mother's training, which meant that you always had to be polite whatever the cost, Cassie led the way to the kitchen.

Natasha sat at the table, unwinding her pashmina to reveal an exquisite pale-blue jumper, also cashmere by the look of it, and Cassie sighed as she filled the kettle. If she tried to wear a top that colour, she would spill something down it and ruin it two seconds after she had put it on, but Natasha looked as if she had stepped out of the pages of a magazine.

Switching on the kettle, she turned and leant back against the worktop and folded her arms. 'What did you want to talk to me about?'

'About Jake,' said Natasha.

Cassie stiffened. 'What about him?'

'I just wanted to know…how he is.' Natasha moistened her lips. 'I'd hoped to see him at the ball the other night, but I couldn't find him.'

Cassie thought about what Jake had been doing while Natasha had been looking for him, and her toes curled. 'He's fine,' she said shortly.

'I see,' whispered Natasha, and to Cassie's horror the green eyes filled with tears. 'I'd hoped…I'd hoped…'

'That he'd be pining for you?'

'Yes.' She nodded miserably. 'I've been such a fool,' she burst out. 'Rupert—he was like a madness. I've always been so sensible, and to be pursued like that by someone so glamorous and so exciting, well, I was flattered. You know what Rupert's like.'

'Yes, I know,' said Cassie. 'But I know what Jake is like too, and so should you. He's worth a thousand Ruperts, and he deserved better than being left without warning—and for Rupert of all people! You must have known how humiliating that would be for him,' she said accusingly.

Natasha bit her lip. 'I can see that now, of course I can, but at the time I wasn't thinking clearly.'

Dropping her head into her hands, she clutched her perfectly straight blonde hair with her perfectly manicured fingers. 'It sounds crazy now, but I just lost my head. I was tired of being clever and careful and doing the right thing all the time. Rupert was such fun and so seductive. Being with him seemed like my only chance to do something wild and spontaneous. It was like my own little rebellion.'

'A little self-indulgent, don't you think?' said Cassie, unmoved. 'Couldn't you have found a way to have fun and be *spontaneous* that didn't involve hurting Jake?'

'I never meant to hurt him, you must believe that!' Natasha lifted her head to look at Cassie with imploring green eyes. 'We never had a very demonstrative relationship. I suppose other people would have looked at us and thought we were cool, but I didn't appreciate what I had. I thought I wanted something different, but then I didn't like it. The truth is that I'm not a rebel. I'm conventional. I'm careful. I like a plan, just like Jake. With Rupert, I never know where we're going to be or what we'll be doing, and I hate it!

'I miss Jake,' she said on a sob, and the tears spilled over at last. 'When I'm with him, I feel so safe. We had so much in common. We were perfect together, but I treated him so badly, and now I don't know if he'll ever forgive me.'

Cassie poured boiling water onto two tea bags. Her face felt tight. Her heart felt tight. 'Why have you come to me?' she asked coolly, squeezing the bags with a spoon before fishing them out.

Natasha wiped tears from under her eyes. Predictably, she was one of those women who looked beautiful even when they were crying. When Cassie cried, she went all blotchy, her nose ran and her eyes turned piggy.

'Because Rupert said he doesn't think you're really engaged to Jake,' said Natasha in a rush. 'He thinks Jake is just saving face, and if…if that's true…then I would like to go to him, to tell him how desperately sorry I am that I hurt him, and ask if he'll give me another chance. I swear I would never do anything like this again,' she promised, an edge of desperation in her voice. 'I can be what Jake needs, I know I can.'

Tight-lipped, Cassie handed Natasha a mug and pushed the carton of milk towards her. She wasn't ready to prove Rupert right just yet, and besides there was last night. Everything had changed now.

Hadn't it?

'And what *does* Jake need?' she prevaricated.

'He needs someone who'll make him feel safe too,' said Natasha. 'I know what a struggle it has been for him to get where he is now. He needs someone who'll let him forget the past and love him for the person he is now. Someone who understands what drives him and doesn't try to challenge him.'

No, thought Cassie instinctively. She shook her head. 'I think you're wrong,' she said. 'Jake shouldn't forget the past. He needs to accept it, accept that it's part of him. You can't just pretend the past never existed.'

'If someone doesn't want to talk about their childhood, you should respect that,' said Natasha. 'Jake knew I would never press him about it. It's one of the reasons he felt comfortable with me.'

Cassie could feel herself prickling with irritation. 'Jake deserves more than comfortable, Natasha,' she said. 'He needs laughter and love and passion and—and *acceptance* of who he was and who he is.'

'I can give him all of that,' said Natasha defensively. 'I do accept him. If I didn't, I would want to change him, and I don't. He doesn't need to change for me.'

But perhaps he needed to change for himself.

Jake needed to let down his guard, to throw away his rule book and his specifications and let himself love and be loved—but that would mean him giving up control, and Cassie wasn't sure he would be able to do that.

He didn't believe in love. Jake had made that very clear. He thought all you needed for a successful relationship was a formula, and Natasha fitted his specifications perfectly. He had told her that.

They had agreed that they were completely incompatible. Two nights weren't going to change that, were they?

Cassie's heart cracked. She so wanted to believe that this magical weekend had been the start of something wonderful, but what, really, did she have to go on? When Jake kissed her, when his hands drifted lazily, possessively, over her body, she hadn't needed to hear that he loved her. Then, the here and now had been enough, but now he had gone, and she could feel her confidence leaking out of her in the face of Natasha's glowing beauty.

It was too easy now to wonder if he had turned to her on the rebound from Natasha, if he had simply been looking for someone different to distract him from the hurt and the humiliation of being left by the woman he really wanted.

Now, too late, she could remember that it had only ever been a pretence, and Jake had never suggested otherwise. Why hadn't she remembered that before?

Because it wasn't a pretence for her, not any more. Cassie loved Jake. She knew that she could give him what he really needed.

But what he needed wasn't necessarily what he wanted.

Stirring her tea, Cassie looked across the table at Natasha, who had dried her tears and was looking poised and elegant once more.

Looking exactly like the kind of woman Jake had aspired to for so long.

A lead weight was gathering in Cassie's chest as she remembered everything Jake had ever told her.

He didn't want to take the risk of falling in love. He didn't want to lose control. He didn't want to change.

Natasha could give him so many of things he had said he *did* want. She wouldn't push him. She would let him keep his emotions all buttoned up— and wasn't that, really, all Jake wanted?

Strange that she and Natasha should love the same man when they were so different, Cassie thought. There was Natasha: so beautiful, so sensible, so classy and so cool, representing the future Jake had worked so hard for—and there was her; clumsy, messy Cassie who muddled through and did her best but would never be more than an also-ran. Who would always be associated with the past he resented so much.

Did she really think Jake would rather be with her than Natasha?

Better to face reality now, Cassie decided. She wasted too much of her life dreaming as it was. This time, she would be the sensible one.

Natasha had been watching her face. 'Is it true?' she asked quietly. 'Is Jake just trying to save face by pretending to be engaged to you?'

Cassie looked down at the ruby ring which she had never got round to taking off the night before. Very slowly, she drew it off and dropped it onto the table, where it clattered and rolled for a moment before toppling over.

'Yes,' she said. 'It's true.'

* * *

'You did *what*?' said Tina in disbelief. She had arrived about ten minutes after Natasha had left to find Cassie a sodden mess in the kitchen.

'I told Natasha the truth.'

'And sent her back to Jake with *your* ring? You're mad, Cassie! You and Jake had something really good going there.'

'We were just pretending,' said Cassie drearily, blowing her nose. Unlike Natasha, she wasn't a pretty sight when she cried, and she had just cried more than she had ever cried before.

Tina wasn't having any of it. 'Don't give me that. I saw the way you kissed each other last night. There was nothing fake about that. Good grief, the top of my head practically blew off, and that was just watching you!' She put her hands on her hips and shook her head at Cassie. 'I can't believe you'd just give up and let that drippy Natasha swan back to him. It's not like you to be so wet. You're crazy about Jake, and you just gave him up without a fight. What's that about?'

'Because it's not a fight I could ever win,' Cassie said miserably. Did Tina think she hadn't thought about it? 'We're completely incompatible.'

'You looked pretty compatible to me last night.'

Cassie's eyes filled with tears again and she swiped angrily at them with the back of her hand. 'We want different things, Tina. Jake thinks he can order a relationship like everything else, and I'm holding out for something he thinks doesn't exist. I want someone to love me, someone who needs me as much as I need him. Jake thinks that's a fairy tale.'

'I'm sure he does love you, Cassie,' said Tina, putting an arm around her shoulders. 'He may not realise it yet, that's all. I bet you anything he'll send Natasha away with a flea in her ear, and come roaring back down here with that ring as soon as he hears what you've done.'

But Jake didn't come. On Wednesday, Cassie sent him a brief, businesslike email saying that she was staying in Portrevick for a while to oversee work on the Hall. She didn't mention Natasha, and nor did Jake when he replied.

Thanks for update, was all he said. *Keep me posted. Regards, Jake.*

Regards? *Regards?* Was that all he could say after he had rolled her beneath him and smiled against her throat? After his hands had unlocked her, made her gasp and arch? After he had loved her slowly, thoroughly, gloriously, and held her, still shaking, as they spiralled back to reality together?

How dared he? Furious, Cassie stabbed at the delete button. How dared he send her *regards* after he had made her love him?

Sheer anger kept her going all afternoon, but when it leaked away it left her more miserable than ever.

'Tell him how you feel,' said Tina, exasperated. 'Put yourself in Jake's shoes. He's got no idea that you care for him at all. You have a great weekend together, and the next thing he knows you've tossed him back his ring and told Natasha he's all hers. What's the poor bloke supposed to think?'

'What am *I* supposed to think?' Cassie protested tearfully. 'He didn't even suggest meeting up in London.'

'He's probably terrified you'll think he's getting too heavy. If you ask me, you're both being big babies,' said Tina. 'At least Natasha had the guts to go and tell him how she felt.'

The mention of Natasha was enough to plunge Cassie back into the depths. 'How can I go? He'll be back with Natasha by now.' She tortured herself by imagining the two of them together. How could Jake have resisted those green eyes shimmering with love and the promise of calm? When Cassie looked at herself in the mirror she saw eyes puffy with tears, awful skin and limp hair. There was no way Jake would want her now, even if he wasn't dazzled anew by Natasha's beauty.

At least work on the Hall was going well, she tried to console herself. Joss was pleased with the way the project was going, and as November was never a busy time for weddings she was happy for Cassie to stay in Cornwall for the time being. It was bittersweet, being up at the Hall every day, but Cassie threw herself into the job. It was all she had left.

Three long, wretched weeks dragged past. The days got shorter, darker and damper, and Cassie got more miserable. It was time to go back to London and pick up her old life, she decided grimly. She had been perfectly happy before, and she would be again. It wasn't as if she was likely to bump into Jake. London was a big city and their lives would never cross, unless he was tactless enough to ask her to plan his wedding to Natasha. Cassie couldn't see that happening. No, she would go back, stick to the job she could do and stop trying to be someone she wasn't.

'I'll be back tomorrow,' she told Joss, and went for a last walk on the beach. The sea was wild, the sky as grey as her mood. It was very cold, and the spray from the crashing waves stung her cheeks.

Head bent, Cassie trudged along the sand. There were no surfers today, no lifeguards, and she had the beach to herself. Except, she realised, for a figure in black leathers that was heading towards her from the dunes. Some biker who must have left his motorbike in the car park, and, not content with roaring through the villages disturbing everyone's peace, was now spoiling her solitude.

Cassie scowled. There were plenty of other empty beaches in Cornwall at this time of year.

Why did he have to come here? She wanted to be miserable on her own, thank you very much.

And he was coming straight for her! Cassie glared at him, and was just about to turn pointedly on her heel when she stopped. Hang on, wasn't there something familiar about that walk? About that self-contained stride? She looked harder. The set of those shoulders, the darkness of the hair.... It couldn't be, could it?

All at once a great hand seemed to close tight around her, inside her, gripping her heart, her lungs and her entrails so that she couldn't breathe. She could just stand and stare, brown eyes huge with disbelief and desperate hope, as he came closer and closer until he was standing right in front of her.

'So this is where you are,' said Jake.

'Jake.' It came out as little more than a squeak.

Cassie was completely thrown, ricocheting around between astonishment, sheer joy and confusion at how different he looked. Standing there in black leather, he seemed younger, wilder, and the guarded look she had become used to had been replaced by a reckless glint. The wind ruffled his hair, and with the angry sea behind him he looked so like the old Jake that she could hardly speak.

'What...what are you doing here?' she stammered at last.

'Looking for you,' said Jake.

He sounded the same. He just looked so...

Cassie couldn't think of a word to describe how he looked, but it was making her heart boom so loudly that it drowned out the crashing waves and the wind that was whistling past her ears.

She swallowed hard. This, remember, was still the Jake who had gone back to London without a word about the future, who had sent her his *regards*.

'What for?' she asked almost rudely.

'I bought a motorbike,' he said. 'I wanted to show you. Everyone thinks I'm having a midlife crisis, but I thought you would understand.'

'I would?'

'You were the one who said that riding a bike wouldn't change me, that I could let go just a little and I wouldn't lose everything I'd fought to be.'

Cassie eyed the leathers. They made him look lean, hard and very tough. Of course, he looked like that in a suit too, but now he was even more unsettling. 'I'm not sure I was right about that,' she said. 'You look like you've changed to me.'

'But I haven't,' said Jake. 'I'm still Chief Executive of Primordia. I still have my MBA, my experience, my career. My world hasn't fallen apart because I bought a bike. I really thought that it would,' he said. 'I was afraid that I might lose myself, but I've found myself instead. I've realised that I can't change the past. I have to accept that my family, my past, that difficult boy I was, all of them are part of who I am now.' A smile lurked in his eyes as he looked at Cassie. 'You were right about that too.'

Cassie moistened her lips. 'I don't think I've been right so often before,' she tried to joke, not knowing what else to do, not knowing what was happening, knowing only that all her certainties were being shaken around like flakes in a snow globe.

'You weren't right about Natasha,' said Jake. 'You sent her to me because you thought she was what I wanted, didn't you?'

'She is what you want.' It was cold in the wind, and Cassie hugged her jacket about her. By unspoken consent, they turned their backs to the wind and started walking back along the beach, the sand damp and firm beneath their feet.

Cassie dug her hands in her pockets and hunched her shoulders defensively. 'You told me she was,' she reminded him. 'You told me she was perfect.'

'I thought she was,' he admitted. 'I thought I needed someone cool and careful, like I was trying so hard to be. I thought I needed someone who would help me fit in, who would help me forget what I'd been and where I'd come from.'

'Someone like Natasha,' said Cassie bitterly.

'Yes. I thought Natasha was exactly what I needed, but I was wrong,' said Jake. 'It took meeting you again to realise that what I really needed was someone who would make me laugh, who would give me the strength to let go of everything I thought

I needed.' He slowed, and Cassie slowed with him, until they had stopped and were facing each other alone on the beach.

'Someone who would make me remember, not forget,' he said, his voice very deep and low. 'Someone who would force me to stop running away from the life I had here and accept it as part of who I am.'

He looked down at Cassie, whose hands were still thrust into the pockets of her jacket, and he could see the realisation of what he had come to say dawning in the brown eyes.

'Someone like you,' he said.

'But—but, Jake, you can't need me,' she said in disbelief, even as Jake was reaching for her wrists and tugging her hands gently from her pockets. 'I'm the last person you can want. I'm not sensible or clever or beautiful or—or *anything*,' she said, but her fingers were twining of their own accord around Jake's. 'I'm useless.'

'Useless?' he said. 'You've transformed the Hall, organised a ball, set up a wonderful marketing opportunity with a magazine, charmed the socks off everyone who met you in London. You're not useless at all,' he said sternly.

'My family wouldn't agree with you,' she sighed. 'I haven't achieved anything, not like the rest of you, with your degrees and your fantastically successful careers.'

'But you can do the things your clever, successful family can't.'

'Oh yes? Like what?'

'Like make the sun seem brighter when you smile,' said Jake. 'Like making me laugh. Like making me happy.' He drew her closer. 'Like making me safe,' he said softly. 'Cassie, tell me I can do that for you too.'

Her eyes filled with tears. 'You can,' she whispered. 'You do.'

They didn't kiss, not at first. They just held each other, very, very tightly. Cassie's face was pressed into his throat, and she could smell the leather of his jacket, just as she had done ten years ago. But this time the shock and anger had gone and in their place was a ballooning sense of joy and relief, as if she had finally found her way home.

Safe—that was what Jake had said he felt. Cassie knew exactly what he meant.

'Tell me you love me, Cassie,' he murmured against her hair, and she tipped back her head to smile at him, her eyes still shimmering with tears.

'I love you,' she said. And then they did kiss, a long, intoxicatingly sweet kiss that dissolved the hurt and the uncertainty and left them heady and breathless with happiness.

'I love you,' said Jake shakily at last. Somehow they had made it to the shelter of the dunes, and sank down onto the soft sand as they kissed and kissed again. 'I love you, I love you,' he said again between kisses. 'I can't tell you how much.'

Cassie drew a shivery sigh of sheer contentment and rested her head on his shoulder, her arms wound tightly around him as if she would never let him go. 'What about the formula?'

'Ah, the formula,' he said with a wry smile. 'I clung to that formula like a life raft! It seemed to make sense,' he tried to explain. 'It worked, or at least it did until I met you again. You don't know what you did to me, Cassie. You turned my world upside down. I had constructed such a careful life, and suddenly everything was out of control.

'You made me *feel* again, and I was torn. I wanted you, but I didn't want you. You were part of the past I'd been running away from for so long. I thought if I could just hold onto my sensible, practical formula I'd be all right, but I can see now that it was just as much a fantasy as the fairy tale that you believe in.'

'Yes, I've learnt that too,' said Cassie, snuggling closer as they lay in the sand. 'I held on to the fairy tale, just like you held on to the formula. I suppose I was always such a dreamer that it was natural for me to fantasise about the perfect relationship, the perfect wedding, the perfect everything.'

She ran her hand over his abdomen. Even through the leather, she could feel the muscled strength of him. 'I don't think you're perfect, though.'

'Oh?' Jake pretended to sound hurt, and she softened the blow by leaning up on her elbow and smiling down at him as she dropped a kiss on his lips.

'No, you're not perfect. You're impatient and practical and oh-so-sensible—or you were until you went out and bought yourself a motorbike just to make a point! When I dreamed of the man I would love, I never imagined someone like you, but it *is* you. I've learnt to love what's in front of me, not a dream. Now I know that you love me back, well…' She smiled, kissing him again. 'I think this just might be the fairy tale after all!'

She settled back into the curve of his arm with a sigh of happiness. 'I've been so wretched for the last three weeks,' she told him. 'Why did it take you so long to come?'

'Because I thought you'd changed your mind after I'd gone,' said Jake. 'I thought you'd just been amusing yourself that weekend, and that you didn't want to get any more involved. I thought you couldn't even be bothered to tell me yourself. You just sent Natasha instead.'

Cassie wriggled uncomfortably. 'I didn't *send* her. I thought you would be happy to see her.'

'Happy? Hah!' Jake snorted. 'There was one moment that day when I was wildly happy. The door bell rang and I convinced myself that it was you, that you'd told the contractors they could go to hell so that you could come up to London early and be with me.'

'Well, I don't know why you would think I would do that.' Cassie pretended to grumble. 'You never said a word. How was I to know you wanted to see me?'

'I know, I was a fool. I should have begged you to come with me.' Jake wound his fingers in the curls that were hopelessly tangled by wind and sand. 'But, Cassie, I was terrified,' he said. 'I'd fallen wildly in love with you. That weekend, when we made love, it all happened so fast. I felt as if I was losing control when I was with you, nothing else mattered. I could feel myself slipping back, becoming the reckless boy I'd been before, not caring about anything except the moment.

'It was as if everything I'd spent the last ten years working for had started to crumble,' he tried to explain. 'I thought I needed a day or two to get a grip of myself and decide what I really wanted.

'And I realised that I wanted *you*,' he told her. 'When I got to London, everything was colourless without you. That life I'd fought to keep under control was still under control, but it was flat and meaningless too. So I knew I wanted you, but I wasn't sure how to win you. You were always telling me how incompatible we were, and you clearly didn't need *me* to have a good time.'

Jake paused. 'There was a little bit of me, too, that was hung over from the past, a bit that didn't feel as if I was good enough for you. You come from such a nice, happy, middle-class family, and when all was said and done I was still one of those Trevelyans with a father in prison.'

'But you're more than that,' said Cassie. 'Your family doesn't matter. It's you I love, and as for my family, well, they're going to see a chief executive, not the wild boy who used to make trouble in the village. They like high achievers, remember? They'll approve of you much more than they do of me!'

'I hope so,' said Jake. 'I suppose I just lost my nerve in London. I told myself I had to take things carefully, so I planned to ask you out to dinner as soon as you got back and ask if you'd consider making that silly pretence of being engaged real. But Natasha turned up instead. She told me you'd admitted that it was just a pretence, and had sent back the ring to prove it.'

'I didn't think you'd be able to resist her,' sighed Cassie. 'She's so beautiful.'

'Well, yes, she is—but next to you she's just a little colourless. I never laughed with her the way I laughed with you. We never talked, or argued, or lost our cool with each other. Natasha's a nice person,' said Jake. 'But she was the last person I wanted to see that day. Once I'd got over my disappointment that she wasn't you, we had a long talk. I think the fact that she was ready to have an affair with Rupert made her realise that we weren't really right for each other. I hope she'll find the right man one day, but it's not me.'

'Why didn't you at least call me *then*?' asked Cassie, thinking of the weeks they had wasted being miserable apart.

'I was angry,' said Jake. 'With Natasha, with you, but mostly with myself—for letting myself fall in love with you, for throwing my whole life into disorder for someone who apparently didn't care enough about me to tell me she couldn't be bothered to carry on pretending. And then, when I *did* hear from you, it was just an impersonal email about the Hall!'

'At least I didn't sign it "regards"!' sniffed Cassie, and he laughed as he hugged her closer.

'I was trying to show you I cared as little as you did. God, I can laugh now, but at the time I was hurt and I was bitter. I was impossible to deal with for two weeks—my PA told me she was ready to shoot me, in the end—until I realised I couldn't go on like that. I used to take myself off for long walks around the streets, and one day I passed a guy on a motorbike. It was just like the one I used to have in Portrevick, and that's when I started to think about what you'd said about accepting the past and letting go of it at the same time.

'I can take a risk, I thought, and I went out and bought a bike of my own. And then I took an even bigger risk. I thought you'd be back in London, so I went round to your office and Joss told me you were still here, so I got straight on my bike and drove all the way down here,' he said, unzipping a pocket to pull out the ruby ring.

He shifted so that he was lying over Cassie, smiling down into her eyes. 'I came to tell you that I love you and I need you, and that more than anything in the world I want you to take this ring back and say you'll marry me. Will you, Cassie?'

Cassie's smile trembled as she took the ring and slid it back onto her finger where it belonged. 'Oh yes,' she breathed, and her eyes shone as she put her arms around Jake's neck to tug him down for a long, long kiss. 'Oh yes, I will.'

The short winter afternoon was closing in, but it was only the first spots of rain that forced them to move at last. 'Have you still got that wedding dress you wore for the photos?' Jake asked as they brushed sand off each other.

'I took it back to the shop the next day.'

'Why don't you go and buy it?' he said. 'We can get married at Christmas.'

'Christmas!' said Cassie, startled. 'That's only a month away!'

'It's enough time for the banns to be read.'

'Just!'

'And the wedding's already planned,' he pointed out as they headed back to the car park. 'We've got the table decorations and we know the menu. We've even had the photos done already. Tina's got her bridesmaid's dress, and I've got my tuxedo—unless you want me in breeches and a cravat, of course! So all you need to do is buy the dress and tell your family.'

'Are you sure you don't mean next Christmas?' asked Cassie. 'What happened to Mr Sensible? I thought you'd be saying it was crazy to rush into marriage!'

'It is,' said Jake with a smile. 'But let's do it anyway.'

A gleaming, mean-looking motorbike had the car park to itself. Jake handed Cassie a helmet when they got back to it and put on his own. 'Hop on the back,' he said, kicking the machine into gear. 'And we'll go and see if the vicar can fit us in for a Christmas wedding.'

EPILOGUE

Christmas Eve

CASSIE woke on her wedding morning to a glittering world. Under a thin, blue winter sky, a hard frost rimed every twig and every blade of grass. But by lunchtime the clouds had blanked out the meagre December light, hanging so heavily they seemed to be muffling the slightest noise, and Portrevick was enveloped in the stillness and strange, expectant silence that comes before snow.

In the pub, they were taking bets on a white Christmas at last, and the children were wild with excitement at the prospect of bulging stockings and presents under the tree. Cassie had always loved Christmas, too, but this was her wedding day, and all she was dreaming about was the moment she stood in front of the altar with Jake. Until then, she hardly dared let herself believe that it wasn't just all a dream.

At four o'clock it was already dark, but there were flares lining the path to the church, and the trees were strung with fairy lights. Tina took the *faux* fur stole Cassie had worn on the brief journey from Portrevick Hall with her father and laid it on the porch seat.

Cassie's father offered her his arm. 'You look beautiful, darling,' he said. 'Your mother and I are very proud of you, you know.' His voice cracked a little at the end, and he had to clear his throat.

'Thank you, Dad.' Cassie's eyes stung with tears. 'Thank you for everything.'

'Promise me you'll be happy with Jake.'

'I will.' It was her turn to swallow a huge lump in her throat. 'I know I will.'

'In that case,' said her father, reverting to his more usual, reassuringly brisk manner. 'Let's go.'

And then they were walking up the uneven aisle of the old church. *How odd*, Cassie found herself thinking with a strange, detached part of her mind. She had spent so long planning weddings for other brides, so many years dreaming about her own, that she thought she would know how it would feel.

Everything looked exactly as she had always imagined it. Lit only by candles, the little church looked beautiful, and was filled with the people she loved. Her mother was there, trying not to cry. Liz had started already, and was wiping her eyes with a handkerchief as she smiled tremulously. Her brothers were doing their level best to look as if they weren't moved, and not quite succeeding.

The flowers were simple, stunning arrangements of white, and tiny wreaths hung at the end of every pew. Cassie had a blurred impression of warmth and colour as everyone turned to smile as they passed. Yes, it was just as she'd imagined it.

What she had never imagined was that none of it would really matter. The only thing that mattered was that Jake should be there, waiting for her at the altar.

And there he was. Cassie's heart gave a great bound of relief as she saw him turn. He was looking serious, but as she got closer she saw that he was not serious so much as anxious, and she knew with a sudden, dazzling certainty that he had been afraid she wouldn't come, that all that mattered to him was that *she* was there.

Her father lifted her hand to his lips and kissed it, and Cassie smiled at him brilliantly before he stepped back to join her mother. Then she turned to face Jake at last.

He smiled at her as he took her hand, and she smiled back, twisting her fingers around his. All at once it was just the two of them in the warm candlelight. They had forgotten the church and the watching congregation, and Cassie could feel herself beginning to sway towards him, turning her face up for his kiss already.

The vicar cleared his throat loudly, and they turned to him with identically startled expressions. He smiled. 'If you could spare us few minutes of your attention…?' he murmured.

'Sorry,' they whispered back, and he raised his voice.

'Dearly beloved…'

The familiar words rang like a bell in Cassie's heart. This was what her wedding was about. It wasn't about the beautiful dress she was wearing, or the gasps when the guests saw the great hall. It was more than an excuse for a party. It was about Jake and about her, about the love they shared and the life they would build together.

Her eyes never left Jake's dark-blue ones. She was intensely aware of his hand, of his voice making his responses steadily, of the smooth coolness of the ring he slid onto her finger. At last she was in the right place at the right time. It wasn't a dream. This was where she was meant to be, and this was the man she was meant to be with.

Cassie's heart was so full, she could hardly say 'I do'. Even when she thought it couldn't possibly be any fuller, it kept swelling, and swelling until the vicar declared them man and wife, and then she was afraid it would explode altogether. Giddy with happiness, she smiled as Jake took her face between his hands and kissed her.

'You look beautiful,' he said.

Cassie had seen how radiant other brides looked, and now she knew exactly how they felt. She was brimming with joy. It felt as if it were spilling out of her, shimmering away into the candlelight.

In a blur, she dropped the pen twice before she managed to sign the register, and then she was sailing back down the aisle, Jake's fingers wrapped firmly round her own.

The church doors were thrown open and a magical scene awaited them. Great, soft snowflakes were drifting steadily to the ground, blurring the warm, flickering glow of the flares and glimmer of the tiny lights in the trees.

'Oh Jake, it's perfect!' gasped Cassie, and promptly tripped over the porch step. 'Just as well we decided not to have a video,' she muttered out of the corner of her mouth as Jake hauled her upright, and behind her she heard Tina smother a fit of giggles. 'Thank goodness I had you to hang on to, or I'd have gone flat on my face!'

Jake's hand tightened and he smiled down at her. 'That's the thing about being married,' he said. 'We'll always have each other to hang on to now.'

Cassie's smile widened. 'So we will,' she said, and then stopped, catching sight of a carriage drawn up outside the lych gate. In the light of the flares there, she could see that it was pulled by two white horses.

A car would be more sensible, Jake had said

once, and it was a car she had expected to take them back to the great hall. But Jake, her sensible husband, must have remembered her fantasy and arranged the carriage for her instead.

Her eyes shone as she looked up at him. 'It's my dream!' she breathed, but Jake shook his head and smiled.

'It's not a dream,' he said. 'It's real.'

* * * * *

This season we bring you
Christmas Treats

For an early Christmas present,
Jessica Hart would like to share
a little treat with you...

JESSICA HART'S TOP TEN TIPS
FOR A SPARKLING CHRISTMAS PARTY!

1. Invite all your neighbours as well as your friends, even if you don't know them very well. Everybody loves to be invited to a party—and it's a great way to meet that person you smile at in the street every day but whose name you don't know…

2. It's much more fun if everyone is jammed in together, so put your guests in a room that's not quite big enough for them all. Don't let anyone sit down, either! It makes it easier for your guests to mingle and meet each other if everyone is standing up.

3. Don't forget to introduce guests to each other—it can be daunting to walk into a room full of people who all seem to know each other, and it makes a big difference if the hostess makes sure everyone has someone to talk to when they arrive.

4. At Christmas you can go to town on the decorations—a Christmas tree is a must, but fairy lights look wonderful strung around the room too. Keep the lighting flattering with candles

and soft lamps, and put out piles of pine cones and crackers. A room fragrance scented with cinnamon, oranges and cloves will get everyone in the mood the moment they step through the door.

5. Greet guests with a glass of mulled wine and a mince pie as soon as they arrive, or impress them with a real Christmas cocktail—see below!

6. Cheese biscuits to nibble on are easy to make, and if you buy a box of Christmas pastry-cutters you can have holly, stars, angels, Christmas trees and all sorts of other Christmassy shapes, or use letters to spell Noel or Happy Christmas on a plate. They can be made in advance, and will make it look as if you've gone to masses of effort even when you haven't.

7. Have a Secret Santa. Give all your guests a (very low) price limit and get everyone to bring a present to put beneath the tree. That way everyone will have a gift to take home—but much more fun will be had watching their re-actions as they open their present!

8. Make sure you leave yourself enough time to make yourself look fantastic. It won't matter if

nothing else is ready as long as you're there to greet people when they arrive.

9. Don't forget the music—the cheesier, the better. Bring out all the old Christmas favourites and your guests will dance the night away.

10. Have a good time and everyone else will too!

JESSICA HART'S CHRISTMAS COCKTAIL

Frost the glasses in advance by dipping the rims first in lightly whipped egg white, and then in caster sugar.

Put a sugar cube in the bottom of each glass and add enough brandy to cover. Let it soak for a while, then pour in some cranberry juice and top with sparkling wine.

Stand back and watch your party take off!

 **ROMANCE 2-in-1**

Coming next month

HER DESERT DREAM
by Liz Fielding

After **Trading Places** with Lady Rose Napier, lookalike Lydia
Young is leaving her job at the local supermarket behind
and jetting off to Sheikh Kalil's desert kingdom!

AND THE BRIDE WORE RED
by Lucy Gordon

Olivia Daley believes the best cure for a broken heart is a
radical change of scenery. Exotic, vibrant China is far
enough from rainy grey England to be just that!

THEIR CHRISTMAS FAMILY MIRACLE
by Caroline Anderson

Finding herself homeless for the holidays, single mum Amelia's
Christmas wish is granted when she's offered an empty
picture-perfect country house to stay in. Then owner
Jake steps through the door...

SNOWBOUND BRIDE-TO-BE
by Cara Colter

B&B owner Emma is about to discover that the one thing not
on her Christmas list – a heart-stoppingly handsome man
with a baby in tow – is right on her doorstep!

On sale 4th December 2009

Available at WHSmith, Tesco, ASDA, Eason and all good bookshops.
For full Mills & Boon range including eBooks visit
www.millsandboon.co.uk

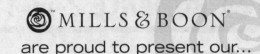

MILLS & BOON®

are proud to present our...

Book of the Month

A Bride for His Majesty's Pleasure
by Penny Jordan
from Mills & Boon® Modern™

A ruthless ruler and his virgin queen. Trembling
with the fragility of new spring buds, Ionanthe
will go to her husband: she was given as
penance, but he'll take her for pleasure!

Available 6th November 2009

Something to say about our
Book of the Month?
Tell us what you think!
millsandboon.co.uk/community

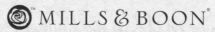

millsandboon.co.uk Community

Join Us!

The Community is the perfect place to meet and chat to kindred spirits who love books and reading as much as you do, but it's also the place to:

- **Get the inside scoop from authors about their latest books**
- **Learn how to write a romance book with advice from our editors**
- **Help us to continue publishing the best in women's fiction**
- **Share your thoughts on the books we publish**
- **Befriend other users**

Forums: Interact with each other as well as authors, editors and a whole host of other users worldwide.

Blogs: Every registered community member has their own blog to tell the world what they're up to and what's on their mind.

Book Challenge: We're aiming to read 5,000 books and have joined forces with The Reading Agency in our inaugural Book Challenge.

Profile Page: Showcase yourself and keep a record of your recent community activity.

Social Networking: We've added buttons at the end of every post to share via digg, Facebook, Google, Yahoo, technorati and de.licio.us.

www.millsandboon.co.uk

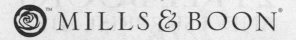

2 FREE BOOKS
AND A SURPRISE GIFT

We would like to take this opportunity to thank you for reading this Mills & Boon® book by offering you the chance to take TWO more specially selected books from the Romance series absolutely FREE! We're also making this offer to introduce you to the benefits of the Mills & Boon® Book Club™—

- **FREE home delivery**
- **FREE gifts and competitions**
- **FREE monthly Newsletter**
- **Exclusive Mills & Boon Book Club offers**
- **Books available before they're in the shops**

Accepting these FREE books and gift places you under no obligation to buy, you may cancel at any time, even after receiving your free shipment. Simply complete your details below and return the entire page to the address below. You don't even need a stamp!

YES Please send me 2 free Romance books and a surprise gift. I understand that unless you hear from me, I will receive 5 superb new stories every month including two 2-in-1 books priced at £4.99 each and a single book priced at £3.19, postage and packing free. I am under no obligation to purchase any books and may cancel my subscription at any time. The free books and gift will be mine to keep in any case.

Ms/Mrs/Miss/Mr_____ Initials _____

Surname _____

Address _____

_____

_____ Postcode _____

Send this whole page to: Mills & Boon Book Club, Free Book Offer, FREEPOST NAT 10298, Richmond, TW9 1BR

Offer valid in UK only and is not available to current Mills & Boon Book Club subscribers to this series. Overseas and Eire please write for details.. We reserve the right to refuse an application and applicants must be aged 18 years or over. Only one application per household. Terms and prices subject to change without notice. Offer expires 31st January 2010. As a result of this application, you may receive offers from Harlequin Mills & Boon and other carefully selected companies. If you would prefer not to share in this opportunity please write to The Data Manager, PO Box 676, Richmond, TW9 1WU.

Mills & Boon® is a registered trademark owned by Harlequin Mills & Boon Limited. The Mills & Boon® Book Club™ is being used as a trademark.